THE DEATH'S HEAD TAVERN

And Other Fantastic Tales

Nancy A. Collins

Hopedale Press

ISBN-13: 9798876431318

Cover design by: Canva/Midjourney

Printed in the United States of America

For Rusty Burke

TABLE OF CONTENTS

Tripping The Dark Heroic Fantastic----------------------2
Ahab: Monster Hunter------------------------------------6
The Sign of the Silver Hand-------------------------------40
The One-Eyed King--74
The Heart of the Dragon---------------------------------117
The Ice Wedding--145
The Death's Head Tavern--------------------------------174
Absalom's Wake--195
Copyright Page---345
About The Author--------------------------------------346

TRIPPING THE DARK HEROIC FANTASTIC

An Introduction

I'm going to make a confession right here and now. Although I have loved fantasy literature and cinema all my life, I have never truly been able to get into ***The Lord of the Rings.*** Granted, to many this is as close to heresy as possible in geek circles. But the truth of the matter is that while I enjoyed ***The Hobbit*** when I first read it in junior high, my heart had already been won over by High Fantasy's red-head stepchild, Sword and Sorcery.

Where High Fantasy has a literary tradition that dates back to Eddic Poetry and features a great deal of world-building, a strong focus on the traditional Hero's Journey ,and invariably involves an apocalyptic world-ending battle between the forces of Good and Evil, Sword and Sorcery is more adventure-based and has its roots in the American pulp magazines of the early Twentieth Century and, as such, its prose possesses an undeniable muscularity and sense of immediacy, as well as protagonists who are closer to Byronic heroes than Sir Galahad.

There is Good and Evil in these stories, but the stakes are much smaller in scale—and often far more personal. Conan the Barbarian is determined to kill the evil wizard not because it's the right thing to do, but because it's the only way he can escape alive—plus, he really hates that son of a bitch.

Like a lot of late-stage Baby Boomers/early Gen Xers, my first exposure to Sword and Sorcery came in the form of Marvel Comics' *Conan the Barbarian* series, adapted by Roy Thomas. I wish I could claim hipster cred for reading the Lancer paperback reprints in the mid-1960s, but I was too young at the time. No, I caught the bug from the spinner rack that announced: *'Hey, Kids! Comics!'*

I had been reading funny books (as they were called back then) for as long as I could remember, starting with kid stuff like *Donald Duck* and *Richie Rich*. But by the time I was twelve I had made the transition from casual reader to genuine fan, picking up such titles as *The Amazing Spiderman*, *Fantastic Four*, and *The Avengers*. Since I was stuck in rural Arkansas, the only way I could buy comics was by haunting the newsstands at the local pharmacy or the grocery store. It was there I bought my first non-superhero comic--*Conan the Barbarian #24*--in early 1973, and for a weird kid growing up in a small southern town it was pretty heady stuff. A couple months later I snapped up the *King-Sized Conan the Barbarian* special, even though it was thirty-cents as opposed to the usual twenty. It reprinted two previous issues from the Windsor-Smith run: *"The Lair of the Beast Men"* and *"Tower of the Elephant"*. Of the two stories, the later genuinely moved and intrigued me, as it combined fantasy with a weird kind of science fiction that was unlike anything I had read before.

While perusing the "The Hyborian Page" editorial column in *Conan the Barbarian*, I learned the character had originally been a reoccurring character in something called 'pulp magazines', and one title in particular, *Weird Tales*. I asked my mother about the pulps and she said she used to read them back when she was girl, and that they were a cross between comic books and paperbacks, with adventure stories involving crime-fighting heroes with names like Doc Savage, The Shadow, and The Black Bat--some of which even had their own radio programs. Needless to say, I was intrigued—and a little bit pissed that I had missed out something that sounded so cool.

Remember, this was in the Dark Ages before the Internet, Google, and YouTube. Conan the Barbarian, Cthulhu, *Weird Tales*—things you can now find with a few keystrokes—were one step away from lost media back then. Luckily, the mid-1970s saw an explosion of commercial paperback reprints of the works of virtually every writer who ever published in the old pulps. I sought out the work of these authors and from there, as Bowie once sang, the song goes on forever.

It wasn't long before I discovered the works of Fritz Leiber—creator of the heroic fantasy buddy team Fafhrd and the Gray Mouser—and C.L. Moore's swordswoman Jirel of Joiry and her star-faring hero,

Northwest Smith. These lead me to more contemporary Sword & Sorcery writers, such as Karl Edward Wagner —creator of the immortal antihero Kane—and Michael Moorcock, whose Eternal Champion series I gobbled up like candy as soon as they hit the shelves. My earliest attempts at fiction were pastiches of my favorite characters—what is now known as 'fanfic'. Some of which I would rework, decades later, into commissioned tales featuring the characters that had inspired them. A few of which you will find in this collection.

Although I am better known for my horror and urban fantasy work, there is still a place in my heart for the brooding sword-slinging heroes—and antiheroes—of my youth. This collection of dark fantastic stories--all of which have never been collected or reprinted before--includes appearances from such well-known characters as Solomon Kane, Prince Corum, Elric of Melniboné, and Robin Hood, not to mention Captain Ahab. It also features a fictionalized retelling of a true story set during the Romanov Empire, and a short novel that poses the question what if instead of writing *Moby Dick*, Herman Melville had decided to create his version of the Cthulhu Mythos? (Hint: It would be far shorter and feature were-sharks.)

I hope you find these dark fantastic tales to your liking. There's a little something for everybody here.

Nancy A. Collins
Macon, GA. 2024

AHAB: MONSTER HUNTER

I am hesitant to relate the tale I am about to tell, largely because it does nothing to bolster my claims of sanity. But if I am to convince others of my innocence in this matter, I have no choice but to recount the singular events that have lead me to this cold cell.

I am first-generation Canadian, my parents having migrated from their native Scotland to this wild and boundless land shortly before my birth. I have long harbored a deep fascination with the rough and tumble lifestyle of the French-Canadian *couriers de bois*, those rugged pioneers who helped shape our fledgling nation. Because of this, I left my home in Toronto for the wilds of what, until recently, was known as Rupert's Land with the intention of becoming a trapper. However, my enthusiasm proved far greater than my woodscraft, and I found it all I could do to survive the first heavy snowfall.

As luck would have it, while on a visit to a trading post I made the acquaintance of a certain Dick Buchan and Ben Martin. They, too, were new to the trapping game and having a hard time of it. We agreed that it was a lonesome and difficult business, especially during the long winter months, and decided to pool our resources and become partners, running our traplines from a home shanty near the vast shores of God's Lake.

Of the three who comprised our rustic enterprise, I was the youngest. Buchan was--at the ripe old age of twenty-seven--the eldest of our group. He was a tall, well-developed specimen with copper-red hair and a beard to match and claimed to have a wife and child in Winnipeg. Martin was a year or so his junior and as stout and strong as an oak barrel, with dark brown hair and a feisty sense of humor.

Come the thaw my partners and I transported our bundles of fur to the trading post at God's Lake. From there they were loaded onto boats and ferried the two hundred miles to the York Factory on the southwestern shore of Hudson Bay. After dividing our profits three ways we discovered we had done far better together than we ever could have alone. We had done so well, in fact, we were able to hire on a Cree Indian who went by the name of Jack to cook for us and keep an eye on the shanty while we were off tending our traplines.

As far as I could tell Jack was older than any of us, and claimed to be the son of an *ogimaa*, which is a cross between a chief and a shaman, to hear him tell it. I don't know about any of that, but I do know he could play a mean fiddle, which he often did to pass the time on those long winter nights.

I am not going to lie and say that our little group went without arguments or differences of opinion. But despite being brought together by happenstance and necessity, the four of us found one another's company agreeable. This I attribute to the fact three of us shared similar backgrounds and admired the hardy voyageurs and colorful Mountain Men who loomed so large in our new-born nation's identity, while Jack knew little English--although he did speak French passing well.

Summer is short in this part of the world, full of mosquitoes and dragonflies, and Fall is shorter still. The first snows came early, turning the towering pines and hemlocks white by the third week of October. The next day Jack frowned at the sky and muttered something about not liking something on the wind, but I did not pay him much heed. Although we cursed the cold and having to trudge about on snowshoes, we knew this meant the beaver, fox, and rabbit would be changing into their prized winter coats all the sooner.

Our humble home shanty was the hub for trapping lines that extended for twenty miles in various directions, like spokes on a wheel. Some followed the borders of the lake and the streams that fed into it and caught mostly beavers, otter, muskrat and mink. Others extended inland and brought us raccoon, fox, lynx, wolf, and the occasional bear. Along these routes were a series of tilts—squat ten by six structures with sharply angled roofs, fashioned from notched spruce logs trimmed by hand to fit tightly together without a single iron nail—that served both as supply depots and shelter. During the trapping season I and my companions would set out along one of these spokes, checking and re-setting our traps along the way, until we reached the end of our territory, then we would head back via an adjacent line.

The snow was already six inches deep--even more where the wind had driven it into drifts—the last time we set out to check the lines. Martin headed west, while Buchan and I headed northeast, leaving Jack to tend the home fires. Each of us was outfitted with an Indian sledge--which we towed behind us—and enough provisions to withstand a fortnight in the bush. The sled dogs were to remain with Jack, to be held in reserve for swift traveling and transporting heavy loads to and from the trading post.

As I said, Buchan and I set out together. The plan was for me to follow him to the first tilt on the line then he and I would go our separate ways. I would head north in the direction of Red Cross Lake while he would head east, towards Edmund Lake.

We set out at dawn and arrived at our destination around noon. We spent the remaining hours of daylight left to us weather-proofing our shelter by gathering moss and alder twigs, which we used to line the walls and roof, while throwing out the rotted remains of the previous season's insulation.

As the sun set, we crawled through the two-foot square opening at the tilt's gable end, tacking off the entrance with a piece of elk hide. In the far corner of the shelter was a portable stove fashioned from a long, rectangular hard-tack tin affixed to a short pipe that vented through the roof. We lost no time in putting the make-shift fireplace to good use and soon the interior was quite warm. It was a snug fit for two grown men, but comfortable enough.

As I bedded down for the night I could hear the wind whistling mournfully about the eaves of the shelter. Every now and again the gusts would rattle the hide that served as our door, as if something outside was desperately trying to find its way in. However, I was too tired to entertain such fancies for long and soon fell asleep.

At some point later I was shaken from a sound slumber to find Buchan's urgent voice in my ear. I opened my eyes to darkness so black I could not see my companion's face, though I knew from the heat of his breath that it had to be inches from my own. Although I had no way of knowing what time it was, I instinctively knew it was midnight.

"What's the matter?" I mumbled.

"Do you hear that?" Buchan whispered.

I focused my senses, still blurred by sleep, but all I heard was the howling of the wind.

"There's nothing out there," I replied tersely. "Go back to bed."

"Are you sure?" Buchan asked, his unseen fingers digging into my shoulder.

I listened again and this time I became aware of a weird noise off in the distance: half-roar, half-wail. "It's no doubt something in one of the traps," I said. "A wolf, perhaps, or maybe a lynx. They can make a hellacious racket when they're caught."

"You're probably right," he said, apparently mollified by my explanation. With that Buchan rolled over and went back to sleep.

I lay there for a long moment, listening to the cry laced within the wind, trying to identify it, but it soon fell silent. I told myself that whatever was responsible for making the sound had either died or moved on and returned to my slumber. However, the dreams that filled the remainder of my night were fitful, providing little in the way of rest.

The next day I rose with the sun, only to find my

companion already up and about. As I relieved myself against a nearby tree, I spotted Buchan kneeling in the snow roughly fifty yards from the tilt, checking one of his traps. Without warning he suddenly cut loose with a string of particularly virulent curses.

"What's the matter?" I called out.

"You were right about that noise last night," he shouted back. "There's something in the trap!"

"What did you catch?" I asked.

"You tell me," Buchan replied, an odd look on his face.

The thing in the trap was unlike anything I have ever seen, alive or dead. There seemed to be something of every animal in it, yet not enough of one to identify the whole. It had the teeth of a rodent, the claws of a lynx, a tail like an opossum's, the build of a fox, a snout like a bear's, and the wide, flat skull of a badger, with deep-set eyes. But strangest of all was it the fact it was hairless. Its naked flesh was ashen and covered with suppurating sores, which stank like rotting meat. Although its left foreleg was firmly clamped within the jaws of the cunningly concealed fox trap, I did not see any signs of blood--fresh or frozen--in the layer of new snow.

"Sweet mother of God—what is that thing?" I gasped.

"I'll be deviled if I know," Buchan replied, eyeing the wretched beast with open distaste. "Perhaps a freakish wolverine, or a raccoon eat-up with the mange. In any case, it's of no use to me or the Hudson Bay Company."

However, as Buchan moved to free the carcass from the trap, the supposedly dead animal miraculously sprang back to life and with a vicious snarl sank its yellowed fangs between the trapper's thumb and forefinger.

"Son of a whore!" Buchan bellowed. Without a

moment's hesitation he pulled the skinning knife from his belt and plunged it into the beast's right eye, killing it once and for all.

"Are you alright, Dick?" I asked, staring at the bright red blood that now stained the white snow.

"I'm fine," he replied stoically, wrapping his wound with a length of cloth from his coat pocket. "It's not the first time I got bit by something I caught." He picked up the empty trap and slung it over his shoulder. "I'm going to move a hundred yards up the line, just in case there are any more like that bastard nosing about."

As I trudged after my friend, I glanced back at the strange creature, only to see its gaunt and hairless body sinking into the snow, as if the very land was conspiring to obliterate all traces of its existence.

After a breakfast of pemmican and black coffee I shouldered my pack and, bidding Buchan farewell and good hunting, headed east, dragging my sledge behind me. I quickly put the strange creature out of my mind. Obviously, it was some kind of diseased freak of nature. What else could it have been? In any case, the beast's days were numbered long before it wandered into Buchan's trap. There was no way it could have possibly survived the winter.

I spent a fortnight in the wilderness along the line, checking, emptying and re-setting my traps, living off the land as well as my provisions, thanks to my trusty rifle. The work was hard and the weather unaccommodating, but nearly every night I enjoyed a meal of fricassee rabbit or roasted spruce grouse and slept in comparative warmth and comfort. There are many who toil in the factories of Toronto and Winnipeg who cannot make such a claim.

As I arrived back at the shanty, my sledge groaning under the weight of the early winter bounty, I saw my other partner, Ben Martin, chopping wood in the dooryard. He had returned the day before with an impressive number of beaver and mink to his credit. That night we sat in front of the camp stove and exchanged tales of our foray into the bush while enjoying Jack's venison cutlets.

I related the tale of the strange, hairless beast Buchan caught, and we had a good laugh at our partner's expense. Rather, I should say Martin and I found it humorous, as the story seemed to unsettle Jack. As I turned in that night, I fully expected to see Buchan trudge into camp the next morning, cursing a blue streak--as was his habit--and bellowing for hot coffee and a plate of beans.

However, the next day passed without Buchan's return. And then another. Come the evening of the fourth day, Martin and I decided to go looking for him. Buchan could have fallen victim to a bear or a mountain lion, perhaps even wolves. But he could have just as easily—and far more likely—run afoul of poachers, most of which would not think twice about killing a solitary trapper for his furs.

The next day we harnessed up the dogs and set out into the vast Manitoban wilderness, with Martin acting as musher and me riding in the sled's basket, my rifle cocked and ready in case of trouble.

Thanks to the dogs we reached the first tilt on the eastern spoke within an hour. Upon our arrival we were surprised to see what looked to be Buchan's Indian sledge beside the shelter, buried underneath a heavy shroud of snow. Martin and I exchanged worried looks.

Whatever fate had befallen our friend, it must have happened shortly after his arrival, over two weeks ago.

I knelt down and lifted the hide that served as the makeshift door of the tilt, only to recoil from the smell that issued forth. I was instantly reminded of the diseased creature that had bitten Buchan, and I wondered—somewhat belatedly—if the beast might have suffered from leprosy or some other communicable illness. After my eyes adjusted from the bright glare of the snow to the dim interior of the shelter, I made out a figure huddled on the floor, wrapped in filthy blankets.

"Buchan-- is that you?" I asked, warily poking the lump with my rifle.

Whatever was inside the mass of blankets stirred feebly and issued a groan so anguished it set the hairs on the back of my neck on end. I put aside my gun and motioned for Martin to help me pull Buchan free of the tilt. As our friend emerged from the rank darkness, I was shocked to see his strapping frame reduced to little more than skin and bones. Buchan's eyes were sunken deep into his skull and seemed as capable of sight as billiard balls. If not for his moaning, I would have thought him dead.

"Merciful God, Buchan—What happened to you?" Martin exclaimed.

The best our partner could do by way of an answer was to lift his right hand, which was swollen to three times its normal size and black with infection. It was from this putrid wound that the smell of rotting meat came from.

Martin and I wrapped him in the bear skin we had brought with us, but as we drew near the sled the dogs began growling and barking--a couple even lunged as if to attack. Martin had to take the whip to wretched beasts--cursing them at the top of his lungs—in order to get them back in line.

I sat in the basket of the sled, holding Buchan tightly in my arms, while Martin drove the dogs. A mile or two out from our base camp, a snowstorm started up. As it grew stronger I thought I heard something that sounded like wailing hidden within the wind. Buchan, who had lain as quietly as a corpse until this point, suddenly began to tremble and twitch, as if taken by a fit. I shouted to Martin to get us home as fast as possible.

By the time we reached the shanty, the snowstorm had become a blizzard, blasting us with sleet that stung like millions of tiny, icy knives. Jack hurried to greet us, only to halt upon catching sight of Buchan, who we dragged between us as if escorting a drunken friend home. The look on the Cree's face was one of utter horror.

"Don't stand there gawking!" Martin snapped. "Get the dogs out of harness and feed them!"

Jack nodded his understanding and moved out of the way, giving us a wide berth. Martin and I entered the cabin, placing Buchan on his own bunk. As I looked down at him I was struck by the peculiar sensation that what lay before me was not, in fact, the man I'd lived and worked alongside for the better part of a year, but an *approximation* of Buchan. I instantly realized how absurd a fancy it was, yet I could not help but feel that someone—or *something*--had hollowed out my friend and climbed inside and was now looking out at me through stolen eyes.

Buchan's moaning became a groan and he began

to writhe underneath the blankets, as if being gnawed upon. His eyes opened and he licked his chapped and bleeding lips with a pinkish-gray tongue. It was clear that he wanted desperately to communicate something to us.

"What is it, Dick?" Martin asked, leaning close so as to hear.

Buchan's voice was as dry and brittle as kindling, but there was no mistaking what he said: *"Hungry."*

"Rest easy, chum," Martin said reassuringly. "You're safe now. I'll have Jack fix you some soup."

This seemed to placate Buchan, and he lapsed back into unconsciousness. Martin took me aside and spoke in a low voice so he would not be overheard. He had been a barber-surgeon before coming to Manitoba, and as such served as the camp physician when necessary.

"He's got a raging fever. He has to lose that hand if he's to survive, no question about it. But I'm going to need laudanum from the trading post to amputate."

"I'll go fetch it."

"Are you sure you want to risk the journey? That's a pretty bad storm out there, and it'll be getting dark soon."

"Buchan would do the same for either of us," I replied. "Besides, the dogs know the way there and back, storm or no. You and Jack try and keep him alive while I'm gone."

"Speaking of which—where'd Jack get off to?" Martin frowned. "It doesn't take *that* long to feed dogs."

I threw my parka back on and went outside, shouting for Jack to get the harness and ganglines out. As I went behind the cabin to where the dogs were penned, I looked around for some sign of the camp cook but he was nowhere to be found. Then I realized two things at the exact same time: the smaller of the two dogsleds was gone, and half the dogs were missing.

Martin was kneeling beside Buchan's cot, wrapping the ailing man's hand in bandages soaked in hot water to draw the infection out. He looked up at the sound of my cursing, which preceded my return by a good thirty seconds.

"That son of a bitch Jack has run off, and he's taken most of the dogs!"

"When this damned storm has blown over and Buchan is on the mend, I'm going to make it a point of tracking that heathen bastard down and skinning him like a beaver!" Martin growled.

"He was always an odd duck, if you ask me," I replied. "When he saw us carrying Buchan, you would have thought he'd seen the devil himself. Something scared him. I'll be damned if I know what."

I lost no time hitching up the four remaining dogs to what was now our only sled and striking out for the trading post, which was twenty-five miles from the camp. Normally it would take two-and-half hours to get there, but that was in good weather. With the storm as bad as it was, I had to trust in the dogs' instincts and sense of direction, as the trail that lead through the forest was all but obliterated by the wind.

After an hour or so the storm suddenly dissipated and the dogs were able to pick up the pace. Just as the sun was about to set, I was rewarded by the sight of the fort-like walls of the God's Lake trading post. My team glided through the front gate just as they were preparing to close them for the night.

Inside the fortified post were several buildings,

including a kennel for visiting trappers to house their sled teams. I paid the old Indian who hobbled out to greet me a few shillings to feed and water my dogs. Taking the bundle of furs I'd brought with me from the sled, I headed into the store to do my trading.

The interior of the Hudson Bay Company store was not that different from the average mercantile in Winnipeg. Inside the large log building a counter ran along the right side of the room, with a glass case on the end displaying such items as horn-handled buck knives and six-shooters. The shelves along the wall behind the counter were stocked with bolts of cloth and other merchandise. Several items of clothing--such as flannel shirts and heavy jackets--hung from the ceiling. Opposite the counter, standing in the very middle of the room, was a large metal stove about which were gathered several wooden chairs.

The clerk behind the counter was a dark-haired Welshman who I had dealt with before and was friendly with. He lifted an eyebrow as I dropped my bundle of furs before him.

"You're here late," he commented as he sorted through what I'd brought him. "Will you be putting up for the night, then?"

"Afraid not, Jonesy," I replied with a shake of my head. "I've got to get back to camp. Buchan's down sick. Martin sent me in to trade for laudanum and rubbing alcohol. I also need a couple of dogs to replace some stolen from me."

"Buchan, eh? That's odd. The gentleman over there was just asking about him earlier."

"What gentleman?"

"The one warming himself by the stove."

I turned to look in the direction the clerk pointed and spotted a figure sitting hunched in one of the chairs drawn close to the stove, puffing on a pipe. He was dressed all in black and sitting so still I had not noticed him when I first entered the room. At least, that is the only reason I could imagine for why I could have overlooked such a distinctive individual.

Judging from the gray in his hair and mustacheless beard, the man was in his fifties, with a physique seasoned by sun and hard work. Indeed, his skin was tanned so deep a brown he looked to have been cast of bronze. As I dropped my gaze, I saw that his right leg was missing just below the knee, beneath which he wore an artificial one made of whalebone ivory.

Although as unusual as his prosthesis might have been, it was nothing compared to his manner of dress, which was not only woefully inappropriate for the harsh climate of Manitoba, but also strangely anachronistic, seeming to be at least twenty-five years out of date. It consisted of a black wool mariner's jacket, a dark-colored cravat, and an odd-looking wide-brimmed black felt hat with a buckled ribbon band.

"Where did *he* come from?" I exclaimed. The sight of a sailor at the trading post was not that unusual, for the merchant marines aboard the ships that ferried the Hudson Bay Company's stockpile of furs to England often came ashore, but that was during the Spring, after the thaw melted the ice.

"I'll be damned if I know," the clerk replied with a shrug. "The old Indian who sees to the gate said he simply walked up out of the snow, just as you see him here. Mighty queer business all around, if you ask me--what with all those 'thees' and 'thous' of his."

As the clerk went about tallying up the furs, I decided to see what this strange, solitary figure wanted with Buchan. "Excuse me, mister--?"

As the old sailor turned toward me, I realized my attention had been so focused on his peg-leg and clothes I had somehow failed to notice the livid white scar that started in the hairline above his brow and ran down his face, disappearing behind the cravat knotted about his neck. Whether it was a birthmark or evidence of some horrific wounding, I could not tell.

The one-legged man glanced at my outstretched hand but did not move to take it. Instead, he removed the pipe from his mouth and slightly bowed his head in acknowledgement. "I was once called captain," he intoned in a rich, deep voice. "But thou may call me Ahab."

"I'm told you've been looking for Dick Buchan..?"

"Aye, that I am, lad," Ahab said, nodding his head once again. "Dost thou know where I might find him?"

"He's one of my partners," I explained. "Are you a friend of his?"

Ahab shook his head as he returned the pipe to his mouth. "I have never met the gentleman. All the same, I have business of the utmost importance with him."

"Might I inquire as to the nature of that business?" I asked

"My own," Ahab replied curtly. The dark look the older man gave me was enough to stop me from pressing the matter.

"I'm sorry if my question offended you, sir. Do you mind if I sit and warm myself?" I asked as I drew up a chair.

The man called Ahab nodded and silently gestured

with his pipe for me to join him. As I sat beside him, I noticed a mark about the older man's neck, partially hidden by his cravat, suggesting a scar. I fought the desire to stare and instead focused my attention on the same thing as he: the glowing embers and flickering flames on view through the vents in the stove's hinged door. After a couple of minutes I grew equal parts bored and bold and decided to resume my questioning.

"So you're a sailor?"

Ahab nodded and replied with a small, humorless laugh: "Aye. Though now I am dry-docked, I once spent forty of my fifty-three years at sea."

"Did your ship come into the Bay before it froze?"

The darkness that had previously filled Ahab's eyes now threatened to reappear. He shook his head and returned his gaze to the stove. "No—I came a different way."

"Do not take my question wrongly; but your manner of speech is most unusual--where do you hail from?"

"I am a Nantucket Quaker, good sir," Ahab replied, not without a touch of pride. "A Yankee, if thou wilt."

"You are very far from home, then."

"Farther than ye can imagine," the old sailor said, his voice melancholy. He took the pipe from his mouth and gave it a sharp rap against his peg-leg, knocking the ashes onto the floor. "Enjoying a good smoke is one of the few solaces those such as me and thee--men who make our living on the knife-edge of the world--can count on," he said, waxing philosophical. "Yet once, in a fit of pique, I threw my pipe in the ocean because it could not soothe me. But now all is forgiven between us, and it provides me comfort once again."

I was about to ask Ahab how he could be possibly

smoking the same pipe he had hurled into the sea when the clerk called out that he'd finished his accounting. I excused myself from the old salt's company and returned to the counter.

"I can trade you the laudanum and rubbing alcohol, but not the dogs," the clerk said, pointing to the bottle of Dr. Rabbitfoot's Tincture.

"Can't you extend us credit? You know we're good for it. The dogs I got now aren't enough to last the winter. If one or two go lame or die on me, I'll be on foot until spring."

"I wish I could help you out, but the Company don't allow credit," the clerk said with a shrug of his shoulders. "Cash on the barrelhead or trade only—them's the rules."

A sun-darkened hand suddenly slapped down onto the clerk's open ledger, placing a gold coin atop the page. "I'll buy thee the dogs thou needeth, my friend," Ahab said. "Granted I ride with thee to thy camp."

The clerk picked up the gold piece and turned it over in his hands, giving out a low whistle of admiration. The coin was a doubloon, the border of which was stamped *Republica del Ecuador: Quito.* On the face were three mountains: on top of the first was a flame, the second a tower, while atop the third was a crowing rooster. Above the three mountains was a portion of the zodiac, with the sun entering the equinox under the sign of Libra. The coin seemed to glow in the dim light of the trading post, as if it possessed a life of its own.

"What say thee, clerk?" Ahab said. "Is that coin enough to buy his dogs?"

"But there's a hole in the middle of it," the clerk

pointed out weakly.

"It is *gold*, is it not?" Ahab said sternly, in a voice that could be heard through a hurricane. "Now give the man his dogs!"

The clerk cringed as if he'd been struck with a cat o'nine tails. "Yes, sir," he replied obsequiously.

As the clerk wrapped the supplies I'd come for in a bundle of rags to protect them from breaking during transport, I turned back to face the man called Ahab.

"I appreciate your generosity, sir. And you are welcome to ride with me back to our camp. But I warn you, Buchan is extremely ill. In fact, I came to the post to trade for medicine in hopes it will save his life. There is a very good chance that he will be dead by the time we arrive."

"All the more important that we leave as soon as possible," Ahab said grimly.

As I headed for the door the sea captain fell in step behind me. There was a line of pegs on the wall just inside the door, upon which were hung several different outer garments, including my own. As I pulled on my gear, I was surprised to see Ahab reach not for a coat, but for a harpoon that stood propped against the door jamb.

It stood taller than the man himself with a shaft fashioned from a hickory pole still bearing strips of bark. The socket of the harpoon was braided with the spread yarns of a towline, which lay coiled on the floor like a Hindoo fakir's rope. The lower end of the rope was drawn half-way along the pole's length, and tightly secured with woven twine, so that pole, iron and rope remained inseparable. The harpoon's barb shone like a butcher's knife-edge in the dim light. It was indeed a fearsome weapon, made all the more intimidating by its incongruity.

"Where is your coat, sir?" I exclaimed, when I realized that my new companion planned to step outside dressed exactly as he was. "It's below freezing outside!"

"Do not concern thyself for my comfort," Ahab said calmly. "I have been in far more inhospitable climes of late."

"Why do you carry a harpoon on dry land?"

"Where a shepherd has his crook, and the cowboy his lariat, this is the instrument of my profession," the old mariner said matter-of-factly. "Wherever I go, it follows with me."

As we approached the kennel to fetch my team, the dogs set up an awful racket. However, it was not the snarling expected from sled dogs jockeying amongst themselves for dominance within the pack, but the growling born of genuine fear. The lead dog--his nape bristling and ears flat against his skull--snapped at me as I moved to harness him. If I had not jerked my hand back when I did, I most certainly would have lost some fingers.

Before I could unfurl my dog-whip, Ahab stepped forward and planted the butt of the harpoon in the frozen mud of the kennel yard, glowering at the wildly barking huskies with those strange eyes of his. One by one, the dogs fell silent, lowered their heads, and skulked away, tails tucked between their legs, without the old sea captain having to utter a single word.

"How did you do that?"

"I have stared down my share of mutineers in my day," Ahab replied. "There is not much difference between a dog and a deckhand; if they smell the slightest whiff of fear, they will tear thee limb from limb."

I added the three new dogs Ahab had staked me to the existing team and harnessed them to my sled. I served as musher while Ahab rode in the basket. With an old horse blanket draped about his shoulders for warmth and his harpoon held across his lap, the dour sea captain looked like some grim Norse king preparing for his final battle.

As we exited through the trading post's gates I looked up at the night sky to find it filled with the shifting radiance of the Aurora Borealis. It was by this light that we made our way back to camp.

Once we were off, Ahab did not utter a single word but instead stared into the darkness, lost in whatever thoughts he kept locked inside his head. As a man who himself had turned his back on the predictability of city life in favor of a wilderness as isolated and unknown as the uncharted ocean, I felt a certain kinship towards the taciturn Quaker who had forsaken the certainty of solid ground for a pitching deck and the vast horizon of the open sea.

The weather for the return trip was cold but otherwise clear, until we came within a mile of our destination. Suddenly the wind picked up and quickly grew to gale-force, accompanied by heavy snowfall. Once again I heard the eerie wailing within the storm, which grew stronger the closer we got to camp. I could not escape the sensation that somehow the blizzard sensed our approach and was not at all pleased by the intrusion.

By the time we made camp the storm was so bad I could barely discern the outline of the cabin. Despite my heavy boots and fur-lined gloves, my hands and feet felt like blocks of ice. I was looking forward to warming myself by the fireplace--the humble chimney of which jutted from the roof of the shanty like the bowl of a giant's pipe. Given my own chilliness, I could only imagine the discomfort Ahab was experiencing. He'd lost one leg to a whale, but I feared he might lose the other to frostbite, as well as some fingers. My concern proved to be ill-placed, however, for he climbed out of the basket as easily as if he was stepping out of a fine horse and carriage. Using his harpoon as a walking stick, Ahab made his way towards the darkened cabin without so much as a backward glance.

"Come back here!" I shouted over the howling wind. "I need help putting up the dogs!"

If the sailor heard me he made no show of it but continued his bee-line to the front door. I grabbed the lantern from the sled and hurried after him, loudly cursing the whole way. I knew Martin well enough to guess what his first reaction would be to the sight of an unannounced stranger armed with what looked like a spear entering his abode in the middle of the night. I caught up with the Quaker just as he was about to put his shoulder to the door.

"Are you daft?" I growled. "If you go barging into a trapper's cabin like that, you're apt to get shot for an Indian or a poacher! And I am in no hurry to clean your brains off my walls!"

"Forgive me, friend," Ahab said, stepping aside so I might go ahead of him. "The prospect of concluding my business has made me--incautious."

Holding up the lantern so that its light would illuminate my face as well as the darkness, I pushed open the door of the shanty. The interior of the cabin was as dark as a well-digger's snuff box.

"Martin! Hold your fire and sheath your knife! It's me!" I called out. "And I have brought a visitor."

I expected to hear my partner's voice in return, telling me to close the damned door before I let in a bear, but there was no reply. I crossed the threshold into the darkness, Ahab's ivory peg-leg tapping against the rough-hewn planks of the cabin floor close behind me.

I hadn't taken more than a couple of steps before I collided with a piece of furniture. I lowered the lantern so I could see where I was going and was shocked to find the interior of the cabin in utter chaos. The table on which my companions and I ate our meals had been reduced to kindling, along with its accompanying chairs. My heart sank at the sight of several sacks of flour and sugar—provisions for the entire winter—dumped amidst scattered traps, furs, cookware, and clothes. The fire in the stone hearth had gone out, its ashes kicked out into the middle of the room, and the cabin was nearly as cold as the wilderness beyond its walls.

"Martin! Buchan! Where are you?" I cried, swinging the lantern about in hopes of it illuminating some sign of my friends. My mind rushed about in circles, as if caught in one of my traps. Had poachers broken into the cabin, looking for furs to steal? Or was this the result of an Indian attack? Perhaps Jack had returned, and he and Martin got into a fight?

I fell silent, hoping I might detect a response. Instead, all I heard was a low, grunting noise, like that of a rooting hog, coming from the back of the cabin, where the shadows were the darkest. Lifting high the lantern, I moved to investigate the sound.

I found Buchan—or rather, what had become of him —crouching in the corner. His back was turned towards me and I could not only see he was completely naked, but every vertebrae along his spine as well.

"Buchan—what happened? Where's Martin?"

In response, Buchan spun about to face me, growling like a cornered dog. Save that he was covered in skin--which was now ash-gray and covered with weeping sores--he was little more than a skeleton. He was so gaunt the ribs in his chest stood out like the staves of barrel and his diseased flesh was pulled so taut across his pelvis it might as well have been wrapped in leather. But the worst of it was that Buchan's face was smeared with gore and saliva and in his boney, claw-like hands he clutched the half-devoured remains of a human liver.

I was so shocked by his wretched condition it took a moment for me to realize that Martin lay sprawled at Buchan's feet, split open from anus to throat, his guts scooped out and piled beside him like those of a field-dressed deer. Strong, iron-hard fingers dug into my shoulder. It was Ahab. I was so horrified I had forgotten he was there.

"Stand aside, friend," the sea captain said grimly. "For this is the business I must attend to." Ahab hoisted the harpoon, his voice booming in the close confines of the cabin like ocean waves breaking against the shore. "*Wendigo! Cannibal Spirit of the North! I am Ahab, hunter of fiends! And in the Devil's name, I have come to claim you!*"

I do not know if the light from the lantern held in my trembling hand played tricks on me or if what I saw was indeed what happened--but as Ahab hurled the harpoon, the thing I knew as Dick Buchan seemed to grow like a shadow cast upon a wall, becoming taller and even thinner than before. As he turned sideways he seemed to disappear and the razor-sharp harpoon sailed past harmlessly and imbedded itself into the wall of the cabin.

Buchan reappeared just as suddenly as he had disappeared, but now he was standing in the hearth of the fireplace. With a terrible shriek--more like that of a wounded elk than a man--he raised his arms above his head, causing his body to elongate yet again, and shot straight up the fireplace chimney. I was so dumbfounded I did not believe my own eyes—until I heard the sound of running footsteps on the roof overhead, followed by a wild, maniacal laughter.

Ahab snatched the harpoon free from the wall and hurried for the door, moving as fast as his missing leg allowed. He charged out into the snowstorm, bellowing curses in seven different languages with the heedless bravery peculiar to those who have hunted and slain creatures a thousand times their size. The dogs—still in harness and attached to their ganglines— frantically barked at whatever it was that was stamping back and forth across the roof over their heads.

As I crossed the threshold to join my companion, I felt something snag the hood of my parka. I looked up and--to my horror--saw a long, boney arm reaching down from the eaves above. I tried to tear myself free of whatever had hold of me but was unable to break its grip. The thing on the roof gave a single tug, as if testing the strength of its hold, and I found my boots no longer touching the ground. As I was dragged upwards to whatever waited me on the roof, my mind flashed back to Martin's fate, and I began to kick and scream as hard as I could. Suddenly Ahab was there beside me, jabbing at my kidnapper with his harpoon.

"Leave him be, Wendigo!" he shouted angrily. *"Thou hast feasted enough for one night!"*

The creature cried out in pain and released its hold, sending me tumbling into a snowdrift. As I got to my feet, I saw it squatting on the roof like a living gargoyle. It no longer bore any resemblance to Buchan, save that it was roughly the shape of a man. Its arms and legs were as long as barge poles and the horns of an elk grew from its skull. Its eyes were pushed so far back in their orbits they seemed to be missing—until I caught a flicker of reddish light in each socket, like those of a wild animal skulking beyond a campfire. Its lips peeled back from its gums, revealing long, curving tusks the color of ivory. Even from where I stood, I could smell the stink of death and decay, just like the horrid freak that had bitten poor Buchan.

"Laugh while thee can, monster!" Ahab shouted at the ghastly apparition. "Thou shalt not escape! I did not drown thirty good men to be bested by thee!"

As if in reply, the creature shrieked like a wild cat, its voice melding with the whistling north wind. It got to its feet and jumped from the roof of the cabin to a nearby pine tree, clearing a distance of forty feet as easily as a child playing hop-scotch. As I watched in amazement the creature darted to the very top of the towering pine--which swayed wildly back and forth in the wind--climbing with the agility of an ape.

Ahab drew back his arm and hurled his harpoon at the abomination a second time. It shot forth as if fired by a cannon, the tow-line flapping behind it like a pennant, only to fall short of its target. Apparently unfazed, the Wendigo leapt into the uppermost crown of the tree beside it, and then the one after that. Within seconds it had disappeared from sight, its scream of triumph fading into the distance.

"Come inside," I said. "The thing is gone. It's over."

Ahab shook his head in disgust as he trudged back into the cabin, his harpoon slung over one shoulder like a Viking's spear. "It will not wander far--not while there is still meat on our bones."

I did not argue but instead busied myself with releasing the dogs from their ganglines. As I returned them to the kennel, I decided it would be wise to keep them in their harnesses, as I foresaw a need to leave camp in a hurry.

Upon returning to the cabin, I found a fire set in the hearth and saw that Ahab had draped a length of canvas over Martin's savaged corpse. The old sailor sat on a stool that was still in one piece, sharpening his harpoon with a piece of whetstone.

"You owe me an explanation, old man," I said sternly. "Whatever your business with Buchan, it now concerns me."

"Fair enough," Ahab replied. "Ask me what thou wilt, and I will answer thee true. But I warn thee, friend—thou might find this truth unbecoming to reason."

"You seem to know what that thing is—you called it 'Wendigo'. What is it?"

"It is a spirit, of sorts. The Indians of the North—the Cree, the Inuit, the Ojibwa--know it well," he explained, pausing to light his pipe. "It comes with the winter storms and is driven by a horrible hunger for human flesh. Some say it overtakes those who stay alone too long in the wilderness, while others claim it possesses only those driven to cannibalism. Of the last I have my doubts, for I have known many a cannibal in my travels, some of whom were men of good character, if not Christian disposition."

I stared at Ahab for a long moment, trying to determine if he truly believed what he had just told me. Under normal circumstances I would have laughed and called him a lunatic. But things were far from normal, as evidenced by poor Martin lying under his makeshift shroud.

"How is it you knew Buchan was afflicted by this spirit?"

"My friend, are thee sure of thine desire for knowledge?" Seeing the steadfastness in my gaze, the old sailor gave a heavy sigh. "Very well, I shall answer thee, as promised. It is my business to know the unknowable, for I have been set a task unlike any since the labors of Hercules. Where once I hunted the great beasts of the ocean, now I stalk the fiends of Hell."

I could no longer hide my incredulity and responded to this declaration with a rude laugh. "Have you lost your mind?"

"I was once mad, but no more," Ahab said sadly. "Would that I had the balm of insanity to allay my suffering; for I am just as sane as thee, my friend, if infinitely more damned."

"What are you babbling about?" I snapped, my patience finally worn thin.

"Once, decades ago, I bragged of being immortal on land and on sea. Now I find I must bear the burden of that boast for all eternity."

As I listened to the old sailor's rant, the hairs on

my neck stood erect. The dark fire deep in Ahab's eyes frightened me in a way the Wendigo's did not. It was one thing to be stalked by a fiendish creature, quite another to be trapped with a lunatic.

"Ah, I see the look in thine eyes," Ahab said with a grim smile. "Thou hath seen what thou hath seen, and yet thee still deem me mad? What of *this*, then?" He pulled aside the cravat about his throat, revealing the marks of a noose no man could have survived. "Aye, I am dead. I have been such since long before your birth. I was once a righteous, God-fearing soul, but I was made wicked by my pride and blasphemous by my wrath. I was determined to avenge myself on the whale that took my leg and offered up my immortal soul in exchange for its annihilation.

"It did not matter to me that I had a child-bride and an infant son awaiting me in Nantucket. Nor did it matter that thirty men, brave and true, had placed their lives and livelihoods in my care. There was a fire in my bosom that burned day and night, and naught would extinguish it, save the blood of the whale that maimed me. Now my child-bride is a withered crone, my infant son dead on the end of a Confederate's bayonet, and my brave crew, save for one, sleeps at the bottom of the sea.

"I chased the accursed beast halfway across the world, and sank my harpoon into its damned hide, only to run afoul of the line. A flying turn of rope wrapped itself about my neck, yanking me below the waves, drowning me within seconds. Yet, to my horror, though I knew myself dead, I was still aware of all that transpired about me. I was helpless witness to the destruction of my ship and the deaths of my men by the whale I had pursued across three seas and two oceans.

"And when it was over, the hated whale pulled me down, down, down—past sunken galleons, past the lairs of slumbering leviathans, past the drowned towers of long-lost kingdoms—down to the very floor of the ocean. With dead man's eyes I beheld a great chasm, from which boiled dreadful beasts with the bodies of men and heads of jellyfish. These abominations freed me of my tether and escorted me into the rift, which lead into the very belly of the world, Hell itself. There I swam not through a mere lake of fire, but an entire ocean, until I came at last to a great throne.

"The throne was fashioned of horn and upon it sat the King of the Fallen, the Devil himself. The Lord of the Damned resembled nothing so much as a gigantic shadow in the shape of a man, with wings of flame and eyes that shone like burnished shields. The Devil spoke unto me, and though he had no mouth, his voice rang like a gong, shaking me to my marrow.

" 'Ahab', he said, 'Thou promised me thine soul in exchange for the life of the whale. Yet here you stand before me, and the fish still swims! Let it not be said that I do not honor my covenants. I have within my kingdom a park unlike any seen on Earth, with trees of bone and rivers of blood. I would populate it with monsters for the pleasure of my sport. Bring me as many fiends as men you led to death, and I shall return thy soul to thee, to do with as thou wish.' "

Although I did not want to believe the outrageous tale the old sailor had just told me, my curiosity got the better of me. "How many men died under your command?"

"Nine and twenty," he replied solemnly.

"And how many monsters have you hunted?"

"This will be the second," he admitted. "There. I have told thee what thou asked, nothing more, nothing less. I have come to this place on the Devil's business and I cannot leave until it is finished. It is as simple as that."

"I have had enough of this lunacy!" I exclaimed, hoping the anger in voice would hide the fear in my heart. "You are welcome to the cabin, but I am taking the dogs and returning to the trading post!"

"The Wendigo will be upon thee within minutes of setting forth," Ahab cautioned.

"I have my rifle and my axe," I countered. "I won't be as easy to kill as Martin."

"Mortal weapons are of no use against that thing."

"It seemed to let go of me quickly enough when you jabbed it with that over-glorified pig-sticker of yours," I pointed out.

"This is no mere harpoon," Ahab said, nodding to spear lying across his lap. "It was forged from the hardest iron there is: the nail-stubs of steel horseshoes —the ones that racehorses wear. I, myself, hammered together the twelve rods for its shank, winding them together like the yarns of a rope. The barbs were cast from my own shaving razors—the finest, sharpest steel to ever touch human skin. But, most importantly of all, it was tempered not in water, but the blood of three pagan hunters, who, at my bidding, opened their veins so that the instrument of my revenge might partake of their strength. Thus I baptized it not in the name of the Father, but the Devil himself. *That* is why the Wendigo feared it."

"All that may very well be true, but I am not a man prone to fancy. If I can see a thing, and hear a thing, and mostly certainly *smell* a thing, then to my mind it is of this world, not the next. And that means I can *kill* it. And if it gets in my way, I will do just that, Devil's menagerie or no!"

"I have no claim on thee," Ahab said quietly as he returned to his whetstone. "Escape if thou can."

I had no idea if Ahab was mad, damned, or a liar, and I had no desire to find which was the truth. Lantern in hand, I left the cabin and hurried to the pen where the dogs were kept. However, before I was half-way there I heard an unholy cacophony of yelps and barks. I quickened my pace--trying not to lose my footing in the knee-high snow and ice--and arrived at the dog-pen just in time to see the Wendigo feed upon the last of the team.

The monster--now easily twice the size of a man--held the hapless animal by the tail as it lowered it head-first into its gaping mouth, the jaws of which were dislocated like those of a serpent. The fiend's belly was hideously distended--far beyond human limits--and I could see the outlines of the other dogs squirming underneath its ash-gray skin as they were digested alive. The Wendigo's jaws snapped shut like a trap, severing the tail of the last dog, which fell to the snow in a gout of crimson.

I had been so horrified by the scene before me I was momentarily rooted to the spot. But the sight of the dog's blood snapped me out of my petrified state, and I turned and fled to the safety of the cabin. I did not dare look behind me for fear of what I might see in pursuit.

As I burst into the cabin, I found Ahab where I had left him, patiently applying the whetstone to his harpoon. "The dogs are dead!" I shouted. "It ate all of them!"

Ahab nodded as if this was something to be expected.

"The Wendigo is hunger incarnate. No matter how much it eats, its belly is never full; it exists in a perpetual state of starvation. The more it eats, the larger it grows; the larger it grows, the hungrier it gets. There is no end to it."

My mind was still reeling from the fresh horror I had just witnessed and was only just realizing I was trapped. While I might have been able to flee the Wendigo using the sled, there was no way I could possibly escape the camp on foot. It was then I surrendered my disbelief and embraced Ahab's reality as my own.

"How can we fight against this monster?"

If Ahab had an answer I did not hear it, for at that exact moment the window in front of which I stood abruptly shattered inward. I turned to see an emaciated arm as long as I am tall reach through the broken sash. I screamed in terror as the Wendigo's fingers--the tips black from frostbite--closed about my leg, dragging me inexorably toward whatever stood on the other side.

Ahab was on his feet as quick as lightning, his harpoon at ready. Without hesitation he dashed forward and plunged the spear into the Wendigo's arm. The monster screamed in agony and anger as it let go of me, the absurdly long extremity withdrawing like a snake fleeing a fire.

"I have cost it an arm, if I'm lucky!" the old sailor said excitedly, pointing to a foul-smelling tar-like substance splashed across the floor. "That bastard won't escape me by climbing the rigging *this* time!"

Harpoon in hand, Ahab rushed out of the cabin and into the snowy night. I followed close behind for fear the creature might return while he was gone. I saw Ahab standing in the door-yard beside the sled that was to have been my escape, surveying his surroundings with eyes accustomed to scanning the open ocean for the fleeting flash of a fluke or the spume of a distant whale.

"*Thar she blows!*" Ahab sang out, pointing to a shambling shape moving off in the near distance. I could make out a gray silhouette framed against the darkness, its right arm hanging uselessly at its side.

Ahab hurled his harpoon at the figure, and because it had its back to us the creature was unable to play its trick of turning sideways and disappearing. This time the harpoon found its target, striking the Wendigo between the shoulder blades.

The creature roared in angry pain and instantly took flight, running faster than any thing on two legs ever could. Ahab quickly grabbed the towline attached to the end of the harpoon and secured it to the brush bow of the sled. "Fare thee well, friend," he said as he took his place behind the handlebars. "Lord willing, we shall never meet again--in this world or the next!"

And with that the sled sped away, shooting across the snow-covered landscape like a longboat dragged by a stricken whale. As the Devil's huntsman and his monstrous quarry disappeared from sight, Ahab's shouted curses were carried back to me on the wind, mixed with the unholy wail of the Wendigo, until they became one and the same.

So exhausted was I by the terrors I had undergone, I returned to the cabin and immediately collapsed into a deep sleep. When I awoke the next day, it was to find the blizzard abated and a gun in my face.

I discovered that a posse had been sent out from the trading post in search of me on account of my stealing three dogs. I insisted that I was innocent of the charges—that the dogs had been paid for--cash on the barrelhead. But even if they had been willing to believe me in regard to the dogs, there was still the matter of the mutilated corpse of Ben Martin that lay twenty feet from where I slept.

I was promptly arrested for the murder of Martin, as well as Dick Buchan--even though his body was never found--and taken back to the trading post and locked up in the stockade. And here I sit, awaiting the thaw, when I will be taken down to Winnipeg and put on trial.

I tried to explain about Ahab, and how he bought the dogs for me, but the clerk who waited on us claims no such person was ever in his store, and that there is no coin in the trading post's coffers that matches the description of the old sea captain's doubloon.

My only hope is that Jack will reappear and vouch for what he saw in Buchan's gaunt, sunken eyes. I realize now the reason for the Cree cook abandoning the camp. If he does not come forward, then I will either be hung as a murderer or imprisoned as a madman. I am not sure which fate is worse.

Perhaps I *am* mad, after all. For sometimes late at night, when the frigid wind blows out of the north and whistles cruelly through the bars of my cell, I can still hear Ahab's voice as he is dragged across the vast, uncharted wilderness by his captured fiend: *"Run! Run! Run to thy infernal master! To the last I grapple with thee; from Hell's heart, I stab at thee!"*

THE SIGN OF THE SILVER HAND

A Prince Corum Story

From *The New York Times*, March 12, 1995

AMATEUR ARCHEOLOGIST SETS OFF IN SEARCH OF FABLED LOST CITY

NEW YORK, NY: Harald Bekk, amateur archeologist and noted eccentric millionaire, announced today that he will be leaving for Peru on a privately funded expedition in search of the legendary city of gold known as El Dorado. During the sixteenth century the city—whose streets were reportedly paved with gold and boasted a ruler that started each day by coating himself with gold dust in order to greet the sun—was the subject of futile searches by Pizarro, de Orellana, Quesada, and Sir Walter Raleigh. Sir Jonas Dabney of the Royal Geographic Society—when asked his opinion of Mr. Bekk's planned expedition—responded: "If Harald wants to waste his family's fortune chasing after fairy tales and hoaxes, that's up to him."

◆ ◆ ◆

From *The New York Times*, August 27, 1995:
ECCENTIRC MILLIONAIRE FEARED DEAD

LIMA, PERU: Harald Bekk—amateur archeologist and heir to the Bekk Chemicals fortune—has been officially listed as missing and presumed dead by the American consulate in Lima. Bekk—who left the United States for the Andes this past May—was on an expedition into the mountain country in search of the legendary city of El Dorado. He was last seen in the community of Santa Ana on May 16th, where was reported to be in the company of two Quechua Indian guides and several llamas, headed in the direction of the Madre de Dios regions—a no man's land of treacherous mountain passes and desolate wilderness that abuts the border of Bolivia and the Amazon basin. It is uncertain, but one eyewitness claims to have seen Bekk talking to a local believed to be a criminal. Bekk Chemicals sent a search party into the region in early July and discovered evidence that the expedition had fallen pretty to bandits. However, there was no sign of the missing millionaire. His younger brother has taken over control of the company until such time as the elder Bekk's death can be substantiated. "I really want to try and remain positive about the whole thing," Sebastian Johann Bekk announced today to reporters. "I keep hoping and praying that the phone will ring and I'll find out Hal's managed to pull it out of the hat, yet again. But I will admit that the outcome doesn't look good. It's such a huge country—most of it still uncharted. We may never find him."

Excerpts from the journal of Harald Armitage Bekk:

May 19, 1995

We're now more than a day's walk from Santa Ana—and in the complete opposite direction I had originally chosen! The new guide, Javier, assures me that what I seek can be found in the wilds of the Madre de Dios. Javier introduced himself to me just as we were leaving the village, begging for a job as a guide. He is a handsome, rather personable young *mestizo.* At first I suspected his claim of knowing an ancient family secret concerning the location of El Dorado was poppycock—just another native out to bilk an Americano of his money. But he was so insistent! There is an intensity to him I find compelling. Felipe was against my hiring him, but I'm now convinced he knows something. If we're on a wild goose chase, at least we have the provisions for high-altitude camping.

May 21, 1995

Juan and Felipe complained to me about Javier this evening. Seems they don't trust him. They think he has ulterior motives for joining us. I told them they were paranoid. As far as I can see, Javier has gone out of his way to be helpful and ingratiate himself. I could tell neither Felipe or Juan liked what I had I had to say, but they did not threaten to quit. The Quechua are a trustworthy folk, and I know they'll stay with me to the end on this. Still, I can't blame them for being on edge. The country is both awesome and frightening in its austere beauty, and its emptiness can prey upon the mind.

Writing. As best I can. Difficult. My fingers ache from the cold. It took me a long time to get the survival tent pitched. I shouldn't complain. I'm lucky I'm not huddled between some rocks with nothing but my parka. Don't know how long the battery on the lamp will hold out. I must put everything down in case I don't make it. So whoever finds this will know.

We were lead into a trap by Javier. Turns out he's the leader of a group of bandits. They heard about the rich Americano searching for El Dorado. Poor Juan and Felipe were right. My judgement was way off this time. Five days from Santa Ana, Javier lead us into a box canyon. The bandits came out of nowhere. Must have been ten to fifteen of them. Javier knocked me unconscious before I had a chance to bring my rifle to bear. When I came to, it was the find myself lying on my side, hands tied behind my back. I could hear Felipe and Juan screaming for mercy as the bastards tortured them.

While I was lying there near the fire Javier strutted up. He was wearing my watch and made sure I saw it as he squatted down to taunt me. All his boyish charm had disappeared and I found his smile cruel and without the slightest trace of humanity.

"Where is the money, American?"

"You took it all. There is no more."

"Don't lie to me!" Javier spat, delivering a swift kick to the side of my head that sent my vision swimming. "You are very rich, Senor Bekk! You have more money! Maybe you hide up your ass, yes?"

It is impossible to explain to a brute like Javier that a man of my wealth doesn't carry it on my person. What funds I'd brought to Peru were spent on kitting out the expedition with high-altitude camping gear, hiring guides, and buying provisions. The barbaric murdering thieves did not believe me, and were going to slice me open like the proverbial golden goose. And there was nothing I could do to prevent it. Javier motioned for one of his men to yank me to my feet by my bound wrists. The pain was horrible.

"You tell me where the money is, American, and you die quick. Otherwise I let my men use you for a woman. They been in mountains long time. Human ass better than llama pussy."

Before Javier could threaten me any further, there was a high-pitched scream. At first I thought it was one of my guides finally being put out of their misery. But there came a strange noise—almost as if the surrounding mountains had cleared their collective throat—and the upper torso of one of the bandits threw through the air and landed in the campfire in front of me.

I didn't get much of a look, but what little I saw was horrible. It was as if he'd been bitten off at the waist and spat out like the butt of a cigar. Even more hideous was the realization that his upper torso was still alive and screaming in doubled agony as his hair and clothing caught fire.

As I stared in horror at the grisly sight before me, a fierce wind came from nowhere. And although it was still early afternoon, a great black shadow blocked the sun, rendering the valley as dark as a moonless night. The bandits began to panic and started shouting and screaming. I used the pandemonium to throw my full weight against my captor, knocking him to the ground. Once I had him down I kicked him hard enough to keep him there and quickly found his knife and used it to free myself.

The brigands' camp was in a state of utter panic. Men were running back and forth, shrieking like children and firing their weapons into the surrounding blackness. Somehow during this madness I succeeded in finding one of my llamas. By sheer good fortune Javier's men had yet to go through its packs, which meant that the tent and survival gear was still intact. I untied the frightened animal and made my way out of the canyon. But before I left that nightmarish slaughterhouse I saw one last horror—and it is something I will carry with me to my grave, whether my dying day be tomorrow or a hundred years from now.

The place stank of gunpowder and blood as the screams of the bandits grew louder and louder. There were bodies—and parts of bodies—strewn everywhere, as if a spoiled child had grown angry with her dollies and broken them in a fit of pique. I saw Javier—spattered with the blood of his comrades—suddenly leap ten feet into the air. At first I imagined he had jumped of his own volition—then I realized he was being lifted by his hair! Then with a single swift motion his midriff twisted completely around as if his spine was made of taffy. There was a wet snapping sound—like that of a celery stalk in a stocking full of gelatin—and his body from the hips down dropped to the ground. The bandit leader screamed for what seemed a very long time but could not have been more than a few seconds. At least I pray to God it was that brief.

Even though he was a murderer, liar, and a thief—and would have, without a doubt, ended my life as horribly as any monster might—I felt pity for the poor bastard. As it is, my last memory of Javier will be of him hanging suspended in mid-air against that unnatural inky void, his mouth opened wide in a rictus of pain as his intestines spilled out like the tentacles of some grisly Portuguese Man O'War.

I don't remember much of what happened after that. I have no idea how long I fled with my pack animal or in what direction—but when I finally came back to my right mind I was on an exposed mesa, shivering as the wind cut through me like an obsidian knife. It was starting to get dark and if I didn't get my tent pitched soon, I knew I'd die of exposure. The Andes is one of the most inhospitable terrains on the planet. During the day it can become hotter than Death Valley, while at night you might literally freeze solid. The air is so thin it can ruin your lungs and shrink your brain. Any rational man finding this journal will already think me insane—or at least suffering delusions brought on by oxygen deprivation. I wish I could believe that was true. I once called this portion of the country god-forsaken—but it has more than its fair share of devils.

The tent is warmer now than when I started on this entry, but I dare not leave the protection of my sleeping bag to check on my llama. I'm very weak and the kick to my head seems to have done some real damage. There's blood crusted on my right temple. I've been writing by the light of the battery-lantern, but the charge is starting to fade, so I must end now. I don't want it to die on me. I managed to eat a little chocolate and drink some tinned milk. Starvation doesn't concern me right now. Instead, I lay here wondering is that monstrous living shadow is still out there. And if so—is it looking for me?

Don't know what day it is. It's so damn cold. So cold I can barely think, much less write. Llama died. It fell to the ground with this awful gasp, like all the air had been let out of it at once. I held its head in my lap as it breathed its last. The eyes seemed so sad, so tired. I wanted to cry but didn't dare. My tears would freeze on my face and in my eyes. As it is, my skin is flaking away like paint on an old barn. The wind never stops up here. It's like a banshee, constantly wailing in my ears and plucking at my clothes.

I spent too much time repacking my tent and what few provisions are left so I can carry them myself, but my fingers don't work as well as they should. I can't kid myself. I have frostbite. Got no idea where I am. Maybe still in Peru, maybe in Bolivia. Hard to say. Crossed a suspension bridge that stretched across a chasm a good thousand feet deep. When I first saw it I thought I'd finally come across civilization. Perhaps a herding community of some sort. But as I got closer I could see it was extremely old—perhaps dated back to the conquistadors. It wasn't even a proper suspension bridge—more a cat-walk with a thick cable of interwoven vines anchored on either end to massive stone plinths, with a second set of ropes running alongside it. Although it was very old it seemed to be in good shape. The grim knowledge I had nowhere else to go drove me onto that precariously swaying rope.

My predicament was made even worse by the pain in my right eye. It's grown progressively worse over the last couple of days. I suspect Javier's boot detached the retina. At least my impaired vision kept me from staring down into the chasm as I inched myself across the divide.

At one point I thought I could hear someone—or *something*—calling my name. At first it sounded like my father. But as I strained to listen, the voice became bubbly and thick, as if a tar pit had been given the power of speech.

Once I crossed the bridge, I noticed there was a glyph of some sort carved into the face of the supporting plinth. It was the outline of a six-fingered hand. Perhaps there was a similar sign on the other side that my poor vision caused me to overlook, or exposure to the elements had scoured away. I certainly wasn't going to go back to check.

Curious. Who made it? Why? What does it mean? The Maya of Central America had a caste of wizard-kings who sported extra fingers and toes as proof of their godly lineage—but the Inca had no such tradition. At least none that I'm aware of.

Tired. Sleep now.

Day One

The date on this entry is due to the fact I do not know the month and date of today. Manco assures me I've been drifting in and out of a coma for at least one moon, possibly longer. I'm going to try and write what little I remember down. It's important that I do this, so I can understand what the hell is happening to me.

It was the day after I'd crossed the bridge. I awoke so tired I was tempted to simply go back to sleep, but I did not dare. If I did not continue moving I would simply die of starvation if the exposure didn't get me first. If I was going to die I was determined it would be on my feet. I would rather plummet to my death down a bottomless chasm than die wrapped in my sleeping bag like some wretched bug.

The first thing I clearly remember is standing on the edge of a cliff that overlooked a valley. I don't know how long I stood there staring before I realized I was looking down on a city. Although the vision in my right eye was all but gone, I could make out enough detail to realize —what with its ziggurats and cobblestone streets—that this city had never seen the Spaniards that ravaged the Inca empire five hundred years ago. My mind was so numbed from cold, pain, and hunger that it took me a very long time to realize that the city before me was none other than El Dorado.

I should have felt something. Joy. Elation. Triumph. But instead there was nothing inside me. I had traveled halfway across the glove to this desolate mountain aerie in search of a city hundreds died looking for. And all I could think of was that I'd found El Dorado and no one would ever know, because I could feel myself dying as I stood on that wind-swept cliff. I wasn't scared, oddly enough. Just sad. And tired. But then I caught sight of something that sent a surge of fear coursing through me like a live wire.

There was a shadow atop the mountain across the valley from where I stood. And as I watched, it began to glide down the peak in my direction. At first I mistook it for a simple shadow cast by a passing cloud. But then I saw it was not so much a shadow as the utter absence of light, moving across the ground with an awful fluidity—like a land-borne oil slick. When the shadow extruded an appendage that looked like a cross between an octopus tentacle and a swan's neck I felt dread that almost made me swoon.

For a brief moment there was no sight, no sound, no smell. Then I was back in the real world, stumbling wildly down what turned out to be rough-hewn stairs cunningly hidden in the cliff-face. I wobbled precariously for a second then turned to see where the pursuing shadow might be. There was a black something towering above me, barely ten feet away. As I stared horror-struck, the shadow-beast stretched upward, waving what looked like a legion of licorice whips the thickness of my wrist. From the depths of its inky heart came a horrible ululation like that of the Dead wailing from the grave. The sound was so blasphemously evil I lost control of my senses.

Again there was darkness, then pain—horrible pain that yanked me from the limbo of unconsciousness. I found myself lying at the bottom of the flight of hidden stairs. I could see enough of my right leg to know it was badly broken. The pain was so severe I almost forgot about the shadow-beast. Almost. There was a touch at my shoulder and I gave out with a great shout—more from fear than pain. A thin brown face with broad features and hair the color of a raven's wing filled my vision. The stranger looked to be Quechua—one of the full-blooded descendants of the ancient Inca—but he spoke in a dialect I could barely understand, Maybe it was the shock coming on, but I could swear what he said to me was: "I have been waiting for you."

I don't remember much of what happened after that. I know now that my savior's name was Manco and that he managed to take me to the city by using a drag hitched to a llama. He brought me to his house and set my broken leg and tended to my other wounds by using herbal potions and salves. If I was aware of his ministrations at the time, I have no memory of it.

Manco assures me that on several occasions during my recovery I spoke to him and I frequently babbled while feverish. I remember none of it, although there are vague flickers at the back of my brain that might be ghosts of memories or the phantoms of dreams. However there are a couple of images that continue to haunt me. I know they cannot be true memories because they are so fantastic and involve people I have never seen before—yet there is a familiarity to these dimly glimpsed faces that makes me doubt they are entirely the creatures of fancy.

There was a man—at least I believe it was a man. His build was so slight and manner so delicate he could easily have been mistaken for a woman. He was walking towards me through a thick ground mist. As he grew nearer I could see that while he was humanoid in shape he was not exactly human. His skull was long and narrow, with slightly pointed ears that were without lobes. Long, fine hair the color of silver threads hung below his shoulder and his eyes were large and almond-shaped. As he drew closer to me he smiled with a wide, expressive mouth. He was dressed in a brilliant scarlet robe with wide sleeves and full skirt that billowed back as he strode purposefully through the heavy fog.

I smiled in return and moved to greet him. Although I have never laid eyes on this outlandish stranger before in my life, he seemed familiar to me. Perhaps he was a long-lost friend or a relative? As we approached one another I could see his right eye was covered by an elaborately jeweled patch and he was wearing a silver gauntlet on his left hand that glittered like the scales of a fish. The one-eyed stranger smiled even more warmly than before and offered his hand in greeting. As he did so I realized that what I had mistook for a gauntlet was actually gleaming, silver skin and that his hand boasted six fingers. And as odd as it may sound, the sight of it did not alarm me.

Before I could grasp the hand of the stranger in scarlet a transformation overtook him. His clothing and body began to wrist and warp, as if something deep within his being was tunneling its way out. The color drained from his rose-pink complexion until it was bleached white as bone. His features became even more ascetic and gaunt, his solitary yellow eye replaced by two that burned as red as the setting sun. The scarlet robe withered and blackened, becoming an elaborate suit of obsidian armor as bat-wings sprouted from the helm atop his head. In his previously empty right hand he now held a great sword, the blade of which was made of black metal carved with strange runes.

My smile of welcome faltered and I took a step back from the albino warrior standing before me. As disturbing as the bone-white reaver was, my attention was riveted on his sword—which was singing to itself.

The fear I felt coursing through me at that moment was very real—for even in my dream I recognized the sound it made as identical to that of the shadow-beast that attacked me. Even now the memory of it makes me shudder with revulsion.

I finally came to my senses and stayed in them a few days ago. My first coherent thought was the realization that I was staring up at a simple roof made of adobe. I felt limp as a wet sock and there was a sharp stab of pain in my leg as I struggled to sit up—but otherwise my mind was clear. My second thought was that my surroundings seemed strangely flat, Then I realized I was only looking out of my left eye. Instinctively I tried to touch my face—but there was no longer a hand attached to my left wrist, just a swath of bandages packed with an odd-smelling poultice. Stunned, I let my arm drop back down.

"You are awake now. Good."

The Incan man I glimpsed before blacking out was at the foot of my bed. He was dressed in a full-length poncho woven from alpaca wool and holding an earthenware bowl in his hands. Although his dialect was obscure I now had no trouble understanding him. Apparently during my convalescence I had learned his language as I drifted in and out of delirium..

"Who are you? Where am I?" I rasped.

"I am Manco, last of the priests of the Sun-God and king of their city, and you are in my house, just as I have told you every day since I found you. Here, I have brought you some soup. It will strengthen you."

Manco helped prop me up so I could drink from the bowl. I clutched at it clumsily, trying to grasp it with a phantom left hand. Manco saw the look of discomfort and grief on my face.

“I had to remove your hand," He explained. "The cold had claimed it. As for your eye—it was withered when I discovered you.”

“You say you found me—but where am I? Is this El Dorado?”

Manco frowned and shook his head. “I know not of this ‘El Dorado’ you speak of. Nor do I know of Tanelorn.”

“Tanelorn?” Now it was my turn to look confused. “What’s Tanelorn?”

“While you fought the fever you kept asking me if you were on the road to Tanelorn. It seemed very important to you.”

“I’ve never heard the word before—although now that you mention it, it seems familiar somehow.”

“Perhaps it is a thing from another life, or a place from your dreams,” Manco said matter-of-factly.

“So, if this is not El Dorado—where am I?”

“You have reached World’s End.”

◆ ◆ ◆

Day Two

From what I’ve managed to pick up so far Manco is a priest. Or perhaps he’s a wizard. Or a king. He uses the phrases interchangeably. Manco also happens to be the last living inhabitant of El Dorado. Except the Inca didn’t (don’t?) call it that. Their name for the city translates into “World’s End.” I haven’t had a chance to see anything of the city except the inside of my sick room. I’m still very weak and Manco says it will be several more days before I’m well enough to walk, even with my leg in a splint. So I occupy my time by scribbling in my journal.

Manco found what little remains of my personal possessions scattered up and down the stairway that leads from the valley to the mesa above. There was not much left that wasn't ruined, but my journal and writing implements were among the few things left untouched. Still, it chafes me to lie here while El Dorado awaits. No. Shouldn't call it that. El Dorado was a Spanish interpretation of an ancient legend, seen through a lens of golden greed.

I told Manco the stories of his city—that it was supposed to have a ruler who covered himself in gold dust at the start of the day in order to greet the Sun God and reflect its rays. He laughed in amazement. He was equally astonished that so many of my people would waste so much time, effort, and blood searching for such a fanciful vision. Then I found myself in the uncomfortable position of explaining to him how those self-same foolish explorers had destroyed his people's empire. To my relief he did not take the news badly.

"I am not surprised the Inca are no more. To tell the truth, the people of World's End came to that conclusion centuries ago. Even though our city is isolated and known to only a few, there had always been commerce between our valley and the empire. But ever since the Shadow Lord returned to our valley no travelers have come here."

"The Shadow Lord? You mean that—thing?"

Manco nodded, a dark look crossing his face. "The Shadow Lord is the enemy of the Sun God. It was this creature that the hero-god Viracocha saved my ancestors from when he first emerged from the sea. This city was raised in his honor and serves as his tomb."

"But surely gods do not die, my friend."

"Gods can do anything. Including die--and come back," Manco replied with a smile. "Many years ago—long before the Inca ruled the Andes—a white-skinned god came from the sea. He was a mighty warrior whose power came from the Sun and he possessed a magic hand and a magic eye. This god—who my people called Viracocha—wore a cloak the color of fresh blood. He killed the monsters plaguing my ancestors and taught them the skills they would need to build great cities and farm the arid highlands. He also taught them wizard-spells and the art of seeing the future. And although he was a god and lived to an age greater than any known by mortal man, there came a time where he passed from this life. But before he died, Viracocha commanded his priests to build a special tomb to house his remains and safeguard his magic eye and hand until the day he would return to claim them.

"So the priests traveled far into the wilderness to build a city composed of priests, wizards, and oracles. These citizens would keep alive the rituals of Viracocha and protect his relics. But to build such a place they needed strong backs. So every village under Incan domination surrendered a number of its citizens to the labor force. And after the workers and artisans completed their tasks, the priests and temple-maidens—those whose destiny it was to tend the sacred things and guard their secrets—put them to death. That way none could tell of the city's location. What commerce transpired between World's End and the rest of the empire was conducted by a handful of tongueless priests.

"Then a century later the Shadow Lord descended upon our valley. It must have finally sensed Viracocha's death. My sixth grandfather knew that the Shadow Lord planned to destroy the magic eye and hand so Viracocha could never return, so he called upon the god's magic to erect a barrier that would protect the valley from the Shadow Lord. He hoped that it would grow weary of waiting and eventually leave. But as the months gave way to years and the years to decades, it became clear that the Shadow Lord would not give up.

"It constantly roams the mountains surrounding the valley, searching for a way to get in. It is a voracious creature, given to feasting on the blood and souls of all it finds. Over the centuries it has claimed more than its fair share of my kinsmen. Although the agricultural oases and llama paddocks that sustain the city were protected by the spell, my people were trapped like lizards in a jug. The Shadow Lord could not get in, but neither could they leave. Over time the population of World's End became increasingly inbred. Uncle married niece. Half-brothers and sisters became man and wife. My own parents were aunt and nephew. The men became sterile, the women infertile. Those who did succeed in bearing young were more apt to produce stillborn monsters than healthy children. The hideously deformed that did not die at birth were left on the mesa to perish of exposure or be claimed by the Shadow Lord.

"During the last century, the wizard-kings of the city grew increasingly desperate. They knew their people would die out soon—and with them would perish the secrets and rituals of Viracocha. There would be no one left to observe the rituals that hold the Shadow Lord at bay, and then all they and the generations before them sacrificed so much for would be lost.

"The best and bravest of the warrior-priests attempted a series of expeditions to the world beyond our valley in hopes of avoiding the Shadow Lord and returning with fresh breeding stock. There were fifteen such expeditions over the years. They all failed. Soon all that was left in World's End were the very old, the very young, and the sick. My mother was well into her fiftieth year when I was born—one of five healthy children born in twenty years. There were no more born after me. The last of my people died six years ago. I have been alone ever since."

"That must have been very terrible for you."

"It was bad. Very bad. But I have my faith. I knew that Viracocha would return as the prophecy proclaims. And now here you are."

"Beg pardon?"

"You were spared the Shadow Lord's wrath because you are blessed by Viracocha. Where the Shadow Lord is the manifestation of Chaos, Viracocha is Order incarnate. They constantly war with one another—with mankind serving as their pawns and champions. The fact you survived the Shadow's Lord attack when the others did not, and found your way to World's End is proof that you are the one the ancients prophesied would return to claim the sacred relics and bring Viracocha back to life."

I wanted to tell Manco that if he is banking on me being his messiah then he is sorely mistaken. But that would be rude. After all, he did save my life and nurse me back to health. If he wants to think I'm his god reborn—well, where's the harm in humoring him?

Besides, he'll figure out his error soon enough.

Day Seventeen

Big day today! Manco finally decided I was strong enough to venture outside! Even though I was prepared for some pain, I nearly blacked out when he helped me to my feet. He gave me some coca leaves to chew on, which helped somewhat, but I was still dripping cold sweat and trembling like a puppy. Still, it felt good to step into the sunshine and breathe fresh air—thin as it is.

This was my opportunity to see World's End close up. I had to hide my dismay that there were no gold paving stones. In fact while the city looked picture-perfect from the mesa above, on closer inspection it proves to be in an advanced state of decay. According to Manco the last few generations of World's End citizens were—to put it kindly—somewhat degenerate. There are huge cracks in the sides of buildings, the streets are missing paving stones, the central temple needs a new coat of whitewash, and the aqueducts leak like sieves. While Mano is a very industrious and able fellow, there's only so much a solitary man can do to maintain a city this size.

Still, World's End is not without its wonders. What immediately caught my attention was the decorative motif on almost every surface in the city: the stylized outline of a six-fingered hand. It is the same as the symbol I saw carved into the bridge-support, save that these are far more detailed and there is an eye embedded in the palm. Everywhere I look the six-fingered hand can be seen—engraved on doorways, woven into tapestries, and even stamped into the paving stones underneath my feet.

I asked Manco what the hand symbolized and he said it was the sign of the returning god, who would arrive missing his left hand and right eye. A strange chill came over me as I recalled my dream. No doubt my feverish imagination fixated on the symbol I'd glimpsed earlier and was subconsciously aware of my own hand being amputated, producing the six-fingered stranger in my nightmare. But how did that explain the eye?

This is starting to unnerve me. I will stop writing now.

◆ ◆ ◆

Day Thirty-Three

Last night was horrible—the worst I've endured since escaping Javier and his band of murdering thieves. It began just before sundown. I was out with Manco, helping him gather maize and potatoes from the oases that ring the city. My leg is now out of the splint and I hobble about fairly easily with the help of a cane. Although the city is crumbling to ruin, the farming terraces Manco's forefathers designed to sustain World's End still thrive, although properly tending them takes up most of Manco's day—and now that I'm well enough to be of some help, mine as well. Just as we were loading the llamas with the day's harvest they began to fidget and spit in agitation.

"What is the problem with these wretched beasts?" I cursed after getting an eyeful of sputum.

Without answering Manco turned to look farther up the valley, so I followed his gaze. I saw what looked like several dozen human figures silhouetted against the setting sun, clustered along the valley's ridge. Manco's face went deathly pale and his hands began to tremble.

"What are they? Bandits?" I asked.

"Worse. They are the Shadow Lord's minions."

"Can they hurt us?"

"Not if we stay in the valley."

Just then the figures on the ridge began wailing, their unified voices thick and bubbling. The air suddenly reeked of boiling pitch as they called out to Manco in Quechan.

"Manco, help us!"

"Manco! Please save us!"

"Save me, Manco!"

"Manco, I need your help!"

My friend bit his lower lip and grabbed the lead llama's bridle. "Come, we must hurry back to the city! It will be dark soon!"

"Manco, you said these are the Shadow Lord's minions—but who are these people? Why are they calling out to you for help?"

"They are my family."

"I don't understand."

"I'll explain once we're safely back inside the city," he promised.

A few hours later—after we'd finished the last of the guinea pig stew--I brought up the people on the hill again. Manco seemed uneasy but did not evade the subject.

"What I did not mention when I told you the story of how World's End came to be is how my people were driven mad. While the majority of my ancestors were resigned to their fate once the Shadow Lord came to the valley, there were those who could not accept the horror of it all. Some of them tried to escape, only to be consumed body and soul by the Shadow Lord. But there were others who were seduced by its evil and went willingly to their doom. Each generation saw more and more of my people succumbing to the Shadow Lord. Some called it suicide, others saw it as self-sacrifice—but whatever their fate, it did not end with death.

"When the moon is full those who the Shadow Lord has claimed are reanimated and gather at the mouth of the valley. There they cry out to their friends and loved ones. This has been their way for centuries. Dozens of my kinsmen have been lured from their homes and into the deadly embrace of the Shadow Lord while attempting to aid family and lovers beyond all help. Those wretched creatures we saw today were my cousins, my uncles, my aunts—my very own parents. Listen." He held up a hand for silence and cocked his head. "You can hear them wailing."

At first I heard nothing—then, as I concentrated I could make out the distant caterwauling of scores of human voices. I felt my flesh creep all the way to the bone. If ever there was madness, this was its call.

"How much longer will they go on?" I asked.

Maco shrugged. "The night is still new and the Shadow Lord very angry. It is scared because it knows Viracocha is returning. It is possible the minions will cry until sunrise. The higher the moon climbs in the sky, the louder they will become. I learned to ignore them as best I can. I suggest you do the same.

I kept Manco's suggestion in mind as I lay on my sleeping palette, trying not to listen to the distant voices. At first it sounded like the yowling of alley-cats in heat, but as the night grew longer I could discern individual voices amongst the undifferentiated mass. Then I thought I recognized one. For a brief heartbeat I heard my father calling my name, as I had heard it on the bridge weeks ago. Then I heard my younger brother, Johann, calling out for me. Then there was Javier, threatening me with sodomy and death if I didn't reveal myself to him. Although these voices were familiar to me, I knew what the Shadow Lord's scheme was. He wasn't going to trick me into wandering out of the valley in search of long-lost family members. I allowed myself a sneer of derision as I drifted off into uneasy slumber.

"Corum--!"

I started awake--calling out a name I do not know. I looked around the empty room wildly. I do not know who—or what—I was looking for, but I know I desperately wanted to see it. After a few seconds I regained control of myself and sat there in the dark, shivering uncontrollably. My heart was pounding so heavily it felt as if it was trying to crawl up my throat.

The voice I had heard was female. But she sounded nothing like my mother, my sister, or any of my ex-wives. Despite this, it was a voice as familiar—and as unidentifiable—as the one inside my head. In any case, the name she called out was not my own—yet it had sparked a response from me the phantom voices of my father and brother had not. And how do I know her name? Who is this Rhalina? And why is it that I feel I should know her?

My head is buzzing like a hornet's nest. I do not dare sleep. That is why I relit the candle and started writing all this down. Please let the dawn come soon.

◆ ◆ ◆

Day Thirty-Five

The shadow people are still keeping vigil atop the ridge and have yet to stop their cursed yowling! It is bad enough for my nerves, but I can only the imagine the hell poor Manco must be going through. After all, these creatures were once his family and friends. On the first day they grew silent come the dawn, but now their lamentations continue throughout the day, growing progressively louder as the sun sinks in the sky. Manco says they have never done this before. He believes that the Shadow Lord is marshaling its forces in preparation of an all-out attack on World's End. I share his fear.

Day Thirty-Six

Today Manco took me to the holy of holies—the secret that lies at the very heart of World's End. He woke me early in the morning—I'd only succeeded in snatching an hour or two of sleep thanks to the Shadow's Lord midnight chorus—and spoke in a dire whisper, although there was no one to hear us.

"Come. It is time."

I followed Manco as he led me through the empty streets to the ziggurat that dominates the center of the city. It is this imposing monument that serves as the city's hub and from which all the lesser buildings and edifices radiate like the spokes of a wheel—or the rays of the sun. Once we arrived Manco lit a torch and motioned for me to follow him as he headed into the bowels of the dead god's tomb. The corridor was narrow, the steps worn smooth by the passage of a thousand feet over a thousand years. It felt as if we were traveling down the throat of some great sleeping beast. Then, without fanfare, we were in the tomb itself.

My first reaction was to gasp in amazement, for now I finally understood how World's End legend had metamorphosized into that of El Dorado. The interior walls were fashioned of silver and decorated with the ubiquitous six-finger hand sigil. Embedded in the palm of each hand was an "eye" fashioned from precious stone—ruby, emerald, diamond, onyx, turquoise. The list goes on and on. The silver hand was literally everywhere I looked—on the doors, on the walls, the floor, the ceiling. In the dim torchlight the room glittered like the heart of a star.

In the center of the room was a sarcophagus, the lid of which was inlaid with gold and studded with gems. The craftsmanship used in creating the likeness of the dead god that lay within was unlike any I've seen of the Inca. However it was not unfamiliar to me, as it was distinctly Gaelic, as were the runes that decorated the tomb.

"This is impossible," I whispered. "These runes predate the Roman occupation of Britain! How could they possibly be in a shrine in the Peruvian Andes?"

"The markings represent Viracocha's magic. He commanded that his resting place be precisely as you see it."

"When did this hero-god of yours die?"

"A thousand years ago. Perhaps more. He was dead two centuries when World's End was completed."

"I don't understand—even a thousand years ago this

language was ancient! No one has spoken this tongue in millennia!"

"What is there to understand? It is the language of the gods, yet you know it. It is still more proof that you are the one foretold." Manco pressed a stud set flush on the sarcophagus and with a great rumbling and grinding of hidden gears the lid—which must have taken a dozen strong men to lower into place—pivoted open to reveal its occupant.

There was a brief whiff of musty old newspapers left to rot in a basement and then I found myself staring at all that remained of the god-hero the Inca called Viracocha. I was so overcome by the enormity of what lay before me I did not know whether to be afraid or elated.

What I noticed first was the mummy's long, narrow skull. Whatever Viracocha may have been, it certainly wasn't human. The second thing I noticed was the elaborate patch looped over the dead man's right eye. It was exceptionally large—resembling more a shield than an eyepatch—and made of jewels and enamelwork. As if in a trance I reached out and slipped it rom its fragile perch. I expected the socket beneath to be empty—after all, isn't that the reason for such apparel? Instead I found myself staring down into a large multi-faceted ruby. The jewel was so large it jutted from the socket like the eye of an insect.

As if from a great distance I heard myself gasp aloud and say: *"The Eye of Rhynn!"*

I allowed my gaze to travel further down and spied folded across the dead god's withered breast the six-fingered hand that was the symbol of the city. At first glance it looked to be no more than a silver gauntlet with five slender fingers and a thumb. But on closer inspection I could tell that the jeweled scales that covered it were far too fine to have even been produced by a smithy's forge. The original owner had worn it not as a glove but as part of his being.

"The Hand of Kwll," I muttered, my mind swimming.

There was no denying I knew these artifacts—even though I had never seen or heard of them before in all my studies of archaeology. Just as there was no denying that I was staring down at the stranger in scarlet cloak I had glimpsed in my dream.

I clutched the lid of the open sarcophagus, trembling like a man in the grip of malaria. I could feel something alien in the back of my brain start to blossom. Although there was no pain I felt a surge of fear as all humans do when confronted by the unknown. Then I was overcome by a sense of—completion. The exhilaration and relief that had proved so elusive on the discovery of El Dorado was finally upon me.

I felt as if I was inside and outside myself as I saw —as if from a great distance—the man Manco's people deified as Viracocha. Somehow I knew him by another name—Prince Corum Jhaelen Irsi, The Prince in the Scarlet Robe, the last of the Vadhagh—a pre-human race with the power to see and move beyond the Fifteen Planes.

I watched him as he whiled away his youth in the study of the arts, swordplay, and sorcery. I observed him as he fought in vain to protect his ancestral home from the ravages of the barbarian army lead by the evil Earl Glandyth-a-Kraw. I stood frozen by horror as he was maimed—much as I was—by brutal captors. I cheered his rescue by Arkyn, last of the Lords of Law. I saw how he pledged his sword to the nefarious godling Skool-an-Jyvim in exchange for the freedom of his beloved human consort, the Lady Rhalina. I marveled at how Skool made him whole again by wedding him to the Hand of Kwll and the Eye of Rhynn. I looked on as he struggled against the Chaos Lords in the years that followed, winning many battles and losing many friends. And I saw how—after suffering the loss of she who he loved more that life itself—Corum set sail upon the Seas of Fate in search of a place called Tanelorn, where all time and space come together, in hopes of altering that which has been and what has yet to be, so that his lady would not die in vain. But he lost his way —or the way was lost to him, to be accurate—and he found himself cast adrift on the shores of a strange land full of primitive humans, where the sorcery that had always been his ally barely worked.

Corum was proclaimed a god by the natives and given the name of their own creator-deity. Since his native magic was greatly weakened on this Plane of Existence, he realized he was trapped until such time as the cosmic balance of Chaos and Order were once again out of kilter and in need of a champion. Resigned to his fate, he set about civilizing his adopted people, teaching them what he knew of agriculture, architecture, engineering, food preservation, law-making, medicine—and magic. The Incas learned their lessons well—going from a tribe of subsistence farmers to an empire second only to that of Rome in record time. And when it came time for him to die, he presented the blueprints for his tomb to the high priests and temple maidens who would become the people of World's End.

Once more I was in my own body. I was dimly aware

that my teeth were chattering and I was dripping sweat from every pore. Manco was standing beside me, a look of grave concern on his face.

"What is wrong my friend? You're burning with fever!"

"I saw it," I whispered, my voice ragged.

"Saw what?"

"Tanelorn."

Day Thirty-Seven

I have seen my future and my past and there is no turning away from it, no matter how much I might wish to. I can no longer play the role of Rational Twentieth Century Man—although there are many who would scoff at the notion that I was ever 'rational.' I have had my destiny revealed to me and I have no choice but to embrace it.

I spent last night preparing myself for the coming ordeal through meditation. I contemplated writing letters of farewell to my brother and one of ex-wives, but decided there was no point. This journal —providing it is ever found—should be explanation enough for those of this Plane of Existence who might care to know whatever became of Harald Armitage Bekk.

Manco came for me very early—the sun had yet to touch the morning sky. He wore his priestly robes and headdress and he carried a heavy sack, which he placed at my feet. In the sack was a hooded robe made of the finest vicuna, dyed a brilliant scarlet. There was also a conical silver helm on which three characters

—identical to those found on the sarcophagus—were carved above the short peak, as well as a double byrnie made of a million tiny links—the upper layer silver, the lower layer brass. The workmanship of all three pieces is outstanding.

"I received a vision of your arrival many months before you appeared," he explained. "In the vision, I was told to prepare these things for the return of the god."

"You honor me with such gifts, my friend."

Manco lowered his head in acceptance of my praise, then left me to change into my new garb. At first the weight on my head and torso was strange and I felt silly, but when I closed my eyes I could hear the clash of sword on shield and the clatter of lances and smell the stench of a blood-soaked battlefield. When I reopened my eyes I no longer felt like a child playing Let's Pretend.

As I pulled on the scarlet robe I thought of how much I missed the original article my mother—the Lady Colatalarna—had made for me with her own hands.

Once I was properly outfitted Manco returned and told me it was time to go to the tomb, for the ritual must be performed as the sun rises. He walked ahead of me, playing a clay flute. When we reached the great temple he turned and peered beyond the walls of the city. I followed his gaze. Although the sun had yet to rise I could make out the movement of scores—possibly hundreds—of figures lurching down the steep stairs cut into the cliff face towards the valley. The bubbling wails were growing ominously closer and the smell of boiling pitch was stronger than before.

"They're marching on the city!" I exclaimed.

"The Shadow Lord grows desperate—and with his desperation comes strength! The magic that has kept the valley safe is no more! We must hurry!

As I write this I am once more in the silver tomb, standing at the foot of the open sarcophagus as Manco —muttering the prayers handed down to him by his forefathers—removes the relics needed for the god Viracocha to reawaken. There is no more time for this. I do not know if I will be writing any more after this—or if there will be any 'I' left to write.

◆ ◆ ◆

The final entry in the journal of Harald Bekk is in ancient Gaelic:

It is done. The prince in the Scarlet Robe has returned, although I find myself much changed. Once I leave this Plane of Existence my magic will grow stronger and my appearance will once again be that of the Vadhagh. The memories of Bekk tickle the back of my mind, but I am used to such things. After all, have I not broken bread with three of my own divergent selves?

The first thing I saw when I opened my eyes to this new age was the body of the Incan wizard-king Manco lying in a pool of his own blood. Although I am not Bekk his memories are still with me and because of this I feel sorrow for the wizard's passing. Manco knew that the return of his god would necessitate the death of the King of World's End. He never told Bekk this for fear his friend would try and prevent his sacrifice. Manco served both his god and the honor of his ancestors nobly, and for this I shall forever be in his debt.

What is left of Bekk compels me to write in this book one final time. Upon my resurrection I went to the secret staircase known only to myself and the slaves who died building it. The stairs lead up to a tiny room at the very pinnacle of the ziggurat. There I found a small altar on which was laid a sword with a blade fashioned from volcanic glass with a silver hilt and matching scabbard. As I fixed the scabbard to my belt I looked out the solitary spy-hole in the room and gazed down upon the city of World's End.

The sun is now up and I can easily see the multitude of ghouls pressed against the walls of the city. The creature Manco knew as the Shadow Lord is one of Arioch's minor servitors, as a Chaos Lord has better things to do than haunt an isolated mountain valley for centuries on end. No doubt the Shadow Lord realizes what will happen if Arioch learns that one of Lord Arkyn's players has been brought back into the game, and is determined to keep me from reaching my ultimate destination.

If I am to reach Tanelorn I mut fight my way through the Shadow Lord's army of the damned. My Vadhagh sensibilities find exquisite irony that those I must destroy were once those dedicated to protecting my mortal remains. Even if I win the day against the Shadow Lord and his minions, I still must make my way across the mountains to the sea. But once I am back on open water I can use my natural abilities to navigate myself onto the Sea of Fate. And this time I will ***not*** *lose my way!*

I go now and leave this journal behind on the altar in place of the sword I take with me. Perhaps this will one day be found by the humans that dwell on this Plane. Perhaps not. It does not matter to me. I go now either to death at the hands of the walking dead or to worlds undreamed of. I must—I ***will****—find Tanelorn, even if takes a thousand lifetimes.*

In the Name of my Lord Arkyn

In the Name of Order
In the Name of the Lady Rhalina:
I remain Corum Jhaelen Irsi, Prince of the Vadhagh; Champion Eternal

◆ ◆ ◆

From *The New York Times*, October 9, 1999:
LOST INCAN CITY FOUND IN ANDES

LIMA. PERU: Bekk Chemicals announced today that an expedition under its sponsorship has discovered a previously unknown Incan city in the Madre de Dios mountain range. The expedition was originally attempting to locate the whereabouts of the company's co-owner, Harald Bekk, who disappeared in the region nearly five years ago while searching for the fabled lost city of El Dorado. Details remain sketchy but the Incan city is thought to be at least eight hundred years old. No one is certain how long it has been abandoned, but from the number of mummified bodies found inside its walls and outside its gate it is assumed that the original inhabitants were wiped out during a war or civil uprising several hundred years ago. Johann Bekk addressed reporters in Lima, stating: "I am both thrilled and saddened by this discovery, While this is a boon to history, it still grieves me that we have yet to find any trace of my brother. I just wish Hal could have been here to see this. We would never have found it if it weren't for him."

THE ONE-EYED KING

An Unknown Tale of Robin Hood

Robert Fitzooth, Earl of Huntingdon, Master of Locksley Hall--known to Saxon and Norman alike as Robin Hood--stood atop the ramparts of his home and surveyed his lands. Not a year ago he was an outlaw, an enemy of the state--hunted by the Sheriff of Nottingham's men like a fox in the wood he held so dear. He had been stripped of his property and chattel, his ancestral home handed over to that Norman cur, Sir Guy of Gisborne--forcing him to take shelter amidst the bowers of Sherwood Forest.

But now here he was, returned to his rightful title--his transgressions against the crown erased by a wave of King Richard's royal hand. Still, there had been much blood and suffering along the way. He had lost his cousin and dearest friend, Will Scarlet, to Prince John's treachery and in repayment he had snuffed out

Gisborne's life. In the months since then he married his beloved Marian in St. Mary's church in the village of Edwinstowe and disbanded his famed Merry Men--save for the most stalwart of his followers.

There was peace in Nottinghamshire once more, but Robin was uncertain as to how long it would last now that King Richard was once more on the road to Damascus. He would have preferred his protector remain in England, keeping his heel firmly planted on his troublesome younger brother's neck. It also worried him that the Lionheart had yet to sire an heir. Should a heathen arrow find its mark, England would once more find itself in Prince John's ungentle hands—but this time not as regent.

"My husband, what is wrong? You seem melancholy."

Robin turned to look at his wife, who had joined him on the rampart. As the wind ruffled the white silk wimple and coverchief framing her heart-shaped face, he was once more amazed that a woman of such loveliness had consented to be his bride. He smiled wanly and shrugged, returning his gaze to the distant canopy of the forest. "I'm homesick, that's all."

"But how can that be? Locksley Hall has been in your family since before the Conqueror!"

"I miss Sherwood," he sighed.

"Ah." Lady Marian slid her slender arms about her husband's waist and laid her head on his shoulder. "I know what you mean. Sherwood was as much a home to us as any built of stone. It sheltered us and fed us, as a mother does her children."

Robin pulled her closer. "I'm pleased you understand. It is not that I am unhappy here with you. It's just that sometimes I miss the old days in the forest."

Lady Marian's voice was gentle but firm. "Those days are gone now, Robin. You have won all you fought for."

"Not all," he reminded her gently.

"But enough," she countered. "Now come inside, husband; there is an edge to the wind."

John Little--late of Hathersage in Derbyshire, better known as Little John, steward to the Earl of Huntingdon--frowned down at the trembling man standing before him. "You are certain of what you saw?"

"As sure as Christ died and walked again," the forester replied, wiping a hand across his lips. "I left my oldest boy to watch the spot."

"And you say the man who spoke with you was a friar?"

"Aye; at least he wore a friar's habit and tonsure."

"Come with me, then." Little John's huge, calloused hand clamped around the forester's upper arm. "We'll soon get this straightened out." He dragged the nervous peasant through the winding corridors of Locksley Hall until they arrived at his master's private chambers. He rapped his knuckles against the heavy oak door, using a code devised during their days spent in Sherwood Forest. The door opened a crack and the Lady Marian peered out at them, frowning first at the forester then at her husband's steward.

"What is it, John?" she asked, clearly resenting the intrusion. Since the moment they first met she had been forced to share Robin with the towering, raw-boned peasant who was both his lieutenant and dearest friend.

"I must speak to Rob," Little John said gruffly.

Marian was about to say something about the lateness of the hour when her husband appeared behind her, pushing open the door. "John! Is something wrong? Please, come in."

Little John brushed past Marian, dragging the frightened man in after him. "This is Ned Willowby, one of your foresters. He claims--well, it's best that he tell you. Well, get on with it, man!" Little John ordered, thumping Willowby on the side of the head with one bear-like paw. "Don't stand there gawping at the Earl like he's got two heads!"

"Leave the poor fellow be, John!" Marian scolded. "He'll tell his tale in good time!"

"I was out in the woods with my boy, Marcus, when we come upon this monk."

"Monk? Do you mean Friar Tuck?"

"Nay, milord. I've seen the good Friar Tuck in church, taking confessions. This monk was tall and thin. He was resting on the side of the road, dressed in a black cassock. When he sees me and my son, he lifts a hand in greeting and asks if we were in the service of the Earl of Huntingdon, known as Robin Hood. When I say yes, he says someone has left a message for you in the woods, just off the foot-path."

Robin scratched his chin-whiskers and exchanged glances with Little John. "Did you see what this message was?"

Ned the Forester turned pale and licked his lips. "Aye. Although now I wish I hadn't! When I returned to the path, the strange monk was gone. I hurried here as fast as I could."

"And what did you see?"

Ned closed his eyes and for a moment it seemed as if

the man was about to swoon. “It was horrible, milord! I dare not speak of it in milady’s presence.”

Marian sighed and set aside her embroidery, excusing herself from the room. When she returned, she was surprised to find Robin and the others gone. She looked out the window to the courtyard below in time to see her husband ride out in the company of Little John and the nervous forester. She glanced worriedly in the direction of the lowering sun. It would soon be dark in Sherwood.

The sun was starting to set by the time they reached the spot where the black-robed monk had spoken to Ned Willowby and his son. The boy, Marcus, was standing by the side of the road, looking pale and anxious.

“What are you doing here?” Ned barked, cuffing his son's ear. “I thought I told you to stay in the clearing!”

“I tried, father,” the boy whimpered, massaging the side of his head. “But the smell...”

Robin dismounted and handed the reins to Ned’s son. “You did well, lad. Stay here with the horses,” he murmured, clapping a hand on the boy’s trembling shoulder.

The smell of death was strong and grew stronger as Robin and Little John followed the forester along a narrow trail through the brambles and undergrowth. Although the sun had yet to set, the thickness of the forest canopy made it seem as if night had already arrived. A few minutes’ walk from the road they came upon a small clearing in the woods. In the failing light they could make out what at first seemed to be three nude figures—a man, woman and a child—standing in a semi-circle before an extinguished campfire. As they drew closer it was revealed that the figures were not standing on their own two feet, but had been nailed to trees.

The man wore the tattered remnants of an abbot's gown about his waist and had been throttled by his own rosary with such violence the beads were imbedded deep into his throat. It was impossible to tell if he had been gelded before or after being disemboweled.

"By the Rood!" Little John's face lost its usual ruddy color.

The outrages done to the woman made those inflicted on the abbot look mild. She, too, was of the Church--judging from what little remained of her habit--and split open like a dressed deer. Robin prayed she had been dead by the time her killers cut off her breasts and shoved the abbot's severed member in her mouth, although the look of horror on the dead woman's face told him those prayers were no doubt in vain.

The final victim--a boy no more than ten years of age--was nailed to the tree as if embracing it. Countless shallow cuts marred his naked back and buttocks. Whoever had tortured the unfortunate youth had finished his work by taking a burning branch from the nearby campfire and thrusting it between the child's hams.

"Who dares?!?" Robin roared, turning his back on the carnage to kick at the remains of the murderers' campfire, scattering its ashes. "Who *dares* defile my woods with such evil! Sherwood is under *my* protection!!"

"Do you think Prince John had a hand in this?" Little

John asked, eyeing the bodies in disgust.

Robin shook his head. "Lackland may be a vicious back-biting ferret, but he's not fool enough to outrage the Church in such a manner. No, whoever did this—and judging by what's left of their camp, there were several of them—swears allegiance to neither State *or* Church."

"You don't think it's anyone *we* know, do you?"

"Don't look so heart-stricken, Little John. The outlaws who committed these atrocities could never have been Merry Men," Robin said reassuringly. As he bent down to study the footprints left behind by the killers he spotted a folded piece of parchment with a rock set upon it near the foot of the abbot. The parchment bore a red wax seal with the imprint of a dragon. He took out his dagger and broke the seal and unfolded the parchment.

"What is it, Robin?" Little John asked, looking over his shoulder. While the loyal steward could sign his name, he was otherwise as illiterate as every other farmer's son in England.

"It would seem to be a letter; one that is addressed to me," Robin replied as he studied the salutation, written in an educated hand.

'To Robert Fitzooth, The False Earl of Huntingdon, Usurper of Locksley Hall, Otherwise Known As Robin Hood.'

Greetings, Brother!

It has been thirty years since we shared the same womb. In that time we have walked very different paths, indeed. News of your pardon by that thick-skulled sodomite Richard has reached as far as my own domain, here in Mordred's Wood. It is rumored our ancestral lands and titles have been returned to you.

I weary of living the life of a shadow, dear lost brother. I feel now is the time for me to come forward and claim my rightful inheritance for you are a pretender! I am the firstborn son of William Fitzooth and the Lady Joanna, not you! If you do not promptly relinquish your claim to my lands and title, I shall wreak upon your house the same fate these worthless fools suffered.

If you do not believe my tale, go to our uncle, Sir William Gamwell, and ask him the truth! If you then continue to deny me what is mine, woe to you and yours!

Signed, Thomas Fitzooth

True Earl of Huntingdon, Rightful Master of Locksley Hall, Known As Tamlane the Dragon.

Sir William, Lord of Gamwell Hall, sat and studied the letter his nephew had given him, stroking his white beard in consternation. He was the older brother of Robin's mother, the Lady Joanna, and now that Will Scarlet was dead his nephew's only living relative. Robin had not seen the old man since the banquet celebrating his and Marian's wedding a year ago. He only wished he had made the half-day ride to his kinsman's home under happier circumstances.

"I have heard tales of this so-called Tamlane," Sir William said grimly. "He is a most foul and black-hearted brigand."

"Yes, but is what he says true, uncle? Do I have an elder brother?"

"Aye," Gamwell grunted unwillingly.

"Why was I never told?"

Sir William heaved an old man's sigh. "It happened

such a *long* time ago, my boy. And, besides, talk of it upset your mother so." He motioned for the servant tending their goblets to leave the wine and vacate the room before continuing with his story. "But my poor sister is fifteen years in her grave, and I see no point in keeping silent now. It is a long story, Robin. And not a pleasant one, I'm afraid. You are familiar with the tale of how your mother and father came to be wed?"

Robin laughed "Of course! Mother never tired of telling the story! My father was the son of a Norman nobleman, and she was the only daughter of your father, Sir George, a Saxon knight. He forbade them to see one another, but they were married in secret. Then when mother became great with child, she and father hid in Sherwood Forest for fear grandfather would have father's Norman guts for garters! Grandfather searched for weeks for the man he believed had ruined his daughter. But by the time he finally found them, mother was in labor. And when Sir George laid eyes on his newborn grandson his wrath was turned aside, and he gladly welcomed his son-in-law into his home and family."

"*Most* of that's true," Sir William grunted. "The bit about your parents hiding out in the woods and my father being madder than a baited badger is right enough. But *you* were not the babe that softened Sir George's heart. That was your older brother—your twin —Thomas."

"I have a *twin* brother?" Robin frowned.

"Aye! You two were as alike as peas in a pod!" his uncle said with a chuckle, his mind going back to those happier days. "Even your mother had trouble telling you apart, so she took to tying a bit of ribbon about your ankles: green for young Robin and black for little Tam, as we called the two of you. At the time, Sir George kept a friar here at Gamwell Hall named Garth, who served as the family's confessor. He was an odd one, even for the clergy. He was a tall, lean fellow--always keeping his nose buried in one scroll or another. He was learned though, and my father respected him for that. He could read and write in Latin, Greek, Hebrew, and a few other heathen languages. Still, there was something *odd* about him.

"When the time came for you and your brother to be baptized by the abbot, your nurse found only one child in the cradle. According to the ribbons tied about the infant's ankles, the one stolen had been Thomas, the heir to the Huntington title.

"Your grandfather had Gamwell Hall turned upside down, but there was no sign of the missing child. It wasn't long before we realized Friar Garth was nowhere to be found as well. Sir George ordered the cleric's rooms be searched." Sir William's demeanor grew even sadder. "We found occult artifacts of unwholesome origin, and it became clear that my poor father had been nursing a serpent at his bosom the whole time.

"My sister took the news very hard. As everyone knows, witches and warlocks use the fat from unbaptized babies in their black Sabbats. It was obvious that poor little Tam had met a cruel fate at the hands of the mad monk. Your father, grandfather, and I decided to make things easier on your mother by not dwelling on it. In time, Joanna focused her love and attention on you, her remaining son. If she ever mentioned poor Thomas' name again after that first year, I never heard it. Still, I know she kept a place in her heart for her lost boy, up to the day she died.

"As for Friar Garth, no one has seen or heard of him for thirty years. Now you tell me he was spotted creeping about Sherwood. I don't like this, Robin. Not in the slightest. I always thought it odd that he would snatch a nobleman's child. If an infant sacrifice was all he wanted, he could have stolen some hapless peasant woman's brat, and no-one would have been the wiser. If this Tamlane the Dragon is indeed your long-lost twin brother, then that accursed monk has raised a monster deserving of Hell."

"You say you know of this Tamlane," Robin frowned. "Why have I not heard of him before now?"

"The past few years have been rather busy for you, have they not, nephew?" Sir William responded with a dry laugh. "Between dodging the Sheriff of Nottingham's men and outfoxing Prince John, I doubt you have had time to keep afoot with the news beyond Nottinghamshire. What little I have heard of this brigand has been exceedingly grim. Tamlane the Dragon is not merely just a thief and a poacher--he is a murderer reveling in the pain and torture of his victims. He has surrounded himself with a band of black-hearted scoundrels called the Dragon's Teeth who are everything the Merry Men shunned. It is said that they attacked the nunnery at Broadholme, subjecting the holy sisters to rape. Then, once finished, Tamlane ordered them sewn shut, so that they would be unable to deliver themselves of whatever issue had been spawned that black day!"

"God's mercy!" Robin gasped in horror. "And this monster is my *brother?*"

"Of that I cannot say for certain," Sir William replied

as he poured himself another tankard of wine. "The only way to know is to see him with your own eyes. And then you must kill him."

"Uncle!" Robin exclaimed in surprise. "You propose I become a fratricide?"

Sir William leaned forward, his eyes hard as beads, and thrust a bony finger at his nephew. "This is no time to be sentimental, Rob! I loved your mother as only a devoted brother can. It would have broken her heart to discover her poor lost little Tam twisted into a murdering ogre! But if Tamlane the Dragon is indeed Thomas Fitzooth, *he* is the rightful heir and master of Locksley Hall, *not* you! The threat this pretender poses is quite clear. I would rather my blood wash the stones of Gamwell Hall than allow such a creature to tarnish the family name!"

"Please excuse me, Uncle William," Robin said, as he stood up from the table. "I will retire to my room now. You have given me much to think on."

Robin sat and stared for a long while at the logs burning in the fireplace of the suite of rooms set aside for him by his kinsman. Normally the discovery of a long-lost brother was something to celebrate with fatted calves and tankards of ale. But there was no joy to be had in claiming a bloodthirsty cut-throat such as Tamlane the Dragon as family.

However, despite his uncle's urgings he could not bring himself to embrace slaying a brother he had never met—especially one said to share his face. He needed to meet this so-called Tamlane the Dragon and take his measure. It was not impossible that the murders in Sherwood were the work of the wicked Friar Garth and his twin knew nothing of them. He was all too aware how easy it was to pin any manner of villainy on an outlaw. When Marian had first met him she was convinced he and his Merry Men were the worst sort of murderous scoundrels, thanks to the slanderous lies spread about by the likes of Sir Guy and Prince John. Perhaps the same was true for Tamlane and his Dragon's Teeth? There was only one way to know for sure.

He would ride for Mordred's Wood come the dawn.

Robin squatted in front of the fire, feeding tinder to the struggling flames while chewing a strip of jerked venison. He had been gone from Locksley Hall for two days and his bones ached and his spirits were weary. Normally traveling the woodlands gladdened his heart, but he had long since left the familiar bowers of Sherwood Forest.

Mordred's Wood was as different from Sherwood as night is to daylight. Where one was full of game, the other appeared bereft of life. Everywhere he looked the saw stagnant bogs and trees stricken by blight. Earlier that day he'd spied a wolf between the trees lining the path. Had he not let fly with his bow, striking the beast between the eyes, it would have surely set upon his mount. Even now he was aware of myriad wild things watching him from outside the ring of light cast by his campfire.

Just then he heard an owl calling to its mate in the darkness. At first he thought nothing of it; then he realized that he had gone all day without once hearing birdsong. He got to his feet, his handgoing to the sword sheathed at his side.

They came out of the woods as quick as a pack of wolves on the hunt. There were six of them, armed with short swords and cudgels. Before he could make a move, the largest of their number hurled a net over him, pinning his arms to his sides. Robin cursed and struggled to free his sword from its scabbard, but it was no good. The bandits descended on him, whooping and screeching like wild animals. One of them struck Robin behind the knees with a quarterstaff, knocking him to the ground as the others set upon him, yowling their delight as they rained blows upon him.

"Enough of that, you fools!" an angry voice called out. "You were told not to kill him—yet!"

Robin's attackers froze in mid-kick and turned as one to the face the tall, hollow-cheeked man dressed in a black cassock who emerged from the shadows. Friar Garth smiled down at the new captive the way a butcher smiles at a well-marbled slab of beef.

"Take him to The Dragon."

As the monk turned away, a big jug-eared peasant stepped forward and kicked Robin in the head hard enough to render him unconscious.

The next thing he knew a damp cloth was being pressed against his face. Robin groaned and tried to lift a hand to probe the swelling over his right eye, only to find himself securely bound. He opened his eyes and stared into the face of a dark-haired woman with pale skin and eyes the color of polished night.

"Marian?" he mumbled in momentary confusion.

"Nay, the name's Morag. Black Morag, they call me." The woman was dressed in a bodice and skirt the color of a raven's wing and her equally dark hair hung loose, obscuring the right side of her face. Her hands were calloused, the nails chewed to the quick. She licked her lips anxiously, peering at Robin as if he was a two-headed calf in a miracle show.

He looked around the best he could and saw he was lying on a bed of willow foliage in a wattle hut with dirt floors. The only light came from a single tallow candle set atop a hand-hewn plank table. He also he noticed for the first time that he had been stripped of his Lincoln green tunic, hose, and boots and dressed in a black robe.

"You're *him*, ain't that so?" Black Morag asked breathlessly. "You're Robin Hood."

"What makes you think that?" he replied cautiously.

Her chapped lips pulled into a knowing smile. "Tam said his brother was Robin Hood. And if you ain't Tam's brother, I'll fuck Dim bowlegged!" she said with a laugh.

Robin flinched, unaccustomed to hearing such coarse language from a woman. "This Tam—is he your husband?"

Black Morag laughed again and spat at the dirt floor. "Husband? To me? Nay, Tam is my leader, nothing more! He's the biggest, meanest, blood-thirstiest bastard there is! I respect that in a man." At that she grinned, displaying stained and crooked teeth.

Just then the blanket that served as the hut's door was thrown aside and a man dressed head to toe in black entered the foul-smelling hut. Morag scuttled away like a dog fearing a boot in its ribs, leaving Robin alone with his visitor.

"Greetings, brother," said Tamlane the Dragon, lifting the tallow candle and holding it so its feeble light fell upon his face. "And welcome to Mordred's Wood."

Although he had known what to expect, Robin still gasped at the sight of his own face grinning down at him. The resemblance was as close as a looking glass, yet there was something different about his twin's features. Although identical, there was a hard edge to the mouth and a cruel gleam in the eye that marked Thomas Fitzooth from his younger brother.

"Yes, the likeness is exceedingly close, is it not?" Tamlane the Dragon said with a humorless laugh. "I'm told not even our mother--the Lady Joanna--could tell us apart."

"Do not mention my mother's name again, or I'll drub you until the blood rises!" Robin growled.

"Mind your manners, brother-dear!" Tamlane laughed, casually striking his prone twin in the side with a booted foot. "You're not in Sherwood anymore! You're in *my* domain!"

"Stop calling me brother!" Robin snapped, struggling to free himself. "What have you done with my clothes?" Before he could continue, Tamlane dropped a knee onto his chest and pressed the cold metal of a dirk to his throat.

"My, aren't we used to giving orders! In that we are *very* much alike."

"What do you want of me?"

"Shouldn't *I* be one asking that question?" Tamlane sneered. "After all, it was *you* who came looking for me."

Robin's face darkened. "You dare accuse *me* of trespass? Do you deny that it was you who tortured and murdered three helpless people in my forest? Even village idiots know that Robin Hood allows pious clergy, honest women, and innocent children safe passage through Sherwood! Any who dares molest them must answer to me!"

"And you called yourself a bandit?" Tamlane scoffed. "Here you are, fêted as the prince of thieves, yet unwilling to dirty your hands with the meat of brigandry! What's the point of being an outlaw if you observe the rules of decency?"

"My rebellion was against unjust laws and corrupt rulers," Robin spat, "not the poor and the righteous!"

"What a prig you are, little brother!" Tamlane said with a contemptuous laugh. "It would seem you and Dim are equipped with the same intellect!" He grabbed Robin by the forearm and dragged him to his feet. "Come! Let me introduce you to the Dragon's Teeth!"

Outside the hut was a large campfire about which were huddled a half-dozen men dressed in filthy rags, worrying greasy gobbets of half-cooked meat like starving dogs. They looked up from their meal both fearful and suspicious as their leader approached. Robin was reminded of the half-wild dogs commanded by his Master of Hounds. As he scanned the faces of the gathered men he saw a hardness in their eyes that reminded him of the hired jackals who'd done the Sheriff of Nottingham's dirty work. These were men who knew nothing of the nobler emotions. What loyalty they felt for their leader was that of feral beasts acknowledging the fastest and strongest of their number.

One of the Dragon's Teeth stood up and came forward. Robin had fancied Little John the biggest man he'd ever seen, but this hulking brute made his steward look like a tubercular old woman. The giant stood nearly three ax-handles high and was a handle wide at the shoulders. His arms were covered with coarse red hair and the seams of his leather jerkin groaned with every flex of his muscled torso. But what Robin noticed most of all was the brigand's hare-lip and drooping left eyelid.

"I caught him good, didn't I, Tam?" the giant said, his voice more child-like than brutish. Moving with surprising speed for his size, he grabbed Robin's throat with huge, sausage-sized fingers. "We gonna gut 'im, like the others?"

"Now, Dim, you remember what Father Garth said, don't you?" Tamlane said in a firm, slow voice, as if speaking to his favorite dog.

Dim blinked a couple of times and sucked on his lower lip for a moment as he effortlessly lifted his captive off the ground. "Uhhh--that he's your bruvver?"

"No, you sluggard!" Tamlane snapped, slapping Dim across the face. The giant let go of Robin as if he'd been scalded, rubbing a rough palm over his stricken cheek. "He said that no harm is to come to him until the moon is full!"

"Oh. That. Yes, I remember now," Dim agreed with a nod of his head.

"Tam!"

The bandit turned and glowered at the tall, gaunt figure standing in the doorway of a small stone hut.

"Bring our 'guest' so that I might prepare him for the ritual," Friar Garth intoned.

Tamlane dragged Robin into the monk's quarters. Compared to the squalid collection of hovels and lean-tos that sheltered the rest of the outlaws, Garth's abode was luxurious.

"What did I tell you about addressing me in such a manner in front of the others?" Tamlane snapped at the black-robed friar. "I take no orders from *anyone*—man or devil! And that includes *you*, old man."

"As you wish, milord," Garth replied with a crooked smile.

The more he saw of them, the more Robin realized his brother and those who followed him were left-hand versions of himself and the Merry Men. Instead of fighting for justice, Tamlane was a scourge to the downtrodden and helpless. Instead of a paragon of noble virtue, Tam's 'Maid Marian' was a foul-mouthed commoner, and his 'Little John' a slow-witted brute with a taste for hurting the helpless. But the most chilling of all was Friar Garth--the counterpart to the Merry Men's kindly Tuck.

Oddly enough, while Friar Tuck resembled the ancient Roman god of revelry, Garth had the look of an ascetic saint. Where Tuck was a plain-spoken but devout holy man, Garth was a warlock sworn to the Dark Lord. Whatever the devil-worshipping monk had in store for him, Robin knew it could not be pleasant.

After Tamlane finished lashing Robin to the chair, he and the wizard spoke in low tones over a collection of yellowed manuscripts spread across a nearby table. The Dragon then turned to sneer at his captive brother before exiting the hut.

"I'm afraid I cannot offer you much in the way of hospitality, Sir Robert," Garth said with a wry smile. "Although I have long since abandoned my vows of poverty, my lifestyle is far from extravagant. The Dragon's Teeth are feared far and wide, but we are not a particularly—how shall I put it?—*prosperous* concern because we never waylay knights or ambush tax-collectors. There is no 'rob the Rich and give to the Poor' here. The Poor *are* our livelihood, scant as it may be. Peasants, palmers, widows, orphans—there are far more of *those* wandering Mordred's Wood than well-fed aristocrats." Garth turned to look at Robin as he lit a candle. "Are you not going to ask me why I stole your brother from his cradle, those long years ago?"

"Because you are an evil man, dedicated to the service of the Foul One!"

"In part, yes," the monk conceded. "But there is more to it than that. Much more." He drew closer, fixing Robin with dark, feverish eyes. "I was there when you and your brother where carried into Gamwell Hall by your grandfather. You were only a few hours old, but I could already see your destiny upon you like a tiny halo. I knew then that you would grow up to be a hero. But I also knew that there can be no light without darkness. No good without its opposing evil. *This* is the way of Nature. And so it was with your brother. When I looked at him I saw a dark light. It was considerably weaker than your own, but *definitely* there! But as you two lay in the cradle, I saw his evil genius begin to fade and flicker, like a candle in danger of being snuffed out by a strong wind. Even though you were not yet weaned, you were already influencing your brother. I realized that if I did not take action, he would turn his face from the darkness. So I decided to steal the child and raise him here, in the shadowy heart of Mordred's Wood.

"I must say, once separated from you he proved himself an apt pupil! He was torturing animals by the age of five and raped his first woman at the age of twelve. He committed his first murder not long after. Out of the raw material that was Thomas Fitzooth, I fashioned Tamlane the Dragon; a villain with a soul blacker than soot! I am proud to say that I raised him a stranger to such small-minded conventions as conscience, shame, and love!"

"You claim my brother loves nothing in this world. But what about you?" Robin countered. "Are you not his foster-father and mentor? Surely he feels something for the man who raised him?"

Garth laughed without humor. "Oh, yes. Dear Tam does indeed feel something for me! If not for a certain protector of mine, my foster-son would have had my guts long before his first whiskers sprouted! Here, allow me to show you."

Garth straightened his back and produced a small brazier, which he lit and into which he began sprinkling various powders, all the while muttering in Latin. It wasn't long before Robin's eyes swam with tears from the overpowering odor of burning myrrh and sulfur. Then Father Garth spoke a name not meant for mortal ears to hear and the fires under the brazier turned first blue, then green.

Something in the shadows that had not been there before grunted and opened its eyes. Robin felt his scalp tighten and his bladder ache as the solid shadow moved forward, sniffing the rank air. Although it had hands, in many ways it resembled a bear, with golden eyes that gleamed like newly minted coins. It stared at Robin down a long, squared snout painted like a carnival buffoon's. As it peeled back its lips--revealing huge, curving tusks--it made a whining noise like a hungry child.

"No, it not yet time to feed, Lucullus," Father Garth smiled, scratching the demon behind the ears. "You must wait until the signs are right."

"What are you doing, summoning that wretched hell-beast?!"

Tamlane was standing in the door of Friar Garth's hut, staring in undisguised hatred at the thing squatting at the priest's feet. Upon espying the bandit, the demon bared its tusks and stood on its hind legs, exposing a wickedly barbed erect penis.

"I was merely demonstrating something to your brother, my dear Thomas," Garth explained. The monk made a gesture with his hand and the beast disappeared like a mist caught in a high wind.

"Stop calling me that! My name is Tamlane!"

"But not for long, eh, milord?"

Now that the demon was gone, Robin realized for the first time that Tamlane had changed out of the black garments from earlier into his own Lincoln green tunic, hose and boots. "What are your doing in my clothes?" he demanded.

"They're yours no longer, brother."

"What evil are you planning, damn you!"

"Can't you figure that out on your own? Surely you're not *that* dense, little brother!"

Robin's eyes widened in horror. "You won't succeed! The others will see you for the pretender you are!"

"Why should they suspect me? You did not divulge the true reason for your trip to your retinue—not even your lovely wife. If you had, they would not have allowed you to ride into these woods alone."

"What do you hope to gain by this unholy charade?"

Tamlane grinned and for a fleeting second Robin

understood how Sir Guy of Gisborne must have felt time and again, looking up into his taunting smile. "My birthright as Earl of Huntington, for one. And the crown of England, while I'm at it."

"You're mad!" Robin gasped. "King Richard still rules the land!"

"But not for long," Friar Garth said darkly. "I have looked into the fires of Hell and seen the Lionheart roasting in its flames alongside his Muslim lover, Saladin. When that time comes, there will only be Prince John to succeed him. You, yourself, know Lackland to be a weak and unpopular man. There will be a brief chance for a usurper to claim the throne, as The Conqueror did a century past. But it must be someone of *noble* background--someone popular with the Saxon nobles and peasantry, who can rally an eager army of knights and hod-carriers alike with just a whisper of his name! And that name is 'Robin Hood'!"

"You're worse than mad—you're a fool if you believe that could happen!" Robin laughed, despite the direness of his predicament. "I would *never* dream of usurping the throne!"

"We're well-aware of that, little brother," Tamlane sneered. "Despite your avowed hated of the Normans, you are still subservient to the status quo. You would never dare step out of your place in the pecking order—unless it was to right wrongs and see justice done. What a pathetic waste of potential! I, on the other hand, do *not* share your qualms and I'm more than willing to take your place in history."

"You'll fail! Little John and Friar Tuck—they'll be able to tell the difference! And you haven't got a chance of deceiving Marian!"

"Are you so sure, brother?" Tamlane leered. "After all, a change is as good as a rest, as they say."

Sir William sat alone in his chambers, staring pensively at the gathering shadows. The hour was late and he had sent his manservant off to bed. He was well into his second bottle of wine but had yet to shake the melancholy that had haunted him since his nephew's visit. He had agreed not to speak of the contents of the letter to anyone, not even Marian. But now he wondered if that had been a wise decision.

When he was younger he wouldn't have had second thoughts about hiding such things from the womenfolk. Over the years he had come to learn that the fairer sex was only weaker when it came to muscle, not heart. Heavens knows his beloved sister Lady Joanna had been stronger willed than any man he'd ever met, save her son. And there was much about her in young Marian, as well.

Just then something moved in the corner of the room, where the shadows were at their deepest. At first Sir William thought one of the hounds that wandered Gamwell Hall had found its way into his room. But when it stepped out of the darkness, he realized whatever else the horrific creature with the golden eyes and long, brightly colored muzzle might be-- it most certainly was not a dog.

The deer looked at the man dressed in Lincoln green sitting astride a chestnut horse for a long moment before quickly turning and bounding away, its tail raised in warning.

Tamlane stared after it, his jaw as slack as Dim's. Having spent his life in the dismal groves of Mordred's Wood—a place notorious for its poor game—Sherwood was a veritable paradise. Everywhere he looked there were quail, fat rabbits and squirrels, as well as a seemingly endless supply of venison. At first he envied his brother such lush and prosperous land, and then he laughed out loud. What did he have to envy Robin for? After all, it belonged to *him*, didn't it?

He was the master of Sherwood Forest now, even though he was obliged to hide behind the name of another. It was all coming true, just as Garth said it would! He would usurp his brother's place as the Earl of Huntingdon without anyone being the wiser, claiming his lands, titles and wife as his own. And why *shouldn't* he? Save for the woman, they were all rightfully *his* to begin with.

Still, he could not help but worry. After all, he was riding into an enemy camp alone. It was up to him to make sure that his brother's household had no cause to suspect their master had been replaced. He had everything to gain if he could pull off the masquerade—and Lucullus' embrace should he fail.

The thought of Garth's familiar made him shiver--something he only allowed himself to do that when he was certain no one else was around. The Dragon's Teeth were on constant watch for signs of weakness--like hyenas waiting for a lion to grow weary. Only Garth knew how deep his fear of Lucullus was, as it was the leash he used to control his foster-son.

Tamlane was uncertain as to the wizard's exact

agenda—but that was nothing new. He'd never fully understood his mentor and was not sure he wanted to. The one thing he was certain of was that the moment he was proclaimed the King of England he was going to order the old man's head stuck on a spike.

"Hail, Robin of Locksley!" bellowed a voice that boomed like good-natured thunder.

Tamlane fought to keep from instinctively grabbing his sword and turned to stare at the short, squat man dressed in a brown monk's cassock striding out of the woods. The friar was ruddy-faced and carried a quarterstaff like other men handled a walking stick. Despite his barrel-like build, it was obvious the cleric was made more of muscle than of fat. The monk strode to where Tamlane sat perched on his purloined stallion and smiled up at him, as he would a friend and equal. It was then Tam realized that this brash, buffoonish creature was one of Robin's boon companions from the days of the Merry Men.

"Good day, Friar Tuck," he said, in his best approximation of his twin's voice. "What brings you this way?"

Tuck gave another laugh and gestured at the distant turrets of Locksley Hall with his quarterstaff. "As if you didn't know! 'Tis time for me to leave the monastery and hear your lovely lady's confession! And yours too, lest you forget!"

"No! No, of course! Of course I didn't forget!" Tamlane lied. "You are welcome in my hall as always, good monk!"

Friar Tuck's smile dimmed and his demeanor grew more serious. "I only just heard of your uncle. I'm deeply sorry, my friend. He was a good man."

Tamlane tried to keep his confusion from being too obvious. “My uncle? What of him? I have been on the road for the past few days and only just returned...”

The priest blushed. “I’m sorry. I thought you knew—Sir William died at Gamwell Hall, not two days ago. It was apoplexy, or so I’m told. He was your only living family, was he not?”

Feigning grief, Tamlane lifted a hand to his face in order to hide his smile. “Yes. There is no other.”

For the hundredth time since they’d left him tied to the chair, Robin tested his bonds. And, for the hundredth time, his bonds held. The frustration made the fear for his life seem trivial. He was not a man to suffer being held captive lightly. Cursing mightily, he strained against the rawhide thongs that held him fast, but only succeeded in overturning the chair. He continued to squirm, his breath growing heavier as rage eclipsed rationality. He’d escaped from worse death-traps than this dozens of times! The Sheriff of Nottingham and Sir Guy had concocted far more devious ways of ensnaring and disposing him, and he always managed to free himself!

But back then he had the Merry Men at his side--good friends and true that knew his predicament and would do all in their power to help him. Now he was alone and no one knew where he was—save for his uncle, Sir William. He cursed himself for worse than a fool. He should have at least told Tuck! If he couldn’t trust a priest to keep a family secret, who else was there? Now here he lay bruised and beaten--trussed-up like a Christmas goose awaiting the butcher’s knife!

He froze at the sound of someone entering the hut. He was afraid it might be that drooling hulk of a half-wit, Dim. The moment Tam had quitted the camp the giant had taken the opportunity to pummel his leader's look-alike into unconsciousness. If Father Garth hadn't intervened, he surely would have been beaten to death. The fact Garth had saved what little was left of his life galled him to no end.

"Are you here, Robin Hood?"

He gave a sigh of relief upon seeing it was the woman called Black Morag. While he had his doubts concerning her, so far she was the only member of the Dragon's Teeth to have shown him anything resembling kindness. "I'm over here," he called out. "Please help me."

Black Morag hurried over and righted the chair with a grunt. She peered anxiously at his swollen, bruise-dappled face. "Are you hurt?"

Robin laughed and spat out a loosened tooth. "Now I know how the wheat feels at threshing time!"

"It was that brute, Dim, wasn't it?" Black Morag growled, unslinging a wineskin from her shoulder. "Here, this will blunt the pain."

Robin gratefully drank from the proffered skin. He was too thirsty to wonder about Black Morag's reasons for being helpful. In any case it was hard to tell what thoughts passed through the girl's head, as the hair hanging in her face made eye contact difficult. But there was something about the way she moved that reminded him of a dog whipped once too often.

"Will you untie me?"

She seemed surprised by the suddenness of his request and for a moment he thought she was going to run away, like a rabbit flushed from cover. "Don't ask me things like that," she whispered. "I may not be like the others, but that doesn't mean I'm in a hurry to be killed."

"You seem to be a decent sort, Morag. Why do you travel with these monsters?"

"Because no one else will have me," she replied bluntly.

"But surely you must have family?"

She giggled and Robin felt his bowels turn to ice. It was not a sane woman's laugh.

"Oh, yes; I had a family, once. My mother died when I was too little to remember. My father and I--we lived in the woods. He was a charcoal-maker. He would go and chop down trees while I stayed home and made dinner. He took care of me and I took care of him. We loved each other very much. And after a while, he loved me like he loved my mother. But then one day I met a boy from the village. His name was Matthew. He was a nice boy--a handsome boy. He would come to see me when my father was away chopping down trees. Then one day father came home early. He found me with Matthew and he chopped him up just like one of the trees. Then he turned on me--calling me names. He said he'd make it so no boy would ever want me again."

Morag brushed aside the hair hanging in her face and showed Robin her scars. He'd seen worse in his time, but those wounds had been inflicted by the royal torturer, not by a father on his own daughter. He winced and looked away.

"After he marked me, he raped me. *Really* raped me," Morag said sadly, letting her hair fall back into place. "After he was finished, he went into the woods and hanged himself. When the villagers found out what happened, they said it was all my fault. They said I had tempted my father and Matthew into sin. They said I was a fornicator and marked by the Devil. I was chased out of the only home I'd ever known and wandered for a long time. I finally ended up in a brothel. That's where I met Tam. He was there selling novice nuns he'd stolen from a monastery. He bought me from the madam because he said he liked my looks."

"And you've been with him ever since?"

Morag nodded as she chewed one of her thumbnails. "He said I could be his Maid Marian. Is she beautiful?"

"Yes. She is very beautiful," he replied wistfully.

"I thought so." She studied Robin with eyes that had suddenly grown remote. "Tam's not coming back, is he?" When he remained silent, she flashed her stained, crooked teeth in what seemed more like a rictus grin than a smile. "I know what he's up to. He's gone off to play at being you. He doesn't need me anymore now that he has the *real* Maid Marian." She frowned at the look of consternation on Robin's face then tickled his beard with her chewed fingers. "Don't look so upset. If I can't be your Maid Marian, maybe you can be my Tamlane the Dragon."

"Robin, my husband--is there something wrong?"

Tamlane started at the sound of Lady Marian's voice. Yes, something was indeed wrong, but there was no way he could explain it to his brother's wife, much less himself.

Marian knelt beside his chair, placing her hand atop his. "You seem so--remote, my love. Does your uncle's death weigh upon you?"

"Yes, that is it," he lied, staring hard at her fair white hand resting atop his far larger, rougher one. The ballads did not do her justice. He had never seen such a woman before in his life. The Lady Marian's beauty was not limited to her face and form but seemed to radiate from within as well. She possessed a self-confident serenity that transcended that of any of the uncounted 'brides of Christ' he'd defiled. Her presence was as soothing to his tortured soul as a cool cloth pressed to a feverish brow. No wonder his brother had gladly faced such overwhelming odds reclaiming her from Prince John.

But there was more to his ill-ease than his unprecedented reaction to this woman. It started the moment he met Friar Tuck. As they made their way to Locksley Hall—Tamlane on horseback, Tuck keeping easy pace on foot alongside him—he found himself starting to enjoy the well-fed monk' s company.

Although the thought of his feeling friendship towards another was laughable, Tamlane had to admit that he found it difficult to remain aloof from the jolly priest's ribald jokes and jests. In all his days as a robber-lord he'd never known such camaraderie with his own followers. The Dragon's Teeth were not his equals--they were a feral band of outcasts used for his own purposes and followed him solely for the crumbs dropped from his table, nothing more. They feared him only slightly more than they hated him, and he knew each and every one of them would gladly stab him the moment his back was turned. He expected and accepted such treachery from others because—well, because he'd known no other way.

He'd been raised to believe that love and friendship were weaknesses that the human race deluded itself into mistaking for strengths. And to prove it Garth went out of his way to crush any signs of affection from his foster-son. When Tam was only four years old he made the mistake of telling Garth--who he still thought to be his father--that he loved him. Garth showed him the error of his ways by summoning forth his familiar Lucullus and allowing it to have *its* way with him. The lesson had not been lost on the child: love nothing; trust no one.

Shortly after his arrival at Locksley Hall he'd been approached by a broad-shouldered fellow with a bristling beard who clapped him on the shoulder. Tamlane had come close to boxing the bigger man's ears as he would have done Dim, only to realize this was none other than Little John, Robin's right-hand man. Before he could react, the taller man swept him into a bear-hug, all the while professing how sorry he was about the death of Sir William. And, to his shock, Tamlane realized that it was not merely an act to curry favor from his superior. Little John was genuinely grieved.

As news of his return swept through the manor, staff and servants poured out to greet their master and offer their condolences. At first he looked into their eyes and tried to spot the hidden hate and secret envy Garth assured him all men harbor towards their betters. But--search as he might--he could not find any trace of deceit. Instead, these people genuinely loved and respected him—or at least the man they thought him to be. This realization shook him to his very marrow. It was as if he'd suddenly discovered the world was not flat but round.

Although he did his best to respond, Tamlane felt his mind reeling. The wealth of emotion surrounding him was threatening to make him lose what little control he possessed. Just as he was about to scream like a madman and draw his sword, the crowd parted and the sun given human form approached him.

The Lady Marian appeared like a vision sent from on high to deliver him. The moment he laid eyes on her something within him changed--like base metal transformed by the Philosopher's Stone. He was no stranger to the bodies of women and the things that they did—or could be made to do—to please a man. But what he felt as Lady Marian embraced the man she believed to be her husband was as far removed from lust as burlap is from silk.

That night he'd come to her as her husband, and she eagerly welcomed him. In all his years, she was the first consenting woman he had lain with who was not a bawd or a camp follower. At first his passion had been fired by the thought of cuckolding his twin in such a manner, but as Marian succumbed to his caresses--and he to hers--he became increasingly aware of something alien about their consummation. Although he had raped, fucked, swived, and fornicated countless times, this was the first time he'd ever been made love to. He felt like a starving man given a chalice of the king's best wine. Afterward, as they lay in each other's arms, Marian smiled at him and Tamlane felt the ice surrounding his heart melt away.

He shook himself from his reveries and returned his gaze to Marian, now seated beside him while she busied herself with her embroidery. Even in the most domestic of scenes, she radiated the nobility of one born to the purple. If ever there was a woman deserving of being made England's queen, it was she. There was so much love there--and all of it was his.

No; not *his*.

Aye. There lay the rub. None of the love, friendship and adulation he had experienced was rightfully his. While Locksley Hall, its titles and lands might be his birthright, the loyalty and love of those around him belonged to his brother and no other.

When he was growing up under Garth's cruel tutelage, the heretic monk was always going on about how mankind was blind to the Great Truths and focused instead on love, friendship, and justice. Those unimpeded by such foolishness could stride the world as gods madeflesh, if only they dared toss aside such petty delusions. As Garth was fond of telling his ward: In the Country Of The Blind, The One-Eyed Man Is King.

Yes, but what did the One-Eyed King become once he entered the Land Of The Sighted?

"You needn't worry that your death will be meaningless," the monk assured Robin, tapping a large, unwieldy tome resting on the table between them. The book was bound in some kind of animal skin, but whether reptile or mammal--or some ungodly hybrid of the two--was impossible to tell. "In fact, your ritual slaughter will insure that a Saxon king will once more rule these lands." He smiled at the startled look on Robin's face. "Your brother wasn't spouting a madman's delusions of attaining greatness. Given my knowledge of the rituals in this book—the fabled *Aegrisomnia*—I can assure you that Tamlane will succeed in his bid for the throne. All I need is the blood of a hero to cement the deal."

"So you intend to sacrifice me to your diabolic master?"

"In a way. You Christian dullards seem to think all a warlock needs to summon power is dance around naked, sprinkling dog's hair and powdered bat on anything that stands still. It's much more complicated than that." The monk produced an elaborately carved rosewood casket big enough to accommodate a newborn child and set it on the table next to the book. "Ritual cleansings and purification rites much be strictly observed, and each has its own set of rules. In your case your blood can not be let by an edged weapon prior to the ritual, nor any seed be spilled beforehand. The signs must be right and the stars in proper alignment before we begin." He opened the lid of the casket, showing Robin the assortment of knives and torture implements kept within. "For instance, the ritual required for this particular spell requires that you be flayed alive. I'm not talking a simple tanner's job, either. Different parts of your body must be stripped at certain times, requiring you to remain alive and conscious as long as possible. Granted, it's time consuming, but results in potent sorcery. I've concocted a special herbal brew to make sure you do not expire prematurely."

"You're not scaring me with this blather!" Robin snarled. "I've been shown the instruments of my torture by far worthier men than you!"

"Indeed," Friar Garth said with a bloodless smile. "Although you will die a hideous and agonizing death, at least you can take pride in knowing that you will go down in history as Good King Robin. And just as Tiberius was an honored general, Caligula a darling of the *vox populi*, and Nero a skilled musician and charioteer, King Robin the First will go down in history as an idealistic freedom-fighter who became a ruthless despot of monumental depravity. And for centuries to come, the people of England will curse the name of Robin Hood." With that, the necromancer exited the hut, leaving Robin alone—but not for long.

The rats--like everything else in the camp--seemed to know he was helpless. He could see their tiny eyes glittering like filthy gems in the dim light of the candle guttering on the table. The biggest of the pack edged forward, sniffing the air. The beast stood on its hind legs, as if challenging him to a duel.

"Get away!" Robin snapped. He was tempted to try and kick at the rodent but was afraid of overturning the chair again. The rats would be all over him in seconds. But then, might that not be preferable to the death lovingly described to him by kindly Friar Garth? Surely the Lord would forgive a suicide, as long as it was committed to keep the victim from dying in a satanic ritual?

Before he could continue any further with that thought, Black Morag entered the hut. She bared her teeth at the rats and rushed forward, snarling and waving her arms. The big rat hissed in return, waiting until the last moment before fleeing with its fellows.

"Hideous creatures! I hate them!" Morag exclaimed with a shudder as she turned her attention to Robin. "I can't understand how the others can bring themselves to eat them!"

"Morag—why do you keep visiting me?"

She paused, chewing her ragged thumbnail in contemplation. "I'm not sure—I suppose it's because you're a hero. I've never seen one before. I just wanted to know what one was like."

"I'm a man, Morag," Robin replied wearily. "Just like any other, nothing more."

"Perhaps."

"Morag—please, help me."

To his surprise, the woman clapped her hands over her ears. She shook her head from side to side and made a strange, droning noise, as if trying to drown out something she didn't want to hear.

"Morag! Stop that! *Listen* to me! Set me free and I'll take you with me to Sherwood! There you can live free and happy under my protection, I *promise*!"

"No!" Morag continued to shake her head. *"No! No! No!"*

"Please, you've *got* to help me! There is no one else here I can trust! You don't belong here with these murderers!"

"You're wrong! I *do* belong here! I can't fit in anywhere else! I killed my father! I killed Matthew! I'm unclean! I *deserve* this place! I *deserve* these people! I'm nothing but a whore who allows murderers and thieves to climb on top of her!"

"Morag, you *have* to do something!" he pleaded. "You *know* what Garth means to do to me!"

"Aye, I know what he plans," she muttered sadly. Her eyes gleamed with sudden realization. "And I know what will spoil his game!" Before Robin could react, she fell to her knees before him and lifted the hem of the black robe he was wearing, pushing it back to expose his nethers.

"What are you doing, girl?" he cried out in surprise as her hands closed on his member.

Morag answered by lowering her head into his lap. He gasped out loud as she took his manhood into her mouth and began to expertly work it into a state of arousal. Half-mad or not, Black Morag was certainly adept in the tricks of her profession.

Robin was at a genuine loss as to what to what he should do. After all, he was married to—and deeply in love with—the Lady Marian. Throughout their long and difficult courtship he had never once indulged in the favors of tavern whores or seduced a peasant's daughter. But what Morag was doing to him—doubtless a sin in the eyes of Church—was something he'd never experienced in or out of the marriage bed.

As she worked feverishly at the task before her, he decided that it was at least preferable to the fate Garth had in store for him and began to thrust his hips in time with the bobbing of her head.

There came a roar of anger and Friar Garth was there, grabbing Black Morag's matted hair with his bony hand. "*Harlot!*" he shrieked. "What have you done?!?" With that he pulled Morag free of her work, sending Robin's seed arcing through empty air.

"Looks to me like I've fucked you side-saddle, old man!" Morag giggled, wiping her mouth with the back of her hand.

Garth emitted a shrill, almost womanly scream of rage as he produced a curved knife from the folds of his cassock. Morag saw the death blow coming but did nothing to deflect it as Garth opened her throat from ear-to-ear, like a butcher disposing of a suckling pig. She smiled and lifted her hand in farewell to Robin, then collapsed onto the floor. Somewhere in the shadows the rats squealed in anticipation of a meal.

Friar Garth stood over the dead body, still clutching the murder weapon in his trembling hand. "Meddling whore! I knew she was trouble the moment Tam bought her from that brothel! Stupid cow! She's ruined *everything!* The ritual is quite specific about no seed being spilled!"

"So your little plan has come to naught, is that it?" Robin laughed. "So much for my brother becoming king!"

"Don't think you're safe, Robin Hood!" Garth snarled. "The ritual would have made Tam's ascension to the throne a certainty, but I can still place him on the throne —provided that there is only *one* Fitzooth left alive!" With that the mad monk advanced on his captive, knife still wet with Black Morag's blood.

"Leave him be, Garth!"

The friar turned to stare in amazement at the sight of Tamlane the Dragon standing in the doorway of the hut, a nocked arrow pointed at his heretic heart.

"Tam? What are you doing here? Are you mad, boy?"

"Of that I have no doubt. Now do as I say!"

Garth frowned and shook his head, as if he couldn't believe what he was hearing. "He's got to die! There's no other way for you to take the throne."

"To Hell with the throne."

"What glamour has been worked on you?" Garth scowled."These are not the words of the Tamlane I know!"

"You mean they're not the words of the Tamlane you *created*," he retorted.

"Damn you, boy! You know what's at stake here!"

"Yes, and I've decided I don't want it! Now stand aside!" he said, motioning with the bow. "I don't want to kill you, but I will if you give me no choice!"

Garth's eyes narrowed as he studied his protégé. "I see, now—it's that woman, isn't it? That bloody Marian! *She's* the one who moonstruck you! I thought I raised you better than that, Tam! Women are no more than fields to be plowed—or salted! Now leave off this nonsense and let me finish what we started!"

Garth turned away from his foster-son and once more raised his knife. The bow sang and an arrow tore through the monk's spare frame. Garth stared down in dumb wonder at the arrowhead jutting from his breastbone as the knife fell from his hand. The look on his face was that of a man bitten by a dog he believed long since cowed into obedience.

The wizard staggered backward, knocking over the table. He pointed a shaking finger at Tamlane and murmured something in Latin before finally collapsing onto the floor, a bubble of blood extruding from his lifeless lips.

Robin waited for a second arrow to take his life as well, but to his surprise Tamlane set aside his bow and fell to untying him. His arms and legs tingled as if beset by a tiny army of fairies wielding embroidery needles. He stared at his brother as he massaged the feeling back into his wrists, uncertain of what might come next.

"It's best you leave as fast as you can," Tam suggested. "He was summoning his pet demon as he died."

"Why did you come back?" Robin asked. "You could have had everything: my name, my property, my chattels—even my wife. You could have even become king! Yet you returned to stop him."

"Believe me; I was sorely tempted to leave you to whatever fate Garth wished to mete out to you. But it did not take me long to realize there can only be *one* Robin Hood. Not because no one is your equal at swordplay or archery—but because of your heart," he replied, striking his breastbone with his fist. "As far back as I can remember, Garth twisted and stunted me, like a freak master creates his dwarves. He wanted me to come to manhood thinking *his* was the True Way. The *only* way. For as long as I can remember, he told me I was evil and it never occurred to me to wonder if that evil was mine by nature—or thrust upon me.

"But now I've seen how men live—*true* men, not the twisted, brutalized things I was raised with. I've seen how even the simplest peasant is a hundred times greater than I can ever be. I am shamed by this revelation. I am angered I have been denied the right to love and know friendship and all that comes with it. I have been sorely cheated. But I know who is to blame for making me the monster that I am," he said sadly, looking down at the body of the man who had raised him.

Despite all that had gone between them, Robin felt sorrow for his brother's predicament. "Thomas, please —I realize your sins have been many. But the Church assures us there is such a thing as redemption. Come, leave this place with me and return to Sherwood. It is your home, as well as mine."

Tamlane sniffed the air and an alarmed look crossed his face. He grabbed his brother and shoved him toward the door. "Go! There's no time for that! Your horse is outside, along with a change of clothes in its saddlebags!"

"But Tam--!"

"Don't argue with me, little brother! You mean well, but a one-eyed man can't see through a glass eye, no matter how badly he may want to! Go back to your castle and lands! Go back to your friends! Return and live out your life as history sees fit! But whatever you do, *never* let the Lady Marian slip from your grasp—for without her all is lost! Now *go*!"

Robin opened his mouth, prepared to argue his case even further, only to fall silent at the tears standing in his twin brother's eyes.

"I know I shouldn't weep for him," whispered Tamlane the Dragon. "But—good or bad—he was the only father I've ever known."

Without further word, Robin turned and left. Within seconds he'd mounted the horse his brother had left for him and was on his way back to his wife.

Tamlane the Dragon seated himself in the chair his brother had recently vacated and crossed his arms. It wouldn't be long. The electrical-storm smell of approaching demon was growing stronger by the second. He glanced down at the bodies sprawled at his feet and something like sorrow flickered in his heart as he saw Morag's twisted body. She, too, had been more a victim of her father's madness than her own. Perhaps that's why he'd fancied her in the first place.

He felt the hair on the back of his neck prickle and with a sound of a thousand angry honey-bees, the air was split and Lucullus appeared. The demon shambled from the shadows, quickly scenting the odor of spilled blood. The beast shuffled over to where the dead bodies lay in a tangled heap, snuffling like a bear. When it saw Garth's pale, blood-smeared face it abruptly froze and emitted a low-pitched whine.

"That's right, familiar! Your master's dead!" Tamlane laughed. "You're trapped here, now, with no one to send you home."

Lucullus swung its fierce, fang-filled snout in his direction. Its brow furrowed and lips curled in a snarl. Tam stood up, kicking the chair aside as he rose. He pulled a long, sharp dirk from his belt and motioned for the demon to approach him with a beckoning twitch of his fingers. His grin was almost as wide and sharp as his adversary's.

"Come, Lucullus. Let us dance."

THE HEART OF THE DRAGON

An Untold Tale of Elric

The White Prince pulled his cloak tighter, trying to block the icy wind sawing his flesh. His horse nickered its discomfort; it knew it was too cold to be standing motionless atop an exposed hill, even if its rider did not.

He stared down into the valley laid out before him like a rumpled blanket. It would be warmer down there. And more dangerous. He frowned as he fumbled with the vial in the pouch fastened to his belt. The elixir that helped fire his weak blood was so cold it burned his lips. His ruby-red eyes dilated as the herbs and drugs did their work.

Elric of Melniboné--last of a royal line that stretched beyond the dawn of Human memory--sank his spurs into the flanks of his trembling mount and descended into the Valley of Dragons.

"We need dragons."

This came from Yaris, the young upstart-king. More than once he had made his distrust of Elric known. Of the seven Sea-Lords who'd entered into the conspiracy with the exiled Melnibonéan to raid ancient Imrryr, the fabled Dreaming City, he was the one who complained the most.

Count Smiorgan Baldhead frowned over his horn of ale. He was the closest to a friend the albino prince could claim amongst the seven and the chief conspirator. "You're speaking nonsense, Yaris! Next you'll be wanting the moon on a string! Where would we get dragons?"

"Ask *him.*" Yaris pointed a finger at Elric, seated at the end of the table. "His people have used them for centuries! That's how they founded the Bright Empire! If we are going to raid the Dragon Isle, I'd rest easier knowing we have dragons of our own to call upon."

"The boy has a point," muttered Naclon of Vilmir, the most patrician and respected of the Sea-Lords. "The Melnibonéans did not become known as Dragon Princes for naught."

Elric shook his head. "The dragons of Imrryr are all but extinct. The ferocity has been bred from them, rendering them sterile. Your men and their ships have little to fear from them."

It was a lie, but he did not want his human co-conspirators backing out now that his dream of avenging himself on his scheming cousin Yrkoon and rescuing his ensorcelled lover Cymoril were finally within his reach.

Naclon stroked his beard pensively. "Still, your people tamed the beasts and bent them to their will enough to build an empire. Surely you could use your knowledge to our advantage."

Elric shrugged. "But where could I obtain dragons--and trained ones at that? Ones capable of responding to a rider's goads and directions? The beasts require a human lifetime to break until they're docile enough to accommodate a rider."

No sooner than he'd spoken, Elric envisioned himself astride a flying dragon, caparisoned in the bat-winged helm and black armor of his ancestors, Stormbringer held aloft as he waved his band of mercenaries onward toward the Dreaming City. The idea of the last of the royal line leading the final assault on the heart of the ancient, decadent Bright Empire astride one of the beasts that made that dynasty possible appealed to his vanity. And--as with all Melnibonéans--vanity was Elric's greatest weakness.

He stood up and fastened his cloak about his broad shoulders. "Gentlemen, I must take my leave of you. The raid that we are planning will require a great deal of mental and spiritual strength on my part. I must go forth and prepare myself. You will not see me for some time, I fear. I will return when the tides are right and the hundred ships promised for this venture are gathered in the fjord."

Count Smiorgan Baldhead left the table and hurried after his friend. While he had grown used to the high-handed manner in which the Melnibonéan dismissed himself from matters he considered boring, the same could not be said of the other Sea-Lords. Each was--in his way--a king and master, used to being heard and having their words acted upon. Granted, their kingdoms were little more than barbaric tribes compared to a lineage as old and powerful as Elric's, but that didn't mean they enjoyed having their noses rubbed in it.

"Elric! Is this wise?" Smiorgan whispered as he grabbed the Melnibonéan's elbow. "For you to take indefinite leave while the combine is at such an early and precarious stage risks disaster! What if Yaris should decide to pull out his support? Fadan of Lormyr would not be far behind in joining him--then where would we be? You're leaving me to tend a house of cards!"

Elric stiffened at the grip on his arm but in deference to his friend did not yank it free of the heavier man's grasp. He turned his crimson eyes toward Smiorgan and spoke in a cold, iron-edged voice.

"Your only hope of successfully navigating the Sea Maze that protects Imrryr' s harbor is through me. *With* me you have an alliance amongst your fellow raider-kings--forged by greed, avarice, and a deep-seated hatred of my people. *Without* me, you are seven reaver-kings constantly battling one another for the meager loot offered by the coastal villages of the Young Kingdoms. We will attack Imrryr when the tides and time are right. My being on display for your fellow Sea-Lords will neither hurry nor delay what will come. But if I do not prepare myself in the proscribed manner, there will be no raid, is that clear?"

Smiorgan' s frown deepened, but he let go of his friend's arm. "Very well. We shall await your return."

Elric nodded a farewell to his companion and left the room, pulling his cloak's hood over his head as he thought to himself: *And when I return I shall be astride a flying dragon.*

Elric's schooling in preparation for ascending to the Ruby Throne of Imrryr had given him knowledge of things and places unknown to the Human races. One such piece of arcana concerned the beings known as the Eldren.

Once the Melnibonéans had worshipped the Eldren as gods, although by the time of Elric's birth they had devolved into a half-remembered legend. As heir to the magicks and lore of the sorcerer-emperors who ruled the Bright Empire for ten millennia, Elric knew more about them than anyone else, with the possible exception of his demented cousin Yrkoon.

It was said that the Eldren had emerged from the swirling, formless mass of raw Chaos that stretches beyond the Cliffs of Kaneloon at the place called World's Edge, twenty-five thousand years ago. An Ordered race born from Chaos, the Eldren were rumored to serve neither aspect of the Balance while mastering both forces. They--and they alone--were successful in harnessing the dual natures of stasis and entropy.

As a youth, Elric had found a series of scrolls written by one his ancestors--Yrik the XVI, also known as The Wandering One--that detailed how twelve thousand years earlier the Eldren had created a race of beings like themselves, yet baser and more animalistic. This degenerate offshoot eventually became the Melnibonéans.

If the story was true, Elric could understand why it had been forgotten. The Melnibonéans had long prided themselves on their superiority to that of the lowly Human race, which it terrorized and enslaved before the first man had wits enough to strike flint against rock. The idea that they were a shadow of a more evolved race did not suit their vanity.

The scrolls went on to describe how after a virus had decimated the dragon caves, Yrik went forth to the Valley of the Dragons--where the Eldren were said to make their home--and successfully bargained for a breeding pair of winged serpents with their ruler, Tanoch the Lord of Dragons. Somewhere shortyly thereafter Yrik lost his reason--or at least the ability to concentrate on one thing for more than five minutes at a time, judging from the passages in his journal. All of this transpired three thousand years ago. Whoever--or whatever--the Lord of Dragons might be, it was clear that the Eldren were not to be trifled with.

Until Yaris planted the seed of using dragons to overthrow his enemy in his milk-white skull, the Eldren and their dragon cavalry had been just another piece of occult trivia cluttering his back brain. Now he was leagues away from his marshalling naval force, forcing his weary mount to trudge through harsh northern weather in search of a lost race sheltered from the roar and press of lesser civilizations by a magically-maintained valley. It was a fool's quest. But since when had knowing his actions were folly ever stopped him?

During his journey north he had caught tantalizing hints that what he sought actually existed. He'd heard blue-skinned barbarians invoking their fearsome, comfortless northern deities, and one they spoke of in the most reverent of whispers went by many names: Tanoch the Storm-Giver; Tanoch the Sky Lord; Tanoch the Night-Bringer. He'd even glimpsed a crude graven image of a winged man with a beard and breasts, the fingers crooked into punishing claws. Could this winged hermaphroditic sky-god be the same being his ancestor had petitioned for dragons centuries ago?

These thoughts ran through Elric's mind as he goaded his horse down the narrow mountain pass into the mist-shrouded vale below. The lush hot-house foliage and steaming jungle below reeked of sorcery. The surrounding mountains were harsh, cold granite giants sheathed in snow and black ice--such a place could not exist without the aid of powerful magicks.

His weary mount nickered nervously as they went deeper into the dense greenery. The trail they'd been following was now little more than a pig-path and Elric was forced to dismount and lead his horse as he hacked back branches and vines with his short-sword.

Suddenly the horse pulled against its reins, yanking them free of his hands. The beast reared onto its hind legs, its wildly rolling eyes showing their whites as it impotently kicked at the air with its forelegs. There was not enough room along the trail for it to turn and bolt, so all it succeeded in doing was tangling its bridle in the underbrush. Elric swore as he tried to calm the frightened animal. He made a grab at the flailing reins, fearful the beast's madly stamping hooves would connect with his head. As he wondered what could have thrown the stallion into such a sudden frenzy, he caught scent of dragon.

It was a rank, reptile stink, reminding him of the boyhood he'd spent playing with his best friend, Dyvim Tvar, in the Dragon Caves below the gleaming spires of the Dreaming City. There came the sound of tree trunks snapping like kindling and the sibilant hiss of a thousand angry serpents and then the dragon was upon them. Elric spun to face the monster that shouldered its way through the forest, snatching Stormbringer from its sheath.

The dragon towering over him was unlike any he'd seen in the husbandry charts of his ancestors. The dragons of Melniboné were winged serpents, their snake-like bodies narrow-snouted and equipped with powerful, whip-like tails. This beast, however, stood on two thickly muscled hindlegs, its forelegs dangling like the withered arms of an old woman. Its head was massive, the jaws capable of breaking a fully-armored battle-horse in two with one quick, dreadful snap. The monster's mouth was full of teeth the size of dirks--and just as sharp.

With a speed surprising for its bulk, the dragon seized the terrified horse in its massive jaws. The horse screamed like a girl as the monster's razor-sharp teeth pierced its vitals. The dragon shook its head back and forth, spraying its victim's blood in all directions. The horse's hindquarters fell to the ground, severed completely from the still-struggling head and forelegs.

Even armed with Stormbringer, Elric could see there was no point in pitting himself against such an engine of destruction. Leaving the dragon to feed in peace, he hurried on his way, least a more fearsome beast be attracted by the smell of blood.

Night came to the Valley of the Dragons. Elric had walked for hours along the narrow trail winding its way across the jungle floor, suffering the hot, muggy weather and the stings of numerous blood-drinking insects without finding any sign of civilization,

Eldren or otherwise. He had, however, narrowly skirted further confrontations with the terrible two-legged dragon--or its nest-mates--and spotted a few lumbering, well-armored four-legged dragons sporting unicorn-like horns. Much to his relief, these seemed more interested in feeding on the lush vegetation than pursuing him.

Now he sat watch in front of a meager fire, his sword ready at hand should the surrounding jungle present him with an unwanted visitor. He anxiously fingered the vial of elixir that kept his thin albino's blood enriched. He had enough for two, perhaps three days--assuming he did not have to call upon sorcery. Working magick always depleted him more than simple physical exertion, which was why he was loathe to call upon the arcane arts except in the direst of situations. In any case, if he did not find the Eldren soon, he would eventually weaken and fall victim to the ravenous giant reptiles that roamed the valley floor.

He scowled at the tiny fire and reflected on how, once again, his willfulness had lead him into a dire predicament. His refusal to accept the mantle of emperor had led to his ouster by his cousin, Yrkoon, and the endangerment of the one woman who had ever held any meaning to him--Yrkoon' s own sister, the lovely Cymoril.

He had turned his back on power and love in exchange for the freedom to wander the world and know life as something other than a noble-born scholar. Now he was plotting with the ancestral enemies of his people to overthrow the kingdom that was by rights his own. And now even that plan was in danger, what with him leagues away from his friends and comrades, none of whom he'd dared tell where he was going and for what reason.

Should he die in this lost, enchanted valley it would all be for naught. Yrkoon would continue to rule Imrryr and, in time, marry Elric's beloved so that their offspring would inherit the Ruby Throne. The thought made Elric's guts roil. His light-sensitive eyes ached from staring so hard into the fire. As he blinked back his tears of outrage, he lifted his gaze from the flames and saw that he was no longer alone.

They stood before him in a rough semi-circle, their armor gleaming like snake-skin. There were six of them, caparisoned in tight-fitting greaves and breast-plates made of an iridescent material that looked like leather but shone like metal. Their faces were all but obscured by ornate winged helmets and they held tridents in their hands.

One of the strangely-garbed warriors stepped forward, removing their helmet in a single, fluid gesture. A thick rope of violet hair, plaited into a single braid, dropped onto the warrior's shoulders. Elric could not keep from gasping at the sight of the Eldren's eerily familiar features.

His race had always prided itself on the delicacy of its features, especially when compared to the brutishness of the Human species. The being standing before Elric made even the finest-bred Melnibonéan courtier look like a scullery slave. The Eldren's cheekbones were high and tilted to give the eyes a cat-like slant. The eyebrows were upswept, the ears coming to a slight point. There was an androgynous beauty to the warrior's finely-chiseled features that defied gender. The most disturbing element, however, were the Eldren's eyes--they were of a solid color, lacking iris and whites, and were the same color as their hair. It was like looking into the painted eyes of a marble statue.

The Eldren warrior held up a six-fingered hand and made a gesture that Elric did not understand. As he got to his feet he felt a sharp pain in the back of his brain, as if it'd been pricked with a pin. His hand closed about the hilt of Stormbringer, which pulsed in his grip.

"I wish to see the Lord of Dragons," he announced, trying to sound as authoritative as possible.

The purple warrior did not smile or frown or show any signs of having understood anything he'd said.

"I am Elric of the Bright Empire. I have come to see the Lord of Dragons," he repeated.

The purple warrior turned to look at one of their fellows. The second warrior removed their helmet, revealing hair the color of seafoam braided into two heavy plaits. The green warrior twisted the six fingers of their left hand into an arcane symbol and twitched their head in a strange bird-like manner. The purple warrior nodded and turned back to face Elric.

The Eldren warrior's thin lips opened and an oddly clipped, almost mechanical voice issued forth. "Kalki informs me your race is Mute. So I shall communicate with you in the manner in which you are accustomed."

"I am Elric of Melniboné--"

"We know who you are. What you are. Your coming was foretold. The Lord of Dragons sent us to gather you, least one of the Eaters accidentally harm you." The purple warrior made another arcane gesture with their long, oddly-jointed fingers. "I am Euryth, First General of the Dragon Cavalry. Please come with us."

The silent, blank-eyed Dragon Generals lead Elric from his rough campsite to a nearby clearing where their flying dragons were tethered. While winged, these dragons were vastly different from their Melnibonéan cousins. The Eldren's mounts resembled monstrous featherless birds, with peaked crowns and cruel toothed beaks that clattered like clashing swords. Their huge leathery wings stretched thirty feet and the Eldren rode astride their backs on ornately tooled saddles.

General Euryth motioned for Elric to climb behind them and without a single look or visual signal exchanged between the six, the Dragon Cavalry took to the air as one. The Dragon Masters of Melniboné manipulated their serpentine mounts by way of sharpened goads and the use of special pitch-pipes that charmed the great beasts, but Elric was unable to determine how the Eldren kept their breed of dragon under control, as the Dragon Generals and their beasts performed as one.

It had been years since Elric had last ridden the great beasts his people had made their tools of war and empire. Now, looking down at the jungle from astride the Eldren's mount--the thunder of its wings and the rushing of the wind in his ears--he realized how much he'd missed such simple pleasures.

As dawn broke they came within sight of the Eldren's walled city, the legendary Arum. The sight of its towering spires and shimmering, glass-smooth walls reminded Elric of the place of his birth. No other city in the whole of the world could claim the knowledge and craftsmanship to create such delicate architecture. The Young Kingdoms were millennia from discovering how to build anything except brooding castles and thick-set keeps. And the truth to be told, the Melnibonéans themselves had long lost the incentive to continue creating such wondrous architectural confections. Imrryr itself was little more than a distant reflection of this wondrous city, glimpsed in a looking glass warped by time and neglect.

The squadron sailed across the lightening sky, circling downward like raptors descending the thermals. Their destination was the tallest of the ornate shimmering towers, its pinnacle open to the elements. One by one, the dragons swooped down, landing in the aerie with incredible precision.

Servants dressed in their masters' livery hurried forward to take possession of the squawking dragons as the Generals dismounted. Euryth removed their helmet and twitched the thumb and sixth finger of their right hand at a young Eldren dressed in a violet jerkin and breeches. The youth lifted an open palm in response and Euryth nodded. The First General turned to fix Elric with a blank gaze.

"The Lord of Dragons awaits you."

Euryth handed the reins to their mount to the youth and motioned for Elric to follow them into the heart of the tower.

Elric had seem many things on his travels, but nothing compared to the halls of the Dragon Palace of the Eldren. What had at first glance appeared to be walls of colored glass proved to be actual Chaos-stuff trapped between twin layers of Order. As he passed through the tortured arches and passageways of the palace, the walls became a giant's kaleidoscope as the Chaos surged and shifted its way through the colors of the universe. Elric was duly impressed. For all their vaunted reputation as sorcerers, the Melnibonéans had never been able to turn the raw stuff of entropy to their will.

They came to a set of doors fashioned to resemble a grimacing dragon, which silently opened inward. The throne room ceiling stretched into infinity, its walls hung with silken tapestries and lit by braziers that gave off light but no heat. On a raised dais sat a massive throne chiseled from a single piece of obsidian into which were carved serpent-dragons, but was otherwise empty.

Euryth arched their long-fingered hands as if they cupped an invisible egg, the fingertips straining but not quite touching. There was a rustling sound from deep within the darkness above Elric's head and a shadow spread itself across the floor. He started as he realized there was a figure crouched before him, dressed in what he at first mistook for a black leather cloak. Then the Lord of Dragons lifted her wings and smiled at the pale warrior-prince,

She was taller than him by a full head, her hair silver and her eyes solid black. She wore black suede riding breeches cinched at the waist by a thick leather belt adorned with the silver-plated skull of a feral cat. At first he thought she was wearing a ram's head helmet, then he realized the luxuriantly curled horns were growing from her forehead. She was nude from the waist up, her chest corded with heavy muscle that connected to the bat-like wings folded against her back like a peaked cape. She lifted a six-fingered hand in greeting.

"Welcome, cousin."

As Elric spied the scabbard hanging from her hip, Stormbringer twitched within its own sheath, emitting a low-pitched cry, as if issuing a warning to a challenger. He rested his hand on the pommel of the black sword and stroked it, silencing its moan.

The First General took a warning step toward Elric, the tines of their trident glowing with a purplish witch-fire.

"That will be all, Euryth," said the winged woman, making a complex gesture with her right hand. "We do not wish to offend our guest."

The crackling aura surrounding the trident disappeared and the Dragon General bowed curtly before retiring from the throne room.

The Eldren ruler stepped forward, her wings twitching like those of a restless bird. "Elric of Melniboné--Agent of Chaos; Master-Slave of Stormbringer; Eternal Champion. Your coming was foreseen by our Oracle." She gestured to a slender, fair-haired Eldren male crouching beside the ornate obsidian throne, his empty eyes hidden by a golden cloth.

"Then you know why I have come to petition you."

"You are in need of dragons. Why else would you venture into Eldren territory?"

"I was not certain if the legends were true. I had read of an ancestor's sojourn to your land on a similar quest, three thousand years ago. But I had no way of knowing if his directions were correct or if your people were extinct."

The Lord of Dragons smiled and gestured with one of her wings. "As you can see, the Eldren continue. As we shall always continue. Here or elsewhere, if need be. And we recall your fore-father, Yrik, most warmly."

"You are *that* Tanoch?"

Her smile widened. "Eldren are a long-lived race. And the Lords longest-lived of all. We were a youth of three centuries when Yrik knew us. But, yes, we are *that* Tanoch." She reached out with her left wing, touching him lightly on one shoulder. "Come, you must be tired after such a long journey. Our servants shall see that you are rested and properly cared for."

A pair of androgynous attendants dressed in silver and black livery appeared as if from nowhere.

"We shall see you come the evening, Child of Chaos," smiled Tanoch. "Until then." And with a single beat of her huge, bat-like wings she shot upward into the shadows of the throne room's vast atrium.

After he slept, bathed, and changed into fresh clothes, Elric was once more escorted into the throne room by the silent, blank-eyed Eldren servants. There he found a large banquet table set for three. The blind Oracle sat at the right hand seat beside the head of the table. Elric glanced about but saw no one else.

"Where is Tanoch?"

The Oracle did not answer, but instead angled his sightless face so it seemed as if he was staring into the shadows above their heads. There was the sound of wings and Tanoch Night-Bringer landed behind the chair at the head of the table.

"Forgive us. We were delayed by affairs of state." She gestured for Elric to seat himself at the foot of the table. "How have you found Arum?"

"Wondrous and mystifying. Yrik did not do it justice in his journals."

Tanoch nodded as she carefully folded her wings

against her back and took her place at the head of the table. “We have often wondered about what happened to him.”

“He went mad shortly upon returning to Imrryr with the dragons you gave him.”

Something unreadable crossed the Lord of Dragon’s finely chiseled features, then was gone. “We feared as much.” A servant emerged from the darkness and filled the goblets with a wine the color of turquoise. “He was a man of great measure. There is much that reminds us of Yrik in you.”

Elric grunted, fumbling with the tableware. The fork and knife were weighted for a six-fingered hand and felt alien in his grasp.

“We have given thought to your request for dragons. We have decided to help you.”

“Then you will give me dragons?” Elric exclaimed.

“More than that. We are prepared to turn our generals and their cavalry over to you for the raid on Imrryr.”

Elric tried to hide his surprise but was not entirely successful. “You know that I plan to raid the Dreaming City?”

Tanoch regarded him with her blank, black eyes. “Of course. ”

The Oracle twitched his head and Tanoch shrugged, making a dismissive gesture. “Don’t be a fool, Auberon. We know what we’re doing.” She smiled at Elric. “Please forgive our Oracle. He feels we are being--injudicious.”

Elric’s initial wariness quickly gave way to elation as he realized what this meant. With the Dragon Cavalry at his side, Imrryr would fall in a matter of hours!

Yrkoon' s still-beating heart would be offered as a sweet morsel on Lord Arioch's unhallowed altar on the first and only day of war! How sweet an irony that the Bright Empire would be reduced to rubble by the races that begat it and were enslaved by it! And surely beings as powerful and wise as the Eldren would have no trouble breaking the magicks that held his beloved Cymoril in stasis.

"Before you proclaim your victory over your usurping cousin just yet, perhaps we should discuss the terms of payment." Tanoch' s voice was tinged with both amusement and seriousness. Elric's chalk-white complexion colored as he realized the Lord of Dragons had been privy to his fantasies of conquest.

The Oracle shook his head violently and brought his closed fists down upon the table. Although his hands were almost feminine in appearance, there was unmistakable power in the blinded man's gestures. Tanoch' s fingers clamped tightly onto the arms of her chair as she lowered her horned brow. Elric massaged his forehead. It felt as if a bladder full of poisoned water was expanding behind his eyes. Tanoch slapped her left hand flat against the tabletop and emitted a weird, high-pitched sound that resembled the ultra-sonic piping of bats. Elric felt something warm and salty trickle from his nostrils. He touched his upper lip and stared at the smear of crimson on his bone-white fingertips. The Oracle made an unmistakably obscene gesture in the Melnibonéan' s direction and left the table, moving with surprising surety for someone without eyes.

Tanoch picked up her cutlery and resumed eating. "Do not mind Auberon. He's just jealous. Here, have some minted jelly with your rump of Grazer. We recommend it highly."

After the meal, Tanoch brought Elric into a room hung with black velvet draperies and dominated by a huge latticework of finely braided silken ropes suspended from rings sunk into the walls like a vast spider's web.

"What is this place?"

"It is our bedchamber."

"You sleep in *that*?" Elric motioned to the web-like net.

"Amongst other things," she replied with a tired smile.

Elric frowned. "You still haven't said what you expect from me in payment for the dragons."

Tanoch laughed without opening her mouth, which made Elric's brain flex and tremble inside its cage of bone. He took a step away from her, his vision swimming. He flinched as she touched his shoulder with one of her wings.

"Forgive us. We meant you no harm, neither here or at dinner."

"I believe you."

"To answer your question, princeling--What we ask in the way of payment from you is the same we asked of your ancestor, Yrik, three thousand years ago. If you wish our aid, then you must spend a night with us in the web."

He thought of Cymoril, his one true love--kept from him by her brother's sorcery--and shook his head. "My love belongs to another."

"Did we ask for your love?"

Elric fell silent, contemplating his next move as Tanoch watched him with her bottomless black eyes.

"Before you make your decision, it is only fair that we warn you of the consequences. You may have noticed that while the Eldren are capable of talking mind to mind, we mostly use hand signs to communicate. That is because there must be a dividing line between individuals, otherwise more powerful personalities might subsume and consume the lesser ones. That is where *we* fit into the Scheme. The Lord of Dragons exists to insure the sanctity of Self is maintained. To mate with a Lord of Dragons is a dangerous thing. We are telepathic, and to join with the body is to join with the mind. And our mind is that of all Eldren, for I am the Heart of the Dragon. Are you willing to risk madness, White Prince? Are you willing to risk the loss of your very self to win my favor? You could emerge from our lovemaking like Yrik before you."

"You bear this burden alone?"

"I have my consort--the Oracle. He is the only Eldren who can embrace me without fear. And there is Mind."

"Mind?"

She smiled and rested her hand on the sword hanging from her hip. "You are not the only one whose well-being is tied to a sword of arcane manufacture. Mind belonged to our predecessor. Mind *is* our predecessor. And in time, we too shall become Mind.

Elric unhooked Stormbringer's scabbard from his belt and held it before him in his pale hands. "I have carried this cursed weapon in the service of Arioch; I have slaughtered innocents to keep my master fed with blood and souls. And you ask me if I fear madness? I would look upon it as a gift!"

She reached for him then with her wings, encircling him with their elongated fingers. The light from the braziers illuminated the capillaries of the skin stretched between the vanes and for a brief moment Elric recalled what it had been like inside his mother's womb.

"Take me, child of chaos," she whispered, her twelve fingers slowly working on the lacings of his shirt. "We are damned, you and I. Chained by fate and biology to roles we would rather not play. You yearn for the Lady Cymoril, but are denied her. I would bear Auberon's child, but his seed cannot grow within me. There will be time enough in what remains of our lifespans for remorse, pain, and grief. Let us enjoy what little pleasure and warmth our liege lords will allow us. Do you understand what we're trying to say, Melnibonéan?"

Elric looked into Tanoch' s face, but her eyes were unreadable. Her kisses were long and deep, as if she was weighing his soul with each taste of his lips. She took his manhood in her hands, using the extra fingers to tease him to erection in ways he'd never before imagined. As he penetrated her body she penetrated his mind.

A rush of sensation and memory filled his skull, blossoming behind his eyes like a flower of fire and ice. It was as if he was standing naked on a sandy beach and had been taken unawares by a massive tidal wave. All that ever was and ever would be Tanoch surrounded him. Past, present, and future lay before him, jumbled together like so much abandoned knitting.

The warmth of the sun on her wings as she swoops through the clouds--

The churning sea of Chaos at Land's End spits forth a winged humanoid clad in chitinous armor that reflects the infant moon's cold rays--

Gently stroking her blind consort's penis with a six-fingered grasp--

A winged woman with sky-blue hair and slender gazelle-like horns draws from her scabbard a sword with a hilt fashioned to resemble mating dragons--

The flash of light from the laser as it severs her umbilical cord--

The coppery taste of human blood as she feeds on the sacrificial victim offered to her by the terrified, blue-daubed barbarians--

The winged woman with blue hair takes the sword and falls on it; the gleaming tip punctures her sternum and exits between her pinions--Mother--Mother--

The delicious, erotic prickling of her skin as she swoops in and out of the gathering thunderclouds--

Mother--

*She holds the sword called Mind for the first time and hears the voices of her ancestors, crooning and cajoling her into triggering her clairvoyance. Feels her mother's love--**is** her mother's love--*

The warmth of Yrik the Melnibonéan's semen on her thigh as he withdraws from her womb, screaming--screaming--

A roiling cloud of Chaos obscures the sun--She spreads her wings, signaling the others to follow her. And the Eldren astride their dragons cross the threshold from this world to some new and unknown universe--

The ground convulses and the sky cracks, spilling

Chaos across the land--Elric stands alone at its heart, the unwilling epicenter of mass destruction, screaming and waving Stormbringer like an angry child--Stormbringer leaps from its master's hands of its own volition and--

Elric cried out, forcing himself back into his body at the very moment of orgasm. The sensation of being both penetrated and penetrator remained, and for a brief moment he saw himself through Tanoch' s bottomless eyes: a pale demon with mad, red eyes, teeth bared in a rictus grin. He tried to push himself off her in self-disgust but was too weak. Instead, he lapsed into sleep.

◆ ◆ ◆

He awoke to find himself curled under one of Tanoch' s wings. The leather was as soft as moleskin and radiated body heat. He lay still under this living blanket for a long moment, studying the Lord of Dragon's sleeping features. Her eyes jerked rapidly back and forth behind closed lids and occasionally a muscle in her face twitched, but she was otherwise motionless.

Elric eased himself out from under her wing and nimbly descended the web, careful not to disturb the sleeping Eldren. His head still ached from the torrent of sensory images and snatches of memory that had sluiced through it, but he no longer felt drained. One borrowed memory had particularly intrigued him. It had to do with the sword called Mind.

The Lord of Dragon's scabbard lay amidst her discarded clothes, the sword's ornate handle gleaming softly in the muted light of the bedchamber. Elric's own weapon stood propped against a nearby table. As the albino reached for the Eldren blade, Stormbringer began to moan to itself like a mistreated pup.

"Damn you, be quiet!" he whispered. "If I didn't know better, I'd say you're jealous! I have no intention of casting you aside. *Yet.* I'm merely curious as to the manner of sorcery used in creating this weapon."

Apparently mollified, the black sword lapsed into silence.

From what little he was able to glean from the memories he had shared with Tanoch, Mind was similar to Stormbringer in that it stored souls and drew its power from them. He awkwardly wrapped his fingers around the sword's hilt, which was designed for a six-fingered grip. Mind's scabbard felt strangely warm to the touch--like a living thing. Dismissing the tingling in his fingertips as simple anxiety, he freed Mind from its sheath.

A dozen voices, male and female, instantly swarmed and yammered inside his head like a cloud of angry hornets.

(who?who?who? stranger! not one of us! access denied! Tanoch!Tanoch!Tanoch! access denied! Tanoch! Tanoch!Tanoch! purge! purge!purge!)

The pain that travelled up his arm and into his head and chest was so immense there was no way he could scream loud enough or long enough to give it proper voice. In the brief moment before his brain and nervous system shut down, he glimpsed Mind's naked length: a roiling tendril of Chaos preserved between two gleaming slivers of Order. Somewhere he could hear Stormbringer keening like a newly minted widow.

There were strange hands with too many fingers

touching his body, probing muscle and tissue with peculiar instruments made from metal and horn. Something was squeezed between his clenched teeth and forced down his throat, billowing his collapsed lungs.

Elric reflexively gagged and struggled to sit up. Tanoch squatted over him, studying him with her onyx eyes. When she spoke, it was with great sadness. "We saw this happen before you ever agreed to lay with us. We knew you would do this. Yet we hoped there could be a way around Fate, just as we had hoped Yrik would find a way to escape the madness that was his destiny."

He shook his head and coughed, spraying the back of his hand with blood. "I bleed inside..."

"Not for long. We have fixed what was harmed. You are not to die here and now, Elric of Melniboné. This we know. Now get dressed."

Elric got to his feet. "The dragons..?"

"There will be no dragons. You forfeited them the moment you touched Mind. It's a miracle you're alive at all! None but a Lord of Dragons can wield it. Had Chaos not put its stamp on you from birth, every cell in your body would have imploded! We will give you another gift in place of the dragons. Name it and it is yours."

"You can foresee the future. Let that be your gift."

Tanoch shook her head. "You don't want to know what we see, Melnibonéan. Choose another gift, princeling, we beg you."

"No. Tell me my future. Will I succeed with the raid on Imrryr?"

"Elric--please--"

"Tell me!"

"Yes. Imrryr will fall before your marshaled forces.

The Dreaming City shall burn and the Bright Empire will be no more."

"And what of Yrkoon, my traitorous cousin? Will he die by my hand?"

"Yrkoon shall die."

"And Cymoril? Will I be reunited with my one true love?"

Tanoch closed her eyes and her wings flinched.

"Answer me!" he barked.

"You will be reunited. But your time together will be brief before she dies, impaled on Stormbringer's blade."

"That can't be true!"

"We cannot lie. That is our curse."

"Damn you, tell me the truth!"

"We *have*, Elric Woman-Killer."

"No! You're lying! By my Lord Arioch, I'll *make* you tell me the truth!" He reached for Stormbringer, intent on hacking the empty-eyed demoness to bits, if that's what it took to negate the future she had cast for him. Stormbringer growled like an angry dog, eager to taste blood. Tanoch did not move to defend herself.

"My people learned to shape and sculpt Chaos and Order when the stars were clouds of cosmic dust. Do not think to threaten me with Stormbringer, Champion Eternal."

Elric's shoulders slumped as he met and held Tanoch's black gaze. "Then it's all for naught. If I sail against Imrryr, Cymoril will die. But if I stand idle, Yrkoon will make her his wife. Either way, all that is mine is denied me. But I would rather Cymoril live in incestuous wedlock than spend my days knowing I am guilty of her murder."

"I fear it is not so simple. The die has been cast, Elric of Melniboné. Your doom began the moment of your conception. Mortal things were not meant to see beyond the Now. Such knowledge would paralyze even the boldest of your kind." She brushed his milk white brow with her long, weirdly jointed fingers. "Let this be my final gift to you: None of this ever happened."

Elric awoke suddenly from his dream, sitting upright in his narrow bed. Something--he wasn't certain exactly what--had disturbed his troubled slumber. He scanned the shadows pooled in the corners of his rented room, but they held neither assassins or demons. He swung his legs over the side of the bed, instinctively reaching for Stormbringer as he did so.

He had leased the attic room a fortnight earlier in order to prepare himself for the coming raid on Imrryr. He had spent the last few days fasting and meditating, secluded from all human company.

There had been a dream of a woman--a woman with the head and wings of a dragon. In his dream, Elric battled the dragon-woman, skewering her heart with Stormbringer. Dreams meant things. Every sorcerer's apprentice knew that. Perhaps it was a favorable omen, foretelling the fall of Imrryr and the destruction of his evil cousin, Yrkoon. Yes, that sounded right.

There was the sound of something moving outside the attic window. Elric threw the shutters back, but the eaves were empty of spies. He stared up at the moon's cold, dead eye and thought of Cymoril, his beloved, held captive by her brother's sorcery.

Soon she would be free and his once more. In a few

days' time the tides would be in their favor and the Sea Lords' hundred war ships would set sail for the Dreaming City. And then Yrkoon's head would look on from high atop a pike as Elric reclaimed both his throne and his betrothed.

"It won't be long, my love," Elric promised the moon.

But that's another story.

Twelve months and thirteen days from the night she took the Melnibonéan into her arms, Tanoch was delivered of a male child. The boy was pale like his father, with pointed ears, garnet eyes, red hair, upswept eyebrows, and five fingers and toes. From his mother he inherited wings. And while they were still little more than crib-buds, his horns promised to become a handsome, curling rack.

She named him Lucifer.

But that's yet *another* story.

THE ICE WEDDING

A True Fairy Tale

"Your Highness, Count Ushakov has returned."

Anna Ioannovna, Empress and Autocrat of All the Russias, looked up from the conversation she had been holding with her chamberlain and court favorite, the German-born Duke Biron. There was an eager gleam in her dark brown eyes. Normally she would not have cared whether one of her courtiers had returned from afar or not, but Ushakov was not just another boyar—he was the chief of the Secret Chancery, and therefore one of her most trusted—and useful—servants.

"Send him in."

Count Ushakov entered the empress' private chamber with the brisk efficiency he was both known and feared for.

"Welcome back, Andrei Ivanovich," the tsaritsa said warmly. "I trust you have news for me?"

"Yes, Excellency," Ushakov said as he bowed before his sovereign. "The rumors are true—Prince Mikhail Golitsyn has indeed married a foreigner. And to make matters worse--he has converted to her faith."

Not an attractive woman to begin with, this unwelcome news made Anna Ioannovna's inelegant features even uglier. "How dare he marry without asking our permission?" she spat. "And he compounds his insult to us by becoming an apostate as well!"

"What else should you expect from a Golitsyn, my empress?" Biron smirked

Anna Ioannovna nodded her head as vigorously as her short, thick neck allowed. Her lover was right. Although they were one of the noblest princely houses in Russia, the Golitsyns, were a perverse and untrustworthy lot. They had proved a thorn in her side for some time, even though it was Prince Mikhail's elder brother, Prince Dmitrii--head of the Privy Council--who had nominated her as successor to the throne when the young tsar Peter II unexpectedly died of smallpox.

Under most circumstances Anna Ioannovna would have been grateful for the old diplomat's championing of her, save for the fact he had only done so in hopes of placing a weak and--so he had assumed--easily controlled puppet on the throne. It had been Prince Dmitrii's intent--along with that of the hated Dolgorukiis--to try and introduce a constitutional monarchy to Russia. It had been Prince Mikhail himself who had traveled to her court in Courland to inform her she would be elevated from her position as the widowed ruler of a poverty-stricken, war-torn duchy-- but only if she agreed to sign the list of conditions the Privy Council had drafted.

Of course, Anna Ioannovna viewed the contract she had signed to win the crown as nothing more than words on paper. This the Royal Guards--led by her cousin, Count Saltykov--made perfectly clear to the reform-minded grandees of the Privy Council upon her arrival in Moscow. Shortly after her coronation she exiled the Dolgorukiis and their entire household to Siberia. Then two years ago she had the elderly Prince Dmitrii sentenced to imprisonment for life while confiscating his estates as punishment for his anti-monarchial sentiments. The sentence proved a brief one, as Prince Dmitrii died after only three months in prison.

Shortly before his brother's fall from grace, Prince Mikhail had been granted the post of Russia's envoy to Italy. But now it was clear he, too, could not be trusted.

"Bring me my secretary," Anna Ioannovna said to Biron. "I would send a letter."

Prince Mikhail's stomach tightened into a knot when he saw the letter awaiting him on his desk. He did not need to open it to know who it was from. The double-headed eagle stamped into the blood-red sealing wax told him that.

"Is something wrong, dearest?" his wife asked. "You look so pale."

"I've been relieved of my duties here in Rome," Golitsyn said in a voice as heavy as lead. "The tsaritsa has summoned me back to St. Petersburg immediately."

"But it's already winter!" Madame Golitsyn protested, placing a protective hand on her swollen belly. "Can't you petition the empress to postpone the trip until the spring? By then the baby will be born…"

Golitsyn shook his head. "Anna Ioannovna has little love for my family, I'm afraid. Even if she was better disposed towards us, she would still insist I do as I'm told. In Russia it is not like it is here in the West. Prince and pauper are no different in the eyes of the tsars--we are both their slaves, to do with as they will."

He should have known news of his marriage would have gotten back to Anna--especially after he converted to his new wife's faith. He had allowed the warmer climes and relative freedom of Rome to affect his judgment. Now he had put not only himself but his new bride and unborn child in grave danger. Even though he dreaded standing before the tsaritsa, there was no question of his ignoring her command. Although he had turned his back on the Orthodox Church in the name of love, it did not mean the Mediterranean sun had thinned his blood to the point of it no longer being Russian.

Prince Mikhail's journey from Rome to St. Petersburg took ten weeks. During it he faced brutal weather, avalanche-prone mountain passes, as well as the occasional hungry wolf pack. Madame Golitsyn--unaccustomed to such extreme cold--quickly developed pneumonia, which spread to both her lungs. By the time they reached her husband's palace in St. Petersburg she was gravely ill. A physician was called for, but with a shake of his head declared it too late. Nothing could be done.

As the distraught Golitsyn sat at his wife's deathbed,

watching her struggle for her last, strangled breath, a messenger from the palace appeared at his door. It was clear Ushakov's spies had been keeping an eye out for his arrival.

"The Tsaritsa Anna wishes to know why, though Your Highness has returned to the capital, you have yet to appear before her court," the messenger asked.

"I have only been in the city a handful of hours, and my wife is dying. Please tell Her Imperial Majesty I will seek my audience with her tomorrow, if it pleases her."

The messenger nodded his understanding and hurried off to relay Golitsyn's message to his mistress. An hour later, the same messenger--looking quite winded and more than a little frightened--reappeared on the prince's doorstep.

"Her Imperial Highness wishes to inform Prince Mikhail that it does not please her to wait until tomorrow. She expects your appearance before her court immediately. I have been told to inform Your Highness should you protest you are to be placed under arrest."

Prince Mikhail's shoulders slumped upon hearing this news. Although he did not want to leave his wife's side, neither did he desire to spend the winter freezing to death in a miserable prison cell like his older brother.

With tears in his eyes, Golitsyn knelt at his dying wife's bedside and placed a final kiss on her brow. He wanted her to remain in Italy with her family, where she would be out of harm's way--but she had insisted on accompanying him. She had believed that once the tsaritsa saw she was with child she would find it in her heart to be merciful towards her husband. It was such romanticism that attracted him to her and won his love in the first place. But in the end it proved the death of not only herself, but their unborn child as well.

His heart breaking with every step, Prince Mikhail put on his great coat and fur hat and followed the royal messenger to the sledge waiting outside, leaving his beautiful, doomed wife to her fate: to die alone in a strange land, without family or friends to comfort her, bereft of the last rites of her faith.

The absolute ruler of all the Russias sat atop a dais on the gold and crimson throne of the Romanovs while the lords and ladies of her court stood at obedient attention in the spacious throne room of the imperial palace. Before her stood Golitsyn, fur hat in hand, the shoulders of his heavy winter coat wet with melting snow.

"So, Mikhail Mikhailovich, you are home at last," Empress Anna said, looking down her overly long nose at the disgraced diplomat.

"I came as quickly as I could, Your Imperial Majesty."

"But not as quickly as I would have preferred," she sniffed. "You have displeased us most severely, Prince Mikhail! We have always thought you something of a fool, but your decision to cast aside the teachings of the church of your fathers in order to lie with an Italian strumpet settles the issue."

"I beg your Imperial Highness' mercy," Golitsyn said, dropping to his knees before his sovereign. "I never intended insult to your majesty."

"Then what possible excuse can you offer us for such a blatant act of idiocy?"

"I was in love, Your Majesty. Love makes idiots of us

all, at times."

The tsaritsa glanced at her favorite, Biron, who was standing next to his wife, watching the humiliation of his old political rival with a pleased smile on his handsome face. "That it does," she agreed. "But it would seem it makes greater fools of some of us than others." She looked about the room, frowning. "Where is this ill-thought bride of yours, then?"

"She is at my home, here in St. Petersburg."

"Then why is she not standing here before me at your side?" Anna Ioannovna demanded, her eyes flashing.

"The trip was too much for her," Golitsyn said in a grief-stricken voice. "I—I fear she is already dead, Your Highness."

The tsaritsa frowned. She had been looking forward to punishing husband and wife alike for their effrontery. Now that the bride had eluded justice, she would simply have to make do with the groom.

"You are a fool, Prince Mikhail! First you marry a foreigner without my permission, and then you become an apostate for the sake of a hothouse love that cannot bear even the slightest breath of a Russian winter! We would be angry with you, except that watching your suffer the consequences of your foolishness amuses us a great deal. It would please us to have you play the fool in court. After all, the winters are long and cold--we must have something to alleviate the boredom."

Golitsyn blinked, taken aback by what his ruler was suggesting. "Beg pardon, tsaritsa—are you commanding that I serve as your *jester?*"

"One of them, at least," Anna Ioannovna replied with a shrug of her meaty shoulders. "You would be the sixth."

"But—but I am a prince of Russia!" the aghast nobleman protested. "A descendant of Saint Dmitri Ivanovich Donskoy!"

"As am I," Anna Ioannovna reminded him coldly. "Except that my ancestor was Saint Dmitri's eldest *son*, not his youngest *daughter*. And if I desire that you become my newest jester, that is all there is to it."

"Yes, tsaritsa," Prince Mikhail replied, bowing his head. He realized that if he protested any further, he was in real danger of having his tongue cut out of his head. "As you command."

And so Prince Mikhail Golitsyn returned to his home and ordered his servants to place his dear wife's corpse in the family crypt, alongside that of his hapless brother. He then had his belongings sent to the imperial palace, where he would now live--along with the other courtiers at the empress's beck and call--until such time as her majesty either wearied of him or she had him killed.

He was given a room in the wing of the palace reserved for those who the tsaritsa had regular need of, such as her ladies-in-waiting, astrologer, and hairdresser. As he was unpacking his things a man entered his quarters without knocking. The stranger wore a powdered wig backwards atop his head and a suit of clothes that was well-made but clearly a size and a half too small, which gave him a ridiculous appearance. Hanging from one of his buttonholes was a decoration consisting of a miniature cross of St. Alexander affixed to a red ribbon.

"I am Jan De Acosta, her imperial majesty's jester-in-chief," he announced, pointing to the badge upon his chest. "What manner of fool are you then? You're clearly not a dwarf. Are you a buffoon? Juggler? Clown? Or are you a sad-head?" De Acosta asked, tapping his forehead.

"I am a noble fool," Golitsyn replied.

"Ah!" De Acosta said knowingly. "That explains much. Follow me to your assignment."

Prince Mikhail followed the royal jester through a maze of corridors until they came to a small, drafty antechamber that looked out on the nearby river. In the vestibule was a large nesting box, like those in a hen house. Golitsyn looked inside and saw three eggs in the fresh straw.

"Until further notice, your duty to the tsaritsa is to sit on these eggs and cluck like a chicken," De Acosta said. "If it is discovered you have crushed any of them, you will be severely punished, is that understood? These eggs belong to her imperial majesty, after all."

Golitsyn nodded as he stared at the hen's nest before him.

"Then what are you waiting for?" the jester barked. "Take your place!"

Prince Mikhail sighed forlornly as he carefully positioned himself atop the pile of straw, making sure to squat atop the nesting box instead of sitting directly in it. He then folded his arms into makeshift wings and began to cluck like a broody hen.

"Bawk-bawk-bawwwwk."

The lead jester took a step back, studying the overall effect as if he was the royal engineer overseeing the construction of a bridge. "You make a passing fool," he said grudgingly.

"How long am I to stay here?" Golitsyn asked.

"You must tend this nest from the break of dawn until sunset," De Acosta told him. "In the future, you will want to bring a chamber pot and a lunch with you."

And with that, the jester walked away, leaving Golitsyn clucking mournfully.

◆ ◆ ◆

During his first day as an official fool, Prince Mikhail learned many things. The first was that the antechamber where he was stationed was very chilly. The second thing he learned was that squatting atop a hen's nest was exceedingly tiring on the legs. The third thing was that there was no guarantee that the empress would walk past him during the course of the day. Still, he had no doubt that if he shirked in his nest-tending duties, news of it would somehow get back to her. Still, as humiliating as it might be to pretend to be a barnyard animal for the amusement of the tsaritsa, it was far preferable to spending his days in shackles or exiled to Siberia.

Once the sun had set Golitsyn found the cramps in his calves so bad he was barely able to make his way back to his quarters. As he hobbled down the hallway, he happened past an open door and saw an elderly man dressed in a red caftan embroidered in silver and seated before a table. The man's posture and facial features spoke of extreme tiredness. His head was drooping and his wig had shifted to one side of his head. He held a rosary in one hand while the other rested on a walking stick. Although it had been a long time since he had last laid eyes on him, Golitsyn recognized the weary old man as the jester to Peter the Great and the Empress Catherine, famed for his witty repartee and clever stories.

"Ivan! Ivan Balakirev!"

The old man raised his head and peered at the figure standing in his doorway. "Prince Mikhail? Is that you?"

"Yes, I am afraid it is."

Balakirev frowned. "What in the name of the Blessed Savior are you doing in this part of the palace?"

"Serving the empress as she sees fit for me to do," Golitsyn replied.

A sad but knowing look crossed the old jester's face. "I had heard that another noble fool had been added to the household. I did not know it was you."

"Another? There are more?"

Balakirev nodded. "Prince Nikita Volkonskii tends to her majesty's greyhound, while Count Aleksei Apraksin feeds saucers of warm milk to her favorite goats."

"But isn't Prince Volkonskii's brother-in-law the chancellor?"

"That he is. And Count Aleksei's family built this palace, which Anna Ioannovna usurped for her own when she outgrew the original imperial palace next door," Balakirev sighed. "I miss my beloved tsar more and more. Peter Alexeyevich may have been mercurial in his temperament, but at heart he was a clever man. There is no place in this court anymore for a well-said fool. Perhaps it is time I claim my pension and retire to my chalet in Sweden."

"Before you go—could you perhaps give me some hints as how to amuse the empress?"

"The first thing you must understand is that it is far easier in Russia for a fool to be made a general than for a wise man to play the fool. Anna Ioannovna has no interests in drollery or witticisms. If you wish to amuse her, you must appeal to her taste for practical jokes and buffoonery. The more absurd your behaviors--the more willing you are to accept the slap to the face and the boot to the arse--the happier she will be."

As Golitsyn returned to his rooms he mulled over what the old jester had told him. If the tsaritsa wanted to make him a fool, then he would have to play it to the hilt to survive. And that meant casting aside his pride in order to be a clever idiot.

The next day Golitsyn returned to his post atop the nesting box and clucked like a chicken, as was expected of him. And, yet again, the empress did not pass by. Nor did she pass by on the third day. It wasn't until the fourth day that Anna Ioannovna finally strolled by--accompanied, as always, by her favorite, Duke Biron, as well as some other courtiers.

"Greetings, Prince Mikhail," the tsaritsa laughed. "We have come to see how you are faring in your new position at court." She pointed to the nesting box on which he crouched. "What have we here?"

"As your imperial majesty has so kindly and rightly pointed out, I am prone to making foolish marriage proposals. Now that I am, again, widowed, I have taken a new wife—this time a most becoming little hen! She has already presented me with what I hope will be three fine, healthy young cockerels. I regret that my wife is not here to greet you, your highness—but the cook sent for her earlier in the day, and she has yet to return!"

"How is your brood faring?" Anna Ioannovna chuckled. "Come, let us see."

Golitsyn obediently hopped off the nest, revealing

three brand-new baby ducklings nestled in the straw.

"These are not chicks, Prince Mikhail!" the tsaritsa laughed. "They're ducks!"

"Ducks?" Golitsyn wailed, tearing at his wig in outrage. "Woe is me! I have been made a cuckold! When I get my hands on my wife, I will wring her neck!"

"You would not be the first husband to play nursemaid to another's bastard at this court," Anna Ioannovna said, wiping tears of laughter from her eyes. "Take this as a small token of my amusement." She reached into the pocket of her gown and removed a handful of corn mixed with bits of gold, which she tossed onto the floor at the feet of her newest jester.

Golitsyn crowed like a rooster and dropped to his knees, pecking at the golden feed. He tried his best to ignore the peals of cruel laughter his antics evoked from the empress and her entourage, telling himself it was better to provoke the tsaritsa's amusement than her wrath.

Later that evening as he sat alone in his room, picking pieces of gold out of the shit in his chamber pot, Prince Mikhail cursed the day he agreed to be the one to offer the throne of the Romanovs to Anna Ioannovna.

And so Prince Mikhail became the empress's favorite jester, eclipsing Jan De Acosta and even the Italian fool, Pedrillo--who had entertained the tsaritsa by wedding a goat and consummating the marriage before the entire court.

As the weeks turned into months and the months grew into a year, Prince Mikhail hoped against hope that the sovereign would either eventually appoint him to a post more keeping with his pedigree or--better yet--allow him to return to his ancestral estate, far from St. Petersburg. However, as time wore on Golitsyn found himself in a unique situation. In his desire to keep his head on his shoulders and his land his own, he had worked hard on his foolery and now Anna Ioannovna was loath to dispense with his services. It seemed no matter how hard he worked to amuse her imperial majesty, the joke always ended up at his expense.

One of Anna Ioannovna's fondest hobbies was that of playing matchmaker. Married off at a tender age by her royal uncle to the King of Prussia's frail nephew--who died six weeks later of alcohol poisoning--she strove to vicariously relive what she considered one of the happiest moments of her younger life: her wedding. Now that she was the Mother of the Native Land, and therefore the sole master of her subjects' lives and property, Anna Ioannovna was in the unique position of not merely suggesting possible pairings but guaranteeing them.

One afternoon she was sitting in her private chambers, surrounded by her ladies and maids, when she summoned her personal secretary to her. "Write a letter to the Voivode Kologrivov's wife. Inform her that she is to give her daughter in marriage to Dmitrii Simonov because he is a kind man and we shall not deprive him of our favor."

"As you command, tsaritsa."

As the secretary hurried off to compose the letter to Madame Kologrivov, there came a heavy sigh from the tsaritsa's Kalmyk maid, Avdotya Ivanovna Buzheninova.

"Why do you sigh so, Avdotya?" the empress asked.

"Because I have never known the warmth of a husband in my bed, and never will," the maid replied.

Anna Ioannovna eyed the maid, who was hunchbacked and had the thick black hair, brown skin and broad, flat features common to the tribes that made the grassy plains of western Mongolia their home. Although Avdotya was a capable maid, there was no denying that she was exceptionally ugly, even by her peoples' standards. Still, Anna Ioannovna liked to think it was her prerogative as tsaritsa to see to the personal happiness of all her subjects, including such savage heathens as the Kalmyk.

It was then a delicious idea came to her—one that made her laugh out loud and clap her hands in delight at her own cleverness. "You needn't mourn long for a husband, my dear! We have just the groom for you! But first--go and bring Pyotr Eropkin to us!"

Eventually Eropkin--the royal architect who had helped build the foundations of St. Petersburg under the command of Tsar Pete--arrived and stood before the tsaritsa. "You wished to see me, Excellency?"

"I would have you build a house for me, Pytor Mikhailovich; one that I wish to present as a honeymoon cottage. I would have it finished within two months' time."

A look of concern crossed the royal architect's face. "Two months? But it is the dead of winter, your majesty!" he protested. "The ground is frozen hard enough to break even the strongest shovel! There is no way I could lay a foundation before the thaw!"

"The house I would have you build does not need a cellar," Anna Ioannovna said with a cruel smile. "I want you to build an icehouse on the River Neva."

At first Eropkin wasn't sure he had heard correctly. "A house made of ice? As a *wedding* present?"

"Yes—and spare no expense!"

"As you command, tsaritsa." Eropkin lost no time in hurrying from the empress's chamber. If his lengthy career in service to the creative whims of the Romanovs had taught him anything, it was best to simply shut up and build.

The winter of 1739 was one of the coldest and most severe seasons ever to grip the continent of Europe. In London the Thames froze over; in Ireland an early frost destroyed the potato crops, leading to famine; in France the Seine froze solid, as did Lake Constance in Germany; sailors on the open seas lost their fingers to frostbite; and in Russia famine and cold drove packs of wolves into the streets of Moscow in search of meat.

As serious as these troubles were, none of them penetrated the walls of the imperial palace of St. Petersburg. And even if they did, they did not bother Anna Ioannovna in the least, as she was far too busy planning the wedding festival to end all wedding festivals to pay heed to such trivialities.

When her uncle married her off to the Duke of Courland thirty years before, he had thrown a marvelous wedding feast in her honor. A giant pie—one that was big enough to feed every guest twice over—had been wheeled in on a cart. When the tsar stepped forward and cut it open with a dagger, out popped a female dwarf in fancy dress. Then the royal dwarf,

Ekim, leapt out of a second pastry shell and the two danced a minuet on top of the table before the delighted bride and groom.

Then seventy more little people trooped into the room, dressed like nobles and military officers, and a dwarf priest married the tiny couple in front of their guests, much to the amusement of the court. Anna Ioannovna had never forgotten the parade of dwarves, and the merriment the mock-wedding had generated, and was eager to recreate it.

She sent letters to the governors of all her provinces, commanding that two of each ethnic group--one of each sex--be sent to the capital to participate in a grand parade, the likes of which not even Peter the Great could have dreamed of.

"I have good news for you, Prince Mikhail," Anna Ioannovna said one day. "I have decided that it is time that you take another wife."

"That is most generous of you, Your Imperial Majesty," Golitsyn said, prostrating himself before the throne.

"However, given your long history of foolish choices when it comes to matrimony—first a Catholic, then a chicken—I have taken it upon myself to pick your bride for you."

"Thank you, most beloved tsaritsa," Golitsyn said, trying to keep the fear from creeping into his voice. There was something about the way Anna Ioannovna was smiling at him that made him more than a little uneasy. "You honor me beyond words."

The empress motioned for her maid, Avdotya, to step forward. "This Kalmyk woman serves me as a maid and it pleases me that you two wed. Is she not beautiful?" she asked with a laugh.

Golitsyn looked at the bride his sovereign had selected for him and felt his heart sink as the courtiers crowding the audience hall burst into laughter. The woman was hump-backed and bow-legged, with a mouth like a frog and one eye covered by a bluish film.

"Yes, she is very beautiful, tsaritsa. Thank you for picking her for me. I'm certain we will be very happy and spend all our days together."

"Of that I have no doubt!" Anna Ioannovna laughed. "You have been a very good jester, Prince Mikhail. I would like to reward you for your service by holding a wedding feast in your honor!"

"That is most kind of you, Your Excellency," Golitsyn said. "Once my future bride and I have set a date for our nuptials, you will be the first to know..."

"Oh, no, Prince Mikhail," Anna Ioannovna grinned. "You misunderstand me. Today is the day of the feast—*this* is your wedding day!"

Before the noble jester could say anything more, Duke Biron stepped forward and clapped his hands. "Prepare the wedding carriage for the happy couple!"

Four strong Cossacks strode into the audience hall carrying a large iron cage between them. Without any further word of explanation, Golitsyn and Avdotya were pushed inside and the door locked with a padlock shaped like a heart. The cage was then taken from the audience hall to the courtyard of the imperial palace with the empress, Duke Biron, and the rest of the court trailing after, laughing and chattering excitedly.

There standing shivering in the snow of the open courtyard was an Indian elephant, it's broad back draped with cloth-of-gold and rich tapestries. Surrounding the jungle beast was a motley group composed of the various races, ethnic groups and tribes ruled by the Russian empire, each costumed in their native dress.

As the elephant was made to kneel before the tsaritsa, the cage containing the frightened bride and groom was placed atop it and lashed into place. As the animal got back onto its feet, Golitsyn and Avdotya clung desperately to one another for protection as they were thrown about like beads in a baby's rattle.

Directly behind the elephant were male and female Ostyaks riding on deer, followed by Rusyny mounted on bulls. There were Novgorodians who sat astride a pair of goats, behind which were a couple of St. Petersburg Finns riding donkeys with wings glued to their sides. A Kamchadal shaman and shamaness sat side-by-side on a sledge pulled by dogs, while--in a demonstration of the power of the empire over the nature and custom of its subjects--a Tatar and his wife were made to ride atop a well-fed hog and sow. The representatives from Avdotya's people--the Kalmyks--rode camels painted white in honor of the bride, accompanied by flame-haired Finns mounted on miniature horses. Behind these guests were White Russians from Belorussia astride reindeer, and Nokhchii on water buffalo.

Following these outlandish ambassadors were a number of dwarves of different shapes and sizes. Some were long-bodied tumblers with stunted limbs, while other had short legs, or a labored under the weight of huge humps, oversized heads and large bellies. Lastly came the deformed, the crippled, the legless and the mindless leading dancing bears on silver chains and trained apes dressed as Turks.

The tsaritsa and her court watched in delight as the fantastical wedding party paraded through the frozen streets of St. Petersburg--past starving children and shivering widows--towards the river Neva, where a honeymoon home rose from the surface of the frozen river like a glittering fairy palace.

It was as smooth and as slippery as a wet rock yet gleamed with a watery light like a newborn moon. Its walls--hewn of glassy ice and cemented into place with buckets of water--stood two stories tall, fifty feet long, and twenty feet wide. Outside its frosty gates stood an ice garden composed of twenty-nine ice trees, the foliage of which was hand-painted green and in whose frigid branches perched birds of ice.

A cannon made of ice guarded the entrance to the palace, whose only enemy was the warmth of the coming spring. As the procession drew near, a guard hurriedly put torch to powder, and the ice cannon fired a salute to the approaching guests. The centerpiece of the fanciful courtyard was a hollow elephant fashioned of ice--inside which could be glimpsed a dwarf, who blew into a curling horn, which made a trumpeting sound so real the flesh-and-blood elephant raised its trunk in answer.

Upon their arrival at the honeymoon cottage the cage containing Golitsyn and his bride was removed from the back of the pachyderm and the lock unfastened. The bruised and frightened couple stumbled out, staring in shocked surprise at the frozen wonder before them.

"Do you like it, Prince Mikhail?" Anna Ioannovna

asked, grinning with pride at the handiwork before her. "I had it commissioned especially for this occasion!"

"It is astounding, Your Excellency," Golitsyn said between chattering teeth. He was still dressed in the clothes he'd been wearing inside the far warmer confines of the palace, with nothing but a heavily embroidered kaftan between him and the frigid weather. "You do me great honor."

"Come, let us see inside!" the empress said.

The interior of the ice palace was even more fantastic than its exterior. The palace was divided into two rooms, the larger of which was the drawing room. The pillars that supported the icy roof had been painstakingly painted to resemble green marble, and from the ceiling hung a chandelier carved entirely from ice. In fact, everything within the winter palace's walls was fashioned of ice.

The dining table--surrounded by twelve high-backed chairs--was as solid as any carved from oak, yet moist to a warm touch. Across the room a cunningly sculpted fire sat heatless within an ice-clad hearth. Above it was an elaborately carved mantelpiece on which sat a translucent clock, its detailed interior mechanisms on display. Indeed, everywhere Golitsyn looked there was some new and clever marvel to greet his eye. It was all quite beautiful and strange, and Prince Mikhail would have under any other circumstance been as enthralled by his surroundings as the lords and ladies of the court, who wandered through this fairy tale made real, laughing in delight. But knowing the tsaritsa's cruel disregard for him, when he looked at the ice palace he did not see a charming novelty but instead a fiendish torture device.

Golitsyn and Avdotya stood before the assembled wedding guests, both royal and exotic, as the tsaritsa's own priest married them. Once the vows were exchanged and solemnized there arose from the crowd a ragged cheer, followed by a wild swirl of music. The ambassadors from the farthest reaches of the empire proudly demonstrated the dances of their peoples as servants brought in a yoked pair of roasted oxen, racks of lamb, a herd of marinated venison, a whole covey of grilled quail, and entire schools of herring, sardines and sturgeon. Bringing up the rear of the feast was a multi-tiered wedding cake on top of which stood realistic ice-sculptures of the bride and groom, right down to Avdotya's hunchback.

"Come, Prince Mikhail—have a taste of your wedding cake!" Anna Ioannovna insisted, handing him a slice served on a plate made--like everything else in the house--of ice.

Golitsyn dutifully bit into the confection only to discover that the cake was not made from flour and eggs, but out of snow flavored with vanilla and almond essence. Already freezing from the outside in, he was now chilled from the inside out.

"A toast!" Biron shouted, lifting an ice goblet filled with flaming absinthe. "A toast to the happy couple! May the heat of their ardor unleash the flood trapped within these walls!"

"Here-here!" the empress said gaily, raising her own burning drink in agreement.

Golitsyn clutched the ice-goblet in numbed hands, staring somberly at the bluish flames licking its frosty rim. He glanced over at Avdotya, who was so badly frightened by the pandemonium of the mock-wedding she was weeping, her tears turning to tiny jewels on her eyelashes and cheeks.

Whatever the empress had in store for them, there was nothing they could do but go along with it. Given that she had recently hung her cook for making pancakes with rancid butter, they knew it best not to disappoint the tsaritsa when it came to her pleasures in life.

The newly minted bride and groom were made to sit in a pair of icy chairs as their wedding guests marched past, presenting them with gifts in honor of their nuptials. The wedding presents ranged from tin whistles to sewing needles made of narwhale tusk to a golden necklace adorned with pearls. The last to approach the shivering couple was the empress herself.

"The gift we would give to you, Prince Mikhail, is one on which no price can be set. We will gladly grant you freedom from our service--but only if you and Avdotya agree to spend one night as husband and wife in the bedroom of this house."

Although he knew there had to be a sting in the tail of the tsaritsa's offering of freedom, Golitsyn's heart still leapt at the prospect of finally being free to discard the fool's cap and return to his home. "Nothing would make me happier, Empress," he replied.

The half-frozen bride and groom were escorted from the drawing room to the smaller of the ice palace's two rooms: the bedchamber. The only piece of furniture in the room was a huge canopy bed chiseled out of ice, complete with ice pillows and sheets and comforters sculpted from hoarfrost. Golitsyn and his new bride then were unceremoniously stripped down to their shoes and undergarments.

Avdotya cringed as the courtiers pointed and laughed at her naked hunchback and dropped her head in shame. Golitsyn, feeling even sorrier for the wretched woman than he did for himself, tried to shield her from the cruel taunts of the gathered nobles by stepping in front of her. This attempt at gallantry sparked even more hilarity from the drunken horde.

"We bid you a fond good night, Prince Mikhail and Princess Avdotya," Anna Ioannovna chuckled. "The sun is setting and we would retire to our own household for the evening. We have stationed a guard outside the door to your honeymoon cottage in case you should try to sneak away. We shall return bright and early come the morning, to see how you fared on your nuptial night."

With that, the heavy ice doors of the winter palace closed, leaving the shivering, half-naked bride and groom huddled in the center of the frigid room. Golitsyn looked around forlornly. No matter where they turned they were hemmed in by ice, as if trapped in the heart of a glacier. The extreme cold was already stealing the breath from his lungs and the warmth from his bones.

"This is all my fault," Avdotya wept. "If I had not lamented over being without a husband, none of this would have happened."

"Do not blame yourself," Golitsyn said, placing his arms around her in an attempt to console the terrified woman. "The empress would have simply devised some other equally monstrous practical joke to inflict on me, regardless of who suggested it. I'm just sorry that you got caught up in her hatred for my family. Like all the Romanovs, she's as mad as a rabid bear. But I refuse to die simply to put a smile on her face. If we are to survive the night—and attain our freedom—we have to stay warm, no matter what." He took Avdotya by the hand. "Come, let us dance."

They waltzed around the room for the better part of an hour, but eventually grew tired. They then tried running in place, but that proved too exhausting, and the sweat from their exertion soon turned to frost on their skin, making them even colder than before. Golitsyn suggested turning somersaults, but Avdotya's deformed spine made it impossible for her to join in.

As the cold in his bones began to spread through his limbs, Golitsyn surrendered his last hope in the face of impending death and flew into a white-hot rage, cursing the stupid, cruel and heartless monster who had destroyed not only his life, but that of his late wife and brother. He charged through the ice palace, screaming in wordless anger as he shattered the ice plates and ice goblets against the ice fireplace. He snatched the ice clock from the ice mantelpiece and hurled it across the drawing room, smashing it against the ice table. Lastly, he threw himself against the closed ice door, hammering his fists against its frozen panels until the blood ran, cursing the guard whose silhouette was visible through the translucent walls. Having finally exhausted himself, Golitsyn slid down onto the snow-packed floor and began to weep.

Avdotya, who had watched her new husband demolish the furnishings of the ice house in silence, tip-toed over the shattered debris and put her mouth as close as she dared to the crack in the door without accidentally freezing her lips to the jamb. When the empress posted the guard at their door, the maid had seen something that no one else had noticed: the soldier chosen for the duty had an Endless Knot--one of the Eight Auspicious Symbols of her faith--dangling from his belt.

"Cousin," she whispered in the language of her people, her voice nearly destroyed by the biting cold. "I beg you in the name of the Awakened One to show mercy upon myself and my husband. All we ask is for a little warmth—just enough to survive this night."

The door of ice opened slightly and Avdotya saw the guard standing on the other side of the threshold, wrapped in several heavy coats against the arctic cold. Although, at first glance he looked Russian, she could tell by the color and the slant of his eyes and cheekbones that they shared Kalmyk blood.

"I wish I could help you, but the tsaritsa will have my head on a pike if I let you two out," he replied. "I am sorry, little sister, but you have to stay inside."

"Then just give us one of your coats to wrap ourselves in," she begged, handing him the gold and pearl necklace she had received as a wedding present. "No one need ever know. You can take your coat back in the morning before the tsaritsa returns."

The guard eagerly accepted the jewelry in exchange for his outer coat, which was made from the skin of a yak. Avdotya and Golitsyn then retired to their icy bedchamber and climbed upon the cold, hard bed and--wrapping themselves in the soldier's borrowed coat--spent the rest of the night huddled together.

As he lay shivering on the bed of ice, clasping his new bride to him, Golitsyn could hear the howling of wolves in the distance as they chased some hapless prey across the frozen river. At that moment, he would have preferred the kindness of wolves over that of an empress. At least wolves kill you because they are hungry, not because they're bored and in need of a way to pass a winter's day.

Although he did not remember doing so, Golitsyn eventually fell asleep, for the next thing he knew he was being awakened by the guard as he roughly reclaimed the yak-skin coat. "The empress will be here soon!" the guard warned them. "I saw her sledge approaching from the ramparts."

"We survived the night!" Golitsyn gasped in surprise. "You hear that, Avdotya? We made it!" He looked down to where the Kalmyk maid lay beside him, only to have his smile instantly disappear.

Avdotya's skin was as white as alabaster and almost as cold and hard to the touch. At first Golitsyn thought she was dead, but then he saw her breastbone rise and fall. He was reminded of Snow White lying within her glass coffin, the victim of an evil and heartless queen.

When the empress arrived with Duke Biron at her side, she was surprised to not only find her jester alive but tending to his unconscious bride, chafing her hands in a desperate attempt to restore blood flow even though he himself was freezing.

"How is it you are still amongst the living, Prince Mikhail?" she demanded.

"The fire of our loins and the heat of our passion kept us warm throughout the night," Golitsyn lied. "But I fear my bride is overcome with exhaustion. I would take her to my home, so that she might recover fully."

"I shall have her removed to your rooms at the imperial palace," Duke Biron said.

"No, I'm taking her to my estate," Golitsyn replied. "As per her imperial majesty's promise, I am free to leave the court, if I so desire. Is that not so, tsaritsa?"

Anna Ioannovna scowled darkly at Golitsyn before grudgingly nodding her head. Although the empress was far from an honorable woman, she was very much a superstitious one and a promise made at a wedding--whether mock or not--had to be fulfilled or else it would invite disaster.

"You're not seriously going to keep that that hump-backed wretch as your wife, are you?" Duke Biron gasped. "It was only a make believe wedding! You're a prince of the realm! You have no duty to this worthless mongrel."

"Be that as it may. Avdotya has proven herself to be a better wife to me than any blue-blooded grandee in St. Petersburg or Moscow could ever hope," Golitsyn replied as he gathered the maid's body into his arms. "I have already let one wife die of the cold—I will not let it claim a second."

With the help of the half-Kalmyk guard Prince Mikhail carried his bride out of the ice palace that was intended to be their tomb and placed her on a waiting sledge, wrapping her in riding rugs. Upon arriving at his palace in St. Petersburg he had his servants warm her body in a hot bath until the blood returned to her face and limbs.

When he was satisfied that she had fully recovered from her horrible ordeal, Prince Mikhail summoned the family priest and the vows he and Avdotya had mouthed out of fear for their lives were spoken once again in earnest.

Eight months later, Anna Ioannovna--Mother of the Native Land, Ruler of All the Russias--suffered a bout of kidney stones and collapsed, dying of renal failure a week later at the age of forty-seven. Her married lover, Duke Biron--who she had appointed regent for her infant great-nephew, Peter III--lasted less than a month before he was chased into the wilds of Siberia by the Russian nobility he had taken so much pleasure in terrorizing for the last ten years.

A month after the death of Empress Anna her former maid delivered unto her former jester a pair of healthy twin boys. The lucky couple was then forgotten by history and--better yet--the Romanovs.

Which is as close to happily ever after one could hope for in those days.

THE DEATH'S HEAD TAVERN

A Solomon Kane Story

"Innkeeper! What's holding up that drink, eh?"

"Coming directly, sir!" the innkeeper called back, forcing his thin lips into a smile as he lugged the last cask of ale from the storeroom.

The great room of the tavern was empty save for a middle-aged merchant from Aberdeen who sat by the hearth, enjoying an evening pipe before retiring to his rented room upstairs. The lodger was as stout as the innkeeper was lean and dressed as befit a man of honest trade, complete with powdered periwig.

"Tell me, my good man—do you have any more of those delightful meat pies your missus served earlier?" the merchant asked, smacking his lips in anticipation.

"Sorry, sir. We be out, I fear," the innkeeper replied, setting the foaming pewter tankard down with a thump on the table next to his guest. "Game's been scarce as of late. This time of year the deer and grouse tend to stay deep in the moors."

The merchant's hopeful smile fell into heavy folds of disappointment. "I see. Perhaps you'll have better luck when I return from visiting my dear sister in Inverness?"

"Yes, sir," the innkeeper agreed without much in the way of conviction.

Just then the door to the tavern opened, allowing for a cold, wet gust of wind to rush into the room that made the fire in the hearth flare in self-defense. Both the merchant and innkeeper turned to stare at the stranger standing on the threshold, rainwater pouring off him in rivulets. Although he wore the solemn garb of a Puritan, he was tall and broad in the shoulders and across his back was strapped a musket and a strangely fashioned stave with the snarling head of a jungle cat atop it.

"I seek shelter and food," the Puritan said simply, one strong, long-fingered hand resting on the hilt of his sword.

"Then you have come to the right place, sir!" beamed the innkeeper. "Welcome to the Death's Head Tavern."

The stranger grunted and moved past the two men, spreading his cloak before the hearth and then leaned his weapons against the coal shuttle and poker. He took off his hat and tilted its brim toward the fire. There was a sharp hiss as rainwater met the banked coals.

"I'll have the woman serve ye up some ale and mutton, sir," the innkeeper said as he hurried off in search of his wife.

"Tis a foul night, indeed, to be abroad. I am Angus McIlhenny of Aberdeen--a dealer in wools. Who might ye be, good stranger?"

“I am called Solomon Kane,” the tall man replied as he sat down in the chair opposite McIlhenny.

“That is an interesting walking stick you have,” the wool-merchant said, pointing to the cat-headed stave. “Wherever did you get it?”

Kane man studied the bewigged man sitting across from him. Although he had never seen the merchant before, his face was familiar to him. It was the well-fed face of civilization that had chased him from the smoky cities of England into the company of pirates and mercenaries.

“Africa,” he replied.

Upon hearing this, McIlhenny eagerly hitched his chair closer to Kane’s. “I knew it! I can always spot a fellow traveler a mile off! Got a certain air about us, we have. I’ve been to London, you know.”

“Have you now?” muttered the Puritan, not without some humor.

“You really get that stick in Africa?”

“Aye; from a native priest.”

“You take it off his body?” McIlhenny grinned, his eyes lighting up in anticipation of a story of adventure in far-flung exotic lands. “Spoils of war and all that?”

“No,” Kane replied as he pulled a tinderbox from his pocket. “He gave it to me. He was a decent fellow—for a heathen.” With that he produced a long-stemmed clay pipe and set about wreathing his dark head with fragrant clouds, signifying the discussion was at its end.

A few minutes later a very pregnant woman entered the common room carrying a plate of cold mutton and a tankard of ale. “Here you go, sir,” she said, setting the humble repast on the bench nearest the

Puritan's elbow.

Kane glanced up from his pipe. The inn-keeper's wife was raw-boned with long, dark unwashed hair, and shared the same sallow complexion and slat-eyed features as her husband, although there was something about her that spoke of an innate shrewdness.

"Thank ye, kindly," he said with a nod.

"Your new guest is a traveler—from Africa, no less!" McIlhenny chimed in.

"Is that so?" the innkeeper's wife declared. "It's a rare day the Death's Head Tavern hosts such a guest, I must say!"

"Death's Head", muttered Kane. "Tis a cheerless name for a venture based on hospitality."

"Why, these be the Death's Head Moors, my good man!" McIlhenny interjected, ever eager to appear knowledgeable. "Legend has it that ancient druids sacrificed victims in the peat bogs that pock the landscape hereabouts, and that ghouls roam the moors at night—thus the name. Pure rubbish, of course. But the locals believe it and give the Moor Road a wide berth. How Mr. Todd and his dear wife manage is beyond my ken."

"By the grace of God and the honest sweat of our brows," the innkeeper said earnestly.

"I come this way at least once a year to visit family up in Inverness," McIlhenny explained. "It's the shortest route from Aberdeen. I make a point of staying one night at this tavern, each way, simply to partake of Mrs. Todd's delicious meat pies. A true culinary delight, I assure you! It appears I consumed the last of them just before you arrived. But perhaps the next time you pass this way you will be luckier?" The wool-merchant looked expectantly at the innkeeper's wife, who was staring at the strange cat-headed stick propped against the fire-tools with a mixture of curiosity and displeasure.

"Aye, perhaps," Kane answered. "Assuming I ever come this way again."

"Father?"

Kane's brooding gaze was drawn from the fire and to a vision of beauty the likes of which he had not seen since his long-lost Bess. Standing poised on the heavy-timbered stairs that lead to the inn's second story was a young woman with hair the color of burnished copper, outfitted in a dress of the finest wool. Her eyes were bright green, shining like emeralds held before a fire.

"What is it, Faith?" McIlhenny grumbled. "Can't you see I'm talking, girl?

" 'Tis late, Father. If we are to be at Aunt Agatha's by tomorrow evening..."

"Yes, yes," McIlhenny grunted with an impatient wave of his hand. "I'll be up shortly!"

Faith nodded demurely and headed back up the stairs, but not before pausing to cast a final look over her shoulder at the lean yet handsome stranger lounging before the fire. Kane felt his heart quicken as her gaze fell upon him and nodded his head to her in acknowledgement. Faith's pale cheeks abruptly colored and she hurried up the stairs like a startled doe.

"I'm taking the girl to stay with my sister in Inverness," McIlhenny explained. "Aberdeen is suffering another bout of the pest. The last time it took her mother, God rest her soul. The air of Inverness is far more wholesome, in that regard. What business brings you out this way, good man Kane?"

"I am searching for a friend of mine. His name was Jerymiah Crandall."

"Was? You make it sound as if he is no more."

"That is what I fear."

"Was this Jerymiah a good friend of yours?"

"We shipped together with Sir Francis Drake and fought the Armada for the glory of the Queen. Jerymiah saved my life more than once during those days. I received a letter from his wife a few months back--that is what has drawn me from Africa, for the nonce. She said Jerymiah had gone in search of his brother, Jobe, after he disappeared on a trip to the Cairngorms. But before he left, Jerymiah instructed his good wife to contact me should he not return in a fortnight."

"Passing strange," muttered McIlhenny. "And you believe your friend and his missing brother both came this way?"

"As you say, the Moor Road is the shortest route to the Highlands."

"Then we shall ask our host if he has seen these men!" the wool merchant exclaimed. "Todd!"

"Yes, Master McIlhenny?" The innkeeper asked, seeming to appear as if summoned by magic.

"Has a man of the name Jerymiah Crandall lodged here?"

"N-no, sir," Todd replied.

Kane turned to look at the innkeeper. "What of a man called Jobe? Has he been a guest?"

Todd twitched and dropped his gaze to the floor, unable to meet the Puritan's cold stare, and shook his head. "N-no, sir. No such person has been here."

"Are you sure? Perhaps you could check your register?" McIlhenny prodded.

"No need!" the innkeeper said sharply. "I would remember such names! Perhaps your friend wandered into the moors and was claimed by the bogs?"

"Perhaps," the Puritan agreed without conviction.

"His brother was off to the Cairngorms?" Todd continued. "They are treacherous mountains. All it takes is a misplaced foot and you'll find yourself at the bottom of a chasm."

"Aye, that is true," Kane said, drawing pensively on his pipe.

"I wager they did not come this way at all, but took the longer route instead," the innkeeper said firmly, nodding in agreement with himself.

"Todd is probably right." McIlhenny said. "After all, he would know who has been under his roof."

"Yes, but Jerymiah Crandall was not the kind of man to disappear without a trace, regardless of how he met his fate," Kane replied.

"It would not be the only time travelers have disappeared in such a manner in Scotland," the wool-merchant said darkly. "Remember the Bean Clan?"

"I'm afraid I am unfamiliar with them," Kane admitted. "Were they brigands?"

McIlhenny eagerly hitched his chair even closer to Kane's, to better share the story. "Worse than that! Fifty years ago, this fellow named Sawney Bean—a low sort with no taste for honest work—took to wife a woman said to be a witch. Forced to flee accusations of human sacrifice, the two moved into a cave down on the coast in Ayrshire, near Ballantrae, if memory serves. They then began waylaying unsuspecting travelers along the cliff road at night, taking the bodies to be butchered and pickled to feed their dark appetites.

"Sawney and his wife then set about raising a family, producing eight sons and six daughters to carry on the Bean tradition of murder, cannibalism, and witchcraft. These children mated among themselves and with their parents, producing eighteen grandsons and fourteen granddaughters, and two great-grandsons and a great-granddaughter—until they were a virtual army of ogres!

"After twenty-five years of such debauchery and blasphemy, a married couple was returning from the fair one night when they were attacked. The young groom, as it so happened, was skilled in sword and pistol and able to hold off his attackers until another, larger group of fair-goers happened upon the scene and chased the villains away—but not before they succeeded in carrying off his hapless bride!

"The next day, a group of soldiers billeted in Ballantrae investigated the beach and cliffs below the scene of the attack and discovered a cave that was two hundred yards deep, the entrance of which was hidden during high tide. Inside they discovered the body of the lost bride, dismembered like a side of beef--along with other human body parts, and vast amounts of old clothes and discarded boots scattered about. Going deeper still, they found the loathsome family that made the place their home, dressed in the rotting rags of their victims.

"As fearsome as the Beans were, they were no match for an armed regiment, and the family was rounded up and marched in chains to Edinburgh, where the entire clan was put to death in the town square by command of the King."

Kane lifted an eyebrow. "Even the children?"

"Aye, for nits grow into lice, do they not?" McIlhenny replied. "Although rumor has it that not *all* of the Bean spawn were in the cave that day. Some say those that escaped moved inland, away from the family's old haunts, and continue their foul practices to this day."

"That is, indeed, a gruesome tale," Kane grunted as he rose from his chair. "But I do not see how it aids me in my mission. The hour is late, and I would rest."

"Right this way, good sir," the innkeeper said, gesturing towards the stair.

Kane gathered up his weapons, leaving the cloak to dry by the fire, and followed Todd to the second floor of the tavern. "I have you beside Master McIlhenny," the innkeeper explained as he opened the room for his guest's inspection. The interior was humble bordering on spartan, furnished with a narrow bed, a straight-back chair, and an unpainted washstand atop which sat a cracked basin and pitcher. The only light came from the candlestick that Todd set on the seat of the chair beside the bed. There was no fireplace in the room, and the innkeeper's breath hung in the air as he spoke.

"The woman prepared the sheets with a bedwarmer. You should be most comfortable."

"I can sleep on a plank, if need be," the Puritan replied tersely.

"Aye, as we all will, someday," Todd muttered as he exited the room.

Satisfied he was alone, Solomon Kane sat down on the bed and removed his boots. He then stretched out, fully clothed, atop the threadbare quilt, but not before making sure his sword and pistol were within easy reach. There was something unwholesome about the Death's Head Tavern that went beyond the establishment's name. The way the landlord reacted to the Crandall Brothers' names did not sit well with him.

A few minutes after retiring to his bed, he heard Angus McIlhenny fumbling about in the room next to his, no doubt blunted by one too many tankards of ale. A few minutes later he could make out the wool-merchant's snores as he succumbed to Morpheus' embrace.

Kane lay in his rented bed as his mind kept turning over the bits and pieces of evidence that had set him on the Moor Road. Jerymiah was a practical, no-nonsense man—stories of goblins and ghouls haunting the moors would have meant little to him. Kane knew from personal experience it would take more than a ghost to frighten his friend away from the shortest distance between two points.

In his own way, McIlhenny was probably right. No doubt the bones of the Crandalls rested in some nameless peat bog, but not because unwary footsteps lead them there. But how to prove his suspicions was another matter. England was far from Africa in more than miles. You didn't just run a man through because you believed him to be a murderer—not if you didn't want to find yourself hanging at the crossroads for your troubles. No, England was a land of laws, if not justice.

As he stared at the rough-hewn rafters over his head, Kane's thoughts turned to the girl. The feelings she stirred in him were far from Christian. He shifted uneasily as he recalled the sight of her on the stairs, her eyes shining like a light in the darkness. Aye, there was lust in his heart, but mixed with something far more tender.

Kane was so lost in thought he did not realize he had drifted off into sleep until he abruptly came awake. He was not certain how long he had been unconscious, but years of living in the teeth of danger had honed his senses to such a sharpness that even the slightest noise would snap him free of deep slumber. The first thing that registered was the candle beside his bed was now guttering in its wax, throwing twisted shadows across the plastered walls; the second was that he could no longer hear McIlhenny's snoring. Perhaps that was what had alerted him?

Just then Kane heard a faint clicking noise, like that of a catch being released, and a panel in the wall next to the bed slowly swung open. Hooding his eyes, he lay as still as possible as the dark area in the wall widened. Out of the hidden portal crept a stealthy figure. Kane did not have to see his face to know that the intruder was the innkeeper.

As Todd stole closer to the bed, Kane saw that the innkeeper's shirtfront was stained with fresh blood, and a horrid vision of Faith McIlhenny struggling helplessly as the Scot slit her dainty throat flashed before his mind's eye. The very idea made him want to cry out in horror, yet by force of will alone did he continue his feigned slumber.

The innkeeper now loomed over the bed. His eyes gleamed wildly and his mouth twisted itself into a bestial grin as he raised a dripping butcher knife in preparation of plunging it into the slumbering Puritan's chest. But as the deadly knife came down, Kane rolled away and onto the floor quick as a panther, leaving the blade to drive itself deep into the straw mattress.

As the innkeeper struggled to free the knife,

Kane leapt up and swung the cat-headed stave at his attacker's head. N'Longa's fetish-stick crashed into Todd's skull with fearsome impact. With a scream of pain, the innkeeper abandoned his knife and--clutching his head-- retreated into the hidden passageway which still stood open.

Kane quickly pulled on his boots and snatched up his rapier before following his would-be killer into the darkness behind the wall. He found himself in a space so narrow he had to turn sideways in order to move. As he cautiously groped his way along the passage, his left palm struck what felt like a lever and the wall behind him abruptly pivoted, sending him tumbling into a dimly lit room.

Faith McIlhenny gave a birdlike cry of surprise, her crimson tresses spilling free of her nightcap as she clutched the bedclothes to her chin. Kane lay frozen on the floor, surprised to see her alive and unharmed. However, his relief was only momentary for the danger they were in was as real as the walls that surrounded them.

"Do not be alarmed, Mistress McIlhenny," Kane said as he regained his feet. "I mean you no harm."

"What are you doing here?" Faith queried, more amazement than fear in her voice. "How did you get in my room?"

"I did not mean to intrude upon you in such a manner," Kane assured her. "But now that I am here, I beg you to awaken your father and hurry from this house of evil as fast as you can!"

"Evil? Whatever do you mean, sir?" Faith asked, drawing the bedclothes ever closer as she pressed herself against the headboard. From the look in her emerald eyes Kane could see she thought him tetched.

"I'm not mad, Mistress McIlhenny. As I told your father, I came to this place in search of a missing friend —only to discover the innkeeper has murdered him in his sleep. By no doubt using a door hidden in the wall of the guest room, same as this. I, myself, have just narrowly escaped a similar fate. I struck the scoundrel a hard blow and followed him into the secret passageway, which is how I came to arrive here uninvited."

"Father!" Faith gasped, her eyes widening in alarm. Oblivious to modesty, the young woman cast aside the blankets--revealing her cotton nightdress--and leapt from the bed. "I must warn him!" she exclaimed as she dashed into the hall, Kane at her dainty heels. She ran to her father's room, only to find it locked. *"Father, wake up!"* she cried as she frantically pounded on the door.

"Step aside, girl," Kane said, and with a single well-placed kick broke the door free of its bolt.

Faith hurried into the room, followed close by the Puritan. The only light in the room was provided by a tallow candle set on the dresser beside the bed, and the scene it illuminated wrenched a horrified scream from the wool merchant's daughter.

The bedclothes on Angus McIlhenny's bed were in wild disarray and the pillow soaked in blood. A wide smear of crimson stained the floor, ending at the blank wall. Faith spun about and burrowed her face into Solomon Kane's breast, her body trembling from the force of her sobs. Without a second thought, Kane embraced the girl, speaking to her in a firm, reassuring voice.

"Go to my room, Faith; Todd is not likely to return there. Here, take this dirk," he said, pressing the hilt of the weapon into her fair hands. "Do not hesitate to use it."

Nodding through her tears, Faith obeyed. Once she was gone, Kane took the candle from the dresser and went to the spot in the wall where the trail of blood disappeared. He fumbled about the wainscoting until he found the hidden latch that opened the secret doorway. As the panel swung open, he was surprised to feel a cold finger of dread trace his spine, for he was not a man to tremble in the face of danger.

Indeed, he had walked the vast, uncharted tracts of Africa and witnessed the fall of foul kingdoms that were old when the Egyptians reared their massive crypts. He had faced creatures of unholy making that would have sent lesser men to Bedlam. He had even wrestled with the very Prince of the Undead himself in the blood-soaked crags of the Carpathians. So why did he tremble now?

Todd was just another blackguard who abused the ancient law of hospitality to profit from the personal possessions of his guests, not some darksome sorcerer nursed on the rituals of some black and hungry god. What horror born of Scotland's stony soil could inspire such trepidation on his behalf? Perhaps his time spent in the company of N'Longa had made him sensitive to evil beyond the ken of most civilized men? Could something far more sinister than murder in the name of profit be at play here?

Kane made his way along the narrow passage between the walls until he reached its end and saw an open trap door in the wooden floor. The feeble light from the candle illuminated the rungs of a wooden ladder that led down into an even deeper darkness.

Extinguishing the candle for fear of alerting his prey, the Puritan climbed down the ladder, his flintlock pistol at ready. Upon reaching the bottom his bootheels struck against an earthen floor. Kane realized he must now be in the cellar, which lay beneath the tavern like an abscess.

Once his eyes were adjusted to the darkness, he could see that he was standing in the middle of a crossroads. Four tunnels branched off from the central room in which he stood, the entrance to each shored up by ancient timbers. A faint glimmer could be seen coming from the opening to his left. Drawing his rapier and his pistol, Solomon Kane stealthily made his way towards the candlelight.

A hundred paces later he found himself in a storeroom filled with barrels and other provisions, lit by a solitary candle set on a low bench that ran the length of one of the earthen walls. Overhead was a ceiling made of the heavy beams that served as the foundation for the tavern above. Hanging from a hook set in one such beam was Angus McIlhenny, dangling by his ankles like a freshly butchered hog.

The wool-merchant had been stripped naked and his throat slit from ear to ear so that the blood drained into a wooden trough beneath his head. Kane grimaced in distaste and thanked his Lord that Faith waited upstairs. No child should see their parent thus.

Kane had dealt with cannibals before, but only in the benighted jungles of Africa. To be confronted with it here--in the very bosom of Anglican piety--seemed a thousand times more horrid. Once again, the carefully painted face of Civilization had cracked wide open to expose the ravening, mindless beast beneath its surface

—much as it had years ago, when it drove him from the fellowship of his Puritan brothers and into the company of brigands, thieves, and pirates.

As he moved to cut down McIlhenny's corpse, the innkeeper's wife leapt from hiding amongst the stacked crates, shrieking like a wildcat as she swung a cleaver at the Puritan's head. Kane quickly sidestepped the attack and smashed the knuckle guard of his rapier into her face, causing her to drop to the ground like a poleaxed cow.

"I told that incompetent fool to make work of you, curse him!" The innkeeper's wife snarled in disgust, spitting blood and bits of broken teeth onto the dirt floor.

"He tried, but all he got was a broken jaw for his effort."

"I knew you were trouble the moment I saw that walking stick of yours! I warned him—but the clod doesn't have the Blood like I do."

"What are you babbling about, ghoul? Not that it matters—you're both going to hang for this, and all the other crimes against nature you've committed!"

"Fool!" The woman laughed, her features taking on an inhumanity only previously hinted at. "You dare to judge us? For generations my folk have passed for members of your puerile, mewling race—even before the Pictish kings warred with the Legions! Fifty years ago, my great-grand rose from the hidden tunnels that honeycomb these moors and set forth into your world. She found herself a human mate—the one called Bean —who was eager to learn her ancient secrets and know the forgotten ways! But then the Scottish King came and dragged my family away in chains, so they could be drawn, quartered, and burned alive in the city square."

"But not all of them," Kane said grimly.

"Aye, not all. My brother and I, along with our sister-mother—we escaped capture that fateful day. Ma fled the coast and came inland—back to the moors great-grand hailed from. Together we reared this inn, and although we changed our names, we still observed the old ways. We are the last of our clan, he and me—but not for long," the ogress grinned as she patted her tumescent belly.

"What of Jobe and Jerymiah Crandall, harridan?" Kane growled, the point of his sword hovering an inch above the mad woman's breastbone.

"Oh, *yesss*," she cackled. "A most delicious pair!"

"Foul harpy!" Kane snarled. "Jerymiah Crandall was worth a hundred of you—nay, a thousand! He was a warrior and a Christian, and he deserved to die as a man, not like an animal lead to the slaughter! I have never slain a woman, even in my most bloody travel--but you sorely tempt me, plague whore! For surely you are not a daughter of Eve, but a hag born of Hell itself!"

" 'Die as a man'? Aye, your friend Jerymiah indeed died like a man!" Her giggle--both girlish and ghoulish--made the hair on the back of Solomon Kane's neck stand up. "Whose loaf do ye think I carry, eh, Puritan? My brother's seed is twisted, and spawns naught but stillbirths! No, this is Jerymiah Crandall's child I bear!"

"You lie!" Kane spat the words out more than spoke them. "Jerymiah may have been an adventurer, but he never would have lain with the likes of you!"

"What makes you think he had a say in it?" the innkeeper's sister cackled. "A few select herbs dumped in his ale and a charm placed under his bed for the night, and he welcomed me eagerly enough! And at the very moment he planted his seed in my womb, my dear brother cleft his skull with a hatchet!"

Solomon Kane's face turned ashen at the thought of his old friend's freshly slain body wrapped in the she-fiend's deadly embrace while laying the foundations for a new life. "I should pierce your black heart right now," he hissed, "and save Jack Ketch from soiling honest hemp."

He pressed the tip of the rapier to the hag's throat and a bead of blood rose from where the blade nicked the skin. Instead of whimpering or begging for the life of her unborn child, the innkeeper's sister-wife glared defiantly at him.

"God's oath!" cried the Puritan as he lifted his rapier from the wretched woman's throat. "May the Lord curse me for a fool—but I cannot do this thing! You are saved, daughter of Satan, by a mercy you do not deserve!"

"Mercy?" The cannibal gave a humorless laugh, her swollen, blood-smeared lips pulling into a sneer. "It is a weakness my kind is free of! Is that not so, brother?"

Only a lifetime of battle saved the Puritan from certain death. He leapt aside as Todd—his lower jaw hanging askew—lunged at him from the shadows. All the rage and hatred Kane had swallowed in his dealing with the ogress, he now unleashed upon her brother-husband—his rapier slicing the innkeeper into bleeding ribbons. The cannibal howled like an animal in pain, swearing in a language that was both alien and familiar to the Puritan's ears. Then, with a fearsome yell, Kane ran his sword through Todd's body with such force the innkeeper's feet were lifted off the floor.

As the body slid free of Kane's blade, the cannibal's

mate got to her feet, her voice trembling in rage. "Your kind have not heard the last of my clan! Mark my words, Englishman, my issue shall slaughter your people like the cattle you are! If not this wee bastard, then from the generations that follow! This is not over, Puritan! It's *never* over!" And with that she turned and fled through the haphazard collection of crates and kegs, escaping through yet another tunnel.

Solomon Kane instinctively gave chase, only to pause at the mouth of the shaft. The passageway was completely without light and the slope of its floor suggested it lead even deeper into bowels of the earth. Rather than follow the cannibal into a lair of her own making, it would be wiser to simply erase the loathsome death house from the face of the Earth, the eye of God, and the memory of Man.

Faith McIlhenny stood in the muck of the road and watched the Death's Head Tavern burn. Despite the heat it generated, she could not stop shivering. She clutched her dark green woolen cape about her and numbly stared into the fire. Her father was dead. This she knew and accepted with a calmness that surprised her, for she had loved him very much.

Her heart surged as she turned her gaze to the Puritan,who stood silhouetted against the inferno. She was both baffled and thrilled by the emotions this lean, panther-like man stirred in her. His demeanor was solemn as he leaned upon his strange cat-headed walking staff, staring into the flames as if they held a secret only he could see.

He had been keeping vigil for over an hour, waiting

to see if the fire would flush out the innkeeper's wife. Or was she his sister? The Puritan had been somewhat vague when recounting what he had endured in the cellars beneath the tavern. Finally, he turned his back to the blaze and walked toward her.

"It will be dawn soon, and safe for us to leave," he said. "I found your father's horse and carriage in the stable behind the tavern. No doubt the Todds planned on selling them. I will escort you to your aunt in Inverness; it is the least I can do."

"You have done a great deal already, Master Kane," she smiled, placing her pale hand atop his own. "If not for you, I would most assuredly be dead."

"Aye, but I could not save your father."

"But you avenged his death—and that of your friends. Surely God sent you here this night."

"Perhaps," Kane said with a fleeting smile as he helped the girl into the waiting carriage.

"Will you be staying in England, now that you have solved the mystery of the disappearance of your friend and his brother?"

"I am not the kind of man who is content to sit idle by the fire," he replied, his dark eyes meeting her shining emerald ones. "But I may tarry for a spell if the company suits me—and would have me."

"I will bear that in mind, good sir," Faith smiled, then abruptly gasped and grabbed Kane's arm, pointing towards the moorlands.

The sun was just beginning to burn its way through the pall of mist mixed with the smoke from the burning tavern. Off in the distance a human figure was running across the heath, carrying something in its arms. And riding on the wind came the thin, high cry of a newborn.

"This is not over," whispered Solomon Kane. *"It's never over."*

ABSALOM'S WAKE

Chapter One

A Proper Introduction—My Uncle Calvin—The Dolphin Amulet—My Bequest

The story I am about to relate to you is a true and accurate account of the fate that befell the crew of the good ship *Absalom*--a whaler out of Sag Harbor--in the Year of Our Lord 1846. But before I begin my tale of amazement and woe, allow me to properly introduce myself.

My name is Jonah Padgett. I realize my Christian name is an unfortunate one, given my profession--for sailors are a superstitious breed prone to seeing mermaids and sea serpents at the slightest provocation. But I don't fault them for their fears, for it is my experience that in order to survive the great oceans mariners must spread their five senses thinner than butter on a poor man's bread. This is especially true of whalers, as they are constantly on the lookout for spouters, so it is only natural for them to perceive signs of danger where others see none.

The ocean is a strange place--and one we humans know too little of to dare claim to be masters of its secrets. Still, it was superstition--in part--that lead to the *Absalom's* doom and why I, alone, survived to tell this strange and fantastic tale. But I am getting ahead of myself.

How is it I have sea water in my veins, you ask? I came by it naturally enough, as my mother's eldest brother was once a whaler. As my Uncle Calvin was born early in my grandparent's marriage and my mother late, there were as many years between brother and sister as are normally found between father and daughter. In any case, the difference in their ages did not weaken their familial bond. So when my uncle retired from the sea, he made his home with my mother and her family in Pennsylvania.

The decision to become landlocked was not my Uncle Calvin's choosing, but one forced upon him. While returning from the Pacific whaling grounds, his ship was caught in a fierce storm that snapped the main mast like kindling. One of the spars collapsed across the deck, pinning my uncle underneath and costing him both legs below the knee. Luckily Uncle Calvin was the First Mate, and luckier still to ship with a captain who knew the whaling grounds like a bridegroom of fifty years knows his wife's backside, so he was able to retire with a goodly pension.

My memories of my uncle are fond ones. Every night

he would sit by the fire and smoke his pipe, spinning yarns of his days on the open seas. He told stories of savage cannibals, wild dolphins sporting in the blue Pacific, and fighting typhoons in open water. While my brothers and sisters listened to these tales from a sense of duty, I was completely enthralled by his adventures. Uncle Calvin quickly saw in me a kindred spirit, and we became boon companions.

My family lived twenty-five miles outside the great city of Philadelphia. It was a pleasant enough place, I suppose, with its gently rolling hills and verdant pastures. It was bucolic and peaceful, the way all farming communities are, and completely lacking when it came to stimulating the imagination and passions of a young boy. I know for a fact there was not a single thing to be found in my hometown that could compare to the contents of my Uncle Calvin's sea chest. What wonders it held! Within its cedar-lined confines were such marvels as a shrunken human head and scrimshawed sperm whale teeth.

The most prized of my uncle's possessions, however, was not kept in his sea chest but worn about his neck. It was an amulet fashioned from a piece coral carved in the shape of a dolphin. Its body was curved so that its nose touched the tip of its tail, and so perfect was the likeness one could easily imagine it would swim away if placed in a pool of water. My uncle claimed it was a good luck charm given to him by a native girl whose life he had once saved. The amulet was supposed to protect him from harm while at sea. Unfortunately, its powers did not extend to the air—or to ship's masts.

Despite my yearning to see the world, I would never have left home while my Uncle Calvin was still alive, for I had come to love him as a grandfather. But when his time came my uncle left me three things: his sea chest, a letter of recommendation to a Captain Wendell Solomon--whom he had known and called friend during his whaling days--and the dolphin amulet.

At the age of fifteen I found myself free to answer the call that had beckoned since I was a small boy seated by the family hearth, enthralled by tales of strange latitudes and stranger lands.

Chapter Two

My Arrival In Sag Harbor—The Blind Man of Bay Street—The Whaler's Rest---I Am Re-Christened

Although many years have passed since the day I left home--and I have since seen much in the way of the world--I shall never forget the day I first set foot in Sag Harbor.

Having grown up in a small village in Chester County, I was green as goose shit when it came to sailing. But that didn't stop me from leaving home for one of the busiest seaports on the East Coast. The first thing I saw as my coach drew within sight of the town was a vast cluster of masts that towered above the rooftops like a mighty forest. As it was the first deep-water port on Long Island over sixty whaling ships--not to mention countless other vessels--called it home. Because of this, the town's narrow streets teemed with people from places as far-flung as Fiji and the Ivory Coast.

There were more people walking up and down Division Street than there was in my entire hometown, and all of them were in a great hurry--as city people always seem to be. An African with skin black as pitch and raised tribal marking upon his face was haggling with an outfitter over the price of a kit, while next to him was a Sandwich Islander--his skin the color of buckwheat honey and raven hair as sleek as the pelt of a seal--quietly studying a broadsheet posted on the wall of a nearby tavern. I approached an old man who was sharpening axes and harpoons from a makeshift tinker's stall built from canvas and wooden planking.

"Excuse me, sir..." I began.

The tinker looked up from his work and fixed me with an incurious stare but did not halt his labors.

"I don't mean to take you from your work, my good sir, but could you tell me how to get to the harbor?"

The tinker gave a dry half-laugh and shook his head. "Don't you know nothing about this town, boy? *All* streets lead to the harbor! As long as you're headed north you'll eventually hit water."

I thanked the old man and followed the general flow of the foot traffic, which--as the tinker said--was northward bound. A hundred different languages could be heard with every step I took, and the closer I got to the water, the more alien and outlandish my surroundings became. At one point I saw an Algonquin Indian striding purposefully down the street, a steel-tipped harpoon clutched in his hand as if it was a walking stick, followed closely by a man with a piece of bone skewering his nose like the ring on a prize bull. After twenty minutes' walk, I finally reached the crowded warren of sail makers, grog shops, and brothels that comprised Bay Street.

The streets fronting the water were even more tightly packed than those I had walked earlier, and the air reeked of smoke from the nearby oil yards. For years I had yearned to see the exotic lands and people described so vividly to me by my beloved uncle, but I was still taken aback when faced with the reality of a whaling town. Being young and inexperienced, I was naturally hesitant to ask questions of any of these very strange strangers, so I set out to find someone who looked like they understood English and would not be tempted to eat me.

I spotted an elderly fellow dressed in the rough wool coat and watch cap of a mariner seated on a bench outside a tobacconist's. He was calmly smoking a pipe as the exotic denizens of Sag Harbor paraded past. He seemed old enough and local enough to possibly be able to answer my questions about the person I was looking for.

"Please pardon my intrusion, but could you possibly tell me where I might find a Captain Solomon?"

The old man tilted his head in my direction, so that I could see his face. With a start I realized his eyes were as blind as those of a baked fish. "Solly-man, is it?" The blind man drawled, taking the pipe from his mouth and giving it a hard rap against the edge of the bench. "He captains the *Absalom*, berthed on Long Wharf. Ye mean to go a'whalin', boy?"

"Yes, sir, I do."

"Are ye colored?" asked the blind man.

"No, sir."

"Then why sign on a whaler? It's hard, dirty, dangerous business. That's why most of the crews are darkies of some ilk or another. They'll work you like a slave, and by the time yer done ye'll owe more to the ship's store than ye can claim as a wage."

"You sound like you know something of it, my friend."

"I spent fifteen year in the foc'sle," the blind man replied as his thumb and forefinger dipped into the tobacco pouch, then quested about like sightless grubs until they found the warm heart of the bowl. "The bad air from the try-works affected the humors in me eyes. Struck me blind, it did."

"Bilgewater!" This was from a clerk dressed in a long white apron, a broom held in one hand, who stood in the doorway of the tobacco shop. "You went blind on account of gin, you old reprobate! And as for you, young man—if it's Wendell Solomon you're seekin', you stand as good a chance of findin' him in the Whaler's Rest than anywhere else in town." He pointed the broom handle at the tavern across the way, outside of which hung a sign made of crossed harpoons.

"How will I know him?"

"Oh, if he's in there, you'll find him soon enough!" The clerk replied with a laugh.

I thanked the shopkeeper and hurried across the street to the tavern. Up to that day, I had never once set foot in a place of drink, so you can imagine my surprise at what awaited me at the Whaler's Rest.

The interior was crammed to the rafters with a wild mélange of humanity, most of whom seemed to either be from some far-off country or missing a part of their anatomy, if not both--all of whom were talking at the top of their lungs. The pipe smoke was so thick I could have cut it with a knife and used it for chaw. The sawdust that covered the rough plank floor was composed of equal parts vomit and urine, mainly because those patrons not drinking, talking or smoking were slumped across tables or stretched out in pools of their own waste.

As I looked about the crowd of unfamiliar faces scattered about the tavern's central room, I despaired of ever being able to locate Captain Solomon. Then I heard a laugh so strong and powerful it cut through the surrounding din like Moses parting the Red Sea. Upon hearing that laugh, I realized I had found my man.

Although I have met many a mariner since that fated day, Wendell Solomon remains--to my mind--the perfect sea captain. Even in a bar filled with Red Indians and cannibal Māori, this native Long Islander cut quite the figure. He was six-foot-four, if he stood an inch, with shoulders as wide as an oar. His face was as weathered as a light-house keeper's watch-shack, framed by a great mass of black hair streaked white at the temples, with matching marks in his beard. His right eye was as blue as a robin's egg and as clear as the sky over Eden, while the left was covered with a patch of plain black cloth. He stood with his back to the bar, facing the door, and was dressed in a pair of black wool pants and a gray cable sweater, his cap pulled low on his brow as he drank from a pewter tankard.

I stepped forward and coughed into my fist, doing my best to control the anxiety in my voice. "Beg pardon, sir—but might you be Captain Solomon?"

"That depends on who's doin' the askin'," the sea captain replied, fixing me with his one good eye. "Do I know ye, boy?"

"No, sir. But I believe you knew my late uncle, Calvin Jenkins. He gave me this letter of recommendation and said I should present it to you, or to any captain I might meet, should you happen to be dead."

The distrust in Solomon's eye dimmed, to be replaced with a warmer humor as he took the letter from me. He opened it, glanced at the handwriting, and then returned his solitary stare to my face. "So, you're Cal's nephew, eh? I remember him sayin' he had family Philadelphia way. And you have a bit of his look about you. Well, son, truth to tell—your uncle was one of the bravest men I ever set sail with, and that's sayin' some. Back when we was on the old *Mount Vernon,* I once seen him rescue a native girl from a shark—leapt right off the deck, he did, and landed on the monster's back! It was a big, mean bastard, but damned if he didn't stab it to death as easy as you please! So, boy, even if you're but a hair on your uncle's ass, you'll still make a worthy addition to my crew."

"So you'll take me?"

"Did I not just say as much? My ship is the *Absalom.* She's anchored on the Long Wharf—you'll know her by her figurehead: a gilded eagle. My second, Mr. Shreve, is handling the signing-on." He fished a pencil stub from the pocket of his coat and took the envelope containing my uncle's letter and made a mark upon it, then handed it back. "Show this to him—he'll know what to do."

"Thank you, Captain Solomon!" I beamed. "You won't regret it!"

"Aye," he said with a nod and wry half-smile. "We'll see if you're still thankin' me a year in from today, eh?"

Strolling down the aptly-named Long Wharf was like walking down a city street where all the houses just happened to have masts and anchor chains. Where the streets of Sag Harbor were a mass of swirling chaos to my young eyes, the Long Wharf had a definite sense of order and purpose to its madness.

Teamsters drove up and down the length of the wharf, making deliveries of everything from sailcloth to crates of live chickens. Scores of coopers, caulkers, and carpenters set up shop alongside their respective ships as they worked, while longshoremen hurried up and down the gangplanks, loading or unloading the holds as necessary.

It did not take me long to find the *Absalom.* The sun reflected off the gilded eagle fixed to her prow, causing it to flash as brightly as an ancient warrior's shield. As I drew closer, I spied a man standing near the gangplank, studying a ledger propped open on a wooden cask. He was short and stout like the stump of a mighty oak, with a neck as thick as a bull's and hair the color of a ginger cat. His complexion was the permanent sunburn you find on fair-skinned folk who work in the open elements.

"Are you Mr. Shreve?"

The stump-like man raised pale green eyes from the ledger and nodded. When he spoke, his voice was surprisingly light and musical. "That I am."

"Captain Solomon said I should show this to you," I said, handing him the marked envelope.

Shreve frowned at the captain's scribble for a long moment, raised a single eyebrow, and removed the letter, being careful not to tear the paper as he unfolded it. I was impressed by the delicacy of movement and voice in a man who seemed so outwardly blunt.

"Cal Jenkins! That's a name I haven't heard in a month of Sundays! I knew your uncle, I did. Not as well as the Cap'n. Him and Cal went back a-ways, to hear the tale. But I shipped with him. It was my first voyage and his last. What? Twelve years ago? I couldn't have been much older than you are now. I was one of the men who helped hold him down when the ship's carpenter took his legs off—or, at least what was left of them. So, boy—

what is your name?"

"Padgett. Jonah Padgett."

Shreve's joviality disappeared as quickly as chalk wiped from a slate. "Is it, now?"

"Is there a problem, Mr. Shreve?"

"Sailors are a superstitious lot, lad, what with most of them being heathens of some sort. Jonah is a bad name for a sailor to have; especially a whaler. From here on in, boy, if you want to bunk on the *Absalom*, or any ship for that matter, your name is *Jonas*, is that clear?"

"Aye, sir. That it is."

"Good lad!" Shreve said, his previous good humor returning as quickly as it had disappeared. "Now, do you claim any skill beyond that of a strong back?"

"My father runs a mill," I replied. "I helped him make the casks and barrels that held the flour."

"Excellent! Our tight cooper is in sore need of an apprentice, as he lost the last one to snail fever. Come make your mark in the books, and I'll put you down for your share."

I did as I was bid, being careful to spell my new name correctly in the ship's ledger. Mr. Shreve smiled broadly and gave me a clap on the back that would make a mule stagger.

"Welcome aboard the *Absalom*, boyo! You're lucky you caught us when you did. This is our last day at dock. We set sail for the Pacific hunting grounds in the morning!"

Chapter Three

A Final Farewell—The Crew of the Absalom—The Forecastle—Captain Solomon At The Rail

As the first rays of the rising sun touched its rigging, the *Absalom* pulled up anchor and slipped into the falling tide that flowed into Gardiner's Bay. As we passed Montauk's rounded bluff, several of the crew--including Captain Solomon and his mates--gathered along the rail. The swearing, laughing and spitting that had seemed so much a part of their collective nature as breathing was replaced by a deep and sudden silence. Curious, I joined their number.

"What are we looking at?" This I asked of Mr. Shreve, who, at this point, had proven himself the most accessible of the mates.

"See that, boyo?" he said in a hushed voice, pointing to the lighthouse situated high atop the bluff. "It's the last any of us will see of Long Island for the next year or three—and, in all probability, there's one or two of us who will ne'er see it again."

I thought about what he had said for a moment, and then gave a sidelong glance to the faces ranged along the rail. Although each man's eye was riveted on the distant lighthouse, I could tell each was seeing something different, be it the face of a sweetheart, child, or beloved mother. No wonder those gathered at the rail were as quiet as churchmen.

Perhaps now is as good a time as any to describe to you the crew whose lives and space I shared aboard the *Absalom*. On a whaler, all the men must rely on one another and work as a team. Yet there remains a very strict social order at work, as rigid as that of the Hindoos.

The highest position held on board was, of course, that of the captain. Below him were his four mates, then the four master harpooners. These nine men slept in special quarters, each set aside for their own station, in the ship's stern, and fed at the captain's table. Next came the craftsmen, those whose jobs were to keep the day-to-day of the ship on an even keel: the cooper, the blacksmith, the cook, and the bo'sun, who slept amidships and dined on fare less than that of the captain's table, but far better than what was served to the deckhands, who shared the cramped and foul confines of the bow. Despite our keeping such close quarters--or perhaps because of it--there was even a hierarchy to be found amongst the deckhands, with the old salts having an advantage over the green hands, regardless of the color of their skin.

The Captain and Second Mate of the *Absalom,* I have already described. I shall attempt to do justice to the others, in descending order of rank. The First Mate, Mr. Godward, was a long, tall drink of water that walked with his shoulders drawn up and his hands clasped behind his back. He reminded me of a stork, wading its way through the shallows. When he was not standing watch, he served as the ship's pilot. Although he was lean in build, his hands were strong enough to snap a harpoon lance in two. A New Bedfordman, he kept his own council and watched the carryings on of the crew with a flinty eye. Where, in my mind, Captain Solomon embodied the very sea itself, Mr. Godward personified the craggy shore the surf crashed against.

The Third Mate, Mr. Levant, was an outwardly unremarkable sort, save for two attributes. The first was a pair of bushy eyebrows that swept outward, like the wings of a bat, shielding the sharpest eyes ever set into a human skull. In the harshest glare from the westering sun, he could spot the flash of a fluke from a league away, aided in no small part by the shade thrown by those magnificent brows. The second attribute was the two missing fingers of his left hand, the digits in question having been severed in an accident with a whale-line.

The ship's bos'un was Mr. Gussett, whose charge it was to oversee the cleaning and maintenance of the *Absalom* while at sea and at dock. He was a broad-shouldered fellow with tattoos of crossed anchors on each forearm. His huge hands belied a surprising delicacy with needle and thread, which he used to mend the sails and sew-up the occasional crewman.

As for the harpooners, they were a motley lot, their single unifying feature being their prodigious size and skill with the long iron. One man was assigned to each of the four boats under the command of the ship's officers. The first harpooner--the one who hurled his iron from the captain's boat--was a strapping Swede named Haraldson, whose blonde brows were so sun-bleached they were all but invisible to the naked eye.

The second harpooner--who manned the First Mate's boat--was the African, Mulogo. Mulogo was without a doubt the tallest man I have ever clapped eyes on, and to my dying day I will carry the image of him standing in the gunwale of his longboat, framed against the blue sky of the Pacific like an ebony watchtower poised on a lonesome cliff.

The third and fourth harpooners were a pair of runaway slaves named Virgil and Homer, who were jokingly referred to as "The Classics" by the rest of the crew. At first it was difficult for me to tell the one from the other, until I noticed that Virgil bore deep scarring across his right shoulder, and that Homer still wore the remnant of a manacle as a grim keepsake on his left ankle.

As for the craftsmen, the ship's cooper was a Portugee by the name of Santo. The blacksmith, who was also in charge of the ship's try-works, went by the name of Cuppy. He was easily the oldest man on board the *Absalom*, with snowy white hair and beard, and a small and wiry build--save for his massive arms, which were as big around at the bicep as a young girl's thigh. He reminded me of the god Vulcan, whose crippled frame hid prodigious strength and stamina.

The cook, if he could be so called, was a fellow named Pedro, who claimed to be from Peru. For all I know he was a wizard in the galley, but you not could prove it by what he served me. While the captain, mates, harpooners, and the ship's craftsmen were fed on beef, fowl, and the like, the rest of us had to make do with jerked beef, cold coffee, watery stew and sea biscuits hard enough to drive a nail through an oaken plank.

This now brings me to my fellow crewmen—and a strange and unlikely lot they were, too. At least half were Negroes and Red Indians of various hues, the rest an odd mixture of Yankees, South-Sea Islanders, and Europeans. Of the white men--no matter what their nationality--they could easily be divided into three categories: those who were born to sea-faring families; romantics seeking adventure; and escaped convicts. Of the three, I fell into the middle category, much to the amusement of the former and the disgust of the latter.

My uncle had told me stories of just how hard the life of a whaling man could be, but in my childish fascination I had chosen to ignore them in favor of the tales of cannibal attacks and native princesses. Imagine my dismay when I was shown what would be my home for the next year or more—a narrow, triangle-shaped room located under the deck in the bow of the ship, known as the forecastle or foc'sle.

It was only accessible by a single hatch on the top deck and was otherwise without windows or doors. It was dark and the walls were literally black with slime and filth. Even in the milder climates the foc'sle could be uncomfortably hot, but in the heat of the Pacific it became a virtual oven reeking of seawater, sweat, smoke, vomit, farts, piss and sperm—in short, it smelled of men in too-close quarters under horrid conditions. The crew slept in narrow wooden bunks that lined the walls, and the only place a deckhand had to sit was on his own sea chest.

Since the foc'sle was at the front of the ship, it took the brunt of the waves, much to the dismay of the green hands—myself included—who spent the first few days of the outward journey attempting to get their sea-legs. As we lay in our hard bunks, spewing vomit with every pitch and roll of the storm-tossed ship, the more seasoned salts smoked, laughed, and chatted amongst themselves. The only time they would acknowledge our existence was by cursing us whenever they slipped in a puddle of sick. Although, at the time, I could not find the humor in my situation, I have since come to see myself through the eyes of the old salts whose berth I shared, and I must admit that I was, indeed, a fool.

Still, as horrid as conditions in the foc'sle were, they were counterbalanced by the beauty and majesty of the sea herself. Each morning, as I clambered out of the stinking darkness, the merest sliver of blue was all it took to raise my spirits and spur me onto the deck to greet the day.

The first few weeks out of Long Island enroute to the whaling grounds of the Pacific were uneventful, in the sense that we were not expected to hunt whales. Instead, the time was spent shaking down the crew, training the green hands in what was expected of them, and doing last-minute repairs and preparations to the ship before the hunt began in earnest. At the time I thought I was being worked far harder than any white man could stand. But I would soon discover what I believed to be a bed of hot coals was, in fact, a feather mattress.

One evening--as I was keeping watch from the deck--I caught wind of the smell of burning tobacco coming from behind me. I turned to find Captain Solomon standing at the rail. Save for the occasional glimpse of him as he went in and out of his cabin, this was the first time I had been within striking distance of the man since our initial meeting at the Whaler's Rest.

"So, young Padgett," he said, the words coming out accompanied by puffs of fragrant smoke. "How do you find the life of a sailor?"

"I-I find it good, sir," I managed to stammer out.

Solomon looked at me, so I could see that he knew he had caught me in a falsehood and smiled with the half of his mouth not busy with his clay pipe. "Is that the truth?"

"It isn't exactly a lie, sir," I replied. "The food is awful, the work is hard, my bed reeks of sick, and I fear half of the men I share my berth with are as likely to kill me in my sleep as look at me. But this--" I pointed to the open water and sky laid out before us like a splendid mirror. "This is as good as the Lord makes it."

"By damn, you *do* have Cal's blood in you!" Solomon said with a chuckle. "He was one for speakin' his heart, no matter who was listenin'. You do realize, son, that most of what you just said could get your back painted with stripes? Still, I can respect a man who says his mind. And your mind, it seems, ain't so far from my own.

"I've witnessed all manner of things in my day, lad: I seen crocodiles and sharks fight to the death in the mouth of the Nile, and tigers swimmin' in the moonlight in the Bay of Bengal. I seen a squid the size of a frigate clamped in the jaws of a Sperm, and a Great White swaller a man in one gulp like he was an oyster on the half-shell. Strange and terrible things they were, indeed. And I reckon there's as much death and suffering on the land as there is on the water. But I never did see anything on dry land that compares to the sun setting in the Pacific.

"I'm not a poet, boy. And God knows I'm no philosopher. But I reckon, if he's lucky, at some point in his life a man knows where he's supposed to be. And I'm supposed to be out here—and perhaps you are, too."

With that, Captain Solomon removed the pipe from his mouth, gave it a light rap against the railing, so that the bowl's contents emptied into the water below, and strolled back to his cabin.

Chapter Four

The Hunt Off Valparaiso—Man Overboard—Bloody Work—King Jim—What Stood Upon The Whale

I engaged in my first whale hunt just off the coast of Uruguay, but I will not bore you with the retelling of every time I set chase after the great sea beasts for, in fact, every pursuit is near identical to the one before and the one after it. And all hunts end in either one of two ways: either a whale is caught, or it is not. However, I will describe to you the hunt that cost us our first harpooner, for it leads--in part--to the final fate of the *Absalom*.

We were four months out of Sag Harbor, cruising the waters off Valparaiso before making the long trek to the Marquesas Islands. By that point I had three chases and two kills under my belt and had already developed a taste for the thrill of the hunt. The killing and rendering of whales--especially the toothed variety--is very hard and dangerous work, but preferable to the drudgery of life onboard a whaler when there are no spouters to be seen.

I was scrubbing down the deck when I heard Mr. Levant, he of the prodigious eyebrows, sing out: *"Thar she blows!"*

Mr. Godward, whose watch it was, came forward. *"Where away?"* he called in response.

"Off the port bow!"

As a man, the crew dropped whatever they were doing and raced to the left hand rails, eagerly scanning the horizon for the telltale plume of spray that marked the passing of their prey.

Captain Solomon emerged from his cabin at the ship's stern, spyglass in hand. He raised it to his good eye and after a second's study a wide grin wreathed his mouth. "It's a pod, by damn! There's six--perhaps more--of the beasties!" With a whoop, he turned and grabbed the clapper of the watch bell mounted outside his door and began ringing it like preacher calling his congregation to prayer. *"To your boats, men! To your boats!"*

With that all hell broke loose, as every man on deck--and those below--scrambled to take his place at the long boats, which hung in eternal readiness from davits alongside the ship. Each boat was sleek, double-ended, and thirty-feet long, outfitted with harpoons, lances, knives, and axes, as well as bailing buckets, emergency rations, a knockdown sail, and provisions.

Each boat housed six men: the header, the harpooner, and four oarsmen. Early during our voyage out, the captain and his mates had put the green hands through their paces, divvying us up amongst them as they saw fit. Thanks to my uncle's tutelage in the manufacture of knots, I found myself assigned to Captain Solomon's boat. My fellow oarsmen consisted of an Orkneyman named Jones, a mulatto called Nicodemus, and a West Indian who went by Marcus. Our harpooner was the Swede, Haraldson.

While there was much about the *Absalom* that did not live up to my romantic notions of the whaling life, the harpooners were one of the few that did not disappoint. I was particularly impressed by Haraldson. Although he did not speak much English and took his meals and bunked apart from the deckhands, the Swede was well-liked amongst the crew. He was jovial in nature and fond of dancing the hornpipe while playing the ocarina when he was not sharpening his harpoon with a whetstone. His booming laugh was as loud and as vital as that of the captain. As the Swede was naturally fair, years of exposure to the sun had bleached his hair whiter than cotton, while imparting a tan so deep his skin looked like seasoned leather. With his face framed by two thick braids and decorated by a flowing mustache, he looked every inch the Viking from whom he claimed descent.

One by one the long boats were dropped into the water, each laden with men and equipment. I took my place at the oars while Captain Solomon seated himself at the tiller and Haraldson took the short seat behind the bow. All I could see of the hunt was the backs of the men seated in front of me and the face of Captain Solomon. As the boat header, it was his job to keep our prey in sight and steer the long boat in its direction. As our backs were to the whale, none of us would know if we were within striking distance of our prey until the captain sang out for the harpooner to stand or, if we were unlucky, the great beast smashed our boat with one of its flukes.

"Faster, men!" Captain Solomon shouted, over the constant hiss and slap of the waves. "She sounded half an hour ago! She'll be coming up for breath sooner than not!"

I put all thoughts of pain and weariness out of my mind and focused instead on the task at hand. Once you are out in the boats on the open ocean, allowing your concentration to wander for even the briefest moment is an invitation to death and disaster.

Foremost in my mind was the desire to stay clear of the whale line, which lay coiled in a tub near the rear of the boat. The far end of the rope was attached to the harpoon stowed in the bow of the boat, then looped around the wooden loggerhead beside the tiller, to provide enough tension to tire the whale. Once the harpoon was fixed in its target, the rope stretched itself tight along the line of the keel between the oarsmen and over the bow into the water. It was the bos'n's business to see that the whale rope was perfectly coiled within its tub, for fear of the slightest kink in the rope catching on the boat and dragging us under. If that was not reason enough to stay clear of the damned thing, should a crewman be careless and get in the way of the unwinding rope he would find himself instantly entangled and yanked overboard. Or--since the rope moved so quickly and without slack--you would lose a finger or thumb, as the line sliced through flesh and bone as easily as a knife.

So there we were--out on the open ocean, under a merciless Chilean sun, rowing until our backs cracked, with the *Absalom* trailing after us like a curious onlooker until we reached the spot where Captain Solomon predicted our prey would surface.

We sat there wordlessly hunched over our oars as the boat bobbed atop the water, while our leader scanned the surface for sign of rising whale. A mile to either side of us the boats piloted by Mr. Godward and Mr. Levant kept their own watch, while Mr. Shreve's boat stayed behind ours an equal distance. After what seemed to be half an eternity, I saw the smile of a hunter whose patience has been rewarded break across the captain's face.

"Row! Row, you bastards! She's coming up starboard!"

There was a deep rumble from both beneath and above the waves as hundreds of tons of water were rapidly displaced, and the sperm whales were amongst us. One of the great beasts broke the surface of the water not a hundred yards from us, rising like a newborn island from the ocean floor. A geyser shot upwards, showering us with thick droplets of hot vapor, as if Neptune himself had let out a mighty gasp.

"Stand!" Captain Solomon shouted over the clamor of the whale.

Although I could not see him, I heard Haraldson put aside his oars and stand to brace himself in the bow. I glanced over at the nearest boat--which was closing in as fast as it could on its own whale--and saw in the figure of Mulogo a mirror of the Swede's actions as he lifted the harpoon from its resting place. Each harpooner had to stand in the front of the heaving boat and propel the heavy, single-flue iron spear with enough force to plant it deep in the whale's back. Should the harpooner miss on his first strike, he then had to reel the weapon hand-over-hand back into the boat and try again before the beast sounded once more.

"Stern all!" Captain Solomon bellowed as Haraldson's iron bit deep into its target.

As my fellow oarsmen changed positions in order to back the boat away from the whale's flukes, the boat struck something unseen beneath the waves—exactly what will never be known—causing the Swede to lose his balance and stumble into the whale line. One moment he was there, the next he was jerked from the bow like a marionette from a puppet stage.

There was no time for mourning the harpooner, though, as the great sea beast--enraged by pain and fear--began to run, dragging line, boat and crew behind it like a child trailing a kite. When it found it could not escape by fleeing it sounded, diving deep into the farthest reaches of the sea. We fought against the wounded creature, hauling on the line until our muscles screamed and our nerves caught fire. Our prey struggled mightily, but, in the end, it could not stay down. Although shaped like a fish, the whale--just like Man--must breathe air to survive.

"Ahoy, laddies!" the captain shouted, as the whale rope began to slacken. "She's comin' up to see us!"

My fellow oarsmen and I began frantically hauling the whale line in hand-over-hand, trying to shorten the distance between us and our prey once it surfaced. Just then the whale arose before us, causing the boat to sharply rise then slap back down, nearly sending me tumbling into the churning water.

"Yo, Padgett!" Captain Solomon shouted, slapping my sunburned shoulder as he moved from the back of the boat to take Haraldson's place in the bow. "Keep us steady!"

I clambered to the rear of the boat and grabbed the tiller, which struggled in my grip like a living thing. From my new vantage point, I could see the toothed whale not fifty feet from where I sat, the Swede's harpoon jutting from its gleaming hide like a needle stuck in a pincushion.

Captain Solomon took up Haraldson's second iron and with a mighty bellow let it fly. The harpoon struck the whale and held fast. With a flash of its flukes, the Sperm swam away and we were once more dragged along on a wild sleigh-ride, leaving our fellows—and the *Absalom*—far behind before the beast once more sounded beneath the waves.

During the hour we waited for the whale to rise, Mr. Levant's boat finally rejoined us, although Mr. Shreve and Mr. Godward were nowhere to be seen. By the time our prey resurfaced, it was evident the beast was considerably weakened. Captain Solomon ordered us to close in on the animal and took up a long, spear-like lance which he plunged again and again into the exhausted animal's vitals.

The whale gave voice to a sound few human ears have known but once heard can never be forgotten, followed by a burst of blood from its spout, which coated everyone in the boat in fresh gore.

"Hurrah, Cap'n!" Mr. Levant shouted from his boat. "You've tapped the claret!"

"That I have!" Solomon agreed as he resumed his place as header. "Now let's put some distance between us, lads! We haven't chased this black devil this long and hard just to get smashed to kindling in its death flurry!"

I returned to my seat and began rowing for my life, the dolphin amulet thumping against my breastbone like a door knocker. The last few minutes of a doomed whale's life are the most dangerous to those who hunt them. Many a sailor has met his end from a wildly flailing fluke at the end of a hunt.

Once we were safely away, we rested on our oars and watched as the sperm whale swam violently about in ever decreasing circles until it had churned the sea into a foamy, bloody chaos. After a half hour of this, the stricken beast abruptly began to beat the water with its tail and then gave a huge shudder. A ragged cheer rang out from our boat and Mr. Levant's as the creature turned fin-out, rolling over on its side. However, our rejoicing proved short-lived, as we were now faced with the daunting task of towing the massive carcass back to the ship.

Jones the Orkneyman stood up and fished the whale lines out of the water with a boat hook--one of which was secured to our boat, the other to Mr. Levant's. Then, after a brief break for fresh water and a meal of hardtack, we began the long, arduous task of rowing back to the *Absalom*, dragging our kill behind us like a hound bringing home a dead rabbit for its master. The ship--which had been following us from a distance--now sat waiting on the horizon, left motionless by a change in the winds

It was during the return journey--towing forty tons of dead weight--that the sharks showed up. They arose from the depths like shadows, summoned by the blood of the slain behemoth, their dorsal fins breaking the surface like knives slitting a throat.

While it was not uncommon for these vultures of the sea to serve as grim escort to a butchered whale, I was surprised to see so many appear at once for--unlike dolphins or whales--sharks are not social animals. There were easily twenty or more of the dreadful beasts darting through the water, snatching mouthfuls of flesh from the carcass like greedy children trying to steal pies cooling on a window sill.

To my horror, one of the damned things swam up to the whale boat and clamped its fearsome jaws about the flat of my oar, as if to yank it from my grip. From what

I could see of it, it was what the Māori call a mako--with a pointy snout and relatively short dorsal fin and overlarge, circular eyes as black and flat as shoe buttons.

Suddenly a lance-like spear stabbed down over my shoulder and into shark's face, striking it in the eye. The mako surrendered its hold on the oar and dove back below the surface, leaving a trail of blood to mark its passing.

"Accursed things!" Captain Solomon spat as he resumed his place at the tiller and tucked the lance—the same one he had used to kill the whale--back into its storage space. "We'll be lucky they don't take a third of the carcass before we finish the cutting-in."

After three hours of hard rowing we finally made it back to the *Absalom.* We brought our catch to the starboard side and the whale line affixed to each boat was untied and attached to a pulley lowered from above. The carcass was then winched into place by its tail and secured to the side of the boat.

Mr. Levant's harpooner, Homer, leapt out of his boat, his manacle rattling as he clambered across the slippery back of the dead whale--heedless of the sharks that swarmed the water below--while a cutting stage fashioned from three heavy planks was lowered over the carcass. The former slave cut a hole in the skin and blubber near the whale's eye and inserted a hook connected through a series of ropes and pulleys to the ship's windlass, so that the body was fastened, head and tail, to the *Absalom.* Then, and only then, was a rope ladder tossed over the railing, allowing the crews of the whaleboats back on board.

"Where be Godward and Shreve?" Captain Solomon called out to Gussett as he cleared the rail.

“They was headed west after a spouter before the wind quit us, sir,” the bo’sun reported.

“Even if our sails were full, we can’t go looking for them until we’ve finished the cutting-in,” Solomon grunted, staring in the direction of the lowering sun.

While the captain and the bo’sun discussed the whereabouts of the other whaleboats, I and the others made a bee-line to the water casks to quench our thirst. After six hours on the open sea, I was burned red as a lobster in the pot and my skin was peeling away from my shoulders and arms like an onion. Still, despite a full day spent behind the oars, we were allowed only the briefest of rests in the shade of the mast--where we were served a meal of salted beef and cold coffee--before being ordered to begin the bloody work of rendering the whale.

Nicodemus and Marcus took up a pair of long-handled spades and shimmied down the ropes to the cutting stage atop the carcass. There they cut into the blubber--slicing blanket pieces five feet wide, fifteen feet long and ten inches thick. Then Marcus boarded the body and fixed a huge hook into the swath they had just cut, which was then peeled off the carcass using the windlass and hoisted aboard, dripping oil and blood down upon the deck and deckhands alike.

As I watched in disgust and amazement, Marcus turned and let fly with a stream of piss on the multitude of sharks not ten feet from where he stood atop the whale, laughing in contempt at the fearsome scavengers as they swarmed the carcass like farrow nursing at the teats of a sow.

When the two blocks of the tackle finally came together and no rope remained to lift it higher, the blanket-piece was sliced away and lowered into the blubber room in the upper hold near the main hatch. There it was cut into smaller horse-pieces of four feet by six inches, and then reduced further still into 'bible leaves'--which were taken back on deck and fed into the copper try-pots set atop the furnaces affixed between the foremast and the mainmast, to be boiled into oil.

My job was to assist Santo, the ship's cooper, in making the barrels used to store the precious cargo and insure they were securely sealed before being stowed in the hold. Santo was a rotund fellow--not unlike the barrels he built--with a silver ring in one ear. He was what they called a tight cooper, who made casks for long-term storage and the transportation of liquids. Although Santo did not speak much English—and I spoke no Portuguese at all—I found his company agreeable, and the same seemed to hold true for him. To tell the truth, even if the man had been the devil himself, I would have still counted myself lucky to work by his side, as the ship's cooperage was far preferable to toiling in the dark, reeking confines of the blubber room or skimming the skin and tissue from the hissing, spitting try-pots.

We labored hard for the rest of the day as the blazing sun gradually sank into the horizon like a fresh-forged sword being quenched in a blacksmith's bath. It was then one of the crewmen sang out from the crow's nest.

"Long boat off the port bow!"

The crew on deck stopped what they were doing to hurry to the rail, to see Mr. Shreve's boat making its way back to the *Absalom* like a chick headed for the protection of the mother hen.

"Where's Mr. Godward and his men?" I asked.

Mr. Gussett took out a spyglass and squinted at the approaching boat. "The First Mate's in the whale boat with Shreve, along with Mulogo," he replied solemnly. "I don't see any of the others from his boat."

As Mr. Shreve put alongside the *Absalom* and its crew was taken up out of the sea, Captain Solomon pushed his way through the men gathered on the deck, cursing and kicking those who did not get out of his way fast enough. "Get back to your stations!" he barked. "Have you dogs never seen a whale boat come back empty-handed from a hunt before?" He then turned to face his First Mate, who stood before him, shivering as if in the grip of fever. "What happened, Mr. Godward?"

"Mulongo sank his harpoon into this nice fat cow on his first throw," the Mate replied. "She started to run—but wheeled about when her calf couldn't keep up. That's when Mulongo got the second iron in her. Then, suddenly, this bull sperm whale—the largest I've ever seen, with skin black as the devil's eyes—breached beside us and stove in the boat with a flick of his tail. The next thing I know, Mulongo has his arm about me and is swimming as fast as he can for Shreve's boat. As for the others--none of them came back up." A look of horror crossed Godward's face, as if part of him was still back in the water. "I've never seen a monster like it before. It had to be him, Cap'n—it had to be King Jim."

A muttering rose from the assembled crew, spurring Captain Solomon to snatch the cat from his belt and angrily strike at those sailors unlucky enough to be closest at hand. "What are you, whalers or old women?" he thundered. "I said get back to work!"

Mr. Levant and Mr. Gussett took up the captain's line, cursing and shouting at the crew to get back to their stations or run the risk of a flogging. The sailors grumbled but returned their duties as the Captain hurried Godward and Mulogo into his cabin for what I can only assume to be further inquisition.

As Santo and I returned to his cooperage, I ventured a question as to this 'King Jim' that seemed to worry the crew so much.

"King Jim is big fish," the Portugee replied. "Very big, very *angry* fish."

"You mean a whale?"

"Sim, a maior das baleia," he said solemnly. "Some say King Jim devil. Some say god. I think both."

"That's blasphemy," I pointed out as judiciously as I could.

"Sim," the cooper conceded. "The earth and the sky, that belongs to God. But the ocean? The ocean belongs to King Jim."

There is nothing filthier than the trying out of a whale. It is ceaseless, backbreaking work that goes on day and night until the last of the blubber is melted down in the copper cauldrons of the try-works. During this time the crew ends up working like horses, their days spent in grueling six-hour shifts, and living like pigs--as there is no point in cleaning oneself until the last drop of oil is poured into the final barrel and the try-pots thoroughly scoured.

Everything--and I mean *everything*--is coated in oil during the trying-out process. It rises in thick, reeking plumes from the boiling pots, covering everything from the decks to the sails to the sailors themselves in a foul, greasy sheen. It even permeates the foodstuffs and the eating utensils, so that everything smells and tastes of blubber. It is made even worse by the fact that the fires beneath the try-works are fed not with wood, but with those pieces of whale deemed unsuitable for the boiling pots. As a result, there is literally nowhere onboard where one can escape the fetid odor of burning, boiling or rotting whale.

It was around midnight when Mr. Gussett told Santo and me to close up shop and get some sleep. We had made over twenty barrels that day and-- after a few hours rest--would have made twenty more if the bo'sun didn't tell us to stop.

As weary as I was, the idea of heading down to the stinking, dank foc'sle was enough to make my stomach cinch itself into a sheepshank. I decided to take a walk around the top deck in the vain hope of catching a breath of fresh air, but instead found myself staring down over the starboard railing at what was left of the behemoth I had helped kill.

In the flickering, orangish light cast by the try-works, I could see that the blubber had been stripped from the carcass and all that remained was for the whale to be decapitated in order to harvest the precious, high-grade spermaceti it carried about in its skull case. I looked around, but the flensers were nowhere to be seen —no doubt they had gone to exchange their cutting spades for the longer, heavier head spades used to chop through the vertebrae in the whale's neck.

From where I stood I could hear the threshing of the sharks in the water below as they fought amongst themselves for the choicest morsels of flesh. Their ceaseless feeding reminded of me of maggots working to reduce a corpse. Just then I saw the figure of a naked man emerge from the shark-infested water and clamber onto the back of the skint whale.

At first my exhausted mind thought Haraldson--the lost harpooner--had somehow miraculously escaped drowning, man-eating sharks and the open sea and found his way back to the *Absalom*. But then I realized that the figure was utterly devoid of hair and had a noticeably hunched back. Whoever—or whatever—it was walking across the dead whale, it most certainly was not the Swede.

As I watched in stunned silence, the hunched figure —still dripping from the ocean—fell to its knees and began tearing at the exposed, rotting meat with bare hands, stuffing gobbets of flesh into its mouth. I cried out in horror and disgust, instinctively clutching the amulet about my neck for protection.

The figure crouched atop the whale's carcass jerked its head in my direction, revealing a gaping maw full of jagged teeth and gill slits along the sides of its neck. The glow of the try-works cast a flickering light on its left eye—which was as round and black as a shoe-button— while revealing the right to be a gouged, red ruin.

Chapter Five

My Eyes Deceived—Sea Changes Amongst The Crew—Nuka Hiva—A Shadow In The Surf—My Uncle's Secret

Upon seeing the face of the horror that knelt atop the whale, I cried out in alarm and fled the rail. Without thinking, I ran to awaken Santo--who slept in a hammock strung up in the ship's cooperage--and informed him of what I had seen crawl out of the shark-infested sea.

"You are *louco* from no sleep," he snarled, unappreciative of having been shaken from his well-earned slumber. "That why you see *sereia*."

"But it's not a mermaid!" I protested. "It's something else—something like a shark, but it walks like a man! And it's real, I tell you!"

"Go sleep, Jonas, or I hit you," Santo grumbled, turning his back to me.

I did not dare try to rouse my friend a second time for fear he would make good on his threat. So I returned starboard and cautiously peered over the rail at the whale carcass tethered to the *Absalom's* side. Although the water was still full of hungry sharks, the grotesque, one-eyed creature was nowhere to be seen.

In its place were a pair of deckhands working diligently from their perches on the cutting platform to separate the deceased sperm's lower jaw and head from the rest of the body. Judging by their blasé manner as they sawed away at the leviathan's neck, neither had recently seen anything as untoward as a human shark.

I rubbed my weary eyes and shook my head in reproof. Santo was right: I was so tired I was hallucinating. If I didn't get some rest, I would soon be seeing angels nesting in the riggings and sea serpents frolicking off the port bow.

Both relieved and embarrassed by this realization, I returned to my lowly, stinking bunk in the foc'sle. Despite the sound of the sharks thumping against the hull of the ship as they continued their ceaseless feeding, I quickly fell into a deep and dreamless slumber.

The weeks following the untimely death of Haraldson proved sad ones for all who shipped the *Absalom*. But his absence was felt most keenly by those of us in the Captain's boat. Although Jones the Orkneyman and Marcus took turns in the bow, neither proved to have the Swede's keen eye and sure hand when it came to the tossing of harpoons.

One would not think it difficult to land a strike against the broadside of something the size of a whale, but more times than not their throws ended up in the drink and had to be reeled back into the boat as fast as possible, before our prey returned to the safety of the depths.

Where once we had hunted down our share of whale, now we found ourselves--more often than not--assisting the other boats in their kills, instead of making our own. Although the pay of a whaling man is decided by the sum of the ship's cargo, there is a tally kept of which officer's boat was responsible for what kills, and bonuses applied to the most productive teams, going from greater to lesser. And where once the Captain's boat was at the top of the list, now it was squarely on the bottom.

But as disconcerting as Haraldson's death may have been for the crew of the *Absalom*, it was nothing compared to the sea-change Mr. Godward underwent following his tragic encounter with the legendary King Jim.

Upon returning to the ship, the First Mate took to his cabin for several days, where he remained in his bunk, afflicted by fever and attended by his loyal harpooner, Mulongo. When at last Mr. Godward returned to the top decks, the crew was shocked to see his hair was now white as snow. Never an out-going soul to begin with, the taciturn New Bedfordman now only consorted with the crew when necessary, preferring to keep to himself--save for the company of the African who had saved his life.

One night I--along with a number of my shipmates--elected to sleep on the foredeck in hopes of enjoying the occasional breeze, as the foc'sle was as stifling as an oven in the heat of the equator. As I prepared to bed down, I spotted Mr. Godward standing at the rail, staring out at the darkness. His eyes shone in the moonlight as if still wracked with fever. His lips were moving, although I heard no words, and at first I thought that he was praying. Then I saw his mouth twist into a hateful grimace, and I realized that whatever the First Mate was doing, it had nothing to do with God.

One would think that after having his boat stove in and all hands drown save himself and Mulongo that Mr. Godward would be hesitant to return to the hunt. But nothing could be farther from the truth. As soon as he had regained his health, the First Mate picked a new crew to replace the one drowned and set forth in pursuit of whales in one of the extra boats stored on the boat-deck with the ever-present Mulongo seated in the bow.

Nearly three months had passed since the day we lost Haraldson the morning we hove into view of the Marquesas. By my estimation it had been fifteen months since we first set sail from Sag Harbor. Nuka Hiva was the largest of the eight islands that compose the archipelago, and although the French had recently laid claim to the island chain, Taiohae Bay had long been a popular destination for ships of all nations looking to take on supplies and refresh their weary crews.

The western side of the island consisted of imposing, rocky coasts girdled by soaring cliffs, which occasionally broke to allow glimpses of deep coves that opened onto lush valleys, separated by towering spires cloaked in clouds and laced with waterfalls. The coastline to the east was equally difficult, with the trade wind generated waves pounding against the cliffs with earthshaking reports. In contrast, the northern and southern sides of the island boasted several deep, sheltering bays that allowed easy access to the interior.

As the *Absalom* made its way between the towering twin islets that marked the entrance to the bay, we were greeted by the sight of a vast, horse-shoe shaped natural harbor beyond which could be seen the island's lush vegetation, pierced by brooding volcanic pinnacles. After so long at sea our arrival at Nuka Hiva was indeed a relief. The crew of the *Absalom* crowded the railings, our hungry senses thrown wide to receive the sights, sounds and scents of dry land. As we drew closer to the verdant shores, the breeze from the island carried with it the perfume of plumeria, jasmine and copra, all of which grew wild in the interior and in great abundance. For a boy raised on a Pennsylvania farm it was the very breath of exotic paradise.

To the east of the bay was a stone wharf that dated back to when America kept a garrison on the island. Beyond it stood the canoe houses, and further still could be seen a small village. Scattered amongst the native huts fashioned from yellow bamboo with thatched roofs made of palmetto fronds were more conventional, European-style structures raised by the French colonialists.

The moment *Absalom* dropped anchor the villagers poured out of their huts and into the canoe house, dragging forth the massive outriggers South Sea Islanders are famous for. Since the Marquesas were very isolated in relation to other islands in the Pacific, the natives were extremely quick to trade with passing ships. Within minutes the *Absalom* found itself surrounded on all sides by bobbing canoes filled with eager, shouting islanders touting everything from coconuts to trussed chickens waved about like living feather dusters.

One of the natives—a lovely young *wahine* with long, dark tresses and dressed in naught but a drape of linen about her waist—was so determined to sell her wares she leapt from her canoe and began swimming in the direction of the ship's anchor chain. The sailors lined along the rail began to hoot and laugh, eagerly waving the girl onward.

I caught sight of a shadow in the water, moving swiftly towards the unwary swimmer. I felt a skeletal hand close about my heart as the dorsal fin broke the surface. *"Shark ho!"* I shouted, pointing to the deadly beast slicing its way through the waves.

As the crew of the *Absalom* scrambled for their harpoons and firearms, I leapt onto the starboard rail--knife in hand--and was about to leap into the bay in a desperate attempt to save the girl from the monster's fearsome jaws when a second, slighter shadow shot through the surf, striking the shark in its side, just below the gills. Stunned by the blow, the mako went rigid and promptly dropped like a stone to the bottom of the bay.

The second, silvery shadow then leapt free of the water in a jubilant pirouette, revealing itself to be a bottlenose dolphin. A mighty cheer rose from the crew as the porpoise continued to sport about the swimming girl like a sheepdog herding its charge into a paddock. Upon reaching the ship, the lovely native ignored the rope ladder that Marcus tossed over the side and instead chose to clamber up the anchor chain like a monkey climbing a tree.

As I hopped back down onto the deck I found Captain Solomon watching me with a smile on his face. "By damn, when I saw you jump to the rail to try and save that girl, I thought I was back twenty-five years ago!" he said, puffing on his pipe. "You have your uncle's guts as well as blood in you, Padgett!"

"Thank you, sir. But I *didn't* save her," I said, gesturing to the girl, who now stood--still dripping from the sea--surrounded by eager, leering deck hands who had not seen a woman since liberty in Peru. She seemed in no way perturbed by the fact she had narrowly escaped being attacked by a shark and, instead, was trying to interest the sailors gathered around her in the breadfruit she had brought with her in a bag made of netting. "The dolphin did."

"Aye, but you were ready to jump in between her and that toothy devil, which is more than any other man on this ship was willing t'do--m'self included. And maybe if you had—and lived to tell the tale—you would have won yourself a wife in the bargain, just like your Uncle Cal did."

"Beg pardon, Cap'n?" I said, blinking in surprise.

"Ah, so he never told you about Amura did he?" Solomon sighed, tapping the bowl of his pipe against the rail as he dumped its ashes into the bay. "She was a lovely thing—barely tattooed, compared to most of 'em. She's the one that gave him that amulet," he said, gesturing to the dolphin pendant about my neck. "She was his wife whenever we were near Tahiti. She was carryin' his child when the mast snapped and took his legs. Cal refused to go back to her after that. Said he didn't want to be a burden, what with him bein' a cripple and all. I have no doubt she would have loved him all the same--legs or no legs--but your uncle had his pride."

"What happened to her and the child?" I asked, stunned to learn that not only did I have an aunt I never knew of, but a cousin as well.

Captain Solomon shrugged. "I suppose they're dead. After your uncle lost his legs, he gave me a packet of money and a letter to deliver to Amura the next time I was in Tahiti. Of course, it took me a year or more to get there. Once I arrived, I went to the hut she and Cal shared, which was built on the beach--only to find it long deserted. I asked around and discovered that when Cal didn't return that season, like he usually did, she took their baby son in her arms and walked into the ocean, never to be seen again."

Chapter Six

Heaving Down—I Am Given My Liberty—The Toad Hole—In The Company Of His Lordship—Cannibals At The Bar

The primary reason for the Absalom putting to port in Taiohae Bay was simple maintenance. Whalers set sail on long voyages anywhere from three to five years in length, assuming they're lucky on the hunt. During that time repairs must be made by the crew if the vessel is to remain seaworthy. That means dropping anchor in a sheltered cove from time to time where--safe from the constant churning of the sea--they can heave down the ship so that the crew can bream, scrape, tar, and sheath and copper the hull below the waterline.

Heaving down a whaling bark is an exacting and time-consuming enterprise. At its worst, it is exceedingly dangerous, grueling work and at its very best merely hazardous, arduous labor. But there is no avoiding it.

After conferring with the resident harbor pilot—a tall, lanky, sunburned fellow with an English accent—Captain Solomon brought the *Absalom* alongside the wharf with the leeward side facing the shore. The crew then began lightening the ship, carrying everything from barrels of oil, casks of hardtack, and the Captain's chamber pot ashore via the gangplanks.

Items too heavy to be carried by hand--such as the try-works--were tackled-rigged from the lower yardarms. By emptying *Absalom* of her contents and leaving only enough ballast to maintain stable equilibrium while heeled, less strain was placed on the careening tackle set just below the crosstrees on the mizzen and foremasts. While half the crew was ferrying everything not battened down onto the wharf, the other half was busily planking over the ports and covering them with tarred canvas, plug, caulk and pitch to make sure no water would enter the hull on the leeward side.

The ship's carpenter--a fellow named Hawley--and his apprentice, as well as Santo and myself, were then sent in to construct angled platforms in the hatchways that would serve as staging areas for the crew manning the pumps required to keep the ship clear of the water that managed to seep in while she was hove down. We were also tasked with building temporary bulkheads--fore, aft, and abreast either side of the keelson, extending from the ship's floor to the orlop deck--in order to prevent the remaining ballast from shifting too far to either side.

While we were busy making sure the leeward side of the ship remained watertight, our fellow crew members were sent aloft to dismantle the rigging, clearing all spars above the lower masts. The careening block and tackle on the fore and main masts were then attached to a capstan on the wharf, manned by nine strong men. As they pushed against the bars, the *Absalom* was pulled leeward via its masts, causing her to tip to one side and reveal her barnacle-encrusted hull.

Once careened, the job at hand began at a rapid pace as the ship had to be returned to its natural position as soon as possible to avoid unnecessary strain on the hull and rigging. Strips of copper sheathing below the waterline that had been lost during our outward voyage were quickly replaced from the ship's stores, while sailors swarmed the exposed bottom like ants on a lump of sugar, vigorously scrubbing at the barnacles that clung to its underside with coconut shells, all the while dangling from Jacob's ladders secured from the upper railings. Meanwhile, another brace of hands cut away at the acres of trailing seaweed that had become tangled in the ship's keel and rudder.

Come dusk the ship was righted to its natural position once more, so that the crew could be fed and bedded down in the foc'sle, in anticipation of repeating the exact same labors the very next day until all the repairs that were needed were finished. As for the captain and his mates, they spent the evening in the villa of the *administrateur d'Etat,* enjoying his table and French wine, while the rest of the crew dined on hardtack, salt beef and cold coffee.

The *Absalom's* stores and cargo remained on shore, watched over by a brace of armed men, who were not there merely to guard the provisions from thieving locals but to also make sure none of the crew snuck off the ship in search of female companionship or escape their contracted servitude by fleeing to the interior of the island.

It says something as to the harshness and general unpleasantness of the average whaling man's s life that there were those on board who would gladly risk cannibal tribes rather than spend another season breathing smoke from the blubber-fires.

◆ ◆ ◆

And so my first week in the tropical paradise of Nuka Hiva was spent scraping barnacles and sweetening the ship's bilge by pumping it dry and then rinsing it with pine oil. Every waking moment was spent at the hardest labor imaginable under a broiling sun, yet I could not bring myself to grumble about my lot, for whenever I raised my eyes from the task at hand I found myself staring at the most gorgeous landscape on God's green earth. I can honestly say I have never busted my back and raised blisters on my hands in lovelier surroundings.

Once everything was taken care of and the *Absalom* was made as sound as possible under such circumstances, the vessel was righted for good and the cargo and equipage returned to their proper places within the holds. After everything was declared shipshape by the bo'sun, the captain had the entire crew gather below the poop deck, from whence he addressed us.

"Laddies, you have done *Absalom* proud! I daresay she's as fit now as she was when she set sail from Sag Harbor! Mr. Godward and Mr. Gussett inform me that morale is so high that they only had to flog two or three of you! As reward for such diligence to the greater good, I am grantin' the starboard watch twenty-four hours liberty, startin' at two bells. Then, once they've returned, the port watch gets its fun."

A loud huzzah arose from the gathered sailors upon hearing this news, with the starboard watch—of which I was a member—cheering the loudest.

"I warn you, though," Captain Solomon continued, shouting to make himself heard above the roar. "Keep to Taiohae, no matter what you do. And under no circumstances are you to go wanderin' off into the interior! I don't care how lovely the young lady may be or how many sisters she has at home—the valleys hereabout are thick with cannibals! And if the savages get their hands on you—well, even if you escape the cook pot, they're just as likely to mark you for life with heathen tattoos."

Having said his piece, the captain returned to his quarters and I and the others headed to the forecastle to set about adorning ourselves in what passed for our Sunday best, in hopes of attracting the favors of some pretty little *wahine.*

I doused myself in bay rum as there were no means of bathing on board, tied a fresh kerchief about my neck and polished my dolphin amulet and arrayed it so that it was plainly visible against my shirt. At the sounding of two bells, I and the rest of the starboard watch hurried ashore across the gangplanks as if the hounds of hell were snapping at our heels.

Standing at the end of the wharf was a native covered in tattoos. He was nearly bent double with age and the designs that crowded his withered body had faded from black to bluish-gray. As we approached, the picturesque Methuselah began reciting in a singsong voice, alternating between French and English.

"Welcome travelers! *Bienvenue voyageurs!* Come to the Toad Hole! *Rendezvous au Trou Crapaud!* Best tavern in Taiohae! *Meilleure taverne à Taiohae!* Only tavern in Taiohae! *Seule taverne à Taiohae!*"

"Very well, grandfather!" Jones the Orkneyman laughed. "Take us to this wondrous 'Toad Hole' of yours!"

The old man grinned, revealing toothless gums,

and motioned to Jones and the others to follow him. Moving with surprising alacrity, he lead the crocodile of laughing sailors past the huge canoe house that dominated the beach and into the grove behind it until, a few minutes later, we emerged in a clearing, at the center of which was a structure that was a mixture of civilized and savage design. Although made of native bamboo with a long, steeply peaked thatched roof similar to that found on the canoe house, it otherwise resembled a standard European dwelling and even included a wide verandah, the supporting posts of which were covered in carvings of the grimacing heathen gods known as *Tiki*.

Standing in the shade of the porch was a short, squat flat-faced European with thinning hair and protruding eyes. He was dressed in a linen suit that may have, at one time, been white but was now closer to ecru, with darker, tea-colored stains under his arm pits and around his collar. Upon seeing the group of eager sailors emerge from the tree line, he smiled and mopped his sweaty brow with an equally dingy handkerchief.

The old native hurried up to the man in the linen suit, speaking rapidly in his savage tongue, eagerly gesturing to the sailors he had brought. The European nodded and handed him a small flask of rum. The old man snatched the proffered liquor and hurried away, no doubt to consume his payment as fast as possible.

"Greetings, *mes amis!*" the Frenchman announced in a hoarse, croaking voice. "Welcome, men of the *Absalom* to my humble establishment! *Je suis Crapaud!* Whatever your heart desires can be had here, for a modest price. Is it cuisine you seek? *Mais bien sûr!* Drink? *Oui, oui!* Or perhaps you hunger for the company of a *une jolie fille,* or *un beau garcon?* Crapaud holds the keys to the house of Venus, no matter which door you prefer!"

Upon entering I saw that the interior of the tavern consisted of a single barracks-like room, with tables and chairs fashioned from rattan and bamboo. Several beautiful young native girls, each lovelier than the last and all of them nude from the waist up, were busy hurrying platters of food and drink to the customers. I stared, open-mouthed, until it felt as if my eyes might grow stalks. Although the last fifteen months aboard the *Absalom* had gone a long way to making me a man, I was still innocent as to the fairer sex.

A *wahine* crossed the room and placed a small bundle of taro leaves bound with twine before a man dressed in the uniform of the French navy. The sailor took his knife and cut the string and the leaves unfurled to reveal a succulent pork loin. Upon catching the scent of the roasted meat, I forgot all about the shameless naked flesh on display. After months spent living off jerked meat, hardtack and the thinnest of stews, the sight and smell of freshly prepared food was enough to make me drool like a starving hound.

"Jonas! Over here!"

I spotted Santo seated at a table near the bar. The ship's cooper was given his liberty far earlier in the day and had gone into the village to barter with the trading post for a new blade for his saw. He must have succeeded in his quest, for he was now drinking rum in the company of the local harbor pilot.

"Come! Have a drink!" Santo's companion said with a laugh, motioning for me to join them. Despite his bare feet, sunburned complexion, and lack of a shirt, he spoke with an educated British accent and held his leather tankard like it was the finest cut crystal. "The name's John Michael Arthur Aubrey Monkeith III," he said, offering me his hand as I sat down. "But the locals call me Your Lordship to my face and His Lordship to everyone else."

"Jona—um, Jonas Padgett," I replied awkwardly. If His Lordship considered the fact I stumbled over my own name awkward, he had the breeding not to show it. "Are you really a lord?" I asked, eager to shift the conversation away from myself.

"Only if two brothers and three nephews die before I do," he laughed ruefully. "I'm what is known as a 'remittance man'. That is to say, my family pays me to stay away—and as *far* as possible. My father was *most* insistent on that last part, thanks to a series of unfortunate misunderstandings between myself a number of creditors in London.

"It might sound cruel on the behalf of the old *pater familias*, but to be honest, I don't miss England —the weather there is miserable—and I *certainly* don't miss my family—save for my mother, bless her. I was originally sent to the Caribbean to oversee the family's sugar plantation, but I ran afoul of yet *another* misunderstanding in Barbados, which necessitated my signing on with a whaler headed 'round the Horn. That's how I ended up on this beauteous island paradise —by jumping ship the first chance I got!

"Of course, back then Nuka Hiva was called Madison Island and was under the American flag. I stayed after your countrymen abandoned their outpost, and when the French staked their claim, they made me the harbor pilot since I know the waters hereabouts like I know the alphabet. The natives know me and like me well enough not to have eaten me yet, and I can speak their tongue as well as French. The colonial government pays me a little stipend for my services, and once a year the mail ship arrives with a packet from my elder brother, the new Earl—my father having succumbed to chronic high dudgeon some time ago—that allows me to keep myself properly amused during the monsoon seasons.

"I suspect, once my mother finally passes away, the remittance payments will cease altogether, but until that time, I am more than willing--and capable--of buying myself and anyone else, should it suit my fancy, a round of drinks. So what will it be, young Padgett?"

"If it's all the same to you, Your Lordship," I replied, wiping at the saliva at the corner of my mouth, "I would like to have something to eat."

"Of course! Poor boy, you must be famished! I remember all too well the filth they served aboard the whaler that brought me here." His Lordship snapped his fingers and one of topless bar maids suddenly appeared at our table like a *houri* summoned from heaven. "Petani, my dear, sweet girl," the Englishman said with a politely drunken smile, "please bring my young friend here the house special—and some more rum, while you're at it."

As I waited for my food to arrive, I took the occasion to study my surroundings a bit more closely. Most of the clientele seemed to be split between French colonists and the crew from the *Absalom,* but there were also a handful of natives mixed amongst them as well. A pair of tribesmen sat cross-legged on woven mats set on the floor, talking amongst themselves as they drank from hand-carved bowls. Both men were as hairless as eggs, with heads that gleamed like polished stones, and wore necklaces made of shark's teeth. Although their limbs were covered with intricate tattoos, their faces were unmarked, save for three long, curving dark lines inked onto either side of their necks.

I also spotted a tall, powerfully built fellow seated by himself at a nearby table, sipping grog from the shorn half-shell of a coconut. But where the other natives bore tattooing on their arms and legs, his were bare of adornment. Instead, his torso was covered in a design that resembled a great tidal wave eternally crashing in upon itself. Thrust through his earlobes were two small, intricately scrimshawed sperm-whale teeth, and a similar piece of ivory pierced his nose. In odd contrast to his barbarous appearance, he wore a watch-cap pulled down over his otherwise hairless head.

"That's an unusual piece you're wearing," His Lordship said, drawing my attention away from the naked savage in the wool cap. He gestured to the dolphin amulet hung about my neck. "Wherever did you find it?"

"It was left to me by my uncle," I explained. "It's my good luck charm." Before I could explain any further, the *wahine* Petani returned with a large wooden platter on which was arrayed a bowl of grayish-purple mash, a bundle of taro leaves wrapped in twine, and a bottle of rum. As she placed my meal before me, Petani flashed me a smile that almost made me forget the gnawing hunger in my belly.

"Don't worry about table manners, old chap," His Lordship laughed as I looked about for eating utensils. "The natives eat everything with their hands, including the *poi*." He demonstrated by plunging two fingers into the sticky substance and--with a practiced twirl--

popped his purple-coated digits into his mouth.

I followed his example, although with considerably less expertise and far more mess. Despite my ineptitude, I still managed to get enough of the *poi* into my mouth to find it sweet, starchy and agreeable to the Western palate. I then eagerly tore open the taro leaf and began stuffing the tender morsels of roast pork into my mouth. After months of whaler's rations, I had to keep from swooning in ecstasy. As I hungrily gobbled down my meal, the Toad Hole's proprietor waddled up to the table.

"I trust you and your companions find everything *satisfaisant*, Your Lordship?" Crapaud asked as he mopped the back of his neck with his sodden handkerchief.

"Everything is *magnifique* as always, *mon ami*," His Lordship replied as he pulled the cork out of the rum bottle with his teeth.

Just then I looked up from my meal to see a third native join the pair seated on the floor. His loins were girt by heavy folds of *tapa* hanging fore-and-aft in clusters of braided tassels, and his limbs were covered in elaborate tattooing that reminded me of my dear mother's lace patterns. But what truly caught my attention was the scar that traversed the right side of his face, and the fact the corresponding eye had been reduced to a withered, gray dead thing hiding in the back of its socket. From the way that his companions greeted him, it was obvious this man was their superior, possibly even a chieftain, although I could not spot any outward sign that differentiated him from the others, save the wound to his face.

As the one-eyed native moved to join his tribesmen,

he glanced in the direction of our table and abruptly froze. He then fixed upon me a flat and unwavering stare with his remaining eye, regarding me with such harshness I instinctively recoiled. I was as much baffled as I was unnerved, for I could not ascertain what I could possibly have done to earn such a hostile glare. The native then said something to one of his companions, nodding in my direction as he did so. As the tribesmen spoke amongst themselves, I was alarmed to discover that their teeth were as sharp as those strung around their necks.

Seeing the look on my face, His Lordship gave an amused laugh. "So you've finally noticed the cannibals at the bar, have you?"

I turned to stare at Crapaud in disbelief. "You allow such beings in your place of business?" I gasped.

The Frenchman shrugged his shoulders. "*Monsieur*, if I was to bar all those who have tasted human flesh from my establishment, I would be out of business in a week! *All* natives on this island--and the others that surround it--partake in the ritual of the cannibal at one time or another in their lives."

"That is true," Santo agreed with a sage nod of his head. "But there are tribes considered cannibals, even amongst the cannibals."

"You mean the Typee," His Lordship said darkly.

"Is that what those three gentlemen are?" I asked nervously.

"*Non,*" Crapaud replied with a shake of his head. "The Typee, they keep to their valley. I do not know what tribe these claim, but they are not of Nuka Hiva. Perhaps they hail from Tahuata or Eiao?" The Frenchman turned to address the harbor pilot, who was busy pouring another finger or two of rum into his tankard. "What do you think, Your Lordship? You know the Marquesans far better than I do."

His Lordship set aside his bottle and contemplated the trio of savages like an ornithologist attempting to identify a species of bird. "Whatever they are, they aren't Marquesans. I do not recognize their tattoos as belonging to the tribes on this or any of the islands in the chain."

"You mean you can tell all that by the scribble on their bodies?" I exclaimed in surprise.

"It may look like meaningless scrawl to you, my young friend—but it is much, much more. In a world where everyone walks around starkers, there's still got to be a way to show that you're a high *muckamuck*, or what's the point of being one? And I say that coming from a long line of *muckamucks,* myself. No, the tattoos on a native tell you who they are, where they hail from, and their role and importance. And each tribe has a style and set of designs unique to itself. I've lived on Nuka Hiva for twelve years, and I have never seen those markings before."

Suddenly the trio of cannibals got to their feet and left, but not before the one-eyed leader threw me a venomous parting glare.

"It would seem their head-man does not care for the cut of your jib," His Lordship commented drily.

"But how could I have possibly insulted him? I didn't even speak to him!" I exclaimed.

"Who knows what goes on in the mind of a savage?" the Englishman replied with a shrug. "I have known them to take offense at the slightest provocation. Perhaps they believe you have broken a *tabu* of their tribe? Not that it matters. Your ship sets sail in a day or two, does it not? So bugger the cannibal bastards and have another drink."

I spent the rest of the day drinking rum and swapping stories with His Lordship and Santo, growing increasingly inebriated as afternoon stretched into dusk then lengthened into evening. Upon seeing both Santo and I stifle a yawn, our newly found friend suggested that we should spend the night at his bungalow. I found the idea of sleeping somewhere besides the fetid confines of the foc'sle quite appealing and had no trouble in coercing Santo into accompanying me.

After settling our tab, the three of us staggered out of the Toad Hole. His Lordship lead the way, armed with a torch provided by the ever-considerate Crapaud, while Santo and I followed close behind, arms linked about one another in the name of comradeship and mutual stability. Thus armed against the night--and whatever dwelt within it--we headed in the direction of the beach.

Chapter Seven

His Lordship's Estate—Santo's Family—Strange Sounds In The Night—The Nightmare Island—Awakened By Cannibals

His Lordship lived in a bungalow cottage located on the wide, horseshoe-shaped beach, less than ten minutes' walk from the wharf where the *Absalom* was anchored. It was built of bamboo, had a thatched roof and sat upon a stone foundation. It also boasted a wide porch supported by heavy wooden posts.

"Welcome to my estate," His Lordship said with a drunken laugh. "It's not much, compared to what my brother inherited, but I daresay the climate and view are a damn sight better." He gestured to the vast, natural amphitheater of the bay, barely a hundred feet from his doorstep. He quickly ducked inside the one-room cottage and returned with a straw-wrapped jug. "I try to keep a little palm wine on hand, should I have visitors," he explained with a laugh. The exiled aristocrat sloshed the milky liquid into a trio of empty tins that had once contained corned beef, but now served as drink ware.

I gave the stuff a wary sniff before trying it, but the moment I tasted its sweetness on my tongue, I tilted the can back and drained it dry. It was like very sweet coconut water, with just a touch of vinegar, and I quickly decided I liked it.

"Be careful, boy," Santo laughed knowingly. "Palm

wine, she is sweet, but she is strong—like my wife!"

"I didn't know you were married, Santo," I said in surprise. Although we had worked side-by-side for months, the cooper and I rarely had time for small talk as we were too busy building casks and barrels.

"Sim," he said, with a proud smile. "She is *muito bonita,* my Magdalena. I go to sea *quarto--cinco anos*, yes? Then I return to my village of Nazaré with my pay. I spend a year with my family. Then I go back to sea. Every time I leave, my wife, she is big in the belly. I have *cinco filhos*: Branco, Gomes, Salazar and Renata."

"That's only four," His Lordship pointed out as he sipped his palm wine.

"Like I said, my Magdalena, she big when I go. When I next return to Nazaré, I see if she has son or daughter for me."

"Your wife doesn't mind you being away from home for so long?" I asked.

"Não!" the cooper said with a laugh. "We are husband and wife twenty *anos*." He held up his right hand, splaying the fingers. "But we only live together *cinco anos*. Every time I return, we are like new, yes?" he said with a wink.

"Doesn't your *Senhora* worry that you will be unfaithful while you're away?" His Lordship queried.

"My Magdalena, she know I never betray her with another woman," Santo replied with a solemn shake of his head. "All this time, I never touch another *garota*—not even a *wahine* or *prostituta*.

"Most commendable," His Lordship said with a crooked smile as he sloshed another round of palm wine into our waiting tins. "I propose a toast to your matrimonial fortitude in the face of temptation!"

I eagerly downed another draught, and then another. But I soon discovered what Santo had said about the drink's potency was indeed true. I found myself too drunk to stand, much less crawl into one of the hammocks His Lordship had kindly strung up on the his porch for us to use, and ended up passing out on a tapa mat, which proved no harder than my regular berth aboard the *Absalom*.

I woke up about an hour later, still drunk and more than a little disoriented. I looked out toward the beach and saw that the moon and stars above the bay had moved in the night sky. I wondered to myself what could have roused me from my sodden slumber. I glanced in the direction of Santo's hammock, only to find my shipmate nowhere to be seen.

It was then I heard a low, muffled sound, like that of someone groaning in pain. As I struggled to push the fog from my mind, I recognized the voice as belonging to Santo and that the sound seemed to be coming from inside the cottage. I got up from my palette and peered through the window, which was covered by a thin curtain of mosquito netting.

Santo stood with his back to me, his pants down about his ankles, revealing his muscular, hairy legs. His head was angled as if he was studying the thatching of the roof, his hands firmly planted on his hips, which rocked to-and-fro. His Lordship knelt before the cooper, his head bobbing up and down rapidly. Whatever Santo was feeling, it most certainly wasn't pain. While I was surprised to see my shipmate in such a compromising position, I was far from shocked. One does not spend fifteen months in the foc'sle without becoming familiar with what lonely men do in the dark when they think no one else is awake.

Seeing that my friend was not in any danger, I discretely returned to my makeshift bed, leaving Santo to remain faithful to his wife, in his fashion. As I lay back down, I turned my drowsy eyes in the direction of the nearby beach and listened to the sound of the surf, which filled my ears like the breathing of a giant, until it lulled me back to sleep.

"Row, you dogs!"

I was in the whale boat, pulling on the oars. I did not know how I had come to be there, nor did I remember anything leading up to that moment. Instead, it was as if I had spontaneously generated between the gunwales. I looked about and saw we were in the middle of the ocean, and that the *Absalom* was nowhere in sight.

Captain Solomon sat at the tiller, his pipe clenched between his teeth, his solitary eye fixed on the horizon beyond my straining back. As my gaze fell upon the others in the boat, I was surprised to find Haraldson amongst their number, his beard and mustaches decorated with strands of seaweed.

"Put your backs into it, laddies!" the captain shouted urgently. "We have to make that island before the storm o'er takes us!"

Upon hearing the words 'island' and 'storm', I paused in my rowing to glance behind me and saw in the near distance a dark mass rising above the waterline and, in the farther distance, a rapidly approaching squall line, its thick, black thunderheads laced with lightning. My heart leapt in terror at the thought of being caught on the open water in such conditions and I resumed my efforts double-time.

It was not long before we reached what Captain Solomon had called--rather optimistically--an island. In truth, it was more a barren hummock of rock. It looked to me like the uppermost portion of an underwater mountain thrust skyward by some recent volcanic upheaval on the ocean floor. As there was no beachhead in evidence, the captain ordered us to maneuver as close as possible, so that Haraldson could leap onto its sloping shore.

Once there, the Swede was thrown the whale-line and then each of us, in turn, shinnied across like rats onto a ship. Once all of us were on the shore of the strange island, we heaved as one on the line, pulling the boat up after us. Once it was safely ashore, only then was I free to turn my attention to our surroundings.

The island looked to be no more than a mile long and half as wide, like a great loaf of bread afloat in the middle of the Pacific. The ground was black as a bible and reeked strongly of fish. There was no vegetation anywhere to be seen on its godforsaken expanse, nor were there any rock formations.

"He's near," Captain Solomon said, taking the pipe from his mouth and tilting his head back to stare at the broiling sun tacked high in the sky. "I can feel him."

"Who do you mean, Cap'n?" I asked.

"King Jim, of course," he replied. "Or did you forget what we've been chasin' all this time?" With that he bit back down on the pipe stem and began trudging towards the center of the tiny island, Haraldson and the others trailing after him.

As I hurried after my shipmates the toe of my boot struck against something, nearly causing me to fall on my face. I bent down to investigate and saw a twisted piece of metal about the length and breadth of my hand jutting from the otherwise smooth surface of the islet. I tugged on it and, to my surprise, pulled it free like Arthur drawing Excalibur from the stone. But instead of a sword, what I held in my hand was a harpoon.

As I did so, the ground beneath me began to tremble and roil, like the skin of a horse seeking to rid itself of flies. Captain Solomon and the others were knocked down like a set of duckpins by the earthquake. Then there came a rumbling sound from deep within the island itself, and suddenly a geyser burst forth not far from where I stood, showering me in bright red gore.

As I staggered backward, wiping at the blood streaming down into my face, I saw Captain Solomon, the dead Swede and the others lose their purchase in the scarlet downpour and slide off the back of the awakened sea-beast and plunge into the ocean below. I watched in horror as my captain and fellow shipmates were torn limb from limb before my eyes by the monstrous sharks that filled the churning waters.

Suddenly there came a noise unlike any I had ever heard before, louder than any roar voiced by mortal throat. I cried out in horror and clamped my hands to my ears, for no man can hear the call of the ocean god and survive unscathed.

I awoke to the sound of Santo cursing in his native tongue. As I opened my eyes, I was greeted by the sight of the Portugee trapped within his hammock, flanked on either side by the cannibals we had seen earlier at the Toad Hole.

The one-eyed headman stepped forward while the others pinned the cooper's arms to his sides, keeping him from rolling free of the hammock, and bared his horrible teeth. The cannibal's mouth seemed to grow to hideous proportions, like a snake unhinging its jaw, then he bit deep into Santo's exposed belly. The cooper's angry shouts quickly dissolved into shrieking, the likes of which I had never heard from a human being before.

As I lay there in the shadows, paralyzed with horror, the one-eyed cannibal yanked free a length of my friend's guts, causing them to unravel from his torso like a magician's scarf. The savage then swallowed the mouthful of pulsing, living flesh whole, without using his hands, his throat expanding as he gulped down his hideous meal.

Excited by the smell of their victim's blood and the sight of his agonized thrashing, the remaining cannibals set upon poor, doomed Santo, ripping into his struggling body like a pair of boars rooting for truffles.

"Get off my porch, you bloody bastards!" His Lordship yelled as he charged out of the bungalow, armed with a native paddle-spear fashioned of *koa* wood.

The Englishman attempted to brain the one-eyed cannibal with the oar blade, but his opponent proved too swift. The savage dodged the blow while sweeping the aristocrat's legs out from under him, causing His Lordship to drop his weapon. The cannibal headman then snatched up the paddle-spear and drove its business-end through His Lordship's chest, pinning him like a butterfly to the floor of the porch. The sight of the blood spurting from the dying man's mouth like the crimson geyser in my nightmare shocked me from my paralysis. Leaping to my feet, I ran towards the beach and the direction of the *Absalom*.

As I sped across the sandy beach, I heard angry shouts behind me. I glanced over my shoulder and instantly wished I had not looked. The trio of cannibals were in close pursuit, their tattooed faces smeared with the blood of my friends, their horrible, shark-like maws opened impossibly wide as if to swallow me whole.

Chapter Eight

An Unexpected Savior—Koro—I Become Ship's Cooper—The New Harpooner—The Watchers On The Hill

I fled my dreadful pursuers as fast as I could, my heart climbing my ribs like a ladder until I feared it would escape from my mouth. I did not dare cast a second look behind me, for fear the sight would unman me completely. Separated from my shipmates aboard the *Absalom*, I was on my own against the dreadful trio of bloodthirsty murderers chasing me like a pack hounds going after a rabbit.

Suddenly a dark shape stepped out from the palm trees that lined the shore, looming before me like one of the natives' stone gods. I cried out in alarm, thinking one of the cannibals had outflanked me. However, to my surprise, the shadowy figure pushed me aside and hurled a spear at the killers behind me.

The savage at the head of the pack gave a single shriek of agony and dropped to the sand like a poleaxed steer, the haft of a harpoon jutting from his chest. His companions halted to stare down at their slain tribesman. The one-eyed headman then looked up and said something angrily in his heathen tongue, loudly slapping his naked chest with a splayed hand.

My unexpected savior took a step forward into the moonlight and, in response, pulled a knife from the handwoven belt about his waist. It was then I recognized him as the solitary native I had seen at the Toad Hole earlier that evening, the one who wore the watch cap. He answered the cannibal with his own stream of heated gibberish, all while making menacing gestures with his blade. Whatever he said must have proved persuasive, for the remaining cannibals abruptly turned on their heels and fled toward the bay.

As I watched in amazement, the tribesmen leapt headfirst into the surf and disappeared, leaving their dead comrade behind on the beach. They were either very strong swimmers and managed to escape, or drowned almost immediately, for I saw no more sign of them. It was as if the water had swallowed them alive.

The native who had rescued me grunted in disgust and strode over to the body of the tribesman he'd just killed. From the casual manner in which he yanked free the harpoon, you would have thought he had just brought down a wild boar as opposed to a fellow human.

"Thank you, my friend, for delivering me from those horrid cannibals!" I exclaimed, offering him my hand. "My name is Jo—uh, Jonas Padgett. What is your name, good sir?"

"I am called Koro of the Aina," the native replied, in surprisingly passable English. After a moment's hesitation, he took my hand and shook it in a firm but friendly manner. The native was naked save for his loincloth, watch-cap, and the ink that covered his torso. And although a veritable giant with muscles like pythons, he seemed possessed of a genial and trustworthy nature.

"I do not know what brought you to this stretch of

beach, Koro, but I am glad of it! I owe you my life, my friend!"

"I was hunting the Mano Kanaka," he said, pointing to the dead cannibal at his feet. "They are the ancestral enemy of my people, and I know their ways. I saw them follow you when you left. I knew they would try and kill you."

"If they were looking for a cannibal feast, why choose the three of us where there are plenty of solitary sailors wandering about tonight?"

Koro pointed to the dolphin talisman about my neck. "*That* is why the Mano Kanaka chose you. It is the totem of my people. That is what made them want to kill you, and it is what made me want to help you."

"My Uncle Calvin, rest his soul, always said this was a good luck charm," I said, patting the amulet like a faithful pet. "I must go now and alert the Captain as to what has happened. I would very much appreciate your company on these errands, friend Koro, in case those fiendish Mano Kanaka, as you call them, decide to come back."

"Whatever you wish of me, it is my honor to obey," the native said, bowing his head in acquiescence.

And that is how the greatest friendship of my life began.

Upon reaching the *Absalom*, I promptly reported to Mr. Levant, who was in charge of the night watch. I related how Santo and I had availed ourselves of His Lordship's generosity—although I left out the part about Santo availing himself of our host's hospitality even further—and the subsequent cannibal attack. By the time I'd gotten to my rescue by Koro, the Third Mate raised his bushy brows and proclaimed: "There's nothing much I would rouse the Cap'n for, save a typhoon or King Jim. But, by damn, I'm waking him up for this."

A few minutes later a bedraggled Captain Solomon emerged from his cabin with a sour look on his face. But upon seeing the harpoon-wielding Koro--dressed in his loincloth and watch-cap--his demeanor quickly changed. I once more related my story, and as I described the cannibals I saw a glimmer of recognition in his eyes.

"Mano Kanaka, you say?" he muttered, rubbing his chin. "The tribe sounds familiar. I believe your uncle and I had a run in with such heathen man-eaters, long years ago. Very disagreeable buggers, if memory serves. Mr. Levant! Grab a lantern and gather a shore party! We've a fallen shipmate to claim."

The shore party sent to gather up what remained of Santo consisted of Captain Solomon, Mr. Levant, Koro, two deck hands, and me. The hands carried between them a roll of sailcloth plus needle and thread, and the rest of us bore lanterns to light our way. Just to be on the safe side, every one of us was also armed with a weapon, whether it was pistol, knife, hand-ax or belaying pin, while Koro--easily the most physically intimidating member of the expedition--carried his harpoon balanced on his shoulder like a soldier on parade.

As we re-traced our route along the beach, Captain Solomon called a halt upon spotting the body of the dead cannibal. “What a dreadful thing to be a man’s last sight,” he muttered as he examined the carcass. He frowned and pointed to the markings on either side of the dead man’s neck. “What manner of wounds are those?”

As I stared down at the corpse, I realized that what I had initially mistaken for tattoos on either side of the cannibal’s throat were, in fact, subcutaneous incisions of some sort, designed to resemble the gills of a fish.

“No doubt it’s some type of heathen adornment, Cap’n,” Mr. Levant suggested. “They’re always muckin’ with their bodies to make themselves look fierce to their enemies. That would explain their jaws as well.” He nudged the cannibal’s unusually wide mouth with its mouth full of jagged teeth. “I hear tell of African savages that stick plates the size of saucers in their lips and Red Indians that wrap their babies’ heads to make the skull come to a point. There’s no tellin’ what fancy will take root in a primitive mind.”

Captain Solomon’s demeanor grew even grimmer once we reached the bungalow and he what was left of Santo and His Lordship. “A harpoon to the heart is too good for the murderin’ savages,” he growled. “Get to work, maties—stitch up a proper sailor’s shroud for the Portugee.” He then nodded in my direction. “As for you, young Padgett—you’re now the ship’s cooper. I’ll have your shares adjusted accordingly in the company books.”

Normally I would have been pleased by such news, but given the conditions under which I found myself being elevated I could take no joy in it. Santo had been a good fellow, and an excellent craftsman--one I would be hard-pressed to surpass. I thought about his beloved Magdalena, back in Portugal, now awaiting her husband's return from the sea in vain, and my heart grew heavier still.

Once Santo's body was sewn up inside his canvas shroud, Captain Solomon ordered Mr. Levant and his men to stand guard over the bodies, in case the cannibals came back to finish their meal. He then had Koro and me escort him into the village, so we could repeat our story, yet again, to the French authorities.

The Governor's mansion was a two-story colonial-style edifice, similar to those found in Fiji, with wide verandas and shady porches built to shelter the wandering citizens of France from the punishing tropical sun. It was far from a palace, but compared to the humble huts of the surrounding natives it was a veritable Versailles. As for the Governor himself, he was not in the least bit pleased at being dragged from his bed at such an hour, and unafraid to say so in every language he knew. But upon hearing my story, he lost no time in sending a squadron of soldiers from the nearby garrison to relieve Mr. Levant's watch and claim His Lordship's body.

It was dawn by the time I returned to the *Absalom*. Upon reaching the boarding plank, Captain Solomon stopped and turned to eye Koro, who had followed me--as silent and docile as a hound--every step of the way.

"I'm in sore need of a new harpooner, Koro. And I don't have to ask if you can throw that thing," he said, motioning to the harpoon. "The question is, are ye interested in signin' on?"

Koro turned to look at me. "Will you be on the ship?"

I nodded my head.

He turned back to Captain Solomon and smiled. "Yes. I will be your new harpooner."

We buried Santo later that same day, along with His Lordship, as the tropic heat is not kind to corpses, especially ones so roughly treated. The cooper's final resting place was on a hillside with a splendid view of the bay. The ship's carpenter and I built a coffin from the lumber used to make the barrels and casks, in tribute to our fallen shipmate.

There was a decent turn out as Santo had been well-liked amongst the crew, and Captain Solomon recited a psalm or two, since there were no missionaries on the island. His Lordship's mourners numbered only the Governor and Crapaud, who seemed genuinely grieved over the loss of his best customer. I wondered how many years the long-suffering brother back in England would continue sending remittance payments before discovering the family's black sheep was dead.

Once all was said and done, we trooped back to the *Absalom*, now re-provisioned and ready to set sail. As we left the island, I went to the rail to bid farewell to its wild, exotic beauty. As I looked toward the mountain spires, I espied two figures standing side-by-side on a grassy, windswept hill, watching the *Absalom* slip its way between Nuka Hiva's guardian islets. I rubbed my eyes and looked again, but all there was to see were a pair of freshly turned graves.

Chapter Nine

Freed From The Fo'c'sle—Reading The Waves—A Holiday Feast—Ghost Stories Before The Mast—A Christmas Swim

Upon being named ship's cooper there was not only an increase in my lay but also an upgrade in my accommodations aboard the *Absalom.* No longer was I consigned to the fo'c'sle, with its trapped farts and piss-soaked corners. Instead, I was to bunk in steerage, with the harpooners and other skilled members of the crew such as the blacksmith, carpenter, and cook. My new digs were entered through the after hatch, located just forward of the main cabin and officers' quarters. On the port side were the bunk rooms, each of which held two sets of narrow bunk-beds fitted with thin mattresses and even flatter pillows. After spending months sleeping on a bare wooden bunk surrounded by twenty-three other men, it seemed like the height of luxury.

Another perk of my new station was a much appreciated change in diet. Where before I had been forced to take my meals on the deck, I now dined in the main cabin--granted, after the captain and the mates had left the table. And where once there was naught but hardtack, jerked beef, beans and cold coffee, now I feasted on fresh meats and fresh-made biscuits. Save for the lack of butter and sugar--and having to use molasses to sweeten my coffee--I daresay I ate as well as Captain Solomon himself.

As was to be expected, I took over Santo's berth and Koro claimed what had once been Haraldson's. And as luck would so have it, both happened to be in the same room. My other bunkmates were the ship's carpenter, Hawley, and the blacksmith, Cuppy, who were my elders by several years. While they proved genial enough living companions, it was clear that they viewed me with the same bemusement old dogs hold for a bumbling puppy. So it was only natural that I would gravitate more towards Koro's company during my off-hours.

There is a distinct social hierarchy on board a whaling ship, and the harpooners are often viewed as a breed apart. Although the late Swede had proven affable enough, the majority kept to themselves and often took their mess seated together in the main cabin. Before my most singular introduction to Koro, I had never spoken more than a handful of words to any of the ship's harpooners, and I had most certainly never known a South Seas Islander before. Koro would prove my introduction to both worlds.

Upon signing on, Koro forsook his native loin cloth in favor of a pair of canvas pants, the cuffs of which halted a good inch or three above his ankles. Out of curiosity, he tried on one of the denim shirts in the Swede's sea chest, only to have it burst at the seams the first time he flexed his biceps. As he could not find a shirt that could accommodate him, Koro decided to go about bare-chested, save for the swirls of ink that decorated his midriff. The only item of clothing he retained from our first meeting was the wool watch-cap, which he wore day and night atop his otherwise hairless head. He even wore it in his sleep.

As was to be expected, Koro's physical prowess made him a worthy addition to the crew. He was a tireless oarsman, whether in pursuit or the hauling-back, and would take his place between the gunnels without complaint. But what amazed me was his ability to read waves.

All mariners, in time, learn how to read the ocean by studying the stars and watching the clouds and birds. But in Koro's case he could rest his hand atop the surface of the sea and divine from its movements how close land might be, and in which direction. You might think that is so much sun-addled balderdash, but I assure you it is the truth.

A stone thrown in a pond results in ripples, does it not? Any object that breaks the surface will affect the pattern of the ripples, whether the body of water is as small as a pond or as vast as the Pacific Ocean. Islands and atolls have the same effect as rocks. When waves hit an island, some are reflected back in the direction from which they came, while others are deflected at angles around the island and continue onward in a different form. The Polynesians are schooled in such navigation from birth, and that is how they can travel from Fiji to Tahiti without the use of compass, maps, or sextants. Simply by using his sense of touch, Koro was able to read the ripples and waves of the ocean the same way a phrenologist reads the bumps on one's head. This also held true for passing ships and the great beasts that we hunted, all of which he claimed generated their own unique patterns.

But as far as the *Absalom* was concerned, Koro's true

worth lay in his skill with the harpoon, and in that there was no equal. If he threw an iron, it was certain to find its mark and sink deep on first strike. He could all but thread the eye of a needle with the damned thing. There was no hauling back of lost throws whenever Koro stood in the bow, and I never once saw him flinch as the behemoths breached the surface, sending spray and spume in all directions. He always stood fast, motionless as a statue, no matter how rough the seas.

Captain Solomon was very pleased with his new hire and sang his praises every chance he got. This did not sit well with the other harpooners, of course--all of whom had been there far longer and considered themselves far more experienced in the business of whaling. However, if Koro was aware of the jealous looks cast his way by Mulogo and the others, he did not show it to me or anyone else.

On those evenings we were both at leisure, Koro and I would sit on the deck and watch the stars as they pinwheeled overhead. I would smoke my pipe while Koro covered a whale's tooth in scrimshaw, and we would talk about the worlds we had left behind or the worlds we hoped one day to see. Although, I admit it was me who did most of the talking, while Koro did most of the listening. Still, those were good times--the kind you tuck away for colder, darker days to remind yourself that there was once a moment in your life where you were content with the world, and your place in it.

Of course, it could not last.

Normally, the life of a whaling man is one of deprivation and hard work that most outside the poor house will never know. However, there are two days of the year where the entire crew is allowed a day of rest and pleasure. The first is the day commemorating the birth of our great country; the second is the day commemorating the birth of our blessed Savior.

In truth, the festivities aboard the *Absalom* began on Christmas Eve, with Pedro the cook preparing a proper holiday feast in the galley. Captain Solomon and his mates were presented with a roast suckling pig, with mashed potatoes and baked turnips, along with bottles of wine, while the skilled hands dined on boiled turkey with oyster sauce, washed down with sweet cider. As for the rest of the crew, in place of their usual meal of hardtack and jerked beef, there was a savory stew, and each hand was presented with a small mince pie and extra rations of rum.

While not all the hands aboard the *Absalom* were Christian—indeed, more than a few were heathens in the truest sense of the word—this did not deter them from sharing in the celebration. Jones the Orkneyman brought out his concertina and played a fine shanty, while Virgil, Homer, Marcus and Mulogo demonstrated the dances of their shared ancestry.

"Why do you rejoice tonight?" Koro asked, frowning in puzzlement as he watched the gathered crew sing and laugh and lift their leather flagons in merry toast.

"We're celebrating the birth of our god," I explained.

"A god has been born on this ship?" Koro exclaimed, looking about in surprise.

"No, my friend," I laughed, clapping him on one broad shoulder. "Our god was born long ago, in a land far away. He died but came back to us, and promises eternity in paradise if we give our love to Him and live by His rules. Tonight we honor His birth and the brotherhood of man, for through His love, all of us are as brothers for we are all His children."

"That is a good thing to celebrate," Koro conceded. "My people also honor our god, Tangaroa--Lord of the Ocean--with celebration."

Fearing I was about to hear a story of hapless virgins hurled alive into volcanoes to appease native gods--thereby ruining my Christmas cheer--I cut Koro short by pouring him some more rum and stuffing a mince pie in his hand, both of which he eagerly consumed.

As the evening progressed and the merrymaking continued, the conversation turned, as it always does on Christmas Eve, to the telling of ghost stories. "Anyone ever hear tell of the *Caleuche*?" Cuppy the blacksmith asked.

"Ain't she a ghost ship what sails near Chiloe Island, off the coast of Chile?" Mr. Shreve replied.

"Aye," the blacksmith said as he lit his pipe. "And a wondrous sight she is, shinin' beautiful and bright in the night, like a star on the water."

"How do you know *that*, Cuppy?" The second mate asked with a disbelieving laugh.

"Because I seen her with me own eyes, sir," the old man replied, tapping his right temple with the stem of his pipe. "It was long years ago, back when I shipped on the *Bunker Hill*. It was midnight and we was off the coast of the archipelago when I seen it. The whole ship were aglow, as if painted in Saint Elmo's Fire! And although I could hear the sounds of people laughin' and playin' music like they was havin' themselves a fine party, there was no one to be seen on deck!

"Then, just as sudden as she appeared the ship began to submerge—but not like she run aground. It was more like the soundin' of a whale, once they've taken their air. I looked down and I could see the ghost-ship glowin' under the water, sailin' beneath the waves as pretty as the *Bunker Hill* sailed atop 'em! And as I watched, I seen a woman leave the captain's quarters and stand on the poop deck. Her body were human on one side, and fish on the other. The side that were human was beautiful beyond compare, with long blonde hair that floated about her head like a cloud. On the side that were fish, she was covered in golden scales."

"What you saw was the *Sirena Chilota*," Mr. Gussett said sagely. "She's a water spirit what escorts the souls of drowned sailors to the afterlife aboard the *Caleuche*. Once the dead are on board, they resume their lives as they were before they died."

"What he saw was the bottom of a bottle of rum, more like!" Mr. Shreve said with a dismissive laugh. "There ain't no such animal as a mermaid! I don't care what you call 'em, or what half of them be fishy and what half be woman!"

"I wouldn't be so quick to scoff, sir," Cuppy replied dourly. "I been on the water longer than most of you been alive. There's things in the ocean that no man can explain. Who is to say mermaids ain't one of them?"

"Not *all* merfolk got the nethers of a fish," Jones the Orkneyman pointed out. "The selkie that haunt the waters of me people wear the skins of seals, they do. On Midsummer's Eve they come out of the sea and cast aside their selkie-skins and appear as beautiful women and handsome men. They dance on lonely stretches of beach and bask in the sun on outlyin' skerries, for they have no human shame. Some even fall in love with mortal men and women and have children with 'em—but in time, they all return to the sea. It's in their nature, y'know."

"Kamoho, King Of All The Sharks, often takes human lovers," Koro said suddenly, speaking in all earnestness. "When he crawls out of the sea to walk amongst the people of the land, he takes on the form of a mighty chief. Dressed in his majestic skin, he walks amongst them, partaking in their sports and enjoying their bounty, always looking for the most beautiful woman of the tribe. Once he finds her, he lies down with her and fills her belly with his seed, then returns to the sea."

"Sounds t'me like ol' Kamoho is a sailor," Mr. Shreve said with a wink and a nod.

"When it is the woman's time to deliver," Koro continued, ignoring the Second Mate's interruption, "she gives birth to a shark pup, not a human baby. Once she sees what she has brought forth, she hurls it into the sea, where it swims off in search of its father and its many brothers. When Kamoho's sons grow to adulthood they, too, leave the ocean in the form of men to search for women and to feast on human flesh. They are the Mano Kanaka: the Eaters of Men; the Children of the Shark-God."

"Mano Kanaka--isn't that the name of the cannibal tribe that killed Santo?" I asked.

Koro nodded his head. "Yes. They are one and the same. One day a princess of my people was swimming in the bay when a Mano Kanaka saw her. The princess was very beautiful, but because the Mano Kanaka was in the water, he did not want to mate with her but wanted to devour her. The princess swam very fast and very hard, but the Mano Kanaka swam even faster. Just when it seemed she could not escape, a sailor on a ship anchored in the bay leapt into the water and onto the back of the Mano Kanaka, stabbing it with his knife and killing it. The princess was so grateful to the brave sailor she became his wife."

"Them native girls, they know how to thank a man proper!" Mr. Shreve said with an inebriated guffaw. "Am I right, mates? None of that hand-holdin' in the front parlor with a pair of maiden aunties watchin' you like hawks! They know what a man needs from a woman, and ain't shy about givin' it to 'em! Why, I remember this little *wahine* in Fiji—breasts like peaches she had, and a bottom as firm as a melon..."

Koro's face flushed bright red and he abruptly got to his feet, leaving the Second Mate to regale his eager listeners about the pleasures of his Fiji conquest. The harpooner stalked over to the railing and stared down at the wine-dark ocean. I trailed after him, surprised by the sudden change in his mood.

"That story you told about the princess and the shark—that was just a legend, wasn't it?" I asked. "Like Jones' seal-people and Cuppy's ghost-ship?"

"No; it is a true story," he replied, not taking his eyes from the dark water. "It is the story of how I came into the world. The princess was my mother, and the sailor was my father."

I stood there for a long moment, thinking about Koro's tale and the story Captain Solomon had told me about how my Uncle Calvin once saved a native girl from a shark. Was it possible that Koro's father and Uncle Cal were the same man? It would certainly explain the strong sense of kinship I had felt towards him from the moment we first met. But such a thing was impossible. Captain Solomon said that Uncle Cal's bride had killed both herself and their son by walking into the sea.

I glanced down and saw that I was clutching the amulet my uncle had given me without realizing it. Perhaps it was the extra rations of rum, but for the tiniest moment the red coral dolphin seemed to stir in my hand.

◆ ◆ ◆

After thoroughly partaking of the holiday's good spirits I stumbled off to my bunk, leaving my fellow shipmates to continue their merry-making without me. I slept so soundly I barely registered the arrival of my bunkmates when they finally trooped in later in the evening.

A few hours later I was prodded awake by my bladder. I crawled out of my bunk and lifted the lid of the wooden commode-box just inside the door of the bunk room and relieved myself in the chamber-pot. As I closed the lid and turned back to bed, I heard Cuppy and the ship's carpenter, Hawley, snoring away. I automatically glanced in the direction of Koro's bunk—only to find it empty.

It had to be well past midnight. Where could he possibly be? Still more than a little drunk, I decided to go in search of my friend. As I made my way above deck, I could tell by the angle of the stars in the sky that it was early Christmas morn, perhaps an hour or two before the dawn. The boat was eerily silent and I saw no one moving about, as Captain Solomon had relieved the night watch of their duties.

As I made my way to the prow of the ship, I spotted a pair of canvas pants neatly folded into a square resting on the portside deck, atop which sat a tidily folded wool watch cap. There was no doubt in my mind as to whom the garments belonged. I looked around, hoping to see some sign of Koro. Then I heard the sound of something splashing in the water below. I looked over the rail and was surprised to see Koro swimming in the open ocean as easily as you or I might swim in a pond. Suddenly a fin broke the surface and sped in his direction. But before I could call out a warning, a small spume of spray shot forth from the top of the sleek gray shape's head, followed by a series of telltale clicks and squeals. As the porpoise drew closer to where Koro was swimming it shot out of the water, pirouetting in midair as if propelled by sheer joy, its wet hide glistening like a polished stone in the early morning starlight.

The harpooner did not seem in the least surprised by the dolphin's arrival or concerned with its close proximity. Instead, he laughed, as one would upon greeting an old friend one has not seen in many years. To my surprise, as the animal swam past him Koro reached out and grabbed its dorsal fin. Not only did the porpoise not seem to mind such familiarity it also willingly pulled Koro along behind it as if this was the most natural thing in the world. Even from such a distance and in such poor light, I could see the look of delight on Koro's face as his aquatic playmate sped through the water.

Then, without warning, the dolphin sounded, taking Koro along with him. I expected my friend to abandon his game and quickly resurface upon realizing the porpoise was headed for deeper water, but his head did not pop up above the waves. A minute passed, followed by another, and still there was no sign of Koro. Trying to control the panic rising in my heart, I hurried over to the starboard rail to see if perhaps the dolphin had carried the native underneath the ship, but there was no sign of him there, as well. I dashed back to where I had last seen my friend, trying to decide if I should raise the alarm of 'Man Overboard!'

Just as I was about to give myself over to despair, a pair of cavorting dolphins leapt from the water and somersaulted in midair. I was so amazed I momentarily forgot all about Koro and instead watched, slack-jawed, as the aquatic tumblers splashed back down. A moment or so later, Koro's bald head popped back up above the waves, gleaming like a pearl. Apparently unharmed and no worse for being underwater for over five minutes, the islander swam back to the ship and grabbed hold of the anchor chain, which he used to climb back onto the *Absalom*.

I dropped back from the railing before Koro could catch sight of me. Whatever his reasons for indulging in his strange pre-dawn swim, they were none of my business. Besides, I sensed that what I had just witnessed was never meant to be seen by civilized eyes. What was it that he had said earlier? *'My people also honor our god Tangaroa, Lord of the Ocean, with celebration.'*

I hurried back to steerage and returned to my berth. If Cuppy or Hawley noticed my absence, they gave no sign of it. A few minutes later Koro entered and crawled into his bunk, still smelling of the sea.

Chapter Ten

The Sugar Bowl—Mulogo's Wager—To The Boats —Koro Stabs The Whale—Man Overboard!

It was a couple of weeks into the new year, and I had all but forgotten Koro's strange Christmas morning swim. We were seated at the table in the main galley, breaking our fast. I was wedged, as usual, between Koro and Mr. Hawley and seated opposite Mulogo. The African scowled at us by way of greeting, as he did most every morning. He had never been the friendliest of the harpooners, but since Koro came aboard his temperament had soured even further.

Pedro the cook set down a large pot of fresh coffee in the middle of the table. Then, to everyone's surprise, he placed a small bowl of sugar lumps down beside it. Normally sugar and butter were reserved for the officer class, but on rare occasions the Cap'n would indulge the skilled hands and harpooners as a reward.

Mulogo grinned and reached for the sugar bowl, only to have Pedro slap away his hand. "Cap'n say only Koro get sugar," the cook said in heavily accented English. "It his reward for killin' more whale."

"I kill as many whale as Koro does!" Mulogo retorted angrily.

"Cap'n not say Mulogo get sugar. He say *Koro* get sugar," the cook said sternly, waving a cleaver in the African's face.

Mulogo grudgingly drew back his hand, for fear of losing it to Pedro's knife skills.

"Go ahead," I said, nudging Koro with my elbow. "Claim your reward."

He warily eyed the sugar bowl as if it was a strange and potentially dangerous animal. "What do I do?" he asked.

"Put it in your coffee," I replied. "Just like you do with the molasses."

Koro tentatively picked up one of the lumps of sugar, turning it around between his thumb and forefinger as if studying it, before dropping it in his coffee. Pedro promptly snatched the sugar bowl off the table and whisked it back to its hiding place in the ship's pantry, where it safely resided under lock and key. The entire table sat in silence, their own meals forgotten, and watched as Koro lifted the cup of sugared coffee to his lips and took a long sip.

"So—how is it?" I asked.

"Too sweet," he replied with a grimace as he set the tin cup back down.

After finishing our meal we trooped out of the galley and onto the deck. Once we were in the open, Mulogo turned to face Koro. "I bet I kill the next whale before you do, Islander!" he said angrily.

"What are you willing to wager then?" I sneered in response. "It's not a proper bet unless you have something to lose."

Mulogo reached into his pocket and withdrew a watch, holding it up so that everyone could see.

The case was much-worn and bore more than a few scratches, but it was obvious to the naked eye that it was gold. "Is this good enough?" he asked.

"It will do," I conceded. I glanced at Koro, who was observing the proceedings with a concerned look on his face. "What say you, my friend? Do you accept Mulogo's wager?"

"I do not have anything of value," he replied simply.

"You needn't worry, I am more than willing to stake you," I laughed. "I gladly bet my good luck charm that you will be first to kill the next whale!"

"You must not do that, Jonas!" Koro gasped, an alarmed look on his face. "That talisman is your protection!"

"It's all right," I assured him, patting the amulet as if it would soothe him as well. "The Cap'n's right: you *are* the finest harpooner on this ship. Every iron you throw finds its mark. I have perfect faith in you, Koro."

As if on cue, a voice sang out from high in the crow's nest overhead: *"Thar she blows! Whale off the starboard bow!"*

Upon hearing the cry, the *Absalom's* crew burst into action, each officer yelling for his crew to launch the boats. Suddenly the decks were swarming with men, like ants crawling over a picnic lunch.

It turned out that the *Absalom* had sailed up on a small pod of Right whales that fine January morning. Although the oil rendered from the blubber of such animals wasn't worth as much as Sperm oil, it was still of high quality. More importantly, the Rights strained the meals they took from the sea with mouths full of baleen—the stuff used to make buggy whips, umbrella ribs, and the stays in ladies' corsets.

Personally, I preferred hunting Rights as they were quite docile as such creatures go and tended not to shy away from the boats. The Sperm whales, on the other hand, were predators by nature and, as such, knew a hunt when they saw it. Also, the Rights--once killed--float in the water and are much easier to tow back to the ship, whereas it was a struggle to keep a Sperm afloat from the moment it was slain.

The news of the wager between Mulogo and Koro spread amongst the hands faster than cholera. There is nothing like a contest of skill to stir the blood of sailors, especially those bored from being too long at sea. The oarsmen of each whale boat were determined to do whatever it took to help claim the honor of the first kill for their respective harpooner. That is why--compared to the other officers--the boats piloted by Captain Solomon and Mr. Godward flew across the waves that day. I was rowing so fast my good luck charm tapped against my breastbone like a door knocker. Every so often I would spare a sideways glance towards Mr. Godward's boat, only to see my opposite number glowering back at me.

Of course, Captain Solomon and Mr. Godward knew nothing about the wager between their harpooners--or what was at stake--for such things are above the officers. But if either man was surprised by their crew's eagerness for the hunt, neither of them showed any interest in finding out why.

Our prey was a large cow placidly feeding on krill much like its four-footed counterpart would graze in a meadow. Like all Rights, she had a rotund body, an arching rostrum, dark-gray skin with rough, white patches atop her head, and an exceptionally broad back.

As we got within striking distance, the Captain sang out and Koro took his stand. As he did so, Mr. Godward's boat suddenly shot forward, bringing them a good fifty feet closer to the target. To my surprise, I saw that Mulogo was already in position, framed against the hard blue sky of the Pacific like a proud African prince, his harpoon drawn back in preparation of its murderous flight.

Mulogo hurled his harpoon with all his considerable might, striking the whale in the shoulder blade. The men in Mr. Godward's boat let out a loud huzzah to celebrate their man landing the first strike. In response, the hands in our boat once more grabbed oars and shot forward another hundred feet.

"Have you fools gone mad?" Captain Solomon shouted. *"We're too close to the damned thing!"*

As my back was to the whale, I did not see what happened next. However, I did have an unobstructed view of the look of horror and amazement that crossed Captain Solomon's face as he cried out: *"Merciful God! Koro! What are you doing?"*

No longer able to contain myself, I shipped my oars and turned about to see what could so shock a man who had seen everything the ocean could possibly cough up, only to find my friend no longer in the bow of the whaleboat. My first thought was that he had fallen afoul of the line, like poor Haraldson before him, and had been jerked into the sea—then I realized that Koro had yet to throw his harpoon.

"I've never seen anything like it!" Captain Solomon exclaimed. "He jumped twenty feet from a standing start, right onto the damned beast's back! The damn fool heathen is going to get his-self killed, and us in the bargain!"

It was then I saw Koro on the swimming whale, armed with one of the killing irons used to sever the arteries. He was racing along its back in a dead run in the direction of the beast's head. Without thinking, I got to my feet and shouted at the top of my lungs: *"Koro! No!"*

If my friend heard my words above the rush and roar of the whale, he did not heed them. He raised the lance on high and plunged it with both hands into the Right's neck. A gout of blood instantly burst forth from the creature's blowhole, followed by it surging forward in a panicked attempt to flee whatever was attacking it. The water was instantly churned into chop rough enough to raise the bow of the whaleboat several feet in the air and slam it back down again, much like an angry child playing with a toy.

One moment I was standing in the boat, the bloody spume from the wounded whale falling upon me like scarlet rain, the nexy I heard Nicodemus sing out *"Man overboard!"* But it seemed so far, far away. It wasn't until the salt water closed over my head and poured into my nose, ears and throat, that I realized he meant *me*.

Chapter Eleven

Saved From A Watery Grave—News From The Pilgrimage—Marcus Feeds The Sharks

Even as I was hurled from the captain's boat into the open ocean, I knew rescue would not be soon coming. The fish had yet to go flukes up, and until it did none of the whaleboats could be bothered to collect me. It may seem a cruel decision to place the death of a fish above the life of a man, but for the *Absalom* to lose a whale would affect every member of the crew, while the loss of a single hand would barely reverberate beyond his next of kin. Assuming he had any to mourn his passing in the first place.

Luckily, I knew how to swim. But there is a difference between the mill pond of my youth and the Pacific. I struggled mightily to keep my head above water, which had been made angry and bloody by the death throes of the hunted whale. It was as if my clothes--in particular, my boots--had been transformed into lead. It seemed the ocean floor had claimed me for its own and was drawing me to its dark, wet bosom feet first. The next thing I knew, the waves closed over my head, reducing the sun's fierce, burning glare to a distant, flickering disc.

As I sank downward, I could hear the splash of my shipmates' oars and the shout of their voices, muted and warped by the water that surrounded me. I also heard the eerie moan of the dying whale, carried through the sea just as the cries of a four-legged beast would travel through the air. My lungs began to burn and I wrapped my hands about the dolphin amulet still looped about my neck. I heard my Uncle Cal's voice in my ear, telling me how it would keep me safe from the dangers of the sea.

I saw a shadow cutting through the water in my direction. And although I was well on my way to death's door, my heart still managed to leap with terror. As far as every sailor is considered, it is better to drown than to be torn to bloody bits by sharks. If ever a man was caught between the devil and the deep blue sea, it was I at that very moment.

But just as my lungs could no longer contain themselves, I realized that the sleek figure swimming towards me was not that of a shark, but a dolphin with something trailing from its mouth. At first I thought it was a small squid it had caught. Then I realized--just as the ocean rushed in to fill my lungs--what it held clamped in its jaws was a woolen watch cap.

The next thing I knew I was staring at the bottom of a whaleboat as strong, callused hands pressed against my ribs from behind. I abruptly coughed and vomited up a foul mixture of salt water and bile. I pulled myself onto the rowing bench and nodded a heartfelt thank-you to Nicodemus, who had been the one to resuscitate me.

"How you feelin', Padgett?" Captain Solomon asked from his seat at the tiller.

"Lucky to be alive, sir," I replied truthfully.

"I dare say you are," he agreed. "I'd given you up for

drown't, to tell truth. Koro as well, the mad Islander! When you went flyin' into the drink, Koro jumped off the whale after you! But I'll be damned if ten minutes later he don't come swimmin' up bare as Adam--save for his tattoos and that damned cap of his--and pushes you over the gunwales!"

"Koro—is alive—?" I asked in astonishment. Seeing how the last I saw of my friend he was standing on the back of a swimming whale, I could be forgiven my surprise.

"He certainly seems lively enough to me," Captain Solomon said, gesturing to the bow of the boat with the stem of his pipe.

I turned and saw Koro seated behind me, dripping water and naked save for the sodden watch cap covering his hairless head. My friend grinned at me, as if everything that had just happened had been nothing more than a schoolboy's lark.

"Mulogo just lost his pocket watch," he announced proudly. "But tell me, Jonas—what do you *do* with such a thing?"

I will give Mulogo credit—he surrendered the watch to Koro with far greater grace than I would have thought possible. Koro, for his part, did not gloat or seek to humiliate his fellow harpooner. However, while he might not have understood its actual function he most assuredly grasped its significance. He fashioned a cord from a strip of leather and used it to hang the trophy about his neck. And every day, when we took our meals in the mess, Mulogo was forced to look across the galley table and know who the greatest harpooner ever to walk the decks of the *Absalom* truly was.

I know people who read travelogues tend to envision the oceans as vast, empty expanses. But, in truth, the whaling and shipping routes are well traveled by vessels of every make and flag, and it was a rare week when we did not spy another ship--whether merchant or military--off our bow.

Some of these we gave a wide berth, especially those flying flags of the more quarrelsome countries. And it would seem others made a point of avoiding us as well, if for no other reason than the smell and grease from our try-works. But for the most part, there was usually a ritual greeting between the captains--a formal tipping of the hat, if you will, along with a brief exchange of news from the mainland, warnings of foul weather or treacherous reefs, most of it conducted via hailing horns.

It was after dinner and I was taking my ease on the weather deck, enjoying the sunset before retiring to my bunk, when I heard one of the hands sing out: *"Ship off the starboard bow!"*

Captain Solomon came out of his quarters with his spyglass in his hand and raised it to his remaining eye. " 'Tis the *Pilgrimage,* out of Nantucket!" he exclaimed. "She's captained by Abner Fastnacht—we shipped together on the *Bonnie Belle,* long years ago."

In ten minutes' time the *Pilgrimage* was parallel with the *Absalom,* with no more than a hundred yards between us. Solomon ducked back into his quarters and returned with his hailer horn, which greatly amplified his voice. *"Ahoy, Pilgrimage!"*

"Ahoy, Absalom!" came the response. Captain Fastnacht—a stout fellow with once-golden hair and whiskers now turned silver—stood on the poop deck of his ship, armed with his own hailer. "Haven't seen ye in dog's years! How's the mizzus?"

"Alive, last time I was home! And yourself?"

"She died of the influenza!"

"Sorry to hear that, Abner!"

"I got me a new one now," Fastnacht replied with a shrug. "She's younger and prettier, but nowhere the cook the last one was!"

"Where are you headed?"

"Back to Chile! We're in sore need of fresh hands! We have barely enough crew to make it back to Valparaiso as it is!"

"Are you poxed, man?" Captain Solomon asked in alarm, his eyes searching the *Pilgrimage's* rigging for the telltale yellow and black plague flag.

"You see no yellow jacket flying from my mast, do ye?" Fastnacht replied indignantly.

"I meant no offense!" Captain Solomon assured his old friend. "What of the whales in these waters? Have you seen sign of King Jim?"

"That I have, God have mercy on my soul!" The *Pilgrimage's* captain exclaimed. "I lost twenty good men to that black devil less than a week ago! He stove in four of my whale boats and drowned all the mates, save the bo'sun! He's the reason we're headed back to the mainland!"

"Where was this?" Captain Solomon asked, unable to hide the excitement in his voice.

"Three hundred miles southwest of Rapa Nui! He's traveling with a harem—larger than any I've ever seen!

But it's not worth it, Wendell. Mark my words! The fish is big as an island and black as Death itself! There's no lance forged that can pierce that monster's heart!"

"I thank you for the warning, Abner! Godspeed!"

"Farewell to ye, as well, Wendell!" Captain Fastnacht responded. As the *Pilgrimage* passed from sight, I saw its captain sadly shake his head, the way one does when you know wise words have fallen on deaf ears.

As for Captain Solomon, he lost no time in hurrying back to his quarters to chart a new course. One that would take us southwest of Rapa Nui, known to the White world as Easter Island.

Two days later, we came upon a small pod of Right whales. But this time--after my previous escape from Davy Jones' locker--Captain Solomon decided it might not be wise to risk his cooper on the hunt and replaced me in the whaleboat for good. Although I admit to missing the excitement of the chase, I was glad to surrender my oars, as hauling back a dead whale is the most onerous task known to Mankind.

Of course, it was not as if I was lolling about on soft pillows and eating bonbons while my shipmates were out among the whales. There is much that must be done to convert a ship into a floating slaughterhouse and oil refinery, and I spent most of my time knocking together the barrels and casks I knew would be soon needed, as well as helping Cuppy set up the try works.

As to be expected--thanks to Koro--the Captain's boat claimed the first kill and was also the first to return with its prize. Once everyone had sufficiently recovered from their row back to the ship, the business of cutting in began in earnest. As usual, Marcus worked the carcass, using the flensing spade to slice the blubber off the whale in blanket pieces and then attach it to the hook so it could be hauled on board and taken below decks to the blubber room. The West Indian sang as he did his bloody work in a strong, lilting voice:

"The one shirt I have, ratta cut ahm,
Same place him patch, ratta cut ahm,
Rain, rain oh! Rain, rain oh!
Rain, rain oh, fall down an' wet me up!"

Then, upon finishing his song, Marcus turned and urinated onto the sharks gathered to feed on the butchered whale, as was his custom. But this time something went wrong—perhaps he lost his footing, or something in the water jostled the floating carcass on which he stood. Whatever the reason, Marcus plummeted from his perch and landed among the feeding sharks. Although I did not see him fall, I *did* hear him cry out—it was the scream of a man who knows he is going to his death in the worst way imaginable.

"Man overboard!" Jones the Orkneyman shouted, although we all knew there was no hope of rescue even as he spoke the words.

Koro and I ran to the starboard rail, arriving just in time to see poor Marcus burst up out of the sea as if standing upright. A shark had come up from underneath him and had his legs in its mouth. Marcus' scream of horror turned into a shriek as primal and awful as the beast that had seized him. As he beat his fists against the thing's snout in a futile attempt to escape, a second shark leapt from the water and bit into his torso, tearing him in half like a Christmas cracker.

As the second shark swam away with Marcus' lifeless upper body clamped in its dreadful jaws, I noticed that it bore a wicked scar along one side of its head, and that it was missing its right eye.

Chapter Twelve

In Search of King Jim—A Rude Awakening—Wither Levant?—The Shadow Of Suspicion— The Middle Watch

As Marcus left no mortal remains to say prayers over, Captain Solomon was forced to make do by having the mates gather the crew in the waist of the ship and reading a passage from the Good Book. Once he was done, he snapped the Bible shut and gave us all a stern look.

"As you all may know, since you gossip among yourselves worse than a gaggle of old biddies at a quiltin' bee, I have been in search of King Jim—the most treacherous whale that swims these Southern Seas. And now I have a clue as to where to find him!"

As the gathered sailors muttered uncertainly amongst themselves at this proclamation, I looked to Mr. Godward, who stood at the captain's side. The First Mate's face was unreadable, although his jaw was clenched so tight I could see the muscle jump.

"I know there are some of you who call King Jim a devil!" Captain Solomon continued. "And others, still, who think him a god! But in my eyes, he's just another fish! Meaner and bigger than most, but a fish all the same! And I have yet to meet a thing that swims in the ocean that I *can't* kill! But the truth is what I'm *really* after ain't King Jim, but his harem! Like any proper monarch, he travels with an entourage—one said to number in the hundreds! If we find King Jim's harem, boys, we can fill our holds to overflowing in record time! Who among you would rather spend this next Christmas Day on dry land, with your loved ones, eatin' figgy puddin' and drinkin' wassail instead of dinin' on mince pies and grog?"

"Aye!" shouted fifty voices as one.

"Very good," Captain Solomon said with a smile. "And this evening, in memory of Marcus, I'm allowing each man a tot of rum!"

That last bit of news was good for another hurrah from the crew, who returned to their duties considerably cheered by the prospect of toasting their devoured shipmate come the evening meal.

A ship at sea, no matter what kind it might be, is rarely truly 'asleep'. The same was true for the *Absalom*. As soon as the ship was first under sail, we had been called aft for watch selection. Mr. Levant headed the starboard watch, and Mr. Shreve the port, and each mate chose from the crew who they wished to serve under them, and then divided them down even further into separate teams. Before my elevation to ship's cooper, I had served port watch—assigned four hours for sleep and four for work, throughout the twenty-four. Once a watch is done, it is sent below, if not to sleep then to keep out of the way of their replacements. Save for special occasions, the only time the entire crew was awake and above decks at the same moment was the dog watch, when we took our meals.

That night, after toasting Marcus, I retired to my

bunk, knowing I would have to be back up and about come midnight, making yet more barrels for still more oil, until the blubber rooms below deck were empty. I had just fallen into a deep sleep when I found myself roughly shaken awake by the bos'un, Gussett.

"All hands on deck! The Captain wants a head count!"

"What in damnation for?" Hawley snarled. He, too, was resentful of being dragged from his bunk before his appointed watch.

"We're missin' a couple of men," Gussett replied tersely.

Hawley and I exchanged puzzled looks. Given the harsh working conditions and piss-poor pay for a whaler, it wasn't unusual for three or four men to jump ship every voyage. But normally they waited until the ship put into port or dropped anchor at an inhabited island. Where was there to run to in the middle of the ocean? We were thousands of miles from land in any given direction.

Grumbling, the ship's carpenter and I threw on our clothes and made our way to the weather deck, where we found the rest of the crew gathered in the waist of the ship. Mr. Shreve and Mr. Gussett walked between the ranks, lanterns in hand, staring hard at our faces and clothes, while Mr. Godward took the harpooners below decks to inspect the holds. As I looked around, I realized that I had yet to see Mr. Levant, he of the bristling brows.

Meanwhile, Captain Solomon stood atop the poopdeck and called the roll like a headmaster. Each man, in turn, answered to his name save two: the Algonquin known as Askuwheteau and a Yorkshireman named Swinton. When Mr. Godward and his team returned from their search below decks, he went to speak to Solomon and the two retired to the captain's cabin.

"You men off-watch, go back to your berths," Mr. Shreve commanded, before quickly heading off to join his fellow officers aft.

Both weary and perplexed, I did as ordered and returned to my bunkroom with Hawley. We found Cuppy and Koro waiting for us. The old blacksmith was covered in reeking soot from overseeing the try-works' fires, fueled by the skin of the slaughtered whale.

"What do you make of the Cap'n's headcount?" I asked.

"I hear that Levant's missing as well," Cuppy said darkly. "Whatever happened to 'em, they didn't desert."

"Perhaps they went overboard?" I suggested.

"In a calm sea?" Hawley replied doubtfully.

"I overheard Gussett tell Mr. Shreve there was blood splashed all over the bow, near the anchor chain," the old blacksmith said.

"Maybe Askuwheteau got too much rum in him tonight and killed Swinton and Mr. Levant," Hawley asked. "You know how Red Indians are when it comes to liquor."

"It's possible," Cuppy replied with a shrug. "I remember, twenty years back there was a hand on the old *S.S. Gallant* who went stark, staring mad. Got up in the middle of the night and slit the throats of every man asleep in the fo'c'sle."

"If Askuwheteau did such a thing, he's got to still be on board." I turned to look at Koro. "Did you find anything below decks?"

"Nothing but rats," Koro replied, with a shake of his

head.

"Maybe he slew Swinton and Levant in a fit of drunken rage and hurled them into the ocean, then jumped in after?" Hawley suggested.

"But why would he do such a thing, drunk or not?" I asked.

"Who knows what possesses a heathen to do anything?" the carpenter replied with a shrug. "No offense, Koro."

"Well, all I know is that I have another hour before I go back weather side," I grunted as I crawled into my bunk. "And wherever Mr. Levant and the others may be, it most certainly is not here."

Three hours later, I was once more up and about my business and half-way into what is called the Middle Watch, which runs from midnight to four in the morning. My cooper's bench was set up in the waist of the ship, between the fore and main masts, and all around me the work of the ship went on as always, mysterious disappearances or not.

It takes three days laboring around the clock to cut in and try out a whale. During this time, the decks become incredibly greasy, until they're as slick as a frozen pond. If not for the amount of blood found before the mast, I would have had no problem believing the missing hands had slipped and fallen overboard while no one was looking. The try-works, which belched out billows of grease-laden smoke into the night sky, also provided the light by which we labored. Bundles of scrap— hard, brittle lumps of blubber that had the oil boiled out of them—burned in an iron basket swung between the twin chimneys, producing a flaring yellow blaze which gave us plenty of light to work by, while also throwing eerie, distorted shadows.

Mr. Shreve stood on the poop deck, overseeing the watch since--unlike the rest of us aboard the *Absalom*--Captain Solomon was allowed the privilege of sleeping eight hours at a stretch. The only real difference the strange disappearance of Mr. Levant and the two hands had made was the addition of the Colt Paterson revolver the Second Mate now wore on his hip.

After a while, Shreve climbed down the ladder from the poopdeck and headed forward to check on the bow. As I was busy with the work at hand, I did not give it much thought until, a few moments later, there came a shout of alarm, followed by first a gunshot, then a scream of terror the likes of which put poor, departed Marcus to shame.

As I turned toward the bow of the ship, I freed my knife from my belt and picked up the adze I used to smooth the wood, hefting it as a savage would a war-club. Just then Shreve staggered out of the leaping shadows beyond the foremast, his eyes wide with horror and his face white as the death that was on its way to claim him. There was no sign of the gun he had been carrying earlier—nor his right arm.

Chapter Thirteen

The Boarding Party–Blood On The Decks—One-Eye Claims His Due

As the hapless Second Mate collapsed onto the deck--his life's blood pumping from the raw stump of his shoulder--there emerged from the darkness at the bow of the ship things vomited from a madman's nightmare.

They walked on two legs just like men, but there all resemblance to humanity halted. Their skin was grayish-blue, still shining and wet from the sea, and their heads jutted forward, parallel with their hunched shoulders. Their faces were a hideous mixture of shark and man, with pointed noses and gaping, lipless mouths filled with jagged teeth. Their eyes were as black and round as shoe-buttons. Along their necks were pulsating gills, and in their heavily webbed hands they clutched koa spears and clubs studded with shark teeth.

At the very head of the monstrous boarding party stood their leader. Although much changed from last I saw him, I recognized the scarred face and withered eye, and knew that this was the leader of the savages who had killed my friends on Nuka Hiva--the cannibal chieftain I had come to call One-Eye.

"Mother of Christ!" Jones the Orkneyman shouted in horror. "They're climbing up the anchor chain!"

"All hands on deck!" Mr. Godward bellowed. *"All hands on deck!"*

As if in answer, One-Eye gave voice to a roaring war-cry and shook his toothed spear as the boarding party charged across the foredeck and into the waist of the ship. At that exact moment, the hatch to the fo'c'sle was thrown open by the hands responding to Mr. Godward's call, only to be immediately set upon by the invaders.

While their brothers pursued the retreating sailors into the forecastle like terriers chasing rats, the remaining shark-men swarmed the try-works--only to be met by old Cuppy, who used the six-foot long bailers to hurl ladles of boiling whale oil at his attackers. One of the monsters shrieked in agony upon catching a face full of scalding liquid, yet still managed to throw its spear, piercing the torso of the nearest sailor.

One of the hideous beasts lunged at me, but I sidestepped its attack and brought the adze down, burying the blade deep in the cartilage of its snout while I drove my knife into one of its eyes. Having dispatched the fiend, I quickly retreated to the quarterdeck, where my shipmates were making their stand.

"God in Three Persons!" Captain Solomon bellowed as he emerged from his cabin, dressed in nothing but long johns, boots and the gun belt buckled about his waist. "What's this madness?"

"We're under attack by demons, sir!" the First Mate replied, his face the color of cold oatmeal.

"Demons?" the captain scoffed as he aimed his revolver and fired down at one of the invaders, blowing a hole in the shark-man's torso. "They're just natives in Tiki masks, nothing more! For God's sake man, I thought you had more sense than that!" He then turned and yelled at Mr. Gussett, who was watching the slaughter play out before him with bulging eyes. "Don't just stand there gawkin', bo'sun! Go below and breakout the long guns from the armory cabinet! Take Godward with you!"

"Aye-aye, Cap'n!" Both men replied in unison, and quickly disappeared.

The dreadful boarding party pressed forward, undeterred by Solomon's gunfire. They were met by crew members armed with whatever tool they had at hand. I saw Jones take a spear to the gut from one of the shark-men and drop to his knees as if to say his prayers. The creature that struck the blow opened wide its mouth and snapped the Orkneyman's head clean off at the shoulders as easily as you would bite off the end of a cigar.

The Classics--Homer and Virgil--stood side by side, stabbing at the creatures with the harpoons they made their living by. But one of the monsters, spotting the manacle on Homer's ankle, grabbed the dangling length of chain and yanked the escaped slave's feet out from under him. Homer screamed in terror as the shark-man raced back toward the bow of the ship, dragging the harpooner along the oil-slicked deck behind it like a child pulling a toy sled.

"Stand your ground, men!" Captain Solomon shouted as he slid down the ladder feet-first to join his crew on the quarterdeck. *"Drive the devils back into the sea!"*

Another of the were-sharks lunged at me, gnashing its teeth as it thrust its spear at my nethers. I leapt back, only to slip on the oily deck and land on my back, knocking the wind from my sails. The creature grinned as best it could with such wicked daggers wedged in its mouth and lifted its spear, eager to drive it into my exposed belly.

Suddenly there was a wild shout and Koro leapt from nowhere, slashing at the two-legged shark with one of the flensing spades, opening my attacker up from shoulder to crotch and spilling its innards onto the deck. Without a moment's pause, the Islander reached down and yanked me back onto my feet. Koro and I then stood back-to-back, blocking and parrying spear thrusts with the tools of our trade, while all around us our friends and shipmates did the same. Everywhere there was blood and screams, both human and inhuman.

I saw Captain Solomon in the thick of the battle, cursing a blue streak as he fired at the abominations assaulting his crew. From the look on his face, I knew the old sea captain realized that he was fighting something far worse than cannibals wearing masks. Suddenly, One-Eye rose up before him, showing every tooth in a wicked snarl. Captain Solomon pointed his Colt at the were-shark's head. One-Eye froze and something like apprehension flickered across its inhuman face. Captain Solomon pulled the trigger—and the hammer came down on an empty chamber with a dreadful clicking sound.

With an exultant growl, One-Eye knocked Captain Solomon's gun out of his hand, plunging its spear into its opponent's right eye socket with such force the point burst through the back of Solomon's skull. I cried out as I saw my captain fall lifeless to the blood-wet deck as if the killing blow had struck me as well.

One-Eye grasped the haft of the spear with a webbed hand and yanked it free, holding it aloft in a roar of triumph. The other Mano Kanaka froze in mid-battle at the sound, swinging their heads in the direction of their leader. Moving as one, the shark-men began to retreat, backing towards the bow.

There came the crack of rifle fire and the smell of gun powder as the head of one of the shark-men disappeared in an explosion of brains and cartilage. I turned and saw Mr. Godward, Gussett, Mulogo and others emerging from the hatches towards the stern of the vessel, armed with long guns,

"Shoot!" Mr. Godward shouted. *"Kill them all!"*

As the *Absalom's* defenders opened fire, the orderly withdrawal of the Mano Kanaka became a rout. The shark-men dropped their weapons and fled to the bulwarks, only to fall in a hail of bullets. Those closest to the railing died in mid-transformation, flopping on the deck like landed fish, their legs fused together below the hip.

The only one to escape the initial volley unharmed was One-Eye, who used the chaos to flee to the bow. Koro and I gave chase, unmindful of the bullets flying through the air. A murderous rage filled my heart unlike anything I have ever known before or since. This monster was responsible for the deaths of men I considered friends. And, in the case of Captain Solomon, the fiend had murdered the only person I held in as high esteem as my own, beloved uncle. At that moment I wanted One-Eye's death more than a starving man wants food, or a drowning man wants air. But, just as we closed in on fiend, One-Eye clambered out onto the bowsprit extending from the prow of the ship and leapt into the ocean below.

Koro and I ran to the rail and stared down into the

water. One-Eye had cast aside its human guise as easily as you or I would toss aside a garment and was now gliding only a few feet below the surface like a gray ghost. The were-shark turned slightly on its left side to look up at the enemies peering down, daring us to follow it into its element.

"The bastard is taunting us!" I spat. "He's not even trying to run away!"

Koro snatched up a harpoon, jumped onto the bulwarks and let fly the iron with such force the spear-point emerged from the other side of One Eye's body. The Mano Kanaka thrashed mightily, lashing the sea into white froth, and after a few minutes it ceased it struggles and floated belly up. It wasn't long before other sharks came swimming up to feed on One-Eye's carcass.

Whether they were true sharks or fellow Mano Kanaka, it is impossible to say.

Chapter Fourteen

A Terrible Silence—Sailcloth Shrouds—A Funeral At Sea—Captain Godward Names His Mates—Mulogo Swings The Cat

Having survived the attempted boarding, the remaining crew of the *Absalom* set about collecting the dead and washing the decks of blood. It was a sad and gruesome task, and one undertaken in near silence. The horrors I and my shipmates had undergone that dreadful night had stunned us so thoroughly not one of us could speak more than the most basic of instructions.

As we hurled the monstrous carcasses of our attackers back into the sea from which they'd climbed, I saw something dangerously close to madness in the eyes of many of the crew. I could tell by the tightness at the corners of the men's mouths and the trembling of their hands that their silence was out of fear that speaking aloud might lead to screaming—a screaming they might be powerless to stop.

When the tally was made, it revealed the *Absalom* had lost seven good men that horrid night: Captain Solomon, Mr. Shreve, Jones the Orkneyman, Homer, and three able-bodies from the fo'c'sle. Taking into account the missing Third Mate, the redskin Askuwheteau and Swinton the Yorkshireman, who fell victim to the devils' scouting party, the final reckoning was ten.

A bolt of sailcloth was brought up from below decks and cut into seven lengths, and Mr. Gussett and a couple of deckhands began stitching together long canvas bags, into which the bodies of the fallen were placed one by one, along with a weight of bricks.

Each dead man had suffered the most gruesome mutilations imaginable: poor Shreve had lost an arm; Homer was missing the leg that bore his old slave shackle; Captain Solomon was now blinded in both eyes; and the only way we could identify the Orkneyman was by the tattoo on his chest. Looking upon them lying there--lined up like so many broken toys--filled my heart with a profound grief.

Although I had been in good standing with them all, I felt the loss of Mr. Shreve and Captain Solomon most keenly. The Second Mate had always treated me square, and I found him to be a likable, solid-sort of man. And as for my captain, I had grown as fond of him as my dear, departed Uncle Calvin. My only solace was the knowledge that he had died as any good captain should —fighting alongside his men, defending his ship to the last of his breath.

Come the dawn, all hands were called on deck and together carried the bodies down to the main deck, placing them with their feet to the sea. The gang plank was removed from the rail and the Captain's shrouded body placed upon it. We stood gathered with solemn faces in the waist of the ship as the rising sun turned the sky a burnished gold.

Mr. Godward--the *Absalom's* only surviving officer--came forward, his back stiff and straight as a ramrod. "We are gathered here, under the eye of God, to say farewell to these, our shipmates and masters," he said in a loud voice. "They died bravely, every one of them, defending the ship against crazed, cannibal natives..."

I and a couple of my fellow shipmates raised our heads at that point in the eulogy and exchanged glances with one another, uncertain if we had heard our new captain correctly, but did not speak up.

"But none fought as valiantly as her captain," Godward continued, and there was a chorus of assent from the crew. "He ruled the *Absalom* as wisely and justly as his namesake. Never have I shipped with a man who knew more about the ways of the ocean, and the things that swim in it, than Wendell Solomon. He died as he lived—as a whaler."

Godward opened the Bible he held clutched in his hands: "As it says in Psalms, Chapter Eight, Verses Six through Nine: 'Thou madest him to have dominion over the work of Thy hands; Thou hast put all things under his feet; All sheep and oxen, yea, and the beasts of the field; The fowl of the air, and the fish of the sea, and whatsoever passeth through the paths of the seas. O Lord our Lord, how excellent is thy name in all the earth!' " This was followed by a heartfelt, if slightly baffled, chorus of 'Amens'. Then the crew sang a couple verses of *Amazing Grace* before tilting the gang-plank upwards, sliding the shrouded corpse of Captain Wendell Solomon into the waiting ocean, where it plunged beneath the waves and sank without a trace. This ritual was repeated another six times, although words were only spoken over the bodies of Mr. Shreve, Homer, and the Orkneyman, the remainder being consigned to Davey Jones Locker in anonymity.

As the last of the *Absalom's* slain disappeared below the foam, Mr. Godward turned to address the assembled crew: "As all of you are gathered here, I will go ahead and announce my mates. As you well know, the attack by the cannibals robbed us of nearly all our officers. Until such time as we can make for Peru, I shall have Mr. Gussett as my First Mate and Mulogo as my Second."

This last bit of news was greeted with scowls and dark mutters from the crew. Hawley the carpenter stepped forward. "I got no problem working alongside heathens and darkies, sir. But I'll be damned if I take orders from one, much less both," he said firmly.

"And I'll be damned if I am addressed in such a manner by a skilled hand," Godward replied curtly.

With just a nod from their new captain, a couple of hands pounced on Hawley, dragging the surprised carpenter to the nearest mast, where the shirt was torn from his back. He was then placed spread-eagled against the shrouds, his wrists tied to the rigging. Mulogo strutted forward, grinning in amusement as he watched Hawley struggle like a fly caught in a web. In one ebony hand the *Absalom's* newly minted Second Mate held a closed cat made of sound, thick rope, the end of which was tightly knotted. Mulogo took his place on the break of the deck, a few feet away from Hawley, so that he could get in a good swing. He raised his muscular arm—the same one used to throw harpoons—and brought it down onto the hapless carpenter's naked back, bending his body as he did so as to give the blow its full force.

Hawley jerked violently with each stroke of the lash, like a puppet on a string. On the third blow, blood began to seep from the welts across his back. By the fifth stripe, he cried out in a ragged voice: *"Jesus Christ! Deliver me, savior!"* But such entreaties meant nothing to Mulogo who--as Hawley himself had pointed out--was of a savage creed.

It wasn't until the poor devil swooned and went limp, his body held upright only by the bindings about his wrists, that Godward finally ordered his Second to stay his hand. "That's enough!" he barked. "Take him down and put him in his bunk." The *Absalom's* new captain then turned to face the rest of the men. "If there are any more of you who question my choice of Mates, you take it up with Mr. Mulogo. Is that clear?"

"Aye, Cap'n," the assembled hands said in sullen unison as they watched Mulogo shake the blood from the cat.

Chapter Fifteen

The Hunt Continues—The Ocean Born—The Drowned City

Given the depletion of our numbers--and the loss of so many of the ship's officers--it was assumed that the *Absalom* would follow the *Pilgrimage's* example and promptly set sail for Peru in order to replenish its crew. However, come the dogwatch--as we were gathered for the evening mess--it was announced that the ship would continue on the course charted by the late Captain Solomon.

"By my calculations, we are a day or so short of our final destination," Captain Godward informed the crew. "We're too close to give up now and turn back. It was Captain Solomon's wish that we find King Jim's harem, and that's how I plan to honor his memory. Are you with me, boys? Will you fill the holds with oil from the monster whale's wives so that the Widow Solomon shall know her good husband's death was not in vain?"

As he spoke, I could see each man was moved--as was I--by the thought of the captain's lady tirelessly pacing the widow's walk, her eyes searching the horizon for sign of the *Absalom's* sails. Whalers may be rough, uncultured men, but there is also a strong streak of sentiment to be found in even the saltiest dog, for rare is the sailor who does not have a mother, sweetheart, or wife waiting news of their return.

"Aye!" cried the crew in unison, save for one. *"We are with you, sir!"*

Who, you ask, was the sole hand who did not add his voice to the chorus? It was none other than Koro.

Later, as we prepared to bunk down, Koro asked me a question that had crossed my mind earlier: "Why did Mr. Godward claim the Mano Kanaka were cannibals?"

"Perhaps it was too much for him to accept," I replied, with a shrug of my shoulders. "Lord knows, I doubted my own sanity when I saw those things. It is far easier for him to explain an attack by cannibal natives than it is men who turn into sharks—or sharks that turn into men. It is a hard thing for a civilized mind to wrap around without it altogether snapping. And he's *Captain* Godward now," I reminded my friend. "And you best not forget it, if you don't want to end up like poor Hawley, there." I nodded to where the carpenter lay face down in his bunk, drifting in and out of delirium courtesy of a fever and a laudanum-laced cup of grog. "But speaking of the Mano Kanaka—are we in danger of them returning?"

"No," Koro replied solemnly. "They will not return. Blood vengeance has been taken for the insult to their chief. Even if they desired to do further harm, they dare not follow us, for the *Absalom* has entered the waters of the Ocean Born. It is taboo to trespass. The Ocean Born are jealous of their territory—especially during mating season."

"What are the Ocean Born?"

"They are the ancestors of my people and the gods of the islands. Long ago, there were beings without form that mated with the creatures of the sea. Their children were the whale-lord Tangaroa, the octopus-god Kanaloa, the shark-god Kamoho, the eel-king Tunaroa, the sea-dragon Waka, the ray-god Punga, and Ikatere, Lord of the Dolphins. My people, the Naia, were born of Ikatere and young girls offered up to him by the islanders."

"So you're telling me you're descended from a dolphin?" I said with a laugh, unable to disguise my amusement.

"No," he corrected gently. "A dolphin *god.*"

That night I dreamt of the Ocean Born.

In my dream, I was standing on the bow of the *Absalom*, naked save for the dolphin amulet about my neck. Above me the Milky Way filled the sky, its cold, distant fire reflected in the dark mirror of the water below. I became aware that I was not alone and turned to see Koro standing on the deck beside me. Save for his eternal watch cap he, too, was naked, and the tattoos covering his hairless torso seemed to writhe with a life all their own.

Koro smiled and gestured for me to follow him as he climbed up onto the railing and jumped overboard. Without pause or fear I followed suit, plunging feet-first into the waiting ocean, just as I used to leap into the old mill pond back home. I sank like a stone, and the salt water flooded my lungs within seconds. But instead of drowning, I found myself breathing just as I would on land.

Koro could also breathe beneath the waves, of course.

He smiled and took me by the hand, leading me deeper still through water darker than any midnight I have ever known. Down, down, down we went, into the vast, hidden belly of the ocean, through sunken valleys and forests of seaweed that towered higher than any tree that grows on land. Although the sun's rays could never penetrate the darkness that surrounded us, I had no trouble seeing the wonders hidden so many leagues beneath the waves. Again, I attributed this to the nature of dreams.

At first I mistook the city for a submerged mountain range, but as we drew closer I realized that they were, instead, a collection of ziggurat-like structures covered in living coral. I was both exhilarated and terrified by the towering structures, which made the Great Pyramids look like termite mounds in comparison. I wondered what might dwell in such a fantastic and alien landscape?

As we swam between the gigantic step-pyramids, I glimpsed windows and doorways carved into their walls and what appeared to be vast, boneless figures stirring sluggishly within the shadows. My heart leapt with fear, for I knew--as only dreamers can--that what dwelt inside these mammoth edifices were the shapeless beings who spawned the gods of the ocean and that they were watching me in return.

I became aware of motion far overhead and glimpsed a great, amorphous blob the size of an unfurled sail silhouetted against the dark water like a cloud in a night sky. The outer edge of its body rippled like a lady's lace shawl caught in the wind, and within its boneless body I saw an array of pulsing colors going from golden orange to blood red to violet to blue and back again. Behind it trailed a forest of tendrils like a ragged bridal train, some as thin as a reed, while others were as big around as a strong man's arm.

As I watched the thing's progress, a green sea turtle swam into view. It was an impressive specimen--easily four feet long and two hundred pounds if an ounce. Without warning, several of the tendrils snapped forth, wrapping themselves about the hapless creature and delivering numerous stings. The turtle struggled briefly before going still and the tendrils contracted, drawing it up into the gelatinous creature's body.

"Do not fear, cousin," Koro said reassuringly, although there was no way he could have spoken, nor I hear him. But such is the nature of dreams. "They will not harm you, for you carry the seal of the Naia." He pointed to the dolphin amulet I wore. "It grants you safe passage among all who share the blood of the Ocean Born."

"It didn't stop One-Eye and his clan from trying to kill me," I pointed out.

"One-Eye broke taboo," Koro replied solemnly. "And he and his tribe paid dearly for it; as will the *Absalom*, and all who sail on her."

I wanted to ask Koro what he meant, but before I could do so there came the sound of whale song. It was louder than any I had ever heard through the hull of the ship, as if a choir of whale were celebrating high mass. It was the most beautiful and eerie thing I had ever heard, either in dreams or the waking world.

A mournful look passed over my friend's face. "Tangaroa's people are offering up their prayers for deliverance. The *Absalom* is doomed."

I awoke with a start, gasping like a man plucked

from the sea. My forehead was damp with sweat and my heart beat against my ribs as if knocking on a door. I automatically glanced toward Koro's bunk and found the harpooner awake. He was looking back at me, still wearing the sad, worried expression I had seen in my dream.

Suddenly, from above decks I heard the lookout's cry: "*Thar she blows!*"

Chapter Sixteen

The Harem Is Sighted—Koro Defiant—Koro And The Cat—The Truth Revealed—Back To The Sea

The dawn sky was red as blood as I emerged from below decks. There were already a number of hands crowding the starboard side, talking excitedly among themselves and pointing toward the horizon. Once I shouldered my way to the rail, I saw what had the crew in such a tizzy.

As far as the eye could see the ocean was full of whales, the great sea beasts dotting its surface like buffalo grazing on the prairie. Not only were there Sperms to be had, but Rights and Humpbacks as well. I have never seen a pod of such size before, comprised of so many different species.

"How many do you think there are?" Nicodemus asked in wonder.

"Easily a hundred, if not two," Cuppy replied. "I gave up countin' at twenty."

"Do you think it's King Jim's harem?" This came from Pedro the cook. He was a thin fellow prone to nervousness and adhered to every superstition known to Man. About his neck he wore a cross, the Jewish star, a rosary and any number of heathen symbols, all of which he constantly fingered during moments of anxiety.

"What else *could* it be?" Nicodemus snorted.

"What if King Jim attacks the ship?" Pedro asked, nervously rattling his collection of icons. "What if he rams us like he did the *Virginia Dare,* seven years ago?"

"Then it will be the last thing the monster does."

Pedro, Cuppy, Nicodemus and I turned around, surprised to find Captain Godward standing behind us. He was staring out at the bounty spread before him, his eyes gleaming as they had when the fever was upon him.

"Where is Koro?" Godward asked, directing the question to me. "He's to serve as harpooner for Mr. Gussett."

Before I could reply, Koro emerged from the nearby gangway, his face as solemn as those that lined the shores of Easter Island. "I will not hunt these whales, Cap'n."

Godward recoiled as if the harpooner's words had been a blow. "How dare you speak to your betters in such a manner, boy?"

"I mean no disrespect, Captain," Koro replied. "But I refuse to break taboo. To kill these whales will bring the wrath of Tangaroa."

Godward's face turned as red as a boiled crab. "I don't care *what* your heathen religion forbids! You're on *my* ship, and I'm giving you an *order,* sailor! You are to report to Mr. Gussett immediately."

Koro shook his head, his mouth set into a resolute line. "What you would have me do is taboo. I cannot be a part of it. I beg you, Captain—turn the ship around. The longer it stays here, the surer its doom becomes."

This last part triggered an uneasy murmur among the assembled deckhands, which did not go unnoticed by Godward. "You *dare* disobey my direct order?" he bellowed, his eyes showing white all-around as if they were about to leap from his skull. "Whale Rider or not, I will take your hide for such insolence! Put that man in irons!" he commanded. A pair of able-bodies stepped forward and laid rough hands on Koro as a third came forth with a set of manacles. With a single flex of his powerful arms the Islander escaped his would-be captors as if he was shrugging off a coat. One of them stumbled backward, landing at Godward's feet.

"Get up, you dog!" the captain bellowed, delivering a swift kick to the seat of the fallen sailor's pants. He then turned to address the others. "Grab him, or I'll have the lot of you flogged as well!"

The threat of the cat was enough to spur the onlookers who had been hanging back into action. Koro struggled mightily as his shipmates grabbed at him, swinging his fists and feet as if they were cudgels, sending strong men flying in every direction. But Koro was but one man, and Captain Godward had an entire forecastle at his command, so it was not long before he was pinned down, three sailors to each limb. Yet still he writhed and bucked like a landed tuna upon the deck. As one of the hands bent down to try and clap a set of leg-irons about the Islander's ankles, Koro lashed out with his foot, breaking the hapless sailor's jaw with a single blow.

"Never mind the irons!" Captain Godward snapped. "Take him to the shrouds!"

The deckhands did as they were commanded, dragging the struggling Koro to the rigging that both kept the main mast from snapping off and provided a rope-ladder to the upper spar above. Although he fought them at every step, they still managed to seize him up and tie him to the shrouds. The intricate tattoos that covered his back jumped and rippled with the movement of his muscles as he tested the strength of his bonds.

Once he was sure the prisoner was secured and unable to escape, Captain Godward shouted: *"All hands witness punishment! Ahoy!"*

The cry was quickly taken up by Mulogo, and then echoed throughout the length and breadth of the ship. The various hands set aside their work to gather in the waist of the ship to watch the flogging. Even Hawley--still weak and feverish from his own beating--joined the throng. Satisfied that everyone from the cabin boy on up was in attendance, the captain turned to the Second Mate, who stood waiting at his elbow.

"Mr. Mulogo! Attend to the punishment!"

The smile on Mulogo's face as he took his place at the shrouds made my blood run cold. In place of the knotted rope he had used previously, the harpooner now carried a cat o'nine tails, the tips of which were barbed with bits of tin. Mulogo looked Koro over like a butcher sizing up a side of beef, then snatched the pocket watch his rival wore from about his neck, snapping the leather thong on which it hung as if it were a piece of string. Then, as an afterthought, he snatched the ever-present watch cap from the Islander's head.

"No!" Koro cried, renewing his struggles to free himself with even greater determination.

The triumphant leer pasted across Mulogo's face dissolved instantly, to be replaced by a look of genuine horror. The African gave out a high-pitched, almost girlish shriek and hurled the cap to the deck as if it was made of fire.

At first I could not understand what could possibly provoke such a show of terror from such a hardened sailor as Mulogo. Then I looked at Koro's head--now exposed for the first time since we had met, revealing the blow-hole at the top of his skull. As I stared, dumbstruck, its muscular flap abruptly dilated and made the clicking-whistle familiar to all mariners. The assembled crew gasped in alarm and more than a few crossed themselves.

"He's one of those monsters!" Cuppy shouted, made angry by his fear. "Like the ones that killed Cap'n Solomon!"

"Kill the bastard!" Pedro the Cook screamed, waving his meat-cleaver for emphasis. *"Gut him like a fish!"*

The rest of the crew yelled in agreement, brandishing knives, belaying pins and boat-hooks like angry soldiers preparing to storm a castle. Within a heartbeat they had forgotten the countless times they had sung Koro's praises as a harpooner, all the meals they had shared with him, and how it was he who had slain the creature who had murdered their beloved Captain Solomon. What had been their shipmate mere moments before was now a fiend from hell, no different in their eyes than a kraken, sea serpent, or any other monster that haunted the uncharted depths of the ocean.

With an inhuman squeal, Koro tore himself free of the shrouds like a dolphin breaking free of a fisherman's net and made a mad dash for the gunwale.

"Stop the prisoner!" Captain Godward hollered. "Don't let him get away!"

One of the hands from the fo'c'sle moved to block Koro's escape, but the harpooner barreled into him and sent him flying like a sack of grain. With a single bound, he leapt half the breadth of the deck, landing atop the gunwale as the angry crew surged forward, howling for his blood. Without a single glance back, my only friend in the world dove head-first into the waiting sea as his former shipmates charged the rail, baying like a pack hounds after a fox.

Chapter Seventeen

The Tattooed Dolphin—I, Jonah—A Moment's Reprieve—I Am Exiled

Without a moment's hesitation, Koro leapt from the *Absalom* and plunged headlong into the ocean, which closed about him with nary a ripple to mark his passing. The outraged crew crowded the rail, hurling everything from curses to harpoons after him.

A few moments later a dolphin abruptly leapt forth from the waves off the port bow, its skin gleaming like polished stone. As it somersaulted in midair, it revealed an intricate tattoo on its under-belly before splashing back down and disappearing for good.

"The devil mocks us!" Mulogo shouted angrily. My bowels turned to water as he then turned and jabbed his finger in my direction. "Padgett is the one who brought the monster aboard in the first place! *He* is the one who brought evil among us!"

The crew of the *Absalom* turned as one to scowl at me. Although I had worked, eaten, slept and shat alongside them for two years, at that moment they were worse than strangers to me.

"Aye, thicker than thieves they were," Cuppy agreed, nodding his snowy head, "always keeping one another's company, like a warlock and his familiar."

"Yes, Koro was my friend; I don't deny that!" I replied,

trying desperately to make myself heard over the collected grumbling of the crew. "But you *must* believe I did *not* know he wasn't human!" Of course, that last part was not exactly true, and the others could hear the nervousness in my voice.

"The man's a wizard!" Mulogo shouted, drowning out my denials. "He controls the creature with that amulet he always wears! That is why he is never without it!"

"It is a bequest from my uncle, nothing more!" I protested, my hand instinctively closing about the pendant. And then, in my eagerness to clear myself of suspicion, I blurted out: *"I am no warlock! This I swear, or my name isn't Jonah Padgett!"*

As I heard myself speak, my heart tumbled from its perch--but there was nothing I could do to make it right. There are no calling back words, once they are spoken—especially those said in front of so many witnesses.

Mr. Gussett stepped forward, eyeing me like a rabid rat he'd flushed from the bilge. "*What* did you say your name was, boy?"

"J-Jonas," I stammered, doing my best to sound truthful.

The First Mate grimaced at my lie as if he'd bitten into a lemon. "This man's a Jonah in both deed *and* name!"

There was a ragged roar of anger, as if every hand aboard the *Absalom* had one throat, and the crew abruptly surged forward. I found myself buffeted about in a human maelstrom, subjected to kicks, punches, and slaps from all sides, before finally being grabbed by a half-hundred hands and lifted bodily from the deck.

"Throw the Jonah overboard!" Mulogo bellowed. *"Toss him to the sharks!"*

And they would have done it, too, without a

moment's thought or remorse, had there not come the explosive report of a gun. The rabble fell instantly silent as Captain Godward waded through their number, a smoking Navy Colt clutched in one hand, kicking aside those who moved too slowly out of the way.

"Set that man down!" he ordered.

My attackers immediately did as commanded, and I heaved a sigh of relief as my boots once more touched the deck.

"We may be on the open seas, but this ship flies under an American flag!" The skipper said, his voice raised loud enough for all to hear. "And I'll not stand by and watch a fellow countryman murdered in cold blood, warlock or not!"

"Bless you, Cap'n," I said gratefully.

"Don't go thanking me just yet, Mr. Padgett," he snarled, eyeing me as he would a maggot crawling about in his breakfast bacon. "The truth of the matter is the men will mutiny if I allow you to remain on board. So I have decided to place you in my gig, along with some provisions, and tether you to the stern of the ship. Once we are done in these waters, I will see to it that you are put ashore at Rapa Nui."

"You're going to leave me in an open boat for a fortnight, maybe more?" I exclaimed. "You might as well put a bullet between my eyes!"

"Do not tempt me, Mr. Padgett," he replied darkly.

Despite his obvious distaste for me, Captain Godward was true to his word and converted the boat that normally served as the captain's private taxi while in harbor into my floating prison. The dinghy was smaller and lighter than the whale boats, but nowhere near as seaworthy, and outfitted with a can of sea biscuits and a cask of water. After removing the oars, Mulogo tied one end of a lengthy coil of rope to the bow-line of the captain's gig, the other end of which was secured to the stern of the *Absalom*, then ordered it lowered over the side. I was then forced at pistol-point to climb down a rope ladder to the waiting boat, which pitched and wallowed in the chop of the ocean. The moment I dropped into the dinghy, the ladder was immediately pulled up and Mulogo hurled a sea bag containing what few belongings I called my own after me.

As dangerous as being in an open boat on the high seas might be, by that point I was eager to escape the *Absalom*. I had noticed more than one crewman eyeing me while fingering their knives, and it was only a matter of time before one of them slipped a blade between my ribs, captain's orders or not.

And so the *Absalom* continued on its course, sailing headlong into King Jim's harem, all the while towing me along like a recalcitrant hound brought to heel.

Chapter Eighteen

In Absalom's Wake—The Hunters Return—A Cradle Rocked By Sharks—A Dream of Gussett—The Blood-Red Dawn

Exiled to *Absalom's* wake, I could do nothing but sit in my open-air prison and watch as Captain Godward and his officers lowered their whaleboats and set out to raid King Jim's harem. Once they finally dwindled from view, I set about making myself as comfortable as possible in my new surroundings.

The sun at such latitudes is brutal, and I knew I was in far greater danger of dying of heat stroke than a shark bite. So I busied myself by tying together what few articles of clothing were in my sea bag and stretching them between the gunwales at the bow, in hopes of creating both shelter and shade. As the sun was extremely hot, it wasn't long before I was completely drenched in sweat and burning with thirst. I inspected the small barrel given me, which held nine gallons of fresh water. While that might sound like more than enough water for a single man, it does not take into account the constant broiling sun which, even on board ship, will parch a sailor's tongue until it feels like sandpaper. Or the fact I was looking at a fortnight or more exposed to the elements. It would take superhuman willpower--and far better luck than I had been enjoying of late--to survive more than a week under such circumstances.

I opened the spigot on the barrel and decanted some of the precious fluid into a battered tin cup. Although the water was stale and warm, I had to fight the urge to fill my cup a second time.

Hours later--just as the sun began its descent--I heard the unmistakable sound of oarsmen singing off in the distance. I squinted in the direction of the voices and saw one of the whaleboats returning with a dead sperm whale in tow. I was not surprised to see that it was Mulogo's boat that had claimed the first kill, for now that Koro was gone he reigned supreme as the *Absalom's* finest hunter.

I watched from afar as my former shipmates set about the cutting-in, turning the sea red with the blood from the dead whale. As the crimson continued to spread, sharks rose from the briny deep like housewives hurrying to the butcher shop.

By the time the sun had all but slipped from the sky, Captain Godward's boat arrived with its catch—this time a right whale. Since the first kill was still in the process of being butchered, the second whale had to be tethered at the ship's prow to await its turn.

For the rest of the night the *Absalom* burned like a barque from Hell, its masts lit by the fires of the try-works as gouts of foul, greasy black smoke rose into the sky. Even in exile, there was no escaping the stink of boiling blubber. I sat there in the flickering darkness, bobbing about on the end of several hundred yards of rope like the cork on a fishing line, listening to my former shipmates shout, curse and sing as they labored to fill the cargo hold. Never, in all my months at sea, did

I pine for my childhood home as I did that night.

Although the sun had finally disappeared, night brought little relief as all it did was replace the broiling heat of the day with a stifling humidity that lay against my skin like a towel in a Turkish bath. It wasn't until I finished consuming a humble repast of hardtack soaked in water that it occurred to me that the third whaleboat —the one piloted by Mr. Gussett—had yet to return. Finding one's way back to the ship in the dark can be extremely difficult, but at least the fires from the try-works could be seen for miles, effectively turning the *Absalom* into a beacon for its errant children. Indeed, there was enough light that I could easily make out the figure of Captain Godward atop the poop deck, awaiting the return of his First Mate.

Having fed myself, I folded my emptied sea-bag into a makeshift pillow and settled down at the bottom of the boat, my head to the bow and my feet toward the stern. With its high gunwales and the unceasing movement of the waves and the occasional thump from a passing shark, it was not unlike being rocked in a cradle and I soon fell asleep.

I dreamt I saw Koro treading water not far from my boat, bobbing up and down like a buoy. Although he did not speak to me, I knew he wanted to show me something and I leapt from the boat without a moment's hesitation. The moment I entered the water, Koro disappeared and in his place was a dolphin with skin that gleamed like a polished stone. I grabbed its dorsal fin and it towed me along at breakneck speed.

When the dolphin finally halted, I found myself staring at the flotsam of what had once been the whaleboat piloted by Mr. Gussett. The bo'sun-turned-first mate was still clinging to the wreckage with the last of his strength. I scanned the surrounding water, but there was no trace of the other men he'd set sail with earlier that day. With an agonized groan, Gussett surrendered his hold and slid beneath the waves, joining his shipmates in Davy Jones' locker.

The moment he sank beneath the surface, there came a dreadful great sound--like the bellow of an animal, but in a register so low it vibrated the marrow in my bones. But as I turned to ask Koro what might possibly give voice to such a frightful call, I found that I was alone and I knew--with the certainty of knowledge that comes with dreams--that whatever voiced that fearsome challenge was headed my way.

I awoke with a start and sat bolt upright, my heart hammering away like a blacksmith at his anvil. The night was no more, and in its place was a dawn that dyed the early morning sky the same shade of red as the whale's blood that surrounded me.

Chapter Nineteen

The Collision—The Wrath of King Jim—The Fate of the Absalom—The Eye of Tangaroa

Shortly after dawn, Captain Godward resumed his watch atop the poopdeck. His manner was noticeably agitated, even from my distant vantage point. As he searched with his spyglass for sign of Gussett and the others, I remembered what Koro had shown me in my dream and knew with dreadful certainty that the missing whaleboat would never return. The day continued to progress, and as the sun crossed the yardarm I heard the lookout in the crow's nest shout: *"Thar she blows! Off the starboard bow!"*

There in the near distance sat a bull sperm whale so large that if I had not seen its flukes, I would have mistaken for a small, barren island thrust up from the ocean floor. The beast's skin was black as a bible and the plume that shot from its spout was taller than a church steeple. There was no mistaking this whale for any other—we were in the presence of his royal highness, King Jim.

Captain Godward began shouting at the crew, yelling at them to ready the boats for the greatest hunt of their lives. Just then--as the deck hands scrambled to launch the whaleboats--a hand emerged from the water just beyond the bow of my boat. The hand was webbed and clutched an obsidian blade, which it used to slice through the rope tethering the dinghy to the stern of the ship.

"Koro!" I exclaimed, and then quickly clamped a hand over my mouth. A few moments later the remaining length of rope attached to the bow-line went taut, like the line on a fishing pole that's hooked a fish, and the dinghy reversed itself and began to move in the opposite direction of the ship. Suddenly there came the sound of the alarm-bell, and I instantly assumed one of the deckhands had noticed my getaway--but that was not the case.

I turned around, fearing that I might still be within rifle-shot of the *Absalom*, and was astounded to see King Jim rapidly propelling itself toward the ship by churning the ocean with its massive flukes. In all my months at sea, I had never seen a whale charge a ship before. But then, King Jim was no ordinary whale, but a ship-killer--made famous when he attacked the *Virginia Dare*, a decade before. As the crew of the *Absalom* ran frantically to and fro, Captain Godward snatched up his harpoon and dashed forward in hopes of spearing the monster from the deck of the ship just as King Jim plowed into her starboard side, just short of the prow.

There came the terrible sound of snapping timbers, followed by horrified screams as those hands still in the rigging were sent flying from their perches. Some of them landed with bone-splintering force onto the decks below, while others were catapulted into the shark-infested water. As for King Jim, the impact barely slowed him down as he passed under the ship, causing the *Absalom* to rock violently from side to side.

A few seconds later the great whale surfaced close on the port side, where it lay apparently stunned, with its head by the bow and tail toward the stern. Both Captain Godward and Mulogo hurried forward with their harpoons, looping the ropes attached to them about a nearby capstan. But upon realizing the leviathan's tail was too close to the ship, Mulogo lowered his weapon. Captain Godward, however, was so given over to the hunt, he either did not notice or did not care, and launched his iron at the monster whale's vast heart.

The moment the barbed lance sank into his ink-black hide, King Jim snapped back to wakefulness and with a single slap of its mighty tail reduced the *Absalom's* rudder to kindling before sounding. As the league of rope played out, the capstan spun like a top and the ship listed dangerously to port, causing everything not nailed down to tumble across the deck, including the huge cast-iron kettles set atop the try works. A chorus of agonized screams rang out as hapless sailors found themselves doused in boiling oil and crushed against the bulwarks by burning cauldrons. Then to add to the horror, the door to one of the brick furnaces flew open, spilling forth fire. Within seconds, the top deck of the *Absalom* was ablaze.

Captain Godward quickly rallied his remaining crew, ordering them to man the bilge pumps in hopes of extinguishing the fire before it reached the sails above or the oil-laden cargo hold below. And for a brief moment it looked like they would succeed—until King Jim returned. But this time he was no longer a whale, but a thing born of myths and nightmares.

From the waist up he was shaped like a man, in that there was a head, torso and two limbs--but after that the resemblance ended. The head was massive, with a bulbous brow that thrust forward like the bow of a ship and was joined to a pair of shoulders as wide as a redwood by a short, thickly muscled neck. The eyes were set way back and far apart, and what I can only call his 'face' lacked nose, cheekbones, lips, or hair of any kind.

King Jim opened his long, narrow lower jaw, exposing peg-like teeth the size of a man's doubled fist, and issued forth the dreadful bellow I heard in my dream. The sound of his royal displeasure was enough to make me clap my hands over my ears. He then tore free the carcasses of the slaughtered whales tethered to the *Absalom*, snapping the ropes and chains of the blocks and tackles as if they were made of twine.

Captain Godward, Mulogo and what men now left--all armed with the rifles from the armory--rushed to the bulwarks and opened fire on the leviathan. The volley of lead seemed to do little to King Jim, save anger him even further. With a second ear-splitting bellow, the behemoth snatched up the captain and his mate as if they were dolls and crushed the life out of them. And even though he was always a devil to me, I will carry the sound of poor Mulogo's death scream to my grave.

King Jim then grabbed the foremast and wrenched it from its moorings, like a barber-surgeon yanking out a recalcitrant tooth, and used it to bludgeon the ship, sending the terrified deckhands that still remained fleeing in all directions. Once the mast was reduced to kindling, the monster brought a massive fist down onto the burning foredeck, like a spoiled child taking out his temper on his toys.

Already weakened by the collision, the hull gave way with an explosive groan and began taking on water. As the ship sank, King Jim continued his assault by snapping the mainmast in half and using it like a harpoon to punch further holes in the body of the ship. Within minutes the *Absalom* was reduced to nothing more than splinters and torn sailcloth, taking all aboard to the depths below.

As the broken masts sank out of sight, I wept like an orphaned child before his mother's grave. For two years the *Absalom* had been my only home, and its crew the only people I knew. And although they turned against me, they did not deserve such a cruel and monstrous fate.

However, my grief for my shipmates was quickly replaced by mortal terror as King Jim swung about his monstrous head and saw the lonesome captain's gig bobbing atop the waves. The fearsome creature closed the distance between us with a single swish of his powerful tail, barreling towards me like a living juggernaut. I cried out in horror and instinctively raised my arms in a vain attempt to block the sight of the monster's upraised fist. But, to my surprise, the blow never fell.

It took all my courage, but I finally lowered my hands and saw King Jim towering over me like a living mountain, his breath hissing and rumbling from the blowhole atop his head like a steam locomotive standing at the station. Although it is foolish to ascribe human emotions to something so inhuman, there seemed to be a look of confusion on what passed for his face.

Without warning, King Jim gave voice to yet another fearsome roar and scooped up the captain's gig in one vast hand. As I clung to the gunwales for dear life, the sight of the monster's gaping maw made me fear I would end up in the belly of a whale, just like my biblical namesake. But, to my surprise, I was not devoured. Instead, the giant carefully brought the uplifted boat closer, like a nearsighted man inspecting the detail on a model ship.

Although King Jim's eyes were the size of grapefruit, they were tiny in comparison to the rest of his massive bulk. As terrified as I was, I could not bring myself to look away as he studied me, and I glimpsed in their depths a vast intellect born before the islands rose from the ocean floor. It was then I finally realized what it was that had caught his attention.

With trembling hands I removed the dolphin amulet from about my neck and held it aloft, like Diogenes his lantern. It was then the flicker of confusion in the giant eye turn into a gleam of recognition. To my relief King Jim gently returned my boat to the water and gave it a small push, like a boy playing admiral in a pond, which sent it shooting forward as if under full sail.

His wrath exhausted and brides avenged, King Jim— known to some as Tangaroa, Lord of the Ocean— rose up on his tail and, with an oddly graceful pirouette for a being of such size, dropped back into the water with a thunderous splash.

Chapter Twenty

Beyond Reason—I Am Adrift—A Gift From Below —The Ship Beneath The Waves—A Savage Savior

As King Jim returned to the crushing depths of his kingdom, my nerves--already stretched to their breaking point--snapped altogether. I collapsed in a heap as I alternated between screams of laughter and gut-wrenching sobs. There is no shame in admitting I succumbed to madness after all I had endured, and anyone who claims they could have kept their sanity intact under such circumstances is a damn liar.

I do not remember much of what occurred while I was beyond reason, save that I traveled so far into madness I eventually came out the other side. In fact, I daresay I emerged far saner than I ever was before—although there are many who would argue this point. My sense of time was lost along with my mind, and I have no true idea how long I remained in such a state. It could have been hours; it might have been days. All I know is that when I came back to my senses I was lying flat on my back at the bottom of the boat, staring up at a sky filled with pin-wheeling stars and my mouth was so dry I couldn't summon enough spit to fill a thimble.

I crawled over to the water cask and slaked my thirst as much as I dared. I then became aware that I was horribly sunburned from scalp to toe. My skin radiated heat like a stove-top, and every movement of my body brought sharp, stinging pain, as if beset by angry hornets. My discomfort was such that it was impossible for me to sleep, despite my exhaustion.

At length, the morning came and the sun rose on a world made of water, without a sail in sight. The fact I saw no wreckage from the *Absalom*—not even the tiniest of splinters—told me I had been at sea both physically and mentally for some time. The dawn also brought the realization that my supply of water was dangerously low and that I was down to two sea biscuits.

As the sun continued its inexorable climb, I did what I could to protect my scorched flesh from its merciless rays. Large swathes of peeling skin hung from my shoulders and arms like cobwebs, but there was only so much shade to be found in my floating prison. I spent most of the day scanning the horizon in hopes of spotting a sail, but all I could see was sky and water, each as blue as the other. At times I felt as if I was suspended between the two elements and in danger at any moment of drifting off through the clouds.

I not only searched for passing ships, but also sought the ever-shifting sea for some glimpse of Koro. But I had yet to see any evidence of him since the destruction of the *Absalom.* Once I thought I saw a flash of dolphin fin, but it was only a reef shark chasing a school of fish. I was truly on my own, with nothing but my own wits and will to keep me alive.

I did not eat until after dark, as the heat of the day robbed me of any appetite. Even then, I had a hard time keeping down what little food was left to me, as my body was wracked with fever and chills. Eventually

I drifted into a fitful sleep, curled up in the bow of the boat. As miserable as it was, that first day out of madness became the template for my life as a castaway.

Each day the sun scorched me to the bone, and each day I spent the daylight hours parched with thirst. I had no choice but to parcel out what little water was left, granting myself only three swallows a day. The food ran out well before the water, of course, and two days after my final meal, my belly began tying itself in painful knots. My hunger even followed me into my dreams, taunting me with visions of suckling pigs roasting on a spit, wheels of cheese and loaves of fresh-baked bread.

Two days after that, the water in the cask began to take on a brackish taste and I knew it would not be long before it would go the way of the food. But what concerned me even more was the fact my strength was rapidly eroding. My body was beginning to cannibalize itself, and soon I would no longer be able to keep watch for ships or be able to signal should one pass by.

Then, on the fifth day, I was jarred from my fitful sleep by something wet slapping against my blistered flesh. I instinctively shouted and flailed about in alarm, causing the dinghy to rock dangerously back and forth. Once I could focus my eyes, I discovered a mackerel lying beside me. At first I thought it had jumped into the boat, as fish sometimes are wont to do. Then I realized that not only was the mackerel quite dead, but it had also been sliced open from gills to tail and neatly disemboweled.

A burst of excitement shot through my exhausted body, spurring me to raise myself up on my knees and gaze about. *"Koro!"* I called out, my voice hoarse from thirst. "Koro, my brother! Where are you?"

As much as I longed for an answer, the surface of the ocean remained smooth as glass. Once I realized there would be no response, I turned my attention to the fish and greedily fed upon its raw, moist flesh. When I finished my feast, I lay back down, secure in the knowledge that while I might still be the sole survivor of the *Absalom*, I was no longer alone.

The next day, I saw--or thought I saw--a vessel. It was dusk, and my eye was caught by a glow on the near horizon. As I struggled upright onto the bench at the stern of the boat, I spotted a sailing ship with three masts with five sails each plowing across the ocean in my direction! As it came closer I could hear music being played and voices raised in song and laughter. I tore my makeshift tent from where it was stretched across the bow and frantically waved it above my head with the last of my strength.

"Ahoy!" I croaked. *"Ship ahoy!"*

But as what I thought was my salvation drew nearer, it occurred to me that the light coming from the ship did not radiate from lanterns but from the vessel itself. I remembered old Cuppy's story about the *Caleuche,* and quickly fell silent. As I did so, the ghost-ship disappeared beneath waves, where it glowed like the moon reflected in the ocean surf. As it continued to sail underwater I saw figures moving about on the deck, some of whom were familiar to me. I could see Cuppy, Hawley, and Gussett, even Mr. Shreve, Mulogo and Captain Godward, laughing and dancing the hornpipe, as if they no longer had a care in the world. And standing on the poop deck, overlooking the festivities, was none other than Captain Solomon, and on his arm was a beautiful woman with blonde hair that floated about her head like a cloud and whose body was half-covered in golden scales.

The next day I drank the last swallow of water. As the sun poured its heat onto me, I was convinced my final hour was at hand. My vision had steadily faded ever since I saw the ghost-ship. And although it was high noon, I couldn't see beyond my outstretched hand.

At some point I must have drifted into unconsciousness, for I was suddenly jarred awake by the sound of human voices. Thinking the *Caleuche* had returned to claim me for its crew, I managed to raise myself up and saw a whaleboat headed in my direction. Standing in the bow was a towering Māori covered in tattoos and holding a harpoon. He smiled reassuringly as he reached out for me, revealing a mouth full of teeth filed to a point. While such a savage visage would have struck horror into the hearts of most, I would have wept at its beauty had the sun not already burned the tears from my eyes.

Epilog

As luck would have it, the ship responsible for plucking me from what would have been my floating tomb was none other than the *Pilgrimage*, back hunting whales after replenishing her crew in Chile. I was full of fever and nothing else when the Māori pulled me into his boat, and it speaks to the Christian charity of Captain Fastnacht that he brought me into own quarters and personally saw to it that I was nursed back to health.

While delirious, I babbled about whale-gods, dolphin-princes and princesses, shark-men, drowned cities and ghost-ships. But given my condition, no one seemed to pay them much heed. Or perhaps, having experienced King Jim's wrath, Captain Fastnacht knew more that he was willing to admit. In any case, once my fever broke, I made sure to say nothing more and never explained how it was I ended up in the captain's gig in the first place. The last thing I wanted was to once more be branded a Jonah and thrown back into the sea.

I spent the next four months aboard the *Pilgrimage*, working as I had upon the *Absalom* to earn my keep. When the ship dropped anchor in Tahiti, I bid my farewell to Captain Fastnacht, who I had grown quite fond of. I never saw him or the *Pilgrimage* again. As it turned out, I had arrived in Papeete at a most fortuitous time. The Franco-Tahitian War had just ended, and I was hired by a Mr. William Stewart to help oversee a thousand Chinese brought in to work on his vast cotton plantation. After five years, I had saved up enough money to do as I liked. So I quit my job and booked passage to the Sandwich Islands, as they were still called back then.

A dozen years ago I bought a parcel of land on the island of Hawaii near the ocean and built a house for myself in the native style. My wants are simple and my needs few. In many ways, I have taken His Lordship--who died so bravely on the shores of his adopted land--as my role model. I dine on what I pull from the sea in my nets or what I pluck from the fruiting trees that grow on my land. When I weary of the native palm wine, I go to the nearest White settlement and barter for rum.

Although I keep to myself, my brush with the fabled ship-killer, King Jim, and status as the sole survivor of the *Absalom* have made me something of a local "character", as they say. Over the years, numerous visitors have found their way to my hut, gifting me with bottles of whisky and tinned meat in exchange for my story. The Europeans--as well as my fellow Yankees--here on the Big Island argue amongst themselves as to whether I am a hermit or a beachcomber, but all agree that I am a drunkard and a sorry excuse for a White man.

As for the Islanders, they view me far differently. To them, I am a *kahuna*—a shaman, of sorts. One touched by the gods of the ocean, as proved by the dolphin amulet I still wear about my neck. They give me offerings of food and palm wine to bless their fishing nets and outriggers, and on occasion send me their daughters to keep me company.

It has been twenty years since I left my family to

go a'whalin'. I am certain my mother and father are no more, and what siblings remain would find me more stranger than brother, should I return. Besides, I have heard disturbing stories of a war amongst the states. Why should I leave paradise for such a Hell?

Not long ago a young man came to visit me. He carried with him a newspaper that claimed King Jim had been hunted down and killed the year before. There was even an engraving of the dead whale placed on a scale, which held in its balance several elephants to better illustrate its immensity. When he asked me what I thought of the report, I laughed at the very idea of King Jim being boiled down and used to light a parlor in Baltimore.

I told him that what they had caught was one of King Jim's many sons, but not the genuine article. The young man was clearly unconvinced by my claims, and I realized that the spoken word of someone with first-hand knowledge was nowhere as real to him as the written word of someone half a world away.

So that is why I am putting the story—the *true* story—of what befell the *Absalom* on paper. However, I do not plan to see it published any time soon, as I am in no great hurry to have myself declared mad. While I may no longer have to fear being called a Jonah and stranded at sea, being clapped up in a lunatic asylum is another matter altogether. No, once I have finished my narrative I will deliver it to my solicitor in Hilo, with the directive that it not be published, until I am dead—or assumed so.

No doubt, if you have followed my story thus far, kind reader, you are asking yourself: 'But what became of Koro? Did you ever see him again?'

The answer to your question is both yes and no.

While I have not clapped eyes on him since the day he cut me free of the *Absalom,* he often comes to me in dreams. Sometimes he is in the form of a dolphin, but most often he appears to me as a man. In my dreams he shows me things--such as how to bring the fish closer to shore, protect against the sharks, and calm the storms. And I know--as sure as the sun is hot and water wet--my kinsman will one day rise from the surf beyond my door to escort me to the sunken city of the Ocean Born.

And so I leave you now, whoever you might be, to read my words and judge for yourself as to whether I am truthful, mad or a liar.

But I warn you: I am all three.

COPYRIGHT PAGE

ABOUT THE AUTHOR

Nancy A. Collins is the author of numerous novels, short stories, and comic books. She is a recipient of multiple Horror Writers Association's Bram Stoker Awards, The British Fantasy Society's Icarus Award, the Dal Coger Memorial Hall of Fame Award, and the International Association of Media Tie-In Writers' Scribe Award, as well as a nominee for the Eisner Award, International Horror Guild Award, John W. Campbell Memorial Award, the Theodore Sturgeon Award, the James Tiptree Award, and the World Fantasy Award.

Her works include the award-winning *Sunglasses After Dark,* the Southern Gothic short story collection *Knuckles and Tales*, the *Golgotham* urban fantasy series, and the weird western *Lynch: A Gothik Western*. She is the first woman to have written *Swamp Thing* and was the first woman to write both the *Vampirella* and *The Army of Darkness* comic book series. Originally from Arkansas, she currently makes her home in Macon, Georgia with her cat, Lux.

Made in United States
North Haven, CT
21 April 2024